There was a second *snap*! and the remaining attendant catapulted from the van. Gisela, instead of dodging around the front bumper of the coupe, vaulted the hood which her dangling coattail struck with a clang. Kelly flattened himself on the ground, reaching up for the passenger-side door as he twisted his head back to see what weapons were being aimed. He had not attempted to clear the revolver attached to his waistband. All it was going to do under present circumstances was tie up his hand and make a target of him.

A better target.

Two of the figures, the men if they were men, ran toward him while the third's radio shouted, "Thomas Kelly, for your planet's sake—"

Look for these other Tor books by David Drake

FORTRESS
FORLORN HOPE

DAVID DRAKE

Tom Kelly is just a platoon sergeant.
But he's made major policy decisions for his country...
and soon he'll be forced to make even bigger decisions.

FORTRESS

TOR

A TOM DOHERTY ASSOCIATES BOOK

FORTRESS

Copyright © 1987 by David Drake

First printing: January 1987
First Mass Market printing: February 1988

A TOR Book

Published by Tom Doherty Associates, Inc.
49 West 24th Street
New York, NY 10010

Cover art by Alan Gutierrez

ISBN: 0-812-53620-7
Can. No.: 0-812-53621-5

Printed in the United States of America

0 9 8 7 6 5 4 3 2 1

To Tom Doherty,

who published my first book also,
and most of those in between.

Among the people who helped with bits of unclassified background on this one are Glenn and Helen Knight; Bernadette Bosky and Arthur Hlavaty; and Congressman Newt Gingrich and his personal assistant, Laurie James. Many thanks to all of them.

Prologue:
Another 1965

Sergeant Tom Kelly listened to John F. Kennedy's
fifth State of the Union Address—his so-called "Buck
Rogers Speech"—at a firebase in the Shuf Mountains, watching Druse 122 mm rockets arc toward Beirut
across the night sky.

The broadcast, carried live over the Armed Forces
Levantine Network, hissed and sputtered in the plug earphone of Kelly's cheap portable radio. Inside the high-
sided command track against which he leaned, the young
sergeant could have gotten a much clearer signal through
some of the half million dollars worth of communications-
intercept equipment which the Radio Research vehicle
carried. This was good enough, though, for a soldier who
was off duty and waiting for the attack Druse message
traffic made almost certain.

Shooooo . . . hissed the green ball of a bombardment
rocket.

"Our enemies, the enemies of freedom," said the President, more distant from Kelly's reality than seven time
zones could imply, "have proven in Hungary, in Cuba,
and in Lebanon that they respect nothing in their international dealings except strength. Their armies are poised on

1

the boundaries of Eastern Europe, ready to hurl themselves across the remainder of the continent at the least sign of weakness among the Western democracies.''

By daylight, the berm which bulldozers had turned up around the firebase for protection was scarcely less sterile in appearance than the crumbling rock of the hills from which it was carved. Now, in the soft darkness, the landscape breathed. Kelly's left hand caressed the heavy wooden stock of his M14, knowing that beyond the berm other soldiers were nervously gripping their own weapons: Mausers abandoned by the Turks in 1917; Polish-made Kalashnikovs slipped across the Syrian border in donkey panniers; rocket-propelled grenades stamped in Russian or Chinese . . .

"In Europe and the Middle East," continued the President in a nasal voice further attenuated by the transmission and the radio's tinny speaker, "in Africa and Latin America—wherever the totalitarians and their surrogates choose to test us, the free world must stand firm. Furthermore, ladies and gentlemen of Congress, we in the United States must undertake an initiative on behalf of the free world which will convince our enemies that we have the strength to withstand them no matter how great the forces they gather on Earth itself.''

The five tubes of howitzer battery—the sixth hog was deadlined for repair—cut loose in a ragged salvo. The white powderflashes were a lightninglike dazzle across the firebase while the side-flung shock waves from the muzzle brakes hammered tent roofs and raised dust from the parched ground. The short-barreled one-five-fives were firing at high angles and with full charges. Nothing to do with the turbaned riflemen crouching to attack, perhaps nothing to do with even the Druse rockets sailing down toward the airport in the flat curves of basketballs shot from thirty feet out.

"We must have an impregnable line of defense and an

arsenal of overwhelming magnitude in the heavens themselves," continued Kennedy through the squeal of hydraulic rammers seating the shells of the next salvo. Clicks of static from command transmissions cut across the broadcast band, but Kelly was used to building sense from messages far more shattered and in a variety of languages beyond English. He was good at that—at languages—and his fingertips again tried to wiggle the magazine of his rifle, making sure it was locked firmly into the receiver.

"Space is both a challenge—" said the President as Kelly's hearing returned after the muzzle blasts of the howitzers which were more akin to physical punishment than to noise. "—Now also the unbreachable shield of freedom and the spear of retribution which cannot be blunted by treacherous attack as our land-based weapons might be."

The breechblock of a fifty-caliber machinegun clanged from the far side of the firebase as the weapon was charged, freezing time and Tom Kelly's soul. Only the sounds of the howitzers reloading and traversing their turrets slightly followed, however. Nothing Kelly had seen in ninety-seven days in the field suggested the hogs were going to hit anything useful, but their thunderous discharges made waiting for an attack easier than it would have been with only the stars for company.

"My detailed proposals . . ." said the radio before the words disintegrated into a hiss like frying bacon—louder than the voice levels had been, so it couldn't be the French dry cells giving out. . . .

"Fuckin' A!" snarled Chief Warrant Officer Platt as he ducked out the rear hatch of the command vehicle. He, the intercept team's commander, was a corpulent man who wore two fighting knives on his barracks belt and carried the ear of a Druse guerrilla tissue-wrapped in a watch case. "We're getting jammed across all bands! What the fuck *is* this?"

Something with a fluctuating glow deep in the violet and

presumably ultraviolet was crossing the sky very high up and very swiftly. A word or two, ''—dominance—'' crept through a momentary pause in the static before the howitzers, linked by wire to the Tactical Operations Center, fired again.

"Commie recon satellite," Platt muttered, his eyes following Kelly's to the bead shimmering so far above the surface of dust, buffeted by hot, gray strokes of howitzer propellant. "You know those bastards're targeting us down to the last square meter!"

Tom Kelly reached for the tuning dial of the radio with the hand which was not sweating on the grip of his rifle. Anybody who could come within a hundred yards of a point target, using a bombardment rocket aimed by adjusting a homemade bipod under the front of the launching tube, ought to be running the US space program instead of a Druse artillery company. The hell with the satellite—assuming that's what it was. If the rag-heads could jam the whole electromagnetic spectrum like that, there were worse problems than Radio Research teams becoming as useless as tits on a boar. . . .

"—domestic front," said the radio just as Kelly's fingers touched it, "the curse of racial injustice calls for—"

Tom Kelly never did hear the rest of that speech because just as normal reception resumed, a one-twenty-two howled over the berm and exploded near a tank-recovery vehicle. It was the first of the thirty-seven rockets preceding the attack of a reinforced Druse battalion.

The only physical scar Kelly took home from that one was on his hand, burned by the red-hot receiver of his rifle as he worked to clear a jam.

Another 1985

The three helicopters were orbiting slowly, as if tethered to the monocle ferry on the launchpad five hundred meters below. When the other birds rotated so that the West Texas sun caught the cameras aimed from their bays, the long lenses blazed as if they were lasers themselves rather than merely tools with which to record a test of laser propulsion.

The sheathing which would normally have roofed the passenger compartments of the helicopters had been removed, leaving the multi-triangulated frame tubing and a view straight upward for the cameras and the men waiting for what was about to happen on the launchpad.

Sharing the bay of the bird carrying Tom Kelly were a cameraman, a project scientist named Desmond, and a pair of colonels in Class A uniforms, Army green and Air Force blue, rather than the flight suits that Kelly thought would have been more reasonable. The military officers seemed to be a good deal more nervous than the scientist was; and unless Kelly was misreading them, their concern was less about the test itself than about him—the staff investigator for Representative Carlo Bianci, chairman of the House Subcommittee on Space Defense.

Sometimes it seemed to Kelly that he'd spent all his life

surrounded by people who were worried as hell about what he was going to do next. Occasionally, of course, people would have been smart to worry more than they did. . . .

The communications helmet Kelly had been issued for the test had a three-position switch beneath the left ear-piece, but only one channel on it was live. He could not hear either the chatter of the Army pilots in the cockpit or the muttered discussions of the two officers in the passenger bay with him, though the latter could speak to him when they chose to throw their own helmet switches forward. The clop of the blades overhead was more a fact than an impediment to normal speech, but the intake rush of the twin-turbine power plant created an ambiance through which Kelly could hear nothing but what the officers chose to direct to him through the intercom circuitry.

"Someday," Kelly said aloud, "people are going to learn that the less they try to hide, the less problem they have explaining things. But I don't expect the notion to take hold in the military any time soon."

"Pardon?" asked Desmond, the first syllable minutely clipped by his voice-activated microphone. The scientist was Kelly's age or a few years younger, a short-bearded man who slung a pen-caddy from one side of his belt and a worn-looking calculator from the other. It was probably his normal working garb—as were the dress uniforms of the public-affairs colonels, flacks of type which Kelly would have found his natural enemy even if they hadn't been military.

"I'd been meaning to ask you, Dr. Desmond," said Kelly, rubbing from his eyes the prickliness of staring into the desert of the huge Fort Bliss reservation, "just why you think the initial field test failed?"

"Ah, I think it's important to recall, Mr. Kelly," interjected one of the colonels—it was uncertain which through the headphones—"that the test was by no means a

failure. The test vehicle performed perfectly throughout
eighty-three percent of the spectrum planned—''

"Well good *god*, Boardman," snapped the project scientist, "it blew *up*, didn't it? That's what you mean, isn't
it?" Desmond continued, snapping his head around from
the officers across the bay to Kelly seated on the portion of
the bench closest to the fully-opened starboard hatch. "I
certainly don't consider that, that *fireworks* display a
success."

Kelly smiled, the expression only incidentally directed
toward the colonels. "Though I gather many of the sys-
tems *did* work as planned, Doctor?" he said, playing the
scientist now that he had enough of a personality sample
from which to work. Even among the project's civilians,
there were familiar—and not wholly exclusive—categories
of scientists and scientific politicians. Desmond had seemed
to be in the former category, but Kelly had found no
opportunity to speak to him alone.

The public affairs officers were probably intended to
smother honest discussion within the spotting helicopter
the same way the administrators had done on the ground.
That plan was being frustrated by what was more than a
personality quirk: Desmond could not imagine that anything
the military officers said or wished was of any concern to
him. It was not a matter of their rank or anyone's position
in a formal organizational chart: Colonels Boardman and
Johnson were simply of another species.

"Yes, absolutely," agreed the project scientist as he
shook his head in quick chops. "Nothing went wrong
during air-breathing mode, nothing we could see in the
telemetry, of course—it'd have been nice to get the *hardware*
back for a hands-on."

"I think you'd better get your goggles in place now, Mr.
Kelly," said the Air Force officer, sliding his own protective eyewear into place. The functional thermoplastic communications helmets looked even sillier atop dress uniforms

than they did over the civilian clothes Desmond, and Kelly himself, wore. "For safety's sake, you know."

Kelly was anchored to a roof strap with his left hand by habit that freed his right for the rifle he did not carry here, not on this mission or in this world where 'cut-throat' meant somebody might lose a job or a contract. . . . He looked at the PR flacks, missing part of what Desmond was saying because his mind was on things that were not the job of the Special Assistant to Representative Bianci.

The colonels straightened, one of them with a grimace of repulsion, and neither of them tried again to break in as the project scientist continued, "—plating by the aluminum oxide particles we inject with the on-board hydrogen to provide detonation nuclei during that portion of the pulsejet phase. Chui-lin insists the plasma itself scavenges the chambers and that the fault must be the multilayer mirrors themselves despite the sapphire coating."

"But there's just as much likelihood of blast damage when you're expelling atmosphere as when you're running on internal fuel, isn't there?" said Kelly, who had done his homework on this one as he did on any task set him by Representative Bianci; and as he had done in the past, when others tasked him.

"Exactly, *exactly*," Desmond agreed, chopping his head. "Just a time factor, says Chui-lin, but there's *no* sign of overheating until we switch modes, and I don't think dropping the grain size as we've done will be—"

"Fifteen seconds," boomed a voice from the control center on the ground, and this time Kelly and the scientist did slide the goggles down over their eyes. The cameraman hunched behind the long shroud of his viewing screen. A guidance mechanism as sophisticated as anything in the latest generation of air-to-air missiles should center the lens on the test vehicle, despite any maneuvers the target or the helicopter itself carried out. Machinery could fail, however, and the backup cameraman was determined that he would not fail—because he was *good*, not because he was worried about his next efficiency report.

The monocle ferry was a disk only eighteen feet in diameter, and at its present slant distance of almost half a mile from the helicopters it would have been easy to ignore were it not so nearly alone on a barren yellow landscape. With Vandenburg and Cape Canaveral irrevocably surrendered to the US Space Command when it was formed in 1971, the Army and Air Force had chosen Fort Bliss as the site for their joint attempt to circumvent their new rival's control of space weaponry.

Not only was the huge military reservation empty enough to make a catastrophic failure harmless, but its historical background as the center of Army Air Defense Training lent a slight color to the services' claim that they were not trying to develop a 'space weapon' of their own in competition with the Space Command.

Not that that would help them if Carlo Bianci decided the program should be axed. The congressman from the Sixth District of Georgia had made a career—a religion, some critics claimed—of space defense, and it wasn't the sort of thing he permitted interservice squabbling to screw up.

"Now, there *may* be a critical limit to grain size," Dr. Desmond was saying, "below which none of the aluminum will form hot-spots on the mirror surface, but at these energy levels it won't take more than a few *molecules* to—"

"Go," said the control center, and the landscape changed in intensity.

The beams from the six chemical laser lift stations in orbit above the launch site were in the near infrared at a wavelength of 1.8 microns. Not only was light of that frequency invisible to the human eye, it was absorbed by the cornea instead of being focused by the lens to the potential injury of the retina. The wavelength was a relatively inefficient one for transmitting power, especially through an atmosphere which would have passed a much higher percentage of the ultraviolet. The five megajoules of energy involved in the test, however, meant that even the least amount of reflection raised an unacceptable risk of blindness and worse if the operation were in the visible spectrum or shorter.

"Go-o-o . . ." whispered Desmond, probably unaware that he had spoken aloud. Tom Kelly leaned outward, bringing his shoulder and helmet into the dry, twenty-knot airstream.

The six-ton saucer quivered as it drank laser energy through the dozen windows of segmented corundum which ringed its upper surface like the eyes of a monstrous insect. The central hub of the ferry contained the one-man cockpit, empty now except for instrumentation, which did not rotate as the blast chambers around the saucer's rim began to expel air flash-heated within them by laser pulses.

Dust, as much a part of West Texas as it was of the hills above Beirut, rippled in a huge, expanding doughnut from the concrete pad. It formed a translucent bed for the ferry, a mirage landscape on which the saucer seemed to rest instead of lifting as planned. Then the dust was gone, a yellow-gray curtain across distant clumps of Spanish bayonet, and the ferry itself was a lens rather than a disk as it shot past the helicopters circling at five hundred meters.

"All *right!*" blurted Kelly, jerking his eyes upward to track the monocle through the frame members and shimmering helicopter rotors against a sky made amber by his goggles.

"Twenty-two g's!" babbled the project scientist happily. "Almost from the point of liftoff! There's no way Space Command's ground-lift barges can match that—or *any* chemically-fueled launcher."

The chopper rocked between paired sonic booms, a severe one followed by an impact of lesser intensity. The monocle ferry had gone supersonic even before it reached the altitude of the helicopters, buffeting them with a shock wave reflected from the ground as well as the pulse streaming directly from the vehicle's surface. The roar of the ferry's exhaust followed a moment later, attenuating rapidly like that of an aircraft making a low-level pass.

"All *right*," Kelly repeated, disregarding the colonels, who he knew would be beaming at his enthusiasm. There was a hell of a lot more to this 'air defense' program than the mere question of how well the hardware worked; but hardware that *did* work gave Kelly a glow of satisfaction with the human race, and he didn't give a hoot in hell about who knew it. It was their lookout if they thought he was dumb enough to base his recommendations on that alone.

Their helicopter and the other two essed out of their slow starboard orbits, banking a little to port to make it easier for the cameras and observers to follow an object high enough above them to be effectively vertical. There were supposed to be chase planes, T-38 trainers with more cameras, but Kelly could see no sign of them at the moment. The ferry itself was no more than a sunstruck bead of amber.

"Normally," Dr. Desmond explained, "we'd continue in air-breathing mode to thirty kilometers before switching to internal fuel. For the purpose of his test, however, we'll convert to hydrogen very shortly in order to—"

"God almighty!" cried Boardman, the Air Force flack, so far forgetting himself that he started to lurch to his feet against the motion of the helicopter. "For the demon*stration* you do this?"

"We're modifying the test sequence in response to earlier results, of course," the scientist said, glancing over at the military man.

Kelly continued to look upward, squinting by habit, though the goggles made that unnecessary. Boardman didn't matter. He was typical of people, not necessarily stupid ones, who cling to a view of reality against available evidence and their own presumable benefit. In this case, the public affairs officer was obviously so certain that the ferry would blow up that he preferred the test do nothing to advance the project rather than have Bianci's man watch a catastrophic failure.

The bead of light which had almost disappeared detonated into a fireball whose color the goggles shifted into the green.

The cameraman had been only a nervous spectator while his unit's servos tracked the ferry with inhuman skill. Now he squeezed the override trigger in the right grip and began to manually follow the shower of fragments picked out by the sun as they tumbled and danced. His left hand made minute adjustments to the focal length of his lens, shortening it to keep as nearly as possible the whole drifting mass within his field of view.

"God damn it to hell," said Dr. Desmond very distinctly before he lowered his head, took off his commo helmet, and slammed the helmet as hard as he could against the aluminum deck of the helicopter. It bounced, but the length of communications cord kept it from flying out the open hatch as it tried to do. The two officers straightened their backs against the bulkhead with expressions of disapproval and concern.

Kelly slid his goggles back up on the brow of his helmet, sneezing at the shock of direct sunlight again. He put a hand on the scientist's nearer shoulder, squeezing hard enough to be noticed but without trying to raise Desmond's head from where it was buried in his hands. " 'Sokay," the ex-soldier muttered, part of him aware that the scientist couldn't possibly hear him and another part equally sure that it *wasn't* okay, that even future success would not expunge this memory of something which mattered very much vaporizing itself in the Texas sky.

"It's okay," Kelly said, repeating words he'd had to use too often before, the words a lieutenant had spoken to him the fire-shot evening when Kelly held the torso of a friend who no longer had a head.

"Maybe switching to straight calcium carbonate'll do the trick," Kelly's lips whispered while the PR men grimaced at the undirected fury in the veteran's eyes.

"Oh, good evening, Mr. Kelly," said the young woman at the front desk—a second-year student out of Emory, if Kelly remembered correctly. She looked flustered as usual when she spoke to the veteran. She wasn't the receptionist, just an intern with a political science major getting some hands-on experience; but the hour was late, and service to the public—to possible constituents—was absolutely the first staff priority in all of Representative Bianci's offices.

"Marcelle, Marcelle," said Tom Kelly, stretching so that his overcoat gaped widely and the attaché case in his left hand lifted toward the ceiling. His blazer veed to either side of the button still fastening it, baring most of the shirt and tie beneath but continuing to hide the back of Kelly's waistband.

He'd been on planes that anybody with a bottle of gasoline could hijack to god knew where; he'd been walking on Capitol Hill at night, a place as dangerous as parts of Beirut that he'd patrolled in past years with flak jacket and automatic rifle; and anyway, he was a little paranoid, a little crazy, he'd never denied that. . . . It was no problem him going armed unless others learned about it . . . and with care, that would happen only when Tom Kelly was still standing and somebody else wasn't.

Kelly grinned at the little intern, broadly, as he had learned to do because the scar tissue above the left corner of his mouth turned a lesser smile into a snarling grimace. "It you don't start calling me Tom, m'dear, I'm going to have to get formal with you. I won't be mistered by a first name, I've seen too much of that . . . and I don't *like* 'mister.' Okay?''

All true; and besides, he was terrible on names, fucking terrible, and remembering them had been for the past three years the hardest part of doing a good job for an elected official. But Marcelle, heaven knew what her last name was, colored and said, "I'm sorry, Tom, I'll really remember the next time."

Filing cabinets and free-standing mahogany bookshelves split the rear of the large room into a number of desk alcoves, many of them now equipped with terminals to the mainframe computer in the side office to the right. Another of the staff members, a pale man named Duerning, with a mind as sharp as Kelly's own—and as different from the veteran's as Brooklyn is from Beirut—was leaning over a desk, supporting himself with a palm on the paper-strewn wood. It was not until Carlo Bianci stood up beside Duerning, however, that Kelly realized that his boss was here rather than in the private office to the left where the closed door had seemed to advertise his presence. Never assume. . . .

"That's all for tonight, Murray," said Representative Bianci, clapping his aide on the shoulder in a gesture of camaraderie as natural as it was useful to a politician. He stepped toward Kelly as Duerning, nodding his head, shifted papers into a briefcase.

Carlo Bianci was Kelly's height and of the same squat build, though the representative was further from an ideal training weight than his aide and the difference was more than the decade's gap between their ages. Nonetheless, Bianci's thick gray hair was the only sign that the man might be fifty, and he was in damned good shape for anyone in an office job. Kelly suspected that Bianci's paunch was really a reservoir like a camel's hump, enabling the man to survive under the strain of constant eighteen-hour days for the decade he had been in Congress.

At the moment Bianci was wearing a blue jogging suit, which meant it was not expectation of a roll-call vote which kept him in his office at ten PM, and something was sticking worry lines around the smile of greeting which accompanied his handshake for Kelly. "Wasn't sure you'd be in tonight, Tom," he said, and there was an undercurrent below those ordinary words. "Thought you'd maybe want to get some rest."

"Well, don't count on me opening the office tomorrow morning," Kelly said, expecting to be led toward the door of the congressman's private office. Instead, Bianci guided him with a finger of his left hand into what was basically the workroom of the suite in the Old House Office Building, a bull pen where the mainframe, the coffeepot, and a crowd of desks and files would not normally be seen by constituents. "I'm on El Paso time and anyway, I always need to wind down awhile after I get off a plane. Figured I'd key in my report if you weren't around for a verbal debrief tonight."

"Well, how was the demonstration?" Bianci asked. He leaned back against a desk whose legs squealed slightly on the hardwood as they accepted the thrust.

"It really *was* a test," Kelly said, frowning as he made the final decisions about what to present to his employer, "and I guess the short answer is that there's bits of graphite composite and synthetic sapphire scattered all over West Texas and New Mexico."

"Sounds like I was right six months ago," said the congressman, with a nod. "Overripe for the ax, *exactly* the sort of boondoggle that weakens the country in the name of defending it."

"That's the hell of it, sir," Kelly said with a deeper frown, the honorific given by habitual courtesy to a man he felt deserved it. "Like you say, typical interservice wrangling. And you bet, the ferry went off like a bomb, she did that. But—" He shrugged out of his overcoat, his eyes concentrating on that for a moment while his mind raced with the real problem. When he looked up again, it was to say, "Damned if I don't think they've got something useful there. Maybe useful, at any rate."

" 'Hard-nosed Investigator Suckered by Military'?" said Bianci, quotes in his voice and enough smile on his lips to make the words a joke rather than a serious question.

"Yeah," said Kelly, sitting straddled on a chair across the narrow aisle from his employer, the wooden chair back a pattern of bars before him, "it bothers the *hell* outa me to believe anything I hear from the Air Force. I remember—"

He looked up grinning, because it hadn't happened to him and this long after the fact it wouldn't have mattered anyway. "I remember," he said, rubbing his scalp with a broad hand whose back was itself covered with curling black hair, "the Skybolt missile that was gonna make Russki air defense obsolete. Hang 'em under the wings of B-52's and launch from maybe a thousand miles out, beyond the interceptors and the surface to air missiles. . . ."

He was tired and wired and there were too many memories whispering through his brain. 'B-52' had called up transparent images, unwanted as all of that breed were unwanted except in the very blackest moods. The Anti-Lebanon Mountains were lighting up thirty clicks to the east with a quivering brilliance, white to almost blue and hard as an assassin's eyes: seven-hundred-and-fifty-pound bombs, over a thousand of them, dropping out of the stratosphere in a pattern a kilometer wide and as long as the highway from Kelly's family home to the nearest town. The flashes could be seen for half a minute before the shock waves began to be heard at Kelly's firebase; but even at that distance, the blasts were too loud to speak over.

"Damn, that was a *long* time back," Kelly muttered aloud, shaking his head to clear it, and Representative Bianci nodded in agreement with what he thought he had heard, part of a story about a failed missile. "Early sixties, yes?" he said aloud, again giving Kelly the impression that he was being softened up for something on an agenda the congressman had not yet broached.

"Oh, right," the younger man said with an engaging smile to cover an embarrassment known only to him. He couldn't lose it with Carlo, couldn't have his mind ricocheting off on its own paths in front of his boss. Kelly and Representative Bianci were as close to being friends as either's temperament allowed, and his support—what he told Kelly he had done, and what the aide knew from the result he *must* have done—had saved the veteran from the very bad time he'd earned by the method of his separation from the National Security Agency. But Carlo couldn't afford to associate with a psycho, a four-plus crazy like some people already said Tom Kelly was.

"Right, they tested Skybolt and they tested it, the Air Force did," the aide continued. "Kept reporting successes and partial successes—to the Brits, too, mind, the British government was basing its whole defense policy on Skybolt—right down to the time the Air Force canceled the program because they never once had gotten the thing to work right."

Kelly leaned back, flexing his big arms against the wood of the chair they gripped. "Turned out on one of those 'partial successes,' they'd detached the missile from the bomber carrying it, and it hadn't ignited, hadn't done *anything* but drop a couple miles and put a new crater in the desert. S'far as anybody could tell, the only thing the flyboys had tested successfully was the law of gravity, and that continued to perform up to specs."

"Which is why you're on my staff, Tom," said Bianci after an easy chuckle. "But you don't think the monocle ferry's another Skybolt?"

Kelly sighed and knuckled his eyes, relaxed again now

that he was back in the present. "Well, Hughes isn't prime contractor," he said, "that's one thing to the good."

He opened his eyes and looked up to meet the congressman's. Kelly was calm, now, and his subconscious had organized his data into a personal version of truth, the most he had ever tried to achieve. "Look, sir," he said, "they've got a glitch in the hydrogen pulsejet mode they need from a hundred thousand feet to, say, thirty miles. Probably soluble, but on this sort of thing you won't get guarantees from anybody you'd trust to tell the truth about the weather outside."

The aide spread his hands, palms down to either side of the chair, forming a base layer for the next edifice of facts. Bianci's eyes blinked unwilled from Kelly's face to the pinkish burn scars on both wrists. The man himself had when asked muttered, "Just a kerosene fire, price of bein' young and dumb," but the file Bianci had read carefully before he'd hired Tom Kelly spoke also of the helicopter and the three men dragged from the wreckage by Sergeant E-5 Kelly, who had ignored the facts that one of the men was dead already and that the ruptured fuel tank was likely to blow at any instant.

"If they *do* get that one cured," Kelly continued, absorbed in what he was saying, "then sure, there's a thousand other things that can go unfixably wrong, all along the line—but that's technology, not this project alone, and the one guy out there in El Paso willing to *talk* gave me a good feeling. Don't think he'd be workin' on a boondoggle. And okay, that's *my* gut and I'm not in the insurance business either."

He looked at the print on the wall before him, then added, "But I think it might work. And I think it might be nice to have an alternative to Fortress."

"Which works very well," said the congressman. The only sign that his own emotional temperature had risen was the way his fingers, playing with the modem beside him on the desk, stilled. Belief in space-based defense, as embodied in Fortress, had more than any other single factor brought Carlo Bianci into politics.

The framed print on the wall behind Bianci was from the original design studies on Fortress. The artist had chosen to make the doughnut of shielding material look smooth and metallic. In fact the visible outer surface was lumpy and irregular, chunks of slag spit into Earth orbit by the mass driver at the American lunar base and fused there into armor for Fortress.

The space station itself was a dumbbell spinning within the doughnut. Living quarters for the crews were in the lobes, where centrifugal force counterfeited gravity, but the real work of Fortress was done in the motionless spherical hub. A great-winged ferry, launched like an aircraft from a Space Command base in Florida or California, was shown docking at the 'north' pole—the axis from which the station's direction of rotation was counter-clockwise.

The array of nuclear weapons depending from the south pole had been left out of the painting. Three thousand H-bombs, each with its separate reentry vehicle, would have been too nightmarish for even the most hawkish of voters. That was often the case with the truth.

Mounted on the shielding were multi-tube rocket batteries intended to smash any warhead that came close enough to Fortress to do harm. The primary defenses were out of the scale of the picture, however, the constellation of X-ray lasers which orbited with the space station. Each was a small nuclear weapon which, when triggered, sent in the moment of its dissolution up to a hundred and forty-four simultaneous pulses, each capable of destroying any missile or warhead which had risen above the blanket of the atmosphere.

"It's everything President Kennedy dreamed of," Kelly agreed, aware of what he was saying and too tired to more than wonder why he was now voicing an opinion that could cost him a job he needed. "An orbital arsenal defended by X-ray lasers and armored with lunar slag that can stop the beam weapons which the lasers can't."

Bianci nodded, both because he agreed and because he *wanted* to be able to agree with his aide on a matter of such emotional importance to him. "A point in vacuum," he said in a voice that carried a touch of courtliness with no sign of accent from his Italian grandparents, "that can be defended as regions smothered in an atmosphere can't be. No matter how many missiles the Russians build, no matter *how* accurate they become, they can't pierce the defenses of Fortress and knock out our retaliatory capability—as they could with missile silos on Earth."

"And could with submarine launchers," Kelly said, nodding in the same rhythm as his employer, "if they can find the subs—which we can't prove they won't be able to do tomorrow with hardware no more unlikely than radar would've seemed fifty years ago."

"Then what's the problem with Fortress?" said Bianci, relaxing.

"Fortress is the ultimate offensive weapon," Kelly said softly, straightening his fingers and looking at the backs of his hands. Philosophy wasn't something he really got upset about, and that's all they were discussing here. If space weaponry ever became more than a matter of philosophy, *all* the survivors were going to get real upset. . . . "Well, nothing's ultimate, say the 'here-and-now maximum' offensive weapon."

"Defensive weapon in our hands, of course," the representative said, more in correction than as part of an expected argument. His buttocks shifted enough that the desk scraped beneath him.

"Boss," said Tom Kelly, standing and swinging the solid chair to the side rather than stepping around it, "it's defensive because the Reds—or whoever the hell—know that if they attack us, Fortress'll blast 'em back to the Neolithic—with bone cancer. You think *nobody'd* do that, not a risk but a guarantee. . . ."

The squat aide had taken two absentminded steps deeper into the bull pen. Now he turned and smiled as he faced his employer. "And I 'spect you're right, Carlo, for the politicians. But I've met folks who weren't going to back off whatever happened to them or behind 'em." He sighed, then added, "Hell, boss. On bad days I've been that sorta folks."

Congressman Bianci looked at his subordinate and, as if he had no inkling of what had just been admitted, said, "Then we can agree that we're safe so long as the politicians control the Kremlin—as they have at least since Rasputin died"—Kelly chuckled—"and that was true even under Stalin."

"Oh, hell, yes, Carlo," agreed Kelly easily and honestly. "Fortress is the most practical road to peace—bottom line peace—that anybody's come up with yet." He grinned in a way that would have been boyish except for the lines in and on his face. "There's just a certain beauty to a fleet of mirrors up there"—he gestured toward the ceiling and beyond with his trigger finger—"reflecting laser beams into however many warheads're coming over."

"We'll think about it," said Bianci, straightening onto his feet again. "Specifically, you'll have me a report in sixty days on the probable result of moving the project to Space Command. If we *do* decide to save it, there's no point in making a 'logical' change that results in a balls-up."

Well, he was still on the payroll, thought Tom Kelly as he nodded and said, "Yeah, like transferring ground-support aviation from the Army that needs it to the Air Force that isn't interested in anything yucky like mud and Russian tanks."

The veteran stretched, figuring that tomorrow was time

aplenty for him to write up the report since he'd given Carlo the core of it verbally. "Well, boss," he said—

—And Representative Bianci said, toward a far corner of the room, "There are two people who said they'd like to talk to you today, Tom."

"My goodness, two of 'em?" Kelly straightened deliberately from his back-arched posture and swept the room with his eyes: nobody but the two of them. He'd have heard breathing or motion if a team were hidden behind filing cabinets and privacy panels. . . . "What'd they want to talk about, Carlo?"

Bianci was not deceived by his aide's voice, though it was as smooth as the lockwork of a fine revolver slipping to full cock. For all that, nothing in the congressman's own background permitted him to translate data from Kelly's file into the shock and flame of reality. "Not Fortress, I believe, Tom," said Bianci. "Not—" He looked up with the appearance of candor, a politician's look, but possibly real this time. "This appears to be a new development of some sort on which they think you can be of some help."

Everything Tom Kelly saw or heard stood out from its background for the length of time he focused on it. Representative Bianci was a figure with only a blur behind him—unless something should have moved in the periphery of Kelly's vision—as he licked his lips and continued, "This isn't in the purview of your employment with me, Tom. But it would be a personal favor to me if you agreed to talk to them."

"Sure, boss, I understand," said Kelly, and he *did* understand. Bianci had been too smart to give him an order regarding a subject on which Kelly took orders from no one; and the kind of pressure that could be exerted on an elected official, even a powerful one, even an honorable man like Carlo Bianci, whose eyes had been pretty well open when he hired a man who'd been training Kurdish guerrillas for the National Security Agency before he separated on very bad terms indeed. . . . "Where do they want to see me? Langley? Meade?"

"I told them," said the congressman with the stumbling ennuciation of a man thinking of the result of what he was saying rather than the specific words his tongue tried to form, "that I'd relay their message, and that they were welcome to wait in my private office, though I had no reason to expect you in tonight." Bianci smiled. "I gather they had a better notion of your schedule than I did."

"Better'n both of us, I guess," Kelly said, unbuttoning his sportcoat and stretching again, bending forward at the waist and raising his hands locked behind his back. It was the position of a man being lifted to the ceiling in the cheap medieval substitute for the rack. The position loosened the great muscles of his shoulders—tension had locked them as tight as the cables winching in a whale for flensing.

If you watch a man carefully over a period of time, you *do* know him better than he knows himself, because the habitual activities that never reach his conscious mind stand out as statistical peaks in the summary of his behavior. Of *course* Tom Kelly would check in at Bianci's office, because he always did after a tour—though there was no necessity to do so, and though Kelly himself thought he was flipping a mental coin in the airport to determine whether he went to his Arlington apartment or the office in the Longworth Building.

"Well," said Kelly, massaging first his left hand with his right, then reversing the activity, "if they've been waiting this long, I guess it's only polite to look in on 'em."

"You don't have to, you know." The congressman stood up faster than he had intended, his muscles reacting sharply to the charged atmosphere. "Believe me, Tom, that wasn't an order."

The veteran clapped Bianci on the shoulder with his left

hand while the right clenched and unclenched in its own set of unconscious loosening exercises. "No sweat, boss," Kelly said. "You're a good enough friend to ask me a bigger favor'n that." He grinned; and though he saw his employer cringe away from the expression, Kelly didn't broaden the grin into something that might have been socially acceptable.

The two men walked into the front office, moving with tight, precise steps and resolutely looking at desks instead of each other. The door to the private office was covered in dark blue leather tacked down by brass studs corroded to a dull similarity. The chemicals used to tan leather were hard on brass, so you should never keep cartridges in leather belt loops for any length of time. . . .

Wrong thing to think about.

"Carlo," said Tom Kelly as they stepped around the receptionist's desk. Everyone was gone from the office but the pair of them and whoever was beyond the blue door. "I can lock up. Probably just as well if you went home and got some sleep yourself."

"I can go in with you, you know," Bianci said, pausing and touching Kelly to bring the younger man's eyes to meet his.

There was sound of a sort, maybe voices, coming from the inner office. Kelly laughed, a barking sound because of the circumstances, but a gesture of real amusement nonetheless. "With all due respect, boss," he said, "I doubt you're cleared for whatever it is. Of course"—the feral grin came back and all humor fled—"the last time I checked, *I* had a negative security clearance, so it's hard to tell. . . ."

He gripped the congressman by both shoulders, continuing to hold their eyes locked. "Go on home, Carlo; it can't be too heavy if they only came with two of 'em," Kelly said. A part of him hated the operative portion of his mind for the care with which it examined Bianci's face, looking for a reaction to "only two of them" that would imply there was a full team behind the leather door.

Nothing of the sort. "Right, Tom," said Representative Bianci as he strode out of his office. He added over his shoulder, "And thanks. You know I appreciate it."

Everybody's got a handle, thought Kelly as he closed and locked the outer door behind his employer. Carlo had fewer than most; but everybody's got things they don't want to lose if somebody thinks it's worthwhile to dig and to push.

Kelly shrugged again to loosen the cling of his jacket. Then he opened the door to the private office, using his left hand.

The sound within the office came from the television monitor facing Kelly above the desk, rather than the man and woman kitty-corner to it at the far end of the room. Gunfire, flattened and compressed by the signal, rasped from the set for a moment before the waiting man touched the remote control of the videocassette recorder. Sound and picture faded almost instantly, but Tom Kelly's mind was bright with echoes and afterimages.

The man strode forward with his hand out and a professional smile on his face. He was a good-looking fellow in his early thirties, too young for his beefiness to become real fat. The dark blond hair was nicely styled, and the cotton shirt beneath his pin-striped three-piece suit had probably cost as much as Kelly had spent on his own sportcoat. The fellow stood six feet three inches, with shoulders to match—which made them as broad as Kelly's. "Glad to see you at last, Mr. Kelly," he said. "I'm Doug Blakeley, and this is Elaine Tuttle."

"Right," said Kelly as he accepted the other's hand, "and I'm John Patrick Monaghan." That was the cover name he'd been issued when he trained Kurdish guerrillas outside Diyarbakir in another life. He was very ready for what would come next, might as well get it over with, he'd *warned* them. . . .

"Doug!" said the woman very sharply. Her companion relaxed the hand he had been tensing to crush that of Tom Kelly, to prove that he was tougher than this aging cowboy whose file he had read. Doug's handshake became just that, perfunctory and as professional as his smile or the names he had given.

Kelly grinned at the woman as he released Doug's hand. He knew the type well enough, because a reputation like Kelly's had made him a frequent target for boys of various ages who needed to prove their manhood. Usually there had been constraints on Kelly's own response: discipline, the mission, or a sheer desire for self-preservation.

This time he'd been pretty sure he had nothing to lose. He had no doubt that the grip in his own right hand, his pistol hand, could have matched any stress Doug put on it. It wouldn't have stopped there, however, within the civilized norms of the tennis club and the smoking room. It would have stopped when Kelly grabbed a left handful of Doug's crotch and used the double grip to swing the bigger man face-first against the mahogany door.

Elaine smiled back at Kelly tightly, with the irritation of a woman who knew that boys would be boys but who didn't in the least like the way such antics screwed up business. She was five four and somewhat fuller in the face than in the trim body beneath it. Her hair was short and as black as Kelly's own, surprisingly black unless she dyed it or was much younger than the forty suggested by the crow's-feet at the corners of her eyes. It was hard to tell with women's clothing, but Kelly suspected she could buy a pretty solid used car for what she had in her linen blouse, skirt, and sequined jacket.

Not that she'd even have considered buying a used car.

And the lady was smart, smart enough to defuse a

situation her companion didn't recognize and Kelly had been willing to play out just to end the waiting.

"We aren't here because of a problem with you, Mr. Kelly," she said in a clear contralto. There was a ring on the third finger of her right hand, a gold wedding band or something with the setting revolved toward her palm.

"Say, I'm really glad to hear that," said Kelly in a voice louder than he had first intended. There was a catch in his throat that he had to clear with volume inappropriate save as an indicator of how wired he was. Elaine already knew that, *that* was obvious, and Doug's concern seemed to be focused solely on striking a properly macho pose now that the woman had startled him out of testing the veteran.

Kelly took the VCR's controller as the bigger man stepped back. Doug looked surprised, but he did not object as Kelly switched the unit on again and began to rewind the tape.

There was an ordinary television in the lounge area, with the refrigerator and coffeepot, but the set here in Bianci's office had been unhooked from the building's cable system after Kelly had come on board. Kelly'd explained how easily the set could be used to monitor conversations within the room; and, when nobody believed him, had hooked an in-line bug to the cable lead outside the office and used the TV speaker itself to pick up sounds in place of a planted microphone. The television had immediately been replaced by a VCR and screen without antenna connections. Nobody in the office questioned Kelly's judgment about security again.

The videotape clicked to a stop and the screen's neutral pattern coalesced to a picture as Kelly pushed the Play switch. "You've got the ABC version," he said in a voice so distant in his own mind that he could not be sure he was speaking aloud. "I always thought that was the best one, too, what with the computer enhancement."

The tape had the stutter and low resolution to be expected from an original made with a hand-held minicam

from the deck of a sixty-ton torpedo boat. The ship filling
the frame looked to be an ordinary cargo vessel of moder-
ate size, unusual only in lacking the swatches of rust
that stain vessels if even inches of their steel sides
are flaked open to salt water. The antenna arrays were
there if you knew what to look for; but even to an expert,
they tended to be disguised by the multiple booms and
gantries dating from the period before the USS *White
Plains* had been converted from an attack cargo ship into a
technical research ship.

The water boiled just forward of the squared superstruc-
ture amidships. Kelly had turned down the audio track, but
network engineers had laid a flashing violet arrow onto the
picture as they magnified and outlined in complementary
yellow the gap blown in the *White Plains'* hull by the
torpedo launched from two hundred yards away. The man
with the camera had not started filming until moments
after the explosion, even as the shock waves pounded his
own vessel.

The engineers isolated on another portion of what was
originally a panorama shot with a short-focal-length lens.
The bow, with its designator TR4, expanded grainily on
the screen, flecks of random phosphor blurring the sharp-
ness somewhat as raster lines were added in processing
between those swept on the videotape original. The amidships three-inch gun installations had been stripped from
the *White Plains* to make room for additional antennas
when she was converted to her new mission, but one twin
turret on the foredeck had remained.

The guns pointed skyward, their outlines slightly jagged
from the computer enhancement. Somebody had told Kelly
that three-inch seventy-caliber guns should always be
mounted in pairs so that there might be one in operating
condition when the need arose. In the case of the *White
Plains,* both tubes had jammed at the first shots at the
fighters diving to strafe the vessel. The crew had continued

to traverse the weapons in a desperate attempt to bluff the attackers, however. Now a helicopter, a big Super Frelon, made a leisurely pass at mast level to fire rockets point-blank into the gun turret. Flashes of white, then orange as ammunition detonated in a secondary explosion, threw bits of men and plating skyward.

The engineers expanded the helicopter again in freeze-frame. This time the arrow and highlight were on the national insignia above the flotation and landing-gear sponson of the Super Frelon: the six-pointed star of the Israeli Air Force.

"Hard to tell," said Tom Kelly in a voice that did not tremble the way his hands did, forcing him to hold the VCR controller against his left leg while his right palm dried itself fiercely on his slacks, "whether it was that scene that bothered people most, or . . ."

The screen flashed back to a full shot of the *White Plains*, listing so that the hole ripped by the torpedo was already beneath the angry surface of the water. A lifeboat, white against the smooth gray hull, was being lowered from the davits amidships. There were about a dozen sailors in it, far fewer than its capacity, but somebody had decided to launch it before the ship's distress made that impossible.

Tom Kelly aimed the controller with a hand which no longer shook, and thumbed up the sound. The picture jumped, the cameraman flinching at the muzzle blasts of the 20 mm cannon near where he was standing. Shells from the automatic cannon burst against the flank of the *White Plains*, then traced from stern to amidships across the swaying lifeboat. The lifeboat's bow plunged as the sailor there on the winch lowered abruptly in a vain attempt to avoid the gunfire. His companion on the stern winch had leaped into the sea an instant before the shells chewed his position into flying splinters and the black smoke of bursting charges.

The gunfire paused and the video camera picked up the sound of men shouting on the deck of the torpedo boat, though the words were indistinct. Then the automatic cannon opened up again, its rate of fire deliberate enough that the crack of shells bursting could be heard as counterpoint to the louder, deeper, muzzle blasts. The bow of the lifeboat exploded just as it touched the water foaming into the torpedo wound. Even without enhancement, one could see the sailor's bare arms fling themselves wide as a white flash hid his torso.

The picture paused a moment later in a crackle of colored static: the Israeli cameraman had either run out of tape or stopped recording of his own volition. The ABC engineers had not ended there, however. As Kelly dialed off the audio again, the final picture flashed back onto the screen. A glowing outline expanded and drew with it the image of the man in the bow of the tilting lifeboat, his hands bracing him upright on the lowering tackle.

In jerky slow motion, his chest exploded and his body, hurled backward, rebounded from the steel hull. At the final degree of processed magnification, nothing could be seen of the American's face but a white blur and the blotch that was his open mouth. The hull behind him was red with the spray of all the blood in his chest cavity.

". . . or maybe," said Tom Kelly as he switched off the picture, "it was that one that caused most of the flap after it was shown on the evening news."

"Which one bothered you, Mr. Kelly?" said Elaine, one of the figures in his peripheral vision, ignored by the part of Kelly's mind that was now in control. . . . Ignored unless they moved suddenly, in which case he would kill them—in this moment he would kill them, and the release would be worth any regrets he had afterward.

"On principle," said Kelly in a voice like a pond of melt water, still and deep and very cold, "it all bothered me. If Israel had a problem with the way we pulled out of the Lebanon so sudden, that's fine—I understand that, getting mad about being left in the lurch. But you don't shoot up an American spy ship off your coast just because you're pissed at people in Washington. None of the poor bastards on the *White Plains* were behind the bugout from Lebanon.''

Kelly tried to set the controller on top of Congressman Bianci's desk, but his fingers slipped and the unit thumped instead to the blue-carpeted floor. The veteran's whole body shuddered and the room sprang into focus again.

''Shouldn't do that to me,'' said Kelly as he kneaded his cheeks and forehead with both hands. ''Really shouldn't.''

His voice had changed back to its usual lilting tenor as he went on, ''If you mean personally, Danny Pacheco was in the SIGINT Tank in the midships hold, right where the torpedo hit. Guess he was one of the fifty or so who drowned there before they knew what was going on. And yeah, he was a good enough friend that it bothered me. But that's already in the file, I guess.''

''You had good reason to hate the Israelis, Mr. Kelly,'' said the woman, giving a hitch to her skirt as she leaned her hips against the ceiling-height bookcase behind her. There was a tiny purse in her left hand, the gold-plated clasps an inch open. If she was smart enough to have *that* good a grasp of the situation, then she was smart enough to know that she had no real chance to clear the gun in her purse in a crisis—unless she planned to preempt Kelly.

The veteran laughed, briefly euphoric with the catharsis of having watched the attack on the *White Plains* for the first time since the slaughter came to its true climax in a military court in Jerusalem. ''I don't hate anybody,'' he said. ''Nobody in the world.''

''You hated them enough,'' retorted Doug, ''that you left your post in Turkey and spent two months tracking down that tape or something like it.''

Kelly looked at the other man, whose present splay-footed stance suggested karate training. Elaine was playing with her subject, a tense game because of Kelly's emotional charge, but all the better thereby to flesh skeletal file data into a man. Doug, on the other hand, was genuinely belligerent instead of professionally playing the bad cop in an interrogation routine. That was fine. . . .

"When I brought my boys back to Diyarbakir," Tom Kelly said in a soft voice and with a smile that gouged, "that was the third time I'd been over the line in Iraq, officially—"

Doug said nothing, though the pause dared him to speak. The Tasking Order had specifically forbidden American citizens to accompany into Iraq the guerrillas they trained at Turkish bases.

"When I came back, I had maybe a year of leave I'd never got around to taking. If I needed some time off, then I had it coming. And—"

"That doesn't—" started Doug.

"And *don't* give me any crap about leaving my post, the way NSA pulled the plug on the Kurds as soon as Iraq kicked out its Soviet techs," snarled Kelly in a voice like machineguns firing.

"It's the Kurds we're here to discuss with you, Mr. Kelly," said Elaine, reaching out with her right hand to stroke Doug's biceps and remind him of who and where he was. "Nobody cares that you released copies of that tape to the media three years ago."

"The Ford Commission came to no decision as to how that tape got into the hands of the press," Kelly corrected, rubbing his eyes and forehead again but with only his left hand, his eyes winking at the others through the gaps between his fingers.

"We're *not* here to trick you into an admission," said the woman in a sharper tone than any she had used earlier this night. "I've told you, it doesn't *matter*."

"Bullshit," said the veteran, the word soft and savage.

He was as wired as he had been the moment he walked into the room.

They were lying to him the way they had lied so often in the past, and through the flashes and roar of that past in his memory Tom Kelly shouted, "I told 'em I'd leave 'em alone if they'd do the same! I wasn't gonna talk to anybody, I wasn't gonna claim a fucking pension, and if they thought the answer was a chemical debriefing, then the team they sent to take me better be ready to play for keeps. Are you ready? *Are you ready, sonny?*"

"The material at the head of that tape," said the other man in confusion and bureaucratic concern, a turnabout so unexpected that it penetrated Kelly's fury as the woman's voice could not have done at this moment, "was simply to explain to third parties why we were bringing it to you, Mr. Kelly. If something happened on the way, that is. The real information's further back on the tape."

"Jesus," said Tom Kelly, the rage draining from him like blood from a ruptured spleen and leaving him flaccid. "Jesus."

"We understand that your fuse is short, Mr. Kelly," said Elaine. "We have no intention of lighting it, none whatever." She snapped her purse closed and set it deliberately on a bookshelf before she stepped over to the VCR.

"Nobody cares about the—incident, do they?" said Kelly, slumping back against the door and almost wishing there were a chair in arm's reach for him to sit on. "Well, that's a relief."

He looked around the office, taking stock as the VCR whirred to eject the tape into Elaine's hand. The only thing that didn't belong was the attaché case lying on Bianci's otherwise orderly desk. Dull black and unremarkable at first glance, the case was in fact a Halliburton—forged from T-6061 aluminum like the plating of an armored personnel carrier. The three-rotor combination lock hidden under the carrying handle was not impossible to defeat, and the sides could be opened with a cutting torch or the right saw—but anything of that sort would take time, and you could park a car on the case without even disturbing the watertight seal.

"It's old news," Doug was saying. "Do you care that somebody blew away the secretary of defense in Dallas in '63? It's like that."

"Like I say, glad to hear it," the veteran said.

It wasn't that he believed Doug in any absolute sense. Public release of the *White Plains* footage had squeezed the US government to take action against the State of Israel in ways that the highest levels had no wish to do once immediate tempers had cooled. A matter that had subsided into legal wrangling and the bland lies of politicians on both sides exploded into popular anger, spearheaded by members of Congress and the Senate to whom the massacre of American servicemen was not to be ignored as a matter of Middle Eastern policy.

There had been an immediate cutoff of aid to Israel—the munitions which fed the war in Lebanon to which US policy had abandoned Israeli troops, and the hard currency which alone kept afloat an economy which could not support its own welfare state, much less a protracted war. The aid had been resumed only after the Israeli minister of defense had resigned and thirty-seven serving members of the armed forces were given prison sentences ranging from two years to life after a public trial humiliating to the State which tried them.

"They buried Danny at Arlington," said the veteran inconsequently. "Seemed to make his widow happy enough. Me, I always figured that I'd want something besides a stone if it happened to me. . . ."

There were a lot of folks in both governments and, less formally, in Shin Bet—the Israeli department of security—who weren't in the least pleased with Tom Kelly since copies of the tape showed up in newsrooms across the US and Western Europe. There'd been one in the hands of TASS besides, just in case somebody got the idea of trying a really grandiose coverup. For sure, nothing Doug Blakeley had to say was official policy above a certain level—but the big blond wasn't a good enough actor to be lying about *his* mission, his and Elaine's.

The woman took from the Halliburton what looked like a small allen wrench and stuck it into a curved slot on the underside of the tape she had just ejected. The narrow slot didn't, when Kelly thought about it, look like anything he'd seen on a tape cassette before. Neither did it look particularly remarkable, however, even when Elaine clicked something clearly nonstandard into a detent at the farther end of the arc, then removed the wrench.

"Now it explodes?" the veteran asked, making it a joke instead of a flat question so that the pair of them wouldn't gain points if they chose to ignore him.

"There's a magnet inside the cassette," Elaine said as she reinserted the tape in the VCR. "The tape pauses at the end of the news segment. If anybody tried to play it beyond that point without locking the magnet out of the way, they'd get hash." She poked Play, picked up the remote control which still lay on the carpet, and stepped back close to Kelly as the tape advanced with a hiss and diagonals of white static across the screen.

"Look, you ought to understand," said Kelly with his eyes on the television, "the people in Israeli service who— got that tape to the guy who released it. It wasn't just personal payoffs, and it wasn't in-house politics alone, either. There were some people who thought shooting allies in lifeboats was a bad idea . . . and thought getting away with it once was an even worse one."

"That really doesn't concern us, Mr. Kelly," Elaine said flatly, and the murmur of empty tape gave way to a segment recorded without an audio track.

"Sonoabitch," muttered Kelly, for the location was unmistakable to him despite the poor quality of the picture. The segment had been shot with a hand-held minicam, like the footage of the *White Plains* before, but the earlier portion had at least been exposed in the bright sunlight of a Mediterranean afternoon. This scene had been recorded at night in the angle of massive walls illuminated by car headlights, while drizzle flicked the beams and wobbled across the lens itself.

But there was no other stretch of fortification comparable to that on the screen save for the Great Wall of China. Kelly had trained Kurds for two years at Diyarbakir. He could recognize the walls of the great Roman fortress even at a glance.

"Corner by where the Turistik meets Gazi Street," the veteran said aloud, a guess rather than an identification—the sort of thing he did to keep people off-balance about what he knew or might know; the sort of thing he did when he was nervous and off-balance himself.

The walls of black basalt were gleaming and lightstruck where their wet lower surfaces were illuminated; the twenty feet above the quivering headlights was only a dark mass indistinguishable from the rain-sodden sky as the cameraman walked forward and jiggled the point of view.

Close to the wall was a clump of figures in dark overcoats, who shifted away abruptly, backs turned to the approaching camera.

"Who filmed this?" asked Kelly, looking up at the woman who watched him while her companion seemed mesmerized by the television itself. "And when?"

"It was taken three days ago," Elaine said, nodding toward the screen to return the subject's attention to where it belonged. "And officially, everyone at the site is a member of Turkish Military Intelligence."

There were two bodies on the ground near where the men in overcoats had been standing. The wall sloped upward at a noticeable angle, providing a broad base of support for the eight-foot thick battlements at the top.

"Didn't think relations between us and MIT had been so close since Ecevit was elected Prime Minister," the veteran said, pumping them because it had always been his job to gather information.

"Watch the screen, please," the woman said as Doug snorted and said, "No problem. Third Army Command, old buddy. No problem at all."

Elaine paused the tape and gave her companion a hard look. Kelly faced the television and grinned, amused at the two others and amused at himself—for gathering data on a situation that didn't concern him and which he wouldn't *allow* to concern him, no matter what.

The tape resumed. One of the cars must have been driven forward as the cameraman walked up to the bodies, because his shadow and those of some others who had scurried out of the scene were thrown crazily across the basalt wall. The point of view moved even closer, shifting out of focus, then sharpening again as the cameraman adjusted.

The screen steadied on a head-and-torso view of a man facedown in a puddle with one arm flung forward. He wore a dark blue coat and a leather cap which had skewed when he hit the ground. A gloved hand on an arm in a black trenchcoat reached from out of frame, removing the cap and lifting the dripping, bearded face into full view of the camera.

"Son of a bitch," Kelly repeated, softly but very distinctly this time. "Mohammed Ayyubi. He was one of my section leaders back, back when I was workin' there and points south. . . . He was from the district himself."

"Ayyubi has been living in Istanbul for the past three years," Elaine said coolly, watching the screen to keep Kelly's attention on it. "Recently he began to travel extensively in Central Europe."

The hand holding the Kurd to the camera dropped him, letting his face splash back onto the puddled stone. It didn't matter to Mohammed, whose eyes would never blink again until somebody thumbed the lids down over the glazed pupils; but Kelly's own body grew very still for an instant.

"He had a brother in Istanbul," the veteran said softly. "Think I met him there once. . . ." When the brother came to see Mohammed in a base hospital so expertly staffed that all but one of the Kurd's fingers had been saved despite the ten days since they were mangled.

"Ahmed, yes," said the woman as the cameraman walked his point of view over to the other body. The same hand and arm reached into the frame to angle the victim's face toward the headlights.

Kelly glanced from the arm's wristwatch, a momentary black smear on the screen before the cuff of the overcoat hid it again, to the Omega which Doug wore. The quality of the data proved nothing but possibility, and the possibilities were endless. . . . "I don't know that one," said Kelly to the television.

"No, you sure don't," said Doug, and there was more in his voice than mere agreement.

The cameraman had panned the second body only incidentally in maneuvering for a head shot. The figure appeared to be of average height, perhaps a little shorter if American rather than Anatolian males were the standard of comparison. Its clothing was ordinary, trousers of a shade darker than the coat—both of them brown or taupe—and a cloth cap that lay beside the head. The features were regular and unusual only in having no facial hair. In Turkey, where a moustache was as much a part of a man's accoutrements as a pack of cigarettes, that was mildly remarkable.

There was a silvery chain and a medallion of some sort

high up on the figure's neck. The hand and overcoat sleeve entered the field of view to touch the bauble.

The camera jumped a moment later, the lens panning a crazy arc of the walls and night sky as the cameraman's heels slipped on the pavement. Doug's right hand gripped his left as fiercely as if it belonged to someone else and was holding a weapon. Elaine was taut, watching Kelly until the veteran glanced at her.

Kelly was affected only at a conscious level, touched by wonderment at the emotional reaction of the others to what was, after all, a fraud. TV trickery, makeup, and muddy camerawork to make the gimmickry less instantly patent. But it couldn't frighten an adult, not somebody like Tom Kelly who knew that the real face of horror was human. . . .

The camera steadied again, though it was six feet farther from the subject than before, and it was some moments before the cameraman thought to adjust his focus. Not makeup at all, thought Kelly, squinting. The 'head' above the necklace was smaller than that of any human beyond the age of six, so whoever was responsible had used a dummy. . . . "Roll back and freeze it where he touches the necklace," Kelly said.

He expected the woman either to make excuses or ignore him. To his surprise, she reached over with the remote control unit and said, "Go ahead, Mr. Kelly. Freeze any part of the film you choose to."

The veteran cued the tape back in three jerky stages, angry that he had not been paying enough attention to get to the point he wanted in two tries at worst. Neither Elaine's stillness nor Doug's outthrust chin disguised the fact that the pair was nervous; and this time the cause was not the very real one of Tom Kelly's anger.

The bland, human face, only partly hidden by the gloved hand reaching for the medallion. Then the hand jerked back and, in the instant before the startled cameraman jumped away also, Kelly was able to pause the VCR into as close an equivalent of freeze-frame as a television's raster scanning could achieve.

Somebody was pretty good. Kelly couldn't see any sign of the transition, but what filled the screen now was nothing close to human.

Not only was the head the size of a grapefruit, it had no apparent eyes. There was a mouth, though, a blue-lipped circular pit lined with teeth hooked like blackberry thorns. The nose was a gash like that of a man Kelly had met in a village near Erzerum, his limbs and appendages eaten away by the final stages of leprosy. Either water droplets were creating an odd effect, or the surface of the dummy was scaly, and the scales divided at the midline of the face in a row of bony scutes.

Kelly thumbed the Pause button and let the tape roll forward. When the camera achieved focus and steadiness again there was a somewhat clearer view of the alien visage, but nothing beyond what Kelly had already seen. "All right," he said, "what happens next? The mothership comes down and vaporizes Diyarbakir? You know, I'd miss the place."

"There's nothing more on the tape," Elaine said shortly. The screen dissolved into diagonal static again as if it were ruled by her voice.

Kelly tried to switch off the VCR. When his thumb touched the Eject button on the controller as well, the tape whirred and cycled itself halfway out of the feed slot. The veteran's anger flared, though no one in the world but he knew the act was nervous clumsiness instead of deliberation. He was allowing himself to be spooked!

"We need a Kurdish speaker," Doug said with a toss of his head that seemed to clear a dark aura from his soul, "and we may need someone who was involved with Operation Birdlike—assuming Ayyubi wasn't the only member of that group who's gotten involved in this new business."

"Go home." Kelly spoke flatly as he shook himself and

set the remote unit back on Bianci's desk. "Go home so I can lock up behind you and go home myself." He rubbed his eyes with his left forearm. "Been a long day, been a long three years. I'm just not in a mood for government-issue bullshit any more."

"It's not bullshit, Mr. Kelly," the woman said as she watched him with the inscrutable eyes of a cat viewing a bird too big to be prey. "Earth has been visited by aliens—*is being* visited, we think. Men who you know have been in contact with them."

"Don't you think," Doug Blakeley interjected, "that it's time the USG got involved instead of leaving things to barbs whose only link to the twentieth century is a machinegun?"

Kelly turned toward the other man, prey indeed if he chose—as he did not. Doug was trash, the discussion was trash, and Elaine—

Elaine stepped between the two men, close enough to Kelly that she had to tilt her face to meet his eyes. "He doesn't matter, Mr. Kelly," the black-haired woman said as if she had read the veteran's mind. "This matters very much, if it's true. You know it does."

"And *you* know a videotape doesn't prove jack shit!" Kelly shouted, as if to drive her back by the violence of his reaction.

"Then come look at the body itself, Kelly," Elaine said with an acid precision. "If you're man enough."

She would not back away from him and he would not face her glare, so Kelly spun on his heel to stare out at the reception area. "Figured you'd tell me that, 'Gee, the Turkish police had it'—or maybe the plane bringing it back to the World had flown into a mountain." Even five years after the last tour in the Lebanon, Kelly had the veterans' trick of referring to the continental United States as 'the World.' "

"The evidence—the body—is at Fort Meade," said the

woman behind him. "We have a car. We can have you there in forty minutes to examine it yourself."

"Are you doing a job on me, honey?" Kelly said as he turned again to face her. "Is this all a way to get me behind walls with no fuss 'r bother?"

"Oh, come now, Kelly," said the blond man standing behind Elaine, arms akimbo. "Don't you think you're being overly dramatic?"

There were only two things in the office which were not Congressman Bianci's—or alive. Kelly stepped toward the VCR. Elaine, who thought he was trying to close with her companion, sidestepped quickly to block the veteran. She was wearing sequined flats rather than the high heels to be expected with the formality of her suit. The sensible footgear saved her from falling when Kelly's shoulder slammed her back as remorselessly as a hundred and eighty pounds of brick in motion.

Doug shouted something that began as a warning and ended in a squawk as his hands by reflex clasped the stumbling woman. Kelly bent, his back to the couple momentarily as he took the videotape from the VCR. The cassette was cool, its upper edge rough beneath his fingers. As Elaine's hands touched Doug's, in part for balance's sake but also to restrain her companion as both stared at Kelly, the veteran pivoted and smashed the tape down on the aluminum attaché case.

The impact did not scar the anodized surface of the Halliburton, but the polystyrene videocassette shattered with a sound like the spiral fracture of a shin bone.

"Hey!" Doug shouted. Elaine's hands clamped in earnest on those of the man behind her.

Kelly slammed the cassette down again. The lower half of it disintegrated like a window breaking, spilling coils of half-inch tape along with the take-up sprocket. The veteran raised his right hand and opened it, letting the remainder of the cassette fall to the floor. Bits of black plastic clung to the sweat of his palm, and an inch-long shard had dug a bloody gouge into his flesh.

Kelly grinned at the others with his hand still lifted like a caricature of a wooden Indian. "You know," he said in a voice so light that only his eyes suggested what he was saying was the baldest truth, "I figured when I walked in here it was fair odds I'd kill you both. Guess I'll go back to Meade with you instead—but no more jokes about me acting crazy, okay?"

"You can call Representative Bianci and tell him where you're going," the woman said, twisting sinuously out of Doug's arms and stepping to the side, her fingertips smoothing the lines of her skirt.

"*I'm* doing this to me," Kelly replied, dusting his palms together like a cymbals player to clear them. Sweat stung the open gash, and he felt like a damned fool; overdramatic just like the blond meathead had said. "I don't want Carlo getting involved if it's me being too dumb to keep my head down."

Doug massaged each wrist with the opposite hand, then knelt and began gathering up the tape and the larger bits of the cassette as well. Elaine said, "It might reassure him, you know."

"He'll be happy enough if he doesn't get a call from Housekeeping about the blood on 'is upholstery," the veteran said with a savage laugh. "Look, let's get this over, okay? I said I was going, didn't I?"

The attaché case contained no files or papers of any sort, not even a manila envelope into which Doug could pour the remnants of the tape cassette, so they had to lie loose on the nylon-covered polyurethane foam instead. There was, however, a compact two-way radio in a fitted niche. The radio had no nameplate or manufacturer's information on it, but neither was the unit a piece of government-issue hardware that Kelly recognized. Well, he'd been out—way out—for three years, and equipment was the least of what might change.

The stub of the coiled whip antenna bobbled as Doug spoke into the radio, glaring unconsciously at Kelly as he did so. All data was useful somewhere, in some intelligence paradise—you couldn't spend a big chunk of your life in Collection and not think so. But it was only reflex that made Kelly's mind focus on the chance of hearing a one-time-only code word, and that no more than the means of summoning a car. Doug's bridling was an empty reflex as well—and both reactions were complicated by the fact that each of the men had been top dog for a long time, in ways that had nothing to do with chains of command.

Kelly was just loose enough at the moment to both recognize the situation and find it amusing. "Hey, junior," he said to Doug as the radio crackled a muted, unintelligible reply, "I think you lost your place in the pecking order."

"Let's go," said Elaine in a neutral voice, waving Doug out the door ahead of her and falling in behind him—separating the men since she knew that Bianci's aide must be last out of the office to lock up.

The guard tonight at the side entrance of the Longworth Building was a heavy black woman. Kelly had seen and smiled at her a hundred times over the years as she rummaged harmlessly through whatever briefcase he happened to be carrying. It wasn't an effective way to defeat a serious attempt to blow up the building, but it didn't hurt Kelly—who, even when he was on active duty, had not traveled with documents he minded other people inspecting.

Today the guard drew back as she saw the trio approaching her post from down the corridor. "Good night, Ethel," Kelly called, never too tired—or wired—to be pleasant to anybody with a dismal job like guard, refuse collector, or code clerk.

This time Ethel only nodded back, her concentration

preoccupied by Doug and the Halliburton he had carefully locked. There was no reason in the world not to have opened the case like a citizen when he entered the building. Instead, Doug had obviously flashed credentials that had piqued the curiosity of even a guard who saw the stream of visitors to members of the House of Representatives. It was the same sort of bass-ackwardness that caused CIA officers operating under embassy cover in foreign venues to be issued non-American cars. They could therefore be separated with eighty percent certainty from the real State Department personnel by anyone who bothered to check traffic through the embassy gates.

"By the way," Kelly goaded in a voice that echoed on the marble, "who do you work for? SAVE? Or are you Joint Chiefs Support Activity?"

"You *stupid* bastard," Doug snarled, twisting in midmotion to glare at the other man, his palm thumping on the door's glass panel instead of the push bar.

"Mr. Kelly," said Elaine as she reached past her companion to thrust the door open, "you might consider whether in a worst-case scenario you wish to have involved a number of outsiders in this matter." Her voice was clear but not loud, losing itself in the rush of outside air chilled by the shower that had been threatening all day.

Two cars pulled up at the curb outside just as the trio exited the Longworth Building. The follow-car was a gray Buick with a black vinyl roof, but the vehicle its lights illuminated was a bright green Volvo sedan. The Volvo's driver got out quickly, leaving his door open, and trotted around to the curb side.

Elaine muttered a curse at the weather and hunched herself in her linen jacket. Doug strode forward as if there were no rain, the attaché case in his left hand swinging as if it weighed no more than a normal leather satchel.

"Sorry 'bout that," Kelly said as he and the woman hesitated under the roof overhang. "Shouldn't let my temper go when I'm around innocent bystanders. Not for silly shit, especially.''

''Let's go,'' the woman said, darting across the wide sidewalk as a gust of wind lashed raindrops curving like a snake track across the pools already on the concrete.

The driver had opened both curbside doors for them. The veteran paused deliberately to see whether or not Elaine would get in before he did. She slid quickly into the back seat, showing a length of thigh that amused Kelly because it really did affect him. There were people who thought that sex was something physical. Damn fools.

''You can sit anywhere you please, Mr. Kelly,'' the woman called from the car with a trace of exasperation. ''All the doors work normally.''

The front seats were buckets, so they really hadn't planned to sandwich him between the two of them—or more likely, between the former driver and Doug, who was now behind the wheel of the Volvo adjusting the angle of the backrest. ''Right,'' said Kelly, feeling a little foolish as he got into the front for the sake of the legroom. The man who had brought the Volvo to them closed both doors and scurried back to the follow-car.

Doug did not wait for the former driver to be picked up before goosing the Volvo's throttle hard enough to spin the drive wheels on the wet pavement. The right rear tire scraped the edge of the curb before the sedan angled abruptly into the traffic lane and off through the night.

''If these're the radials I'd guess they were,'' said Kelly, angling sideways in the pocket of the seat, ''then that's a pretty good way to spend twenty minutes in the rain, changing the tire with a ripped sidewall.''

Doug glanced at his passenger, but then merely grunted and switched the headlights to bright. Raindrops appeared to curve toward them as the car accelerated.

Doug's face had a greenish cast from the instrument lights. Kelly glimpsed the woman between the hollow headrests, her features illuminated in long pulses by the oncoming cars. The black frame of Elaine's hair made her face a distinct oval even during intervals of darkness.

You couldn't really see into a head like that, thought Kelly as the hammer of tires on bad pavement buzzed him into a sort of drifting reverie. Not in good light, not under stress. Sometimes you could predict the words the mind within would offer its audience; but you'd never know for sure the process by which the words were chosen, the switches and reconsiderations at levels of perceived side-effects which a man like Kelly never *wanted* to reach.

The veteran straightened so that his shoulder blade was no longer against the window ledge. He was physically tired, and the meeting in Bianci's office had been as stressful and disorienting as a firefight. If he didn't watch it, he'd put himself into a state more suggestible than anything an interrogation team could achieve with hypnotic drugs. Even the thought of that made Kelly's skin crawl in a hot, prickling wave which spread downward from the peak of his skull.

"Which of you's in charge?" he asked. The hostility implicit in the question was another goad to keep him alert.

"You'll meet some of the people in charge tonight, if you care to," the woman said, her face as expressionless in the lights of an oncoming truck as it was a moment later when backlit by the follow-car.

"No," Kelly said. "I mean which of *you* two has the rank. When it comes down to cases, who says 'jump' and who says 'how high?' "

Doug turned with a fierceness which their speed and the turnpike traffic made unwise, snapping, "For somebody who claims he doesn't intend to talk to anybody, you show a *real* inability to know when to shut the fuck up!"

Kelly grinned. The woman in the back seat said to his profile, "Would you take a direct order from either one of us, Mr. Kelly?"

The veteran looked at her directly and laughed. "No," he said. "No, I don't guess I would."

"Then our ranks don't matter," she said coolly, and Kelly decided that wasn't much of a lie in comparison to other things he'd heard tonight.

And would hear later.

"Oh, Christ on a crutch," Kelly muttered, locking his fingers behind his neck and arching his shoulders back as fiercely as he could in the cramped confines. "You know," he said while he held the position, headlights flicking red patterns of blood to his retinas behind closed eyelids, "This's going to be a first for me. I worked eighteen years for NSA, more'r less, and I never set foot in the building."

He opened his eyes, relaxed, and as he stared through the windshield toward the future added, "Can't say I much wanted to."

Kelly hadn't intended to draw a reaction from Doug, but the driver half-turned—realized that the woman was sitting directly behind him, out of his sight no matter how sharply he craned his neck—and then tried to catch her eye in the rearview mirror.

"Mr. Kelly," Elaine said, and Kelly surmised that she was speaking with greater circumspection than usual, "I don't want you to be startled by something you misunderstood. We won't be going to NSA headquarters or any portion of Fort Meade dedicated to the National Security Agency. Some disused barracks within the reservation were—taken over for present purposes. You shouldn't be concerned that we enter at a gate different from the one you may have expected."

Kelly laughed. "Well, that explains the *big* question I still had."

Doug glanced at him, but the veteran had been pausing for breath, not a response. "Couldn't figure," he went on, "how you'd gotten NSA to cooperate with *any* damn body

else—which you are, even though I don't much care who,
not really."

Headlights picked out a tiny smile at the corners of
Elaine's lips as she said, "We're government employees,
Mr. Kelly. As you were, and as you are now—through
Congressman Bianci."

The Volvo and the Buick behind it had cloverleafed
from the Baltimore-Washington Turnpike onto the cracked
pavement of Highway 1. Dingy motels and businesses
lined both sides of its four undivided lanes. There was
very little traffic in comparison to the turnpike, and Doug
made only rolling stops at the signal lights, presumably
counting on his ID to get him past a late-cruising Maryland
cop.

'If you've got it, flaunt it' had always been the motto of
the intelligence community. It wasn't a great way to do
business, but it attracted to the profession bright, aggressive people who might otherwise have done something
socially useful with their lives.

Christ, Kelly thought, he was too tired for this crap.
Too tired in every way.

The gates in the chain link fence encircling Fort Meade
were open, but there was a guard post and a red and white
crossbar, which a GI lifted after a glance at Doug's identification. As the car accelerated again, Kelly got a glimpse
of the unit patch on the left shoulder of the trooper's
fatigues: a horse and bend dexter worked in gold embroi-
dery on a shield-shaped blue field.

"Goddam," the veteran muttered as the car swept by,
"Twelfth Cav, wasn't it?"

"You were assigned to them, weren't you?" said the
woman, finding in a mis-memory of Kelly's file a safe topic
for an interval of increasing tension. "During operations in
the Anti-Lebanon?"

Kelly laughed, glad himself of the release. He got antsy
nowadays around uniforms, even when he was just mixing

with brass at a Washington cocktail party or visiting a research installation far too sensitive to be compromised by an attempt to hold Thomas James Kelly for questioning.

The only sensible explanation for tonight's affair was that it was an operation intended for just that end: to close the doors around Tom Kelly unless and until folks in DC and Jerusalem decided they should be opened again. But he was going along with it, he'd said he would, and he was in favor of anything that took his mind off the barracks they drove past and their insulation from what civilians thought was the real world.

"That was a different armored cavalry regiment," Kelly said, lifting himself by his left shoulder and feet so that he could hitch up his trousers. The Volvo had leather upholstery, and he was sweating enough to stick slightly to the seat cushion. "Close, but no cigar. These guys—" They were coming to another checkpoint, and this time the gates were shut. The fencing gleamed in the headlights as the car paused for a soldier with a small flashlight to check Doug's ID. The earth raked smooth around the postholes had a raw, unweathered look.

"These guys are a public relations unit," Kelly said, trying to control his voice the way he would clean a bad signal on tape—trimming out everything but what communicated data, as if there were no such things as static, bleed-over, or fear. "The President needs troops for a parade, visiting brass wants to review something—you know the drill—the Twelfth takes care of it. Nicely painted tanks and APCs, troops in strack uniforms—you know. They even paint the roadwheels of the tanks. Rots the rubber, but it sho' do look black from the reviewing stands."

"You may pass, sir," said the guard, and as the gate opened he saluted.

There was a second chain link barrier twelve feet within the first, with its gate inset further to permit a car to stand between the checkpoints while both gates were closed. The inner fencing was covered with taupe fiberglass panels, translucent and sufficient protection against anyone trying to observe the compound from ground level. The soldiers manning the inner guard post wore fatigues and carried automatic rifles with a degree of assurance very different from that of the Twelfth Cav guards with pistols in patent leather holsters.

The man who examined the credentials this time stooped to look at all three occupants of the car. He wore neither a unit patch nor rank insignia, but there were chevrons and rockers in his eyes when he met Kelly's.

There but for the grace of God, the veteran thought, if his gift for languages was really a manifestation of grace rather than a curse. Being able to process intercept data in real time had put Tom Kelly farther up the sharp end than he ever would have gone if he knew *only* how to sight a cal fifty and handle twenty-ounce blocks of *plastique*. He'd spent a lot of years in places where discipline was something you had yourself because there was nobody around to impose it on you.

When the people who thought in hierarchies realized that Platoon Sergeant Thomas J. Kelly was both willing and able to make a major policy decision for the United States government, it made him very frightening.

"*Christ,* I'm scared," Kelly said with a lilt and a bright smile to make a joke of it as the guard stepped away.

The woman in the back seat smiled with the precision of a gunlock. "I've read your file, Mr. Kelly," she said as the gate squealed open. "If I had any doubt about the purpose of this exercise, I promise I wouldn't be the person nearest by when you learned the truth."

Doug glanced up at the rearview mirror again as he drove forward, his expression unreadable.

Within the second enclosure were four frame buildings, a number of cars—Continentals and a Mercedes, all with opera windows—and more armed men in unmarked fatigues. Incandescent area lights were placed within the fencing on temporary poles, throwing hard shadows and displaying every flaw in the peeling, mustard-colored paint on the buildings. They had probably been constructed during the Second World War as temporary barracks, and had survived simply because military bureaucracy misfiled a great deal more than it discarded.

Well, Kelly had once been very glad for a case of Sten guns hidden against need, decades before, in a warehouse in Homs. It wasn't the sort of waste that bothered him.

Three of the buildings were two-story, but the fourth was one floor with a crawl space, like the shotgun houses built in rural areas at about the same period. It would have been a company headquarters and orderly room; now it was the prize which the troops billeted in the other three buildings were guarding.

Drivers stood by their limousines, one of them polishing a fender with his chamois, as they watched the newcomers. Instead of parking along the fenceline with the other cars, Doug pulled up to an entrance at one end of the low building and shut off the engine. Kelly reached across his own body to open his door left-handed. The latch snicked normally, permitting Kelly to step out of the car while he tried both to observe everything around him and to look relaxed.

Neither attempt was possible under the circumstances. When Kelly met Elaine's eyes across the roof of the Volvo he laughed as he would have done at sight of his own face in a mirror.

"Hell," he said to the woman, "when I was a kid there was a lotta people thought I'd be hanged before I was old enough to vote. I beat that by just about twenty years, didn't I?" He followed them inside.

There were no guards within the building, no women besides Elaine, and only one uniform—Major Redstone when Kelly served under him in the Shuf, and now, from the star on each shoulder, a brigadier general. He was one of the six men waiting in what had been the orderly room, the east half of the structure. The others wore not uniforms but suits, and suits—in this sort of setting—tended to blur together in Kelly's mind. Fight-or-flight reflexes pumped hormones into his bloodstream. It wasn't the sort of situation he handled very well.

"Hey, Red," the veteran said with a nod. "Hadn't heard you were gonna be here."

"Hi, Kelly," said the general. "Glad you could make it." Even as he spoke, Redstone's eyes were checking the faces of the men to either side of him. Any intention he might have had to say more was lost in whatever he saw in those faces.

They had prepared for this business by moving into the orderly room a massive wooden table, scarred and as old as the building, and a complement of armchairs whose varnish was ribbed and blackened by long storage. No one was seated when Kelly entered the room, and if they expected *him* to lock himself between a heavy chair and a heavy table, they were out of their collective mind.

The men, the Suits, ranged in age from one in his late twenties—younger than Doug—to another who could have been anywhere from sixty to eighty and with eyes much older than that. That one's motions were smooth enough to put him on the lower end of the age range, but the liver spots on his gnarled hands were almost the same color as the fabric of his three-piece suit. "Tuttle?" he said with a glance at the woman.

"Mr. Kelly has agreed to look at the physical evidence, Mr. Pierrard," Elaine said in her most careful voice. "He has his own life to live, and he certainly won't become involved in the present matter unless he's convinced it is of the—highest order of significance."

"Well, does he think *we'd* be here?" Pierrard snapped. He stared up and down Kelly with a look not of contempt but superiority—the look a breeder gives to someone else's thoroughbred. "*Do* you, Kelly?"

The veteran had instinctively frozen into a formal 'at ease' posture: feet spread to shoulder width and angled 45° from midline; shoulders back, spine straight, hands clasped behind his back—and the hard feel of the weapon there was no comfort now. He was furious with himself and with everyone around him because the simple answer hadn't been right: they hadn't brought him here to arrest him.

Reflex wanted to say, "No sir." Very distinctly, Tom Kelly said, "Why don't you get to fucking business and show me this thing?"

"Take him in," Pierrard said curtly, with an upward lift of the chin which Doug and Elaine took as a direction to them.

"This way, Mr. Kelly," Elaine said without looking back at him. She walked toward the room to the side, which had been an office for either the company commander or the first sergeant. She took a deep breath, and Doug echoed the sound hissingly as he followed the others. Perhaps it was the smell in the smaller room, but Kelly did not think so.

There was a white-enameled cooling case in the office, purring with a normality belied only by its present location. Condensate on the slanted glass-and-chrome top hid the contents until Doug threw a switch. Floodlights mounted on the ceiling illuminated the case starkly, and the odor which had been present even through the tobacco smoke in the orderly room became so overpowering now that its source could not be denied.

The creature under glass was the same as whatever Kelly had seen on tape, and it stank like the aftermath of an electrical fire in a spice warehouse. Neither the chemical nor the organic components of the odor were particularly unpleasant, and even the combination could have been accepted in another context. Somebody in the other room swore.

"Didn't look this big," said Kelly as he walked over to the case and the flaccid gray thing within. "This tall."

Without clothes, the creature—or construct—but the men in the other room wouldn't be playing games with a little scut like Tom Kelly—looked very frail; but the height should have been more than six feet. When the veteran bent over the case his shadow cut the direct reflection from the glass and gave him an even clearer vision of the creature. The arrangement of torso and appendages was that of a human being, but the limbs had the appearance of flat-wire antenna lead rather than the more nearly circular cross section of a man's.

Of the limbs of an animal that belonged on Earth.

Elaine lifted the center section of glass; the cooler really was an ordinary grocery case. "It's a refrigerator, not a freezer," she said while Doug muttered something unintelligible in the background. "Freezing would have broken down the cell walls. Of course, it can't be kept this way forever. When they've completed the autopsy, they'll . . ."

The torso had been laid open in a long curving incision, but the flap of fine-scaled integument had been pinned back in place when the pathologists paused in their examination. Doctors tended to be self-ruled men in whom arrogance was a certain concomitant of ability if not proof of that ability. Kelly wondered who was handling the autopsy, whether the men in the other room had chosen to go with the best pathologists available or rather to use doctors whom they knew they could control.

They were trying to deal Tom Kelly in on this business. That gave him a notion of where their heads were.

Christ on a crutch. It really was what it seemed to be.

Kelly's left hand reached into the case, his fingers tracing but not touching the surface of one of the arms. The hand had four fingers and no thumb, but it looked as though the two halves could be folded over one another along the central axis.

"There're surgical gloves, if you want," the woman said. She was looking at Kelly while she held the lid open. Only the flare of her nostrils implied that her eyes were on him to excuse them from having to view the alien. "It doesn't have knee and elbow joints the way we do. Each arm is a double column of bones like paired spinal columns, and they're connected only by muscle."

"You can close it," the veteran said, jerking his hand out of the cooler and flexing it repeatedly to work off the damp miasma that clung to the skin. The lid thumped behind him as he turned, and he thought he heard a grateful sigh. "How did it die?" he asked, facing Doug. "Did Mohammed kill it?"

Men waiting in the other room either glanced away when Kelly caught their eyes or matched his with stares of their own. Pierrard nodded coolly as he tamped a tiny meerschaum with a pipe tool shaped like a pistol cartridge.

Doug shrugged, his expression less nonchalant when it remained fixed even though the rest of his body moved.

"They were both killed by nine-millimeter bullets," Elaine said as she walked into the veteran's field of view again. "Turkish service ammunition lots, though of course that indicates nothing. We'd had reports that bullets didn't— affect them, fired at very close range. Those reports appear to be in error."

The palm of Kelly's right hand stung where he had gouged it, partly from his sweat and partly from the aura of burned pepper and phenolic resin which emanated from the thing in the cooler. "You can't be too close to miss what you're aiming at," Kelly said. "Take my word for it, honey."

He walked back into the larger room, again facing the men whom he'd never wanted to see and who didn't see him even now that he stood in front of them. Except for maybe Redstone, Kelly was no more human to the eyes sliding over him like water over a statue than was the dead thing in the cooler behind him. Not officer material, that was god *damned* sure, and both sides would feel thankful for that. . . .

"Where's his clothes?" Kelly asked Pierrard in a harsh, hectoring tone. "And the necklace he had on? Was that all?"

Pierrard took a deep pull on his pipe. Its bowl was discolored almost to the shade and patterning of briar.

The youngest Suit said, "The clothes were probably of Turkish manufacture—handwork, no labels, but local manufacture. The shoes were Turkish, made in Ankara. The legs must have *twisted* to form an ankle joint, the sockets in the leg and arm columns are offset enough to do that."

Kelly stepped closer to Pierrard, so that he was wrapped in coils of pipe smoke whose bitterness underlay the cloying surface odor. "Where's the hardware, Pierrard?" he demanded. "If this isn't all phony, then that damned thing had a gadget to make him look like a man, not a lamprey. Where *is* it?"

Pierrard's lips quirked as he lowered his pipestem. He blew a careful smoke ring toward the low ceiling.

"There were six items of equipment which couldn't be identified," said the young Suit, who was too beefy to be really aristocratic and whose forehead now glistened with sweat. Redstone knuckled his jaw and grimaced, but nobody else Kelly could see appeared to be breathing.

"None of them were larger than a cigarette case, and none of them did anything noticeable when they were tested. We think that when—" The young Suit glanced up and beyond Kelly. "—We think that when the medallion was first touched, all of the equipment shut down. The units we've sectioned after testing appear to have melted internally, but we can't be sure what they looked like before they came into our hands."

"Shit!" Kelly said and turned abruptly. He slapped the doorjamb, shaking the partition wall and making the overhead light jounce. Doug jumped aside, though this time the veteran's anger was directed against the situation rather than any human.

Any human except himself and the fact that he didn't seem able to walk away—that he had buttons that cynical bastards in suits could still push.

"Kelly," said General Redstone from the far side of the room, "we need you on this one. It's no time to fuck around."

"Yessir," said Kelly, slowly facing around and taking a breath that lifted his eyes back into contact with those of the others in the room. "What did you think you could get me to do? Give you names?"

"Because members or at least a member of the Kurdish separatist community had contact with the aliens," said Pierrard, "we need a knowledgeable person in place in that community at the earliest possible moment." His lengthened vowels had probably been natural for him before they were popularized by the Kennedy and Culver presidencies.

"You've got other Kurdish speakers." Kelly walked over to a window and stared out at the lighted fence with his hands on the sash. "Hell, you've got agents, CIA's got agents, every damn body in the *world's* got Kurdish agents."

"We've had no reports regarding—alien presences," said a voice Kelly hadn't heard before, a Suit of his own age with more gut and less hair. "It may be that depending on foreign nationals in this venue cannot guarantee satisfactory results."

"We aren't looking for a translator, Kelly," said General Redstone as the veteran turned to face them again. "We don't need somebody to man an intercept receiver. To get on this as fast as we've got to, there's got to be somebody the sources'll trust—and somebody who can go

to them. There's some other training officers—paramilitary
types—but they *don't* speak Kurdish, not really. You were
the only real NSA staffer in Birdlike, the only one with a
real language specialty. Otherwise the operation was slotted there just to keep clear of the Freedom of Information
Act.''

"Got a problem with Kurds not trusting the USG all of
a sudden, hey?'' Kelly said, his voice struggling against
the leash his conscious mind was trying to keep on it.
Pierrard's face was the only thing in the room which was
not receding from focus. "Couldn't be because of the way
Operation Birdlike was wrapped up with all the finesse of
a hand grenade, d'ye suppose?''

"Yes, of course that had something to do with it,'' the
old man agreed unemotionally as he lifted his pipe again.

"There were people in fucking *Iraq* waiting for the
C-130 to duck in with the pallet of *supplies,* you bastard!''
Kelly shouted. "And instead folks are shaking hands in
some air-conditioned hotel and there's not a problem anymore. There was a fucking *big* problem for the men on the
ground, believe me! And the secretary of state tells the
Senate, 'You must remember, international diplomacy isn't
Boy Scouting,' and gee *whiz,* how foolish those Kurds
were to have believed the word of the United States government. It was all right, though, because they weren't
'pro-Western freedom fighters' anymore—they were just
an Iraqi internal problem.''

"They never were pro-Western freedom fighters,'' said
the middle-aged Suit who had spoken before.

Kelly stared at him. "They were men,'' he said in a
voice that quivered like the blade of a hacksaw. "That's
more'n I see in *this* room.''

"Are you always this offensive, Mr. Kelly?'' said Elaine,
as clear and hard as diamond.

The world collapsed back to normalcy, a room too
warm and far too smoky, filled with men who didn't like

Tom Kelly any better than he liked them. Nothing to get worked up about, just the way the world generally was.

"Only when I'm drunk or scared shitless, Miz Tuttle," Kelly said as he heaved himself away from the sash against which he had been braced. "And I could really use a drink right about now."

He walked past Doug and Elaine, flanking the side door to the office. One of the Suits muttered, "Where's he going?" but only the woman fell in behind Kelly as he approached the grocery cooler for the second time.

The handle was cool and smooth, vibrating with the purr of the refrigerator motor in the base of the cabinet. Kelly raised the lid and reached toward the alien's face. The floodlights had been switched off, but the analytical part of Kelly's mind doubted that he would be able to see much anyway in his present emotional state.

"There are gloves," Elaine said sharply.

"You can't not do things because you're afraid," Kelly said in a crooning, gentle voice, more to himself than to the woman beside him. "I can't not go back in because I'm scared of international flights and dark alleys . . . and because this thing scares me, scares the livin' crap outa me. . . ."

He placed his stinging right palm on the head of the creature, the portion that would have been the forehead if the thing were instead human. The tips of the scales were lifted enough to give the surface the feel of something covered with hairs too fine to be seen. With firmer pressure there were differences in the way the alien flesh and bone resisted the weight of Kelly's hand, but the texture of the covering was the same over hand and head. He lifted his hand away and let the lid thump closed.

"You're not afraid of it anymore?" said Doug, standing hipshot in the doorway like a gunslinger ready to go into action.

The veteran dusted his palms together. The electric

tingle in his right hand had spread to his throat and chest. It was probably psychological rather than a physical reaction to the alien's chemistry; and either way to be ignored.

"Sure I'm scared," Kelly said, looking at the big man and thinking how young the fellow was—and biological age had little to do with that. "That's nothing to do with the price of eggs, is all."

Pierrard stepped into the doorway. He touched Doug on the shoulder with an index finger, removing the younger man from his path abruptly. "Have you reached a decision, then, Kelly?" Pierrard asked. His mouth trembled with wisps of pipe smoke.

"I'll make a deal with you," Kelly said to Elaine. "You call me Tom from here on out, I call you Elaine."

"With a proviso." The dark-haired woman met his eyes with enough of a smile to indicate her amusement at the operational necessity of ignoring Pierrard for the moment. "If you ever 'honey' me again, you can expect to be 'Sergeant Kelly' for the duration. I think I'd prefer the honesty of being called 'you dumb twat' if you can't remember my name."

"We'll work on it," Kelly muttered with an embarrassment he had not thought he was still capable of feeling. To the old man in the doorway, he said, "Can she brief me?"

Pierrard rotated his pipestem in a short arc. "If you wish." Kelly could see others in the orderly room staring at the old man rather than the couple in the office beyond.

"Okay, that'll work," the veteran said, half his mind already considering the people to whom he was going to have to excuse himself if this went the way it looked to. Meetings to cancel, phone messages to be taken and ranked for action. . . . "Some place that isn't here to sit down at—"

Pierrard gestured. "Of course," he murmured.

"—and Dougie goes home or to his kennel'r whatever. I don't need the aggravation, I really don't."

"All right," said Pierrard with no more expression than before, and Elaine looked down at her fingers, which had begun to fold a pleat in her skirt.

"Sir, I don't think—" came Doug's voice from behind the partition wall, out of Kelly's sight. Pierrard turned his head just enough that Blakeley would have been in the corner of his vision. Doug's words stopped.

"Let's roll." Kelly took a shudderingly deep breath before stepping toward the doorway. "Elaine?"

Nobody came out of the building after them. Kelly reached for the driver's side door to open it for the dark-haired woman. The door was locked, and Elaine brushed Kelly's hand away from the latch before she inserted the key into a slot in the doorpost, then unlocked the door itself.

"Very gallant, M—Tom," she said with a smile to dull the sting of the words and the situation. "But on this car, the alarm is set automatically when it's locked, and the last thing we need right now is for everybody in three blocks to lock and load before they come looking for the problem." She smiled brightly at the nearest of the uniformed gunmen. Dazzled, the soldier smiled back.

Kelly walked around to his side of the car. The lock button had risen when the key was turned on the driver's side. Well, the world had never had much real use for chivalry.

He sat down again, finding the seat a great deal more comfortable now than it had been before. Heading toward the meeting, his body had been a collection of bits and pieces as rigid as the parts of a marionette. He could bend at all the normal joints, but tension had kept the muscles taut as guy wires except when they were being consciously relaxed. "Bad as an insertion," Kelly muttered to himself, knowing that the back deck of a tank would have given him as good a ride as the leather upholstery had on the way to Meade.

Elaine was still struggling with her seat, repositioning it from where the long-legged Doug had left it. "It adjusts on four axes," she snapped, knowing that Kelly was smiling, "which gives you the theoretical possibility of finding the perfect solution, and the high likelihood that *every* acceptable solution'll be lost in the maze of other alternatives."

She sat back, grimaced, and started the car anyway. "It's a lot like the information business, isn't it?" she added, and her wry smile mirrored Kelly's.

It had stopped raining, and the overcast had broken patchily to let a few stars glitter down. The air was so clear that lights reflected like jewels from all the wet surfaces around them. "The Buick going to be tagging along again?" Kelly asked, nodding at the follow-car as the inner gate opened. The bigger vehicle's engine was running and its park lights were on while it waited outside the enclosure.

Elaine pulled through the second gate and clutched, looking over at the veteran. "Unless you don't want it to," she said in a voice whose surface brightness Kelly had already learned to associate with a mind nervously in overdrive.

"No problem." He chopped his left hand down the road as if the woman were a squad he was sending forward. "Dougie-boy got on my nerves, that was all. But I really don't bite, I promise."

"Sure, Kelly." Elaine gassed the car and shifted directly from first to third after revving smoothly to the top of the powerband. "And one of these days I'll get a job instead of living off my daddy's money." After a moment she added, "But I know what you mean. Thanks."

There was no bar for traffic outbound from the fort, but the woman slowed and waved toward the guard post. This time she accelerated away fast, keeping the back tires just beneath the limit of traction throughout the radius of the turn and beyond as she straightened onto the highway.

"You didn't get the keys from Doug before you came out," Kelly said while they waited at what he remembered as the last of the traffic lights, if they were headed back into the District as they seemed to be.

"I'd given him my spare set," the woman said, coming off the light as if she were dropping the hammer at a drag strip. "I'll pick them up tomorrow."

Eyes on the entrance ramp and the possible traffic on the turnpike into which they were merging, she added, "Blakeley doesn't get *only* on your nerves, Tom. But let me keep my mind on what I'm doing right now, okay?"

They were heading south for the skyglow above the capital much faster than Doug had brought them to Meade, though there was no similarity between the styles of the two drivers. Doug had a heavy foot for brake and accelerator, and a muffled curse for other vehicles which did not behave in the manner he wished them to.

Elaine dabbed, sliding diagonally through interstices in traffic with a verve which Kelly had thought only a motorcycle could achieve. She was anticipating not only the cars nearest in front and beside them, but the next tier of vehicles as well, so that the drive had the feel of a chess game. Most of the time she kept the Volvo's engine snarling in third gear or fourth. Only on the rare stretches of really empty pavement did she shift up into the overdrive fifth, trading acceleration for the car's absolute top end.

"Motor's to European specs," she called in satisfaction over the engine note at one of the fifth-gear upshifts. "And the suspension's had a little work."

The team in the follow-car must be royally pissed, thought Kelly as he relaxed against the seat cushions, but they had a destination and might even be used to this sort of run if they were assigned regularly to Elaine. She wasn't in a hurry, particularly, and she wasn't trying to prove her competence—or manhood, though it was a joke to think about it that way—to Kelly.

Driving on the edge of control—and control was what was important, not speed—was a hell of a good way to burn away hormones and emotions which had to be bottled up in social situations. If you understood what was going on, you could achieve catharsis without acting as if you were furious with everyone else on the road at the same time. Elaine knew that very well, and she drove with a razorlike acuity not muffled by the need for false emotions to justify it.

"You know," said the veteran as they halted at the first traffic light in downtown Washington, "you could fool me into thinking that you don't like the people you work for a whole lot better than I do."

"You had an escape valve in that meeting." Elaine proceeded through the intersection sedately. The sodium-vapor street lights emphasized the color raised on her cheeks by the high-intensity drive. "You could always decide you were going to try to kill everybody else in the room. I didn't have that luxury."

Kelly turned sharply to stare at her profile. Her hair had fluffed during the drive, shading her cheeks, but she cocked her head enough toward the veteran to let him see her grin.

He smiled as well, releasing the catch of his seatbelt in order to shift the weapon in the hollow of his back. "I wouldn't have, no sweat," he said. "But yeah, sometimes it's nice to know that endgame's *your* choice, not some other bastard's."

Kelly was wondering idly at the facades of Central Washington buildings, lower and more interestingly varie-gated than those of most comparable cities, when the Volvo cut smoothly toward the curb. The veteran glanced from Elaine, thumbing the trunk-latch button on the console, and back with new interest to the hotel at which they had stopped. The ground level expanse was of curtained glass and glass doors printed with 'The Madison' as tastefully as gold leaf can ever be. Despite the hour, a uniformed attendant was coming out almost simultaneously with the muffled pop of the trunk.

Elaine had her door open and was stepping into the street before Kelly could even start around the car to hand her out. "They're gonna confiscate my shining armor, lady," he called plaintively over the green roof.

"Get the case, Tom," she replied as she pointed out the keys still in the ignition to the attendant, who slid behind the wheel.

The sound from above was unmistakable, but it was so unexpected in the present context that Kelly could not fully believe what he was hearing even after he paused to stare up into the darkness. "What the hell?" he said as Elaine walked back to him and glanced upward as well. "There's a helicopter orbiting up there."

The clop of rotor blades was syncopated by echoes from building fronts and the broad streets, but the whine of the turbine waxed and waned purely as a result of the attitude of the aircraft to the listeners below.

"Get the case," Elaine repeated calmly. "It's not us—not that they told me." She shrugged and pursed her lips in a moue. "The President of Venezuela's in town. He's probably staying here."

Kelly hefted out the black Halliburton in the trunk. The attaché case was not so much heavy in the abstract as it was disconcertingly heavier than the norm for things that looked like it. "I congratulate you on the excellence of your expense accounts, ah—" he said as he slammed the trunk, "Elaine."

He followed the woman at a half step and to the side as they strode through the lobby, heeling really, as if he were a well-trained dog. Which was true enough, very true indeed, though he wasn't sure just whose dog he was right at the moment. Not NSA's, certainly not that of the bastards he'd just met at Meade, whatever their acronym turned out to be for the moment.

The hell of it was, the *hell* of it was, Tom Kelly probably still belonged to an abstraction called America which existed only in his mind. It didn't bear much similarity to the US government; but he guessed that was as close as you came in the real world.

Fuckin' A.

Elaine had fished a key from her purse as they walked between a quietly-comfortable lobby and the reception desk. She ignored the clerk as she strode toward the elevators, but Kelly noticed the man turned and spun his hand idly in the box that would have held messages for room 618. Kelly winked, and the clerk waved back with a broad grin.

The graveyard shift was boring as hell, even if you were pretty sure the other side had you targeted for a night assault.

Kelly entered the brass-doored elevator at the woman's side and pushed the button for the sixth floor before she lifted her hand. "This isn't the briefcase you had earlier?" he said, staring at his poker-faced reflection in the polished metal.

"No, it's the one that stayed under guard in the car until we knew we'd want it," Elaine said, eyeing the veteran sidelong with an expression resembling that of a squirrel in hunting season.

Keep 'em off balance, Kelly thought as his expression of wide-eyed innocence looked back at him. Especially when you don't know which end is up yourself.

Room 618 had a king-sized bed, a window that would show a fair swath of the city by daylight, and a Persian carpet which didn't look like anything near the money Kelly knew its equivalent would cost in the shop in the lobby.

There was also a small refrigerator in one corner.

Kelly set the attaché case down on the writing desk and knelt beside the refrigerator. "Gimme the key," he said, holding out his left hand behind him. When nothing slapped his palm, he turned and seated himself on one buttock on the edge of the desk.

Elaine stood with the thumb and index finger of either hand on the keys, the larger one for the door and the small one that unlocked the refrigerator which formed the room's private bar. Her face was as blank as it would have been if construction workers had whistled at her from across a street.

"You've got no right to judge me, woman," Kelly said. His right leg was flexed, and his hand gripped the raised knee in a pattern of tendons and veins. "No fucking *right!*" he shouted as if volume could release the pressure inside him or crack the marble calm of the woman who met his eyes.

"I have the job of judging you, Tom," she said with no emphasis as she bent and handed the paired keys to him. "Shall I get a bucket of ice?"

"Naw, I'm not warm," the veteran said, his throat clogged with residues of the emotion he hated himself for having let out. "Thanks." He fitted the key into the lock and opened the little door. "I'm not warm, just thirsty. Anything for you?"

"Orange juice," Elaine said as she rotated the three-dial combination of the attaché case. "Grapefruit, something citrus."

At least, and for a wonder, it wasn't Perrier—which Kelly had always found to taste like water from a well contaminated with acetylene. And at least she did not stare at what Kelly brought out for himself, a minibottle of Jack Daniel's and a can of Lowenbrau.

"There's a really good Pilsener beer in Turkey," he said as he twisted a chair so that he could see both the woman and the files that she was beginning to place on the desk. "I got to like it." He twisted the cap off the bottle of whiskey, took a sip, and washed the liquor down with a swallow of beer.

When Elaine still said nothing, the veteran prodded, "You've got a dead Kurd and a dead alien. And you've got me, until I drink myself into a stupor, hey? So why don't we get to it?"

"I don't like self-destructive people," the woman said as she set the emptied case to the floor and sat at the other chair by the desk. "I like it even less when an exceptionally able person I have to work with seems bent on destroying himself. But I don't like it when an airline manages to lose my luggage, either, and I've learned to live with that."

Kelly finished the whiskey, his eyes meeting the woman's. "My work gets done," he said, wishing that his tone did not sound so defensive.

"And it'll continue to get done," Elaine responded coolly, "until one day it doesn't. Which may mean that people get dead, or worse. But since it's like the weather, something that can't be helped, then we don't need to talk about it any more."

She wasn't particularly tall, Kelly thought, but she looked just as frail as her black linen jacket, through which light showed every time the fabric fluffed away from her body. He felt like a pit bull facing a chihuahua which was smart enough to be afraid, but wasn't for all that about to back down.

He got up, carrying the can of beer, and walked toward the bathroom. "What is it you think I can do for you?" he called over his shoulder, the phrasing carefully ambiguous. He poured the rest of his beer down the sink and ran water into the aluminum can.

Elaine, still seated, twisted to face him when he returned from the bathroom. "Your personal contacts with the Kurds are more likely to get you information about what's going on than the formal information nets are. The fact that we've heard so little about something so major proves that there's a problem.''

"What *do* you have?" Kelly asked, stretching himself out on his back on the carpet between the bed and the window. He set the can of water down beside him and cupped his hands beneath his skull as a pillow.

"Reports of men going off for military training," the woman said. "Many of them men we'd had on the payroll ourselves during Birdlike.''

"Mohammed Ayyubi one of them?" Kelly asked from the floor. Rather than relaxing, he was bearing his weight on shoulders and heels with his belly muscles tensed in a flat arch. Elaine could not tell whether his eyes were closed or just slitted, watching her, and the effect was similar to that of being stalked in the darkness.

"No," she said, "but he'd been closely associated with some of the people who disappeared. He was living in Istanbul, living well and without a job, you know? He'd make trips east and we think probably to Europe, though we were never able to trace him out of Turkey. Or even far in-country, except after the fact. Somebody would tell us that somebody's wife had a lot of money, now, and her husband had gone off with Mohammed Ayyubi, in a new struggle for Free Kurdistan. That sort of thing.''

Kelly rolled onto his side, facing Elaine, and took a deep draft of water from his can. "Haven't found much use for hotel glasses but to stick your toothbrush in," he said with a disarming grin. "The .22 Shorts of the container world." Without changing expression, he went on, "What do they say when they come back, Elaine? Who's training them?"

"Russia, we thought," the woman said. She shifted on her chair, crossing her right thigh over the left and angrily aware that there was no normal etiquette for discussions with a man who lay at one's feet. "Now, of course, we're not sure. And none of the—recruits we've targeted seem to have come back, on leave or whatever, though their families get sizable remittances in hard currency, not lire."

"You've tried to get people close to Mohammed before now," Kelly said, his flat tone begging the question. "I don't think money'd do much to turn his head if he's—he was—convinced somebody was offering a real chance for Kurdish independence . . . but you people'd think money was the ticket, wouldn't you? What'd he say?"

There was nothing lithe about the man sprawled on the carpet, Elaine thought. He was as close-coupled as a brick, built like a male lion—and with all the arrogance of the male lion's strength and willingness to kill his own kind.

"We don't know," she said carefully. "There was a car bomb explosion—in Diyarbakir—the day before the shooting. Three people were killed, two of them as they came out of the hotel in which they were to have met Ayyubi. We don't know whether they did or not, or what was said."

"Hardball, aren't we?" said the veteran in a very soft voice to the beer can. He held it between thumb and middle finger, at the top where the braced crimp in the cylinder would have made it impossible for even Godzilla to crush the can with two fingers. The mottled skin and the way the tendons stood out proved that Kelly was trying, though, or at least spending in isometrics an emotional charge that would otherwise have broken something. "Amcits, I suppose?"

"Our personnel were American citizens, yes," Elaine said. "They were assigned TDY to the missile tracking station at Pirinclik, just out of town."

"NSA's being cooperative after all." Kelly put the can down again. His eyes, as calm as they ever had been, were back on hers. Elaine had read enough between the lines of the psych profiles in the veteran's file to know that he

really didn't have as short a fuse as he projected under
stress. The anger was there, but there was a level of
control that could handle almost anything.

The flip side of that, and the thing that made him so
much more dangerous than a man who simply lost his
temper, was that Kelly did not go out of control when he
chose to act.

People were entering the room next door, jostling and
cursing as more than one husky man tried to get through a
narrow hotel doorway at the same time. Kelly grinned and
thumbed toward the common wall. "The cavalry's arrived," he said. "You can breathe normally again."

Elaine scowled, realizing that she was just as tense as
the words implied—not that the arrival of the team from
the follow-car would change anything to her benefit if the
shit really hit the fan. She stretched in her chair, twining
her fingers behind her neck and, elbows flared, arching her
chest forward.

Nothing in the file indicated whether Kelly was a leg
man or a breast man.

"You know," he was saying, "you're a hell of a
driver."

She relaxed her body and said, "For a girl."

"Goddam," said Kelly as he twisted to his feet and
walked toward the bathroom with the can emptied now of
water. "You know, I hadn't noticed that."

His delivery was so deadpan that the woman's mouth
opened in shocked amazement—replaced by a flush by the
time he returned with more water and a broad smile at how
effectively he had gotten through her professional facade.

"They're not going to talk to me either, you know?"
the stocky man said as he seated himself normally on the
chair beside Elaine's. "Some folks I worked with might
remember me, sure. But I was US, just as sure as the boys
who got blown away the other day. Free Kurdistan is a lot

more important to—to somebody like Mohammed—than any personal chips I could call in.''

''Word of how you terminated from the service got around very quickly when you didn't return from leave,'' Elaine said. Her voice had never lost its even tenor, and her mind was fully back to business as well. ''Around the personnel of Operation Birdlike. Even though there was an attempt to stop it or at least replace the''—she smiled—''truth with rumors less embarrassing to the USG.

''Since the indigs—the Kurds—were Muslims and strongly religious, the fact that you'd dynamited the government of Israel did you no harm with the men you'd been training. And they're quite convinced that you aren't—won't ever be again—an agent of the United States.''

Elaine paused. Then she added, ''Besides, I think you underestimate the level of personal loyalty that some of your troops felt toward you. It was a matter of some concern during the interval between the time you—terminated and Birdlike was wrapped up.''

''You wouldn't believe,'' said Kelly to his hands flat on the desk, ''how many people'd follow you to hell if you're willing to lead 'em there. We got thirty-seven MiGs in their revetments at Tekret the one night.''

He looked up and his voice trembled with remembered emotion. ''The whole sky was orange from ten klicks away. Just like fuckin' sunrise. . . .''

Kelly stood abruptly and turned away. ''Shit,'' he snarled. ''Don't fuckin' *do* this to me, okay?''

''The only reason,'' Elaine said softly, ''that we'd ask you to use the people you know is that it might take too long to reopen normal channels. We don't know how long we have before the—apparent hostiles—execute whatever plan they have in progress.''

''Don't *bull*shit me, Elaine,'' he said as his hands clenched and the muscles of his shoulders hunched up like a weight lifter's. He faced her again and went on deliberately,

"You wouldn't be where you are if you had a problem with asking your grandma to penetrate massage parlors. You sure as *hell* don't have a problem with askin' me to burn people who trust me."

"I've got a problem with wasting my time," she said calmly, leaning back to look up at the angry man. She uncrossed her legs. "I wouldn't waste time asking you to do something you wouldn't do with a gun to your head. This one's necessary, you know it is—and you know that whatever your friends may think, nobody's coming to Earth from another *planet* to set up an independent Kurdistan! Don't you?"

"Well, there's that," Kelly agreed with a sigh. He sat down again on a corner of the bed. "How many recruits are we talking about? Kurds, I mean." He was studying the backs of his hands with a frowning interest that would have been justified for a fat envelope with a Dublin postmark.

"About twenty that we're pretty sure of," Elaine said, genuinely relaxing again. She gestured toward the files with red-bordered cover sheets, which she had spread on the desk. "It's here, what we have. Certainly we've got only the tip of the iceberg—but at worst we're not talking about—" She smiled; it made a different person of her, emphasizing the pleasant fullness of her cheeks and adding a touch of naughtiness to features which otherwise suggested wickedness of a thoroughly professional kind.

"—a land war in Asia," she concluded.

"I'm not subtle, you know," Kelly said. "If I go in, I'll make a lotta waves. If I think it's the best way to learn what's going on, I'll tell people every goddam thing *I* know. And if it gets rough, it's likely to get *real* rough."

"Slash and burn data collection," the woman said with a grimace, though not a particularly angry one. She shrugged. "The more waves you make," she went on, "the more likely it is that the wheels come off before you—or we—learn anything useful. But there isn't a lot of time, and the people who picked you for this operation had seen your profiles too.''

''Goddam, goddam, goddam,'' the veteran said without heat as he lay back on the white bedspread and began to knuckle his eyes. His feet were still flat on the floor. ''It's going to take me a while to get my own stuff on track. Maybe a week. Couple three days at least.''

''You won't need a cover identity,'' Elaine said. Because Kelly's eyes were closed, it was only in his mind that he saw her face blank into an expression of professional neutrality. ''Your job with Congressman Bianci has taken you out of the country in the past, and—''

''No,'' Kelly said. He neither snapped nor raised his voice, but there was nothing in the way he spoke that admitted of argument. ''Carlo doesn't get involved in this.''

''The congressman will agree without question, Tom,'' Elaine said in a reasonable tone. ''I don't mean we'd put pressure on him—you can clear it with him yourself. He's a, well, a patriot, and if you tell him you're convinced yourself that it's a matter of national security then—''

''Stop,'' said Kelly. He had taken his hands away from his eyes, but he continued to look at the ceiling, and it was toward the ceiling that he spoke in a voice as cold and flat as the work-face of a broadax: ''Carlo hired me to keep him *out* of shit. He doesn't get into this bucket if he swears on a stack a' Bibles he wants to.''

Kelly paused, for breath rather than for rhetorical effect. ''I'll go in as a civilian tech advisor, Boeing or RCA, that sorta thing. There must be a couple thousand Amcits like that. Pick one with the right build who's rotating home and make me up a passport. God knows you can square it with Boeing. I may be carrying some electronics, so make that reasonable enough for Customs.''

Elaine did not even consider arguing the Bianci matter

again. "Check," she said. "Though there's no need for you to carry things in country yourself."

"There's no need for me to carry a lucky charm," said Kelly, shifting his weight a little, though the mattress was too soft to make more than a mild discomfort of the weapon in the hollow of his spine, "but if it ain't broke, you don't fix it.

"Besides . . ." As he spoke the planes of his face changed, tiny muscles reacting to mental tension. "I want to keep clear of whatever you've got on the ground already. I for *damn* sure don't want to be showing up at the US Mission to collect my mail."

"If you need something in a hurry and it isn't pre-positioned," the woman warned, "the chances are it'll have to come in by pouch."

"If I *ask* you for something, it's my lookout," the veteran said as he sat up and met Elaine's eyes. "But don't hold your breath, because, because I'd rather call in favors of my own than trust—" The woman smiled, and perhaps for that reason Kelly softened the remainder of his sentence to, "—people who don't owe me."

He stood up again, stretched his arms behind him as the woman watched in silence, and went on. "What I *want* from you people is to be tasked and left the fuck alone. Don't ask me for sitreps, don't try to help, and for *god's* sake, don't get in my way."

"You expect too much," Elaine said calmly.

"I *expect* to be fucked around to the point I can't work," Kelly answered in a harsh whisper, "and *then* I expect to pack up and go home. That's what I *expect*."

"You'll have a case officer," Elaine replied as if there had been no threat. "Me, unless you prefer otherwise. And there'll be support available in country. If you don't need it, that's fine, but throwing a tantrum doesn't give you the right to flout common sense. Mine. But nobody's going to hamper your activities, Tom."

Kelly smiled broadly and rubbed the heavy black stubble on his chin. "Well, that's something for the relationship," he said mildly. "You tell the lies you gotta, but it seems you stop there. Hell, maybe this thing's going to work."

He stepped over to the desk and riffled one of the files there. "Look," he said, "go off to your friends or wherever"—he gestured toward the partition wall behind him—"for however long it takes me to read in. It'll go quicker if I'm alone in the room." He didn't bother to add that he wasn't going to try to leave.

Elaine nodded, stood up, and walked toward the door. She paused just short of it and said, with her back toward Kelly and the well-stocked refrigerator, "Would you like some coffee from room service before you start?"

"Don't press your luck, Elaine," the veteran said in the glass-edged whisper again.

She turned, wearing her professional smile again. "And don't press yours, Tom," she said. "Don't pretend, even to yourself, that you can walk out on this now that you're in."

Kelly laughed. "Hey," he said with a cheerful lilt, "who greased Mohammed?"

"We presume," Elaine replied in a neutral voice from a neutral face, "that the car bomb and the shootings were the work of the same parties. Either the aliens or their agents made an error, or there are third parties already involved in the matter.

"Good night, Tom."

The brass bolt and wards clacked with finality as Kelly's case officer drew the door shut behind her.

It had been a long night. Around the edges of the rubber-backed outer drapes, saffron dawn was heralding what would probably be a long day. The veteran sighed, set the chain bolt behind Elaine Tuttle, and got to work.

There was a telephone on the bedside table and another extension, weatherized like a pay phone, on the wall of the bathroom. Kelly unplugged the modular jack from the base unit of each phone. He was too tired to trust his judgment, though his intellect floated in something approaching a dream state, functioning with effortless precision in collating information. By allowing habit to take over, Kelly could for the time avoid the errors of judgment he was sure to make if he tried to think things out.

There were a lot of ways to bug a room. Some of the simplest involved modifying the telephone to act at need as a listening device. A fix for the problem was a small, battery-powered fluorescent light. When it was turned on and set near the phone, the radio-frequency hash which its oscillators made in raising the voltage to necessary levels completely flooded the circuitry of most bugs. Unplugging the phone was even more effective, though no one could call in or out while the unit was disconnected. Kelly didn't need the phone, so that didn't matter.

Of course, no sound he was going to make in room 618 mattered either—but it was habit, and it wasn't going to hurt either.

Kelly unplugged the television set next to the refrigerator and then wiggled loose the bayonet connector of the coax to the hotel's common antenna. Lord! how people worried about bugging—some of them with more reason than others—and how rarely any of them hesitated to have cable TV installed. There is a perfect reciprocity in many aspects of electricity and magnetism: if you reverse cause and effect, the system still works. As a practical matter here, that meant that the television speaker also acted as a microphone monitoring every sound in the hotel room— and that the data was available for pick-off through the antenna connection or, with more difficulty, through the hotel's power circuitry.

"If they want to know what I'm doing, they can damn well ask me," the veteran said as he straightened.

The key ring clinked against the face of the refrigerator as his knee bumped it. Kelly looked down. For a moment, the unobtrusive appliance was the only thing in his mind or in the universe. It had been a long time since the whiskey, a *bloody* long time.

"You're too goddam smart for your own good, woman," Kelly muttered; his palms were sweating. "Too smart for mine for sure."

The hell of it was, she didn't think he *couldn't* stop drinking, she thought he could. She was right, of course; Tom Kelly could do any goddam thing he set his mind to . . . but why he cared about disappointing some bitch he'd just met, some hard-edged pro who'd spend him like a bullet, that part of his mind was beyond his own understanding.

Coffee'd do for now.

Kelly tossed his jacket on the bed, then went over to his own zippered, limp-leather briefcase to remove the small jar of instant coffee and the immersion heater. He looked at the beer can and grimaced. He could cut the top off to insert the heater, but that would leave a jagged edge, and a thin aluminum can wasn't a sensible man's choice for drinking hot liquids.

A few ounces of coffee at a time was better than none. He needed fluids to sip while he worked, and if coffee was the choice this time—there were four glasses in the bathroom; he filled them all, brought them to the writing desk where he dusted them with instant coffee, and inserted the immersion heater in the first.

Next, from his briefcase, Kelly took a radio rather smaller than a hardcover book. It was an off-the-shelf Sony 2002, and for less than $300 it would pick up AM, FM, and short wave signals with an efficiency NSA would have spent $15,000 a copy to duplicate a few years before.

Hell, governments being what they are, NSA was probably still paying fifteen grand for similar packages.

The little world-band radio ran either from batteries or from an AC/DC converter; but the latter caused a hum on shortwave, and batteries—unlike public power grids—were the same voltage worldwide. Sound in the background, even if it was no more than the hiss of static, was as necessary to Kelly's study habits as something beside him to drink. He used the scanner to pick up an FM station, classical music, something he had last heard on Radio Sophia when he was a long fucking way from the United States.

Funny. Music cared less about time and nationalities than just about anything except stones. Of course, politicians were pretty similar worldwide, too. As were spies.

Tom Kelly unplugged the immersion heater. There was one final preliminary to getting comfortable. He drew the snub-nosed revolver nestled at the small of his back and set it on the desk beside the bubbling glass of coffee.

The exposed metal of the weapon had been sandblasted and anodized an unattractive dull gray about the color of phosphate-protected steel. There was a line of wear around the cylinder where the registration lug rubbed, but the weapon had actually been fired only a handful of times in the thirty-five years since its manufacture.

A patch of Velcro—hook-side—had been epoxied to the right side of the barrel just ahead of the five-shot cylinder, and there was a corresponding patch of Velcro fuzz sewn at the back of the waistband of every pair of pants Kelly owned. There were a lot of circumstances in which a holster was slower to ditch than the gun itself. The Velcro was unobtrusive, added neither bulk nor weight, and was actually more secure than the usual belt-clip holster.

Apart from its finish and the nylon hooks, the revolver looked like a standard Smith and Wesson Chief's Special, the choice of tens of thousands of people who wanted the punch of a .38 Special cartridge in a small, reliable package. Kelly's gun was something more than that. Though it was dimensionally identical to the ordinary version, the only steel in the weapon was the slight amount in the lockwork: frame, cylinder, and barrel had all been forged from aluminum in response to an Air Force request for the lightest possible revolver to equip pilots who came down behind enemy lines. Almost the entire run had been melted down shortly thereafter, when the decision was countermanded; but not quite all.

Tom Kelly didn't care that the gun weighed ten ounces empty instead of the steel version's nineteen. He cared very much that its magnetic signature was so low that it would not show up on airport magnetometers unless they were set low enough to trip on three or four dimes in a pocket as well.

The ammunition Kelly had handloaded for the revolver was also nonstandard, though the components were off-the-shelf items. He'd used commercial 148-grain wadcutter bullets, swaged from pure lead instead of being cast with an alloy to harden them, ahead of three grains of Bullseye, a powder fast enough to burn almost completely within the snubbie's short barrel. The bullets were formed with a hollow base, a deep cavity meant to be upset against the rifling grooves by the powder gases in the manner of a Civil War minié ball. Kelly had loaded them back to front, and the deep cup had expanded the soft metal very efficiently in a gelatine target despite the relatively low velocity of the bullet on impact.

Keeping pressures within levels that a cartridge-company engineer would have found acceptable in 1920 had been the bottom line for the load. The all-aluminum revolvers had been tested by the Air Force with ordinary ammunition and with blue pills—proof loads developing forty percent greater pressure than normal. There was no reason to believe that in the ensuing thirty-five years the metal would have work-hardened into a state that made it more likely to rupture.

Still, better safe than sorry. . . . Kelly wasn't particularly worried about being hurt if the revolver blew up—the person holding a handgun at arm's length is the one least likely to be harmed if the chamber bursts. He was very much concerned that in a crisis so severe that he had to use the weapon, it would fail and give him one shot when he desperately counted on having five.

The master sergeant who'd sold him the gun at Wheelus had said that no government was going to put an unsafe weapon in the hands of its troops. That would have been more confidence-building if Kelly hadn't seen the USG issue a tactical nuke, the Davy Crockett, with a fallout radius greater than the range of the launcher. Not that anybody'd explained that at the time to the Marines who were expected to fry themselves with the thing.

For the remainder of the morning, the veteran read files and made plans. He had two bars of Bendicks chocolate, the Military and Sportsmen's blend, in his briefcase. They did little to quell the roiling of coffee and fatigue in his stomach, but the caffeine in the dose of fifty-seven percent pure chocolate did its own share of good.

The files were a maze, reports pared to the bone and beyond, filled with agent designators which could be collated with real names only through separate documents. There had been no evident attempt to censor what Kelly was being given: his own name appeared in one report as the source of a case of M14 rifles said to have been received by another Kurd who had disappeared shortly thereafter. Kelly remembered the agent from Operation Birdlike and was amused to note that the man's present reporting officer classed him as "generally reliable." Kelly wouldn't have taken the fellow's word for whether the sun rose in the east.

And that was the problem with most of the information:

the three agents among the Kurdish community whom Kelly did know were venal, cowardly, and thoroughly untrustworthy. Results suggested that the remainder of the reports were from similar trash, men and women who had, at best, secondhand information on whatever Mohammed Ayyubi was involved in. Had been involved in, until somebody shot him and a monster dead on a rain-sodden street.

The files covered approximately the past year. There was nothing in them regarding aliens, and for all but the past two months they were concerned solely with the normal collection from a nationalist movement: money and arms; smuggling and training camps; foreign contacts in general and the dark suggestions of Russian involvement certain to show up in reports approved by American station chiefs.

Not that the KGB and other Russians paid to meddle in Third World problems were any less likely to be doing so than their US counterparts.

There was a change in March which was so abrupt that it must have resulted from a change in emphasis at client level—the members of the US government who received the information—rather than a watershed in what the agents themselves chose to send in. Suddenly Kurds were making UFO reports which would have been right at home in small-town papers throughout America.

There were no, thank god, conversations with little green men, although one case officer had sent a number of reports of angelic revelations before somebody further up the line had rapped his knuckles. There were airplanes that flew straight up, huge cylinders with lighted windows along their sides, and a score of other shapes and styles. Some reports referred to incidents as much as thirty years in the past, proving to a certainty that the sudden spate of reports was only a result of tasking.

In general, the only similarities between objects sighted

occurred when two or more reports were made by the same agent. There was a single exception: disks twenty meters in diameter which lifted silently, wrapped in auroral splendor—from locations separated by a hundred miles, and with no duplication in the chain of data. That could mean something; and certainly there *was* something to be learned; the dead alien proved that. But even if one or all of the reports were true, they were garbage which did absolutely nothing to indicate what was really going on.

And that was all there was. No wonder Pierrard and his crew were willing to try a card as wild as Tom Kelly.

A thing with a mouth like a lamprey, and a couple dozen—maybe a few hundred—Kurds whose families thought they were going off to be armed and trained in the cause of Kurdish nationalism. Well, the connection would be obvious just as soon as Kelly learned what it was.

When the files were stacked neatly again on the top of the desk, the veteran walked to the bathroom. The toothbrush and toothpaste from his briefcase, and the hot shower that he let play over him helped but could not wholly remove the foulness throughout his system. Fear and anger and fatigue, but most especially fear, leave their hormonal spoor on a man.

Kelly looked at himself in the fogged mirror when he stepped out of the shower, but that was another mistake. His outline was intact, but the condensate on the glass turned his hundred and eighty pounds, tank-solid and scarred with experience, into a wistful ghost. He was crazy to get back into this; aliens or no, none of it would matter when he was dead.

But death would come regardless.

He lay down on the bed, his skin warm with the harsh toweling he had just given it. He'd have them book him into the Sheraton in a room facing the Golden Horn. He'd treat it as a perk—they understood perks, these folk in suits they never saw the bills for, and no eyebrows would lift because Kelly wanted a room in the most expensive hotel in Istanbul. They would understand the implied test, also, the precise instructions which they could either carry out or not—and the implications if they did not or even chose to argue.

And because they understood both those things, they would not foresee their agent's—'their agent's'—real reason for wanting a room just there.

He needed to talk to people after he shook free from the box Elaine would try to put around him no matter what she said. There were folks who owed him, though the good ones didn't keep score any more than Kelly did himself. Individuals, unlike nations, were capable of keeping faith.

For now, however, what he needed most of all was sleep. He closed his eyes, and sleep came with the fireshot dreams Kelly had expected. But the dreams changed, and by the time he awakened at twilight he could remember nothing but moving figures and black walls that reached toward heaven.

Airport terminals have certain worldwide similarities, but Istanbul's had more in common with the military portion of Beirut Airport than with any civilian structure Kelly'd walked through. Luggage from the Pan Am flight that had just landed was arrayed on a single long, low table in the center of a hangar converted for baggage examination.

Each individual claimed his or her own suitcases under the eyes of armed guards, and carried them to the examination booths—porters took the weight for some passengers, mostly foreigners, but no one else could accept the responsibility.

Beyond hand luggage Kelly had only one suitcase and that—a solid, vinyl case of Turkish manufacture—held clothing. He had no need, himself, to bring unusual hardware into Turkey, as it had turned out, because his overseas phone calls had been more successful than he had dared hope. Funny. It always surprised him when other people came through the way he would have done for them—120 percent and no questions asked that didn't bear on the fulfillment of the request.

It would have been easy for Kelly to snatch his bag and stride ahead of the remaining passengers, and reaching an empty examination booth would have saved half an hour of waiting for civilians—nervous, belligerent, or both—to be processed through ahead of him.

But even though the stocky veteran had nothing to fear from Customs, he let his training override his instinct to go full bore and finish whatever he was doing by the most direct route possible. He kept a low profile, deliberately followed a middle-aged man with a bag in either hand and a brown Yugoslav passport held with two fingertips and the side of the smaller case.

The Customs agent for whom Kelly opened his bag wore khaki pants with a tie and white shirt. The uniform of the National Policeman watching him was of gray-green wool and included a Browning Hi-Power in a holster of white patent leather. Beyond the line of booths was a squad of soldiers in fatigues, smoking and occasionally adjusting the slings of the Thompson submachineguns they carried.

Prine Minister Ecevit had taken the Defense portfolio for himself, but that was cosmetic. He was also making a real attempt to control the radical violence from both sides before a military junta ousted him to cure the problem more directly. The open display of armed force seemed to concern most of the foreign passengers. Kelly himself had enough other things to worry about.

"I love Istanbul," Kelly joked in Turkish with the Customs agent, "but do they let me stay here? Surely there must be runway sweepers to be maintained in a more lovely part of Turkey than Incirlik!"

"You are a Turk?" asked the National Policeman, running a knowledgeable hand along the hinges of the suitcase instead of prodding through the shirts as he had done with the Yugoslav minutes before.

"No," said the Customs agent, flipping from the front to the back of the artistically-worn passport, but sizing Kelly up sidelong as he stamped the entry data. The American was a hair taller than the Anatolian norm, but his stocky build was right as were the dark complexion and straight black hair. With a moustache and a few days polish on his Turkish, he could pass as a native—of the country, though not of any specific district.

He might have to do just that.

"Not, but should be," Kelly agreed with a smile. "It's good to be back. Even headed for Incirlik."

"Go with God, Mr. Bradsheer," the Customs agent said, closing the suitcase with one hand and returning Kelly's false passport in the other. The currency declaration form went into a file beneath the examination table.

Kelly smiled, snapped the latches of the case—no time to buckle the safety straps as well—and said, "Go with God, brother," as he walked out the rear of the canvas booth.

Elaine Tuttle was standing at the back of the building, beyond the low barrier that separated incoming passengers from those waiting to greet them.

She wore a long-sleeved blue dress today, with ruffles at wrists and throat and a belt of light gilded chain. It had been three days since Kelly last saw her, and his recognition now was not instantaneous. Partly it was the beret that covered the rich curls of her black hair, partly that Tuttle carried a large purse on a shoulder strap for the first time since he had met her. In large measure, Kelly did not recognize Elaine because the physical reality of her was so different—so much less threatening—than memory suffused with the woman's personality.

He did not dream about her, but he had begun to dream—and if the strange landscapes he remembered on awakening were not nightmares, they would do till worse came along.

Kelly stopped at the barrier and rested his suitcase on it while he buckled the straps over the latches. None of the soldiers paid him any particular attention. There were enthusiastic greetings in half a dozen languages, chiefly Turkish and German—a Turkish Airways flight from Frankfurt had just disgorged its load of 'guest workers' from West Germany. Kelly had to wait for a large family reunion at the nearest opening in the barrier, but he wasn't in such a hurry that he would attract attention by scissoring his legs over it instead.

Elaine, who had not moved while Kelly meandered through the entry building, stepped to his side as he began to walk out the door. "It's a long way to the car," she said, nodding toward the parking lot set off from the terminal area by barbed wire and cyclone fencing. There were more troops outside, and an armored car painted blue to match the berets of the paramilitary police. "Do you want to wait for me to bring the car around?"

"No sweat," said Kelly, swinging the suitcase at arm's length in front of him to prove that he could handle the weight. He continued to saunter toward the pedestrian gate at which Elaine had gestured. "You know, I was afraid you people were going to walk me through Customs and make a fuss. I should've said something before. Glad you had better sense than I—gave you credit for."

"Given the present political climate," Elaine said with her eyes on where they were going, "with Ecevit using America as a whipping boy for all the troubles of his administration, I don't know that we could have done much. Not in the Istanbul District, at any rate."

She looked up sharply at the man beside her. "Not that you seemed to need help very badly."

"You wanted somebody who was comfortable in Turkey," Kelly said. "That much you got."

He shifted the case from one hand to the other as she led him through a row of parked cars and, on the other side, wrapped his arm around her shoulders in a hug. "Hey, Elaine," he said, releasing her almost before her light frame began to stiffen beneath the dress, "I'm pumped, but right for the moment I'm feelin' good."

He grinned across at her as they continued to stride along, switching the suitcase back to his right hand to prove that the hug had been no more than a friendly gesture. "Look," he explained, "going—back to work's—my equivalent of riding the roller coaster, I guess. It'll be a rush while it lasts, and you don't have to worry about how I'll get along *with you* so long as we're on the same side, okay? And you handle your end the way I'd want to be able to handle it if it was my job."

"Rather than handle it like you, you mean?" Elaine asked with the beginning of a smile.

"Right," agreed Kelly with a broader one, dodging a little Ford Anadol that was being backed from its parking space with more verve than discretion. "Rather than by getting the admin types so mad that they insist on fucking with the operation, which is exactly what I'd do if anybody were silly enough to put me in that slot. I never had a lotta tact, and when things get tense for one reason'r the other—"

He laughed, and stopped. They passed, one to either side, a dejected-looking palm tree in an island protected from cars by empty oil drums. When they rejoined on the other side, Kelly chuckled in embarrassment and said, "After all, there aren't a lot of times it's helpful to point a gun at your colonel's eye and tell him he's history if he makes a peep in the next ten minutes."

"You did that?" Elaine said, her tone one of amusement rather than the cool appraisal Kelly had expected.

"Yeah," Kelly admitted. "Seemed like a good idea at the time, and I figured we were far enough back in the boonies that he wouldn't have to report it later to cover his own ass. Neither of us got anything in our jackets for that one, and he stopped tryin' to be a big hero like his old man—at least when he was in sight of me."

"This is the car," Elaine said. "We'll put your luggage behind the seats."

The car was a Porsche 944, new enough that the treads on both front and rear tires were almost unworn. It was painted a metallic green, the gloss overlaid by a light dusting of yellow grit from the parking lot.

"What," asked Kelly as Elaine unlocked the Porsche, "were you going to do if I showed up here with a steamer trunk?" An obvious answer struck him, and he looked around for a follow-car big enough to handle any possible load of baggage. Though he craned his neck and raised himself onto his toes, looking like a gigged frog because of his squat build, Kelly could see no likely vehicle nearby.

"There isn't one, Tom," Elaine said dryly, flipping the dirver's seat forward, "but don't worry"—she patted his left arm, whose muscles were rock solid with the weight of the suitcase they were supporting—"I'm packing."

" 'Yea, though I walk through the valley of the shadow of Death . . .' " quoted Kelly as he set the case into the car. It was a snug fit, but because the driver's seat was well forward there *was* a fit.

"And as for the rest," she went on when he straightened, "if you got off with more luggage than you'd boarded with in Frankfurt, we were going to have to hire a taxi for it—yes." She smiled.

The veteran held both hands out in front of him, palms down, and looked at them for a moment. Then he met Elaine's eyes and said, "Look, I know how I get. Don't—" He swallowed. "I've got real problems working close with people when it gets tense, I don't usually do that. I don't wanna, you know, somebody get hurt because I was pissed and there wasn't a whole lotta time.''

Elaine touched his hands with hers, fingertips to palms and her thumbs lying gently on his scarred knuckles. "You haven't had anyone you could trust before, Tom," she said. "You've got that now."

Kelly grinned and squeezed hands that felt so delicate that he could have crumpled them like cellophane. "Yeah, that's a change," he said, stepping around the back of the car to get to the passenger side. His fingers tapped idly on the black rubber spoiler as he passed it, wondering whether there would be any chance of putting the Porsche through its paces one of these days. He was going to need some relaxation. . . .

And he could've used somebody to trust as well, but he didn't have that on this operation either. You could trust the people beneath you, sometimes, if you'd trained them and worked with them before. But your superiors in a hierarchy could *never* by definition be expected to do exactly what you told them to—especially if the time were too short for what they thought was proper respect. People didn't get into positions of responsibility by abdicating responsibility.

Elaine Tuttle would be welcome any day as a member of a team Kelly put together, for her driving and her mind if nothing else. But right now she was, at a guess, a lieutenant colonel—and he was a master sergeant in the only scheme of things that a light colonel's mind could accept.

It would've been real nice to trust her, though.

Traffic on the long stretch of four-lane highway between the airport in Yeşilköy and the city proper was heavy. Elaine, though she did not waste any time, wasn't pushing with the little car the way she had the first night on the Baltimore-Washington Turnpike.

"You haven't asked me," she said, "whether we'd gotten you the accommodations you'd asked for."

Kelly laughed. "Demanded, you mean," he said. At eye level out his side window were the rear axles of a fourteen-wheel semi, just like the ones immediately before and behind the Porsche. He had no doubt that the little car was as sturdy as anything its size could be, but the low seating position emphasized vulnerability to the trucks in a way that not even a motorcycle would have. "Look, I don't say you couldn't have failed, you know—maybe terrorists blew the place up this morning, that sorta thing. But you weren't going to fail and not tell me about it right off."

He turned to look at her profile, unexpectedly softer than any of the angles of the woman's frame—pleasant in itself, and much more pleasant than the angle-iron bumper with a Bulgarian license plate ten feet beyond the hood. "At worst, I'm going to decide you're a vicious bitch who's dangling me for whoever, the Russians, to bite. You won't *ever* convince me you're stupid."

It was the right thing to have said, because Elaine's reaction was wrong—to the speculation, not the flattery. The face compressed itself momentarily into the neutral expression that gave nothing away save the fact that something was hidden. She smiled so quickly that Kelly could have thought he had mistaken the reaction . . . except that long, bloody years had taught him when his instincts must be trusted and no human being could be.

"This is the route from Europe," she said, waving to the truck ahead of them, "traffic from as far as Sweden and England, on the way across the Hindu Kush, some of it."

"Rather have your company than theirs," the veteran replied, his hand paralleling hers in a gesture toward the red airport bus ahead in the other lane. "Though mind you, the next time you pick me up, a fifty-passenger

Mercedes like that one'd be a little more in keeping with the rest of the traffic than a two-seater Porsche."

Elaine laughed and made a pair of lane changes, cutting between bumpers more closely than she had previously that afternoon. The Porsche's exhaust blatted at the downshift followed by swift acceleration. "That make you feel better?" she asked, nodding toward the little Anadol—a license-built version of an English Ford—now just ahead of them. "You see, your wish is my command."

Istanbul was an exotic city with a history that went back long before the Roman conquest, much less that of the Ottoman Turks. Along the highway from Yeşilköy, however, it resembled nothing so much as Cleveland, Ohio: another major industrial city decaying beside a major body of water.

It had ceased to be the capital in 1920, when the Allied powers had anchored warships in the Golden Horn—and had found that the only Turks they ruled were those literally within range of their guns. The Turks had been on the losing side during World War I, but their armies had defeated major attacks both at Gallipoli and in Mesopotamia. There was no longer an Ottoman Empire, but there was a new nation called Turkey. Other failed empires in the region—the Persians and the Greeks both came readily to mind—had their pride. The Turks had in addition an army ready to kick whoever's butt was closest. The planners in Washington who persisted in considering Turkey a client state of the US had no one but themselves to blame for the current anti-Americanism.

"What do you expect to do in Istanbul?" Elaine asked as they waited to cross the peripheral road surrounding the walls begun at least seven hundred years before Constantine renamed the city after himself.

"Talk to some people," Kelly said, shrugging. "Ahmed Ayyubi for one, Mohammed's brother. There had to be some reason Mohammed moved to Istanbul—or stayed

here, if he was just catching his breath with his brother
after Birdlike came apart. . . . Look, I'm playin' it by ear,
that's as much data as I've got.''

Elaine sent the car growling across the intersection and
into the Old City proper. ''We can help you locate people
if you need that,'' she said with a nod—approval, or more
likely reassurance. ''As we did with Ahmed Ayyubi.''

Kelly had asked her for a location on the dead Kurd's
brother even though he would much sooner that his present
employers not know of his interest. What can't be cured,
though . . . Any damned fool would know that Kelly had
to start with or near Ahmed Ayyubi; and though he could
have gotten the man's address without official help, he
could not—in Istanbul—have been sure that his interest
would not have leaked back anyway.

Better to be up front about what you couldn't hide—it
disarmed the brass hats who thought they owned your
soul.

The Porsche turned left at Ataturk Boulevard, steeply
uphill so that by twisting around Kelly got a good view of
the Sea of Marmara. Though they had been driving parallel to the water for some time, the high corniche and the
remains of ancient brick walls had hidden it from him.

Elaine, driving with the intention of making the best
possible time, looked at her passenger in surprise. ''Is
somebody behind us?'' she asked, and as she spoke her
eyes flickered to the mirrors and the traffic around her.

I only get that paranoid in the boonies, thought Kelly,
*but that's probably because she's spent more time in cities
than I've done.* Aloud he said, ''Oh, no problem. I just
like to see something big and real now and again—to
anchor me, you know?''

Elaine nodded acceptance rather than understanding and
concentrated on her driving again. Though she hadn't any
right to be pissed, Kelly knew that nobody likes to be
frightened needlessly, even in innocence. Well, she could

have let him take the bus and a taxi instead of picking him up at the airport.

The Old City of Istanbul was on a finger of land project-ing into the Sea of Marmara, separated from the equally-steep ridge of the Pera District by the deep gash of the Golden Horn. All of the bodies of water—the Horn, the Sea of Marmara, and the Bosphorus, which connected the latter to the Black Sea—were the results of separate fault lines as the continental plates that were Europe and Asia clashed. The earthquakes that were a certain concomitant of those faults meant that all but the most massive struc-tures were brought down on a regular basis or were de-voured by the fires that resulted.

It was a city of apartments of concrete and yellowish brick, built in the late nineteenth century or the twentieth—not unattractive, many of them picked out by balconies or iron grillwork, but all the colors muted by the soft coal that had been the city's fuel for centuries. Only from above was there anything brighter, and that was the omni-present red-orange of tiled roofs the shade of the rouge on a badly laid out corpse.

They crossed the Golden Horn on the Ataturk Bridge, early enough to miss the worst of the northbound traffic—tourists returning to the big luxury hotels in the Pera, and returning with them many of the personnel who had been catering to them among the ancient beauties of the Old City. Istanbul still had heavy industries, but there had been virtually no new development here since World War II. Only the tourists offered to preserve the city from sinking back into the state of somnolent ruin to which it had been reduced by the time the Ottoman Turks conquered it in 1453.

Elaine hadn't used the long drive to pump him, which was just as well since the Porsche was too small a box for the hostility that would have resulted. Such of his plans as she didn't know were things he hoped she wouldn't learn, and the reality of what he was to do faded as the time for execution approached. It was hard to believe that he was really back in Turkey; and the notion that he was here to track down aliens with too many bones and far too many teeth in their circular mouths was as absurd as it would have been the day before he saw the dead thing.

"Doesn't really matter if I believe any of it, does it?" Kelly said as Elaine swung the car around the rank of cabs waiting to load at the entrance of the Sheraton. "Just so long as I do my job."

He had spoken as much to himself as to Elaine, but the woman raised an eyebrow over her smile and replied, "Are you going to have difficulty working under those conditions?"

Before Kelly answered, she stopped the Porsche and handed the keys to the attendant, who had scurried in a failed attempt to open the door for her. "It might be as well," she said over her shoulder as Kelly too got out of the car, "if you carried the suitcase yourself. There'll be people waiting in the room."

"There's no difficulty," the veteran said as he tugged out the big case. "I spent years without thinking any of the people giving me orders knew what the hell they were doing. Doubting that *I* do's something of a pleasant change."

They took the elevators from the ground-floor service area. Kelly noted with amusement that Elaine waited a moment, watching him from the corner of her eye, before she touched the button for the seventh floor. Kelly grinned broadly at her, letting her wonder whether or not he knew which floor their rooms were on this time.

He didn't want to talk business with Elaine, and he didn't have anything but business—one way or the other—to talk with her. Unless—and he looked toward the ceiling of the elevator—he asked the question to which his mind kept returning, whether or not she ever wore a bra. His smile, carefully directed away from anything human, became innocence. A question like that struck him as a pretty good way to get his hand bitten off to the elbow, which would complicate his job a lot. . . .

"A penny for your thoughts," Elaine said, her voice more guarded than the words.

Kelly shrugged and faced her, the bulk of the suitcase on the floor between them. "Just thinking that maybe my first priority was to get my ashes hauled," he said, "so it doesn't get in the way."

She laughed as the elevator cage quivered to a halt. "Are you asking for a list of addresses," she said, "or would you just like the equipment delivered to your room?" She pointed down the hall, her arm a shadow within the puffy translucence of her sleeve. "Seven-twenty-five."

"Naw, no problem," the stocky man said. He wasn't embarrassed—cribs in the Anti-Lebanon had been ponchos pegged into three-sided windbreaks, which pretty well blasted the notion of sex being a private affair. It was useful to note that his case officer wasn't embarrassed either.

"Well, it wouldn't be a problem, you know," Elaine said cheerfully as she, a pace ahead of Kelly, stopped at a door and tapped on it. "All part of the unobtrusive luxury service you've been promised."

"Unobtrusive will do just fine," Kelly replied. Doug Blakeley opened the door with a frozen scowl on his face. There were two other men within the room carrying radio-detection equipment. One of them was smoking a cigarette.

"You've met Doug," Elaine said as she entered 725, moving Blakeley back away from the door by stepping unnecessarily close to him—giving Kelly and the suitcase room without need for the macho games of which both men were capable. "George"—she pointed to the fat, balding man with the tone generator—"and Christophe," she indicated the pale, almost tubercular smoker who wore headphones connected to the wide-band receiver slung from his right shoulder.

"Christophe, put the cigarette out in the toilet and flush it," Elaine continued. She kept her voice as neutral as if she were commenting on the view, being very careful not to raise the emotional temperature. "And where's Peter?"

"What's the matter with the cigarette?" demanded Christophe, taking the half-smoked cylinder out of his mouth to examine it rather than to obey. His English was accented, but it appeared to be German—Flemish?—rather than the French Kelly had expected.

"He's next door in your room," Doug was saying. "I thought we'd sweep his first, before we did yours."

The tone generator which George carried put out a known signal which would trip sound-activated bugs and cause them to broadcast. Christophe swept up and down as much of the electromagnetic spectrum as his receiver covered, unless and until he picked up the tone signal in his earphones. At that point, George could lower the intensity of the generator and move it around the room until the bug was physically located.

If the bugging device was combined directly with a tape recorder, then there was no signal to pick up on the receiver—but that sort of installation required that someone enter the room at regular intervals to change tapes, and it very considerably increased the bulk of the bugging unit. Similarly, a hardwired bug was possible but impractical in a hotel room like this because of the holes that had to be drilled through walls between the bug and the listening post. No sweep could be perfect, but this team appeared to know what it was doing—especially if the piece of hardware in a separate case by the door was the spectrum analyzer Kelly assumed it was.

"Christophe, when you get an order from me you *do* it," Elaine said in a deadly voice to the man at least a foot taller than she was.

Kelly walked over to the window, smiling, leaving behind him the suitcase and the incident developing in the room.

There was more to the woman's reaction than her authority, though there was that too. She'd picked up on the way Kelly felt about cigarette smoke—surely *that* wasn't in his psychiatric profile—and she had a not unreasonable concern that the veteran would use that as the excuse to void his grudging acquiescence to the wishes of a government he hated.

Hell, nobody'd twisted Kelly's arm; he was a big boy. He'd go through with the deal, whatever that meant and whatever roadblocks his superiors threw in his way.

But it didn't hurt to keep 'em nervous.

The window had a nice view of Taksim Square and the Monument of the Republic. The square served for major ceremonies and public gatherings because there was nothing of suitable size in the Old City. The Golden Horn, to the south, was invisible beyond the buildings of the Pera District, and the skyline was dominated by the twenty-story tower of a nearby hotel—the ETAP Marmar, the city's tallest building. Rooms on this side of the Sheraton were considerably cheaper than those with a view of the Bosphorus, but Kelly did find it pleasant to look out at the trees of Taksim Park—probably the only place in Istanbul that contained so much greenery.

Not that his choice of a room had anything to do with that aspect of the view.

Kelly turned. The exchange between Elaine and now both members of the sweep team had continued. Christophe's cigarette had burned almost to his fingers and scattered a lump of ash as he gestured with it.

"Goddammit, Christophe," Doug said sharply with his arms akimbo. "Put out the cigarette!"

The man with his headphones now loosely clasping his neck scurried to comply.

Kelly could afford to smile sardonically at Elaine's slim, tense back. And these were Europeans, not Arabs or even

Moslems. Female officers must have a *really* great time working with locally-recruited teams. . . .

"Tell you what," said Kelly, "let's all just go next door, shall we?" He offered a clown's broad smile, keeping his lips tight. "That way the boys can do whatever they need to do there. And from now on, just for fun, let's not you or anybody you know come into 725, unless I invite him, huh?"

Doug started to bridle, but before he could reply Elaine said tiredly, "Yeah, that sounds like a good idea to me too." She looked at Christophe returning from the bathroom, and added, "And when they've swept my room, Doug, I don't want to see them again myself till you're told different."

Nobody moved for a moment. Then Doug snapped, "Well, why aren't you packing your gear, dammit?" George and Christophe eyed one another as they obeyed, but they obeyed the blond man without question.

There was no door through the partition wall between rooms 725 and 727, but neither was there anyone in the hall to watch the four men and the woman—forming almost as many subgroups as there were individuals—traipse from one room to the other. The gray fiberglass cases holding the debugging equipment were not standard luggage, but neither did they hint that they contained more than expensive cameras.

George tapped on the door of 727. As Peter opened it, Elaine said to Doug, "Give him his own room key now."

"Eh?"

Peter was black haired and heavily moustached, a very solid-looking man and younger than the sweep team. Kelly gave him a cautious once-over. There was no obvious reason why, but Kelly's gut wouldn't have let him keep Peter in a unit he commanded. Now he gave the man a friendly smile as they passed in the doorway.

"Give Tom the key to seven-two-five, I said," Elaine snapped.

Doug reached into the side pocket of his suitcoat, which sagged, Kelly had guessed, with the weight of a spare magazine. That guess had been wrong: the key which Doug handed him was attached to a brass bar rather than a tag or thin plate. Guests were intended to leave their room keys at the desk when they went out, and the management did what it could to make that easy to remember.

The sweep team was already unpacking its equipment, though Christophe paused to light another cigarette first. George got out what was indeed a spectrum analyzer and began walking around the room with it, staring at the peaks and valleys on its cathode ray tube display. His partner waited to rezero his own equipment because the oscillators in Christophe's wide-band receiver would themselves affect the electromagnetic spectrum within the room.

The view from Elaine's window was practically the same as that of Kelly's, something the veteran had counted on without being able to influence. So far, so good. Both rooms were of luxury hotel standards common across the portions of the world which served tourists. The spread of the double bed was a brocade of rich blue which clashed badly with the dress Elaine was wearing but matched the upholstery of the love seat facing the window.

Kelly sat down on the love seat and spread his arms across the back, his big scarred hands dangling to either side. Peter watched him with a flat expression that Kelly recognized: the look that said the mind behind it was considering endgame in the most final and physical sense of the term, just to be ready when the time came.

"We have a car for you," Elaine said. The light through the window behind her silhouetted her body against a sky that otherwise held from Kelly's perspective only the upper stories of the ETAP Marmar.

"I don't need a car," the veteran said. "What I need is

a cup of coffee, black; and I think it'd be real nice if you sent Peter down to get it''—he nodded toward the younger man, so nearly a physical double for Kelly himself—"instead of waiting for room service to bring it up.''

The woman looked sharply at Kelly. Then she turned her head slightly in Peter's direction and said, "Yes, all right, get it. Get two. Anyone else?"

"Yeah, for god's sake, bring up six coffees and be done with it," said Doug to his subordinate. Then, proving that he had better judgment than Kelly would have credited him before, Doug added, "And don't argue about it, just do like you're paid to, take orders."

Peter frowned, but he left the room without the objection that would have really lit Elaine's fuse.

When the door closed she went on, "This is a Ford Anadol, like a million others in Turkey, Tom. You'll need transportation."

"I'll take taxis," he replied. He gestured to the door. "You know," he went on, "that one, your Peter, he could *really* get on my nerves in a hurry. I'm not gonna shout and scream about this, but if I see him again after he brings up the coffee, I go home. This time it's no shit."

Doug looked from Elaine to Kelly in genuine puzzlement. Elaine nodded and said, "All right, we'll see what we can do." She cleared her throat. "It's absurd for you to trust taxis to be where you need them. We can give you a driver, if you like."

It'd be absurd to accept a car with the array of tracking beacons that anything she'd provide would have, Kelly thought. Aloud he said, "I'm a tourist, I take cabs. When I change my mind, I'll let you know."

The sweep team had moved into the bathroom. The receiver in the spectrum analyzer was of lower sensitivity than the one Christophe used to listen for the tone they would generate in a few minutes. In order to pick up a hump on the display, which was the low-powered signal of a bug, the unit needed to be fairly close to the transmitter. "What's the band width on that thing?" Kelly asked, nodding toward the bathroom.

"What?" said Doug. Elaine decided not to argue further about the car. Both of them followed Kelly's nod toward the bathroom.

Kelly slipped the cavity resonator, a three-inch metal tube with a nine-inch antenna of flexible wire, between the back and the cushion of the love seat. "I mean, what range in megahertz does the display cover? Eighty to three hundred? More?"

"I can't imagine, but you can look for yourself if you feel you must," the woman said in exasperation.

"That all we need to cover?" Kelly said, no more relaxed than he had been a moment before. "The car, I mean? Because if it— "

"There's money," Elaine said, lifting a Halliburton from the floor to the bed and opening it, "though you can always say you don't need *that* either."

"I don't," the veteran agreed, "but I'll take what's going." Hard to tell whether the asperity in Elaine's voice was fatigue, the difficulty in getting subordinates to take orders from a woman, or simply Kelly's own arrogance. Probably a combination of the three; and probably things weren't going to improve for the duration, because none of those factors were likely to change for the better.

Elaine tossed a fat, banded packet of Turkish lire onto Kelly's lap. They were used bills, bearing, as did all denominations of Turkish currency, the face of Kemal Atatürk, the republic's founder. "That's a hundred thousand," she said, closing the attaché case. Doug, literally and figuratively the odd man out, looked with his hands clasped from Elaine to the sweep team, which was beginning to make its circuit with the tone generator and receiver.

"It'd seem like a lot more," said Kelly as he stripped

off the banding, "if I hadn't checked the exchange rate in the terminal. Do I sign for it?"

"It's over a thousand dollars, Kelly," said the woman, "which ought to be handy—unless you plan to pay your bloody taxi fares with credit cards. There's more if you need it"—she spun the lock dials of her Halliburton with grim determination—"and if you need large sums, we'll talk.

"And the answer is no, *I* signed for it," she concluded with her eyes fierce.

Kelly wondered if she'd shoot him if he asked if she were on the rag just now. Probably not: she wasn't the type who ever really lost it, any more than Kelly himself did. "I appreciate the way you're covering for me," the veteran said calmly as he rose.

He slipped half the lire—pounds, from the Latin, just like the Italian equivalent and the British symbol for currency—into the breast pocket of his jacket, and the other half, folded, into the right side pocket of his slacks. "I suppose I get this way because I figure the best way to be left alone is to make you'all"—he smiled around the room—"want to keep clear. But I do understand that you're keeping your side of the bargain. And that it can't be easy for somebody in your position."

He walked toward the door. Behind him, Doug called, "The coffee hasn't come yet."

"No," agreed Kelly as he stepped out into the hallway, "but Peter left, which was all I had in mind."

Room 725 had a pleasant feeling for Kelly as he shot the deadbolt lock behind him; not home, but a bunker. Bunkers were a lot more useful than homes.

A glance out the window at the sun told him that he had time to put his gear in order and still catch Ahmed Ayyubi at work. Before starting to unpack, he sat his little Sony radio up on the window ledge and scanned the FM band until he found a station—probably Greek, but that didn't matter one way or the other—playing music. There was a good deal of static, and the red diode that indicated tuning strength fluctuated feebly—which mattered even less to ears trained like Kelly's in the hard school of communications intercept.

He had not brought a great deal of clothing, and his choices emphasized variety rather than several versions of the same garb. He stripped off the sportcoat, hung it up with the slacks he had taken from the suitcase, and tossed the long-sleeved polyester shirt he was wearing on the bed. In its place he donned a checked wool shirt and a nylon windbreaker, both of them well-worn and of Turkish manufacture, as was the short-brimmed cloth cap he put on. He'd look a little strange to the lobby personnel at the Sheraton, but that was a cheap trade-off for avoiding comment when he talked to Ayyubi. The money in the sportcoat could stay there for the time being.

The last thing Kelly did before leaving his room was to walk over to the Sony receiver and poke number seven of the ten station preset buttons. The apparent effect was the same as if he had pushed the Off button: the sound clicked off, the LED went dark, and the liquid crystal display of the tuning readout went completely blank as if the power were off also.

What actually happened to the receiver, which a stateside acquaintance of Kelly's had hastily modified, was a good deal more complex. Preset seven tuned the unit to 88.35 megahertz, squarely in the midst of the upper sidelobe of Istanbul's sixty-kilowatt commercial FM station. The hump which a spectrum analyzer would show there was exactly what was to be expected, and a separate transmitter would have to be very powerful indeed to affect the appearance of the band on the display.

The Sony's output when operating on that preset was not to the speaker as an audible signal but rather through a shunt into the case intended for an external battery pack holding four C cells. It now contained a miniature tape recorder with a voice-activated switch. The false battery pack could be exposed by anyone who cared to open it; but Kelly had deliberately left an unmodified Sony and its accoutrements unattended at his apartment in Arlington during the week he was preparing for the mission, giving anyone who was curious ample opportunity to be reassured about its innocence.

It would be nice to learn that he didn't have to spy on the folks with whom he was working just now. But given Pierrard, he was going to be very surprised if Elaine and her friends were playing straight.

The breeze from the Bosphorus was cool enough to be bracing now. A few hours after sundown it was going to be damned cold, but that itself would be a help in returning Kelly's mind to operational status, like the process of scaling rust from armor plate. Working for Carlo Bianci, he had been able to stay warm enough all the time. That wasn't something you counted on in the field.

The lead taxi in the rank was a Fiat, older than the driver, who cheerfully haggled in Turkish on a price to the Mosque of Sinan. It made a reasonable destination for Kelly, due east of the Sheraton and close to the Bosphorus— as well as being within two narrow, winding blocks of the agent's real destination, a neighborhood mosque in an alley off Maskular Street.

The neighborhood mosque was named for Sidi Iskender— Saint Alexander—and Kelly wondered fleetingly whether Alexander the Great himself might not have been sanctified in the myths of Turkish tribesmen riding westward through the land which the Macedonian had conquered centuries before. The west side of the courtyard looked as if it had sustained battle damage, but that was the result of ongoing refurbishment: the wall had been knocked down and was in early stages of replacement by a portico of four column-supported barrel vaults.

Precast concrete arches leaned against the side of the neighboring commercial building, but the stones of the square pillars were being fitted on-site from the pile of rough limestone ashlars delivered from the quarry. Two stonecutters and the half dozen short-haired boys kibitzing sat in a waste of rock-chips and yellow dust from the stone.

The older of the stonecutters stood straddling the column which he was forming into a hexagonal pilaster. His partner wore a cloth cap like Kelly's, a tan sweater pulled over a dark blue shirt, and baggy black trousers almost hidden by rock dust and the one-by-one-by-two-foot stone prism behind which he squatted with an adze. He was in his late thirties, clearly the elder Ayyubi brother, for his broad, dark face was a near double of that Kelly had last seen videotaped on a rainswept street in Diyarbakir.

Ahmed Ayyubi glanced up at the man approaching and struck the stone again with a blow deceptively light. Rock exploded, and the adze stopped half an inch beyond the point of impact.

"You," said Ahmed Ayyubi as he rose. The arm holding the adze fell to his side, but the tendons of the hand on the haft stood out with the fierceness of the Kurd's grip.

"We need to talk, Ahmed," Kelly said as he walked closer. He was trying to appear calm, but he stumbled on the rock chips—some of them the size of a clenched fist—covering the ground. Danger had made a tunnel of his viewpoint, and the peripheral vision that guides the feet had vanished under stress. The boys continued to chatter for a moment, but the other stonecutter paused with his own tool resting on the work face.

"Get out of here," Ayyubi said in Kurdish, and in a voice so guttural that Kelly could not have understood the words had they not been the ones he expected.

One more step put the American agent as close to the

workpiece as Ayyubi was, well within reach of the adze.
"We *need* to talk," Kelly said. Tiny bits of stone floated
in the sweat that sprang out suddenly from Ayyubi's brow.
"Otherwise Mohammed's killing will be unavenged."

"*You're* responsible for his death, you know," the Kurd
snarled.

Kelly reached out and touched the back of the stonecutter's right hand while he held eye contact. "Whatever
responsibility I have for Mohammed's death, I will wash
away in the blood of his killers. But you must help me find
them."

And only when he felt Ayyubi's hand relax on the adze
helve did Kelly realize that he had succeeded.

The stonecutter grimaced and set his tool on the workpiece. "Come," he said, gesturing beyond a pile of finished blocks toward the street. A couple of the boys
jumped up to follow. "You go away!" Ayyubi said.
"This is man's business." Though there was love in his
gruffness, the hand he batted at the nearest lad would have
flung the boy across the rubble if the blow had landed.

Traffic noise on Maskular and the adjoining streets was
a white ambiance that may have been what Ayyubi was
seeking. More probably the Kurd had needed time and the
movement to clear his thoughts of limestone and his sudden fury at seeing Kelly again.

"I don't know what Mohammed was doing," Ayyubi
said abruptly. Standing, he was three inches shorter than
Kelly, but his neck and shoulders made even the stocky
American look slight by contrast. "I wanted him to get
into decent work, come in with me and Gulersoy"—his
calloused thumb indicated the older stonecutter—"but he'd
gotten the taste for being a hero, for getting rich without
working. *You* did that to him."

"Yes, easy money," Kelly murmured. His right hand
caressed the jacket over his left elbow. There was a four-
inch scar there, where the skin had been laid open by the

same bomb blast which had knocked him silly. Mohammed Ayyubi had carried him to safety a hundred and fifty feet up the sides of a ravine that a goat would have thought was sheer.

But soldier ants probably can't explain what they do to the workers in the colony, either. It was that sort of world, is all.

"This I know, and all I know is this," the stonecutter continued, prodding toward Kelly's chest with a thumb-thick finger. "He met a blond whore, a dancer, and let her get him into this. As you got him into the other."

"I didn't get Mohammed into anything I didn't get him out of," Kelly said softly, with his eyes on the middle distance and his mind on memories that had nothing to do with the business at hand. His body shuddered, and his eyes focused on Ayyubi again. "Tell me about the dancer. Is she a Turk?"

"No, a foreigner," the other man said. Something in Kelly's expression a moment before caused Ayyubi to frown, not in fear but with a different awareness of the situation and the man who questioned him. "I know nothing about her, only the name—Gee-soo-lah. A belly dancer, very expensive. Dances at the best clubs and parties of the very rich because she's blond, you see, and foreign."

"Right . . ." Kelly said. "Know where she's at just now?"

Ayyubi shook his head emphatically. "Sometimes here, sometimes she travels. Not with Mohammed, I think, but I know she was responsible." He paused and added, "Mohammed showed me a billboard once, but that was months ago. I never saw her, and I never let him talk to me about freeing Kurdistan and the big money he was making."

The stonecutter spat into the street. Some of the cars had their lights on by now. "Big money. It helped the family bury him."

"I'll let you know how things work out," Kelly said, wondering if anybody was watching him just now. Pierrard's people or others, not necessarily people. "Thank you, Ahmed."

"Wait," the Kurd said, touching Kelly's arm as the agent started to turn away. When their eyes met again in the dusk, Ayyubi said, "I thought it was friends of yours who killed him. Americans. They came to talk with me the week before Mohammed was shot, and I didn't know where he was to warn him. My *brother*."

Kelly clasped the other man's hand against him. "Ahmed," he said, "nobody who kills one of my people is a friend of mine." He squeezed the Kurd fiercely, then strode back toward the Mosque of Sinan and the hope of finding another taxi.

There was nothing particularly difficult about what came next, but the first three hours of it were simply preparation. He had to lose whoever might be tagging him on Pierrard's behalf or Elaine's—if there was a difference.

A properly trained team of at least a dozen agents could keep tabs on just about anybody in an urban environment, but that was a lot of personnel for anyone but the local security forces. Among US intelligence organizations in Istanbul, the Drug Enforcement Administration could probably put together such a team, and very possibly CIA could as well.

Pierrard, whoever he was and whatever funds he could disburse on special operations, had an insolubly different problem. You can't bring a tracking unit into a city where the street patterns and the language are both unfamiliar, not and expect the team to function. Money alone won't do it. And the most practical answer, to borrow trained personnel from friendly intelligence organizations, was also the least probable. There *were* no friendly intelligence services to people like Pierrard, least of all the other services employed by the US government.

Pierrard's attitude, of course, was fully supported by

that of his CIA and DEA colleagues, who would have been delighted to get their fingers into a rival's turf.

For the moment, Kelly could be pretty sure that he could be being followed by only Doug and the three foreign nationals he had met at the Sheraton, perhaps with an equal number of Turkish drivers and the like. The Covered Bazaar—the Kapali Carsi in the center of the Old City—was the perfect place to dump any such tail.

There were eighteen entrances to the Bazaar and sixty-five separate streets within it, all covered by plastered brick arches with internal iron bracing. Kelly entered the three-acre maze of shops and pedestrians on Fuad Pasha Street across from the campus of the University of Istanbul. He ducked out again fifteen minutes later on Yeniceri Boulevard, spending no longer in the streetlights than he needed to hop into a brightly-painted Skoda taxi.

The trip back across the Golden Horn to the apartment on Carik Street in the Beyoglu District, not far from Taksim Square, was complicated by the fact that Kelly changed cabs twice more. The friend who was arranging this pickup owed Kelly less than he was risking by going up against Pierrard. The least Kelly intended to do was to prevent fallout in that direction.

The apartment was one of a series of six-to-ten-story new constructions filling the block. The street level held a branch bank whose steel grating had been rolled down for the night, a jewelry store, and a rug shop with a silken Herike on display beneath concealed spotlights. There was a guard in the small elevator lobby, chatting with a policeman who probably found it worth his time to spend his entire shift right there.

Both men shifted to their feet with interest and hostile concern when Kelly stepped into the lobby. "I'm to pick up a case from Miss Ozel on the sixth floor," Kelly said in Turkish. "For Nureddin."

Mollified but still cautious, the civilian guard pressed

buzzer six on the wall beneath the intercom grating while the policeman studied the taxi waiting outside.

"Yes?" a voice responded, its sex uncertain due to the distortion of the intercom.

"Lady, a man to pick up a package for Nureddin," the guard explained.

"Oh—thank you. Could you send him up yourself, as a favor to me?"

The guard nodded obsequiously to the speaker grating, causing the policeman to laugh and wink at Kelly.

"Of course, lady," the civilian said. He unlocked the elevator call button and gestured Kelly into the cage. Theoretically, someone from the apartment itself should have come down to accompany the visitor to the proper floor; but those who could pay for security like this could be expected to circumvent those aspects which caused inconvenience to themselves.

The sixth floor was a single suite. Its door was already ajar when the elevator stopped, and the woman waiting in the opening motioned Kelly within. "Robert—could not be here," she said in fair English. "He say—he say that this is what you look for."

What Kelly could see of the apartment was opulent with brassware and wall hangings, but a little overdone for his taste. The same could be said for the woman in a house-dress of multilayered red gauze over an opaque base. She had a fleshy Turkish beauty, with lustrous hair to her waist and breasts that would have been impressive on a much heavier woman . . . but there are no absolutes of taste, and only her smile was greatly to the taste of Tom Kelly.

"Thank you," the American said, stepping to the travel-trunk set in the entranceway to await him. "And more than thanks to Bob. It—it's just as well he's not here now, but—tell him I'll see him again. And I won't forget."

Kelly had met Bob's wife, a slim blond of aristocratic beauty whose ancestry went back several centuries in Virginia. Very cool, very intelligent, very nearly perfect . . . and thinking of that as he reached for the case, Kelly could understand Miss Ozel more easily.

"It's heavy," warned the woman. "I can get—"

"Thank you," Kelly repeated, lifting the trunk by the central strap as if it were an ordinary suitcase. Bob could be depended on to make sure the load was balanced.

Danny Pacheco, who had died below decks on the *White Plains*, had been a friend of his as of Kelly.

"I guess I need a key to get down, too," the American said apologetically. The weight of the case forced him into a counter lean as if he were thrusting against a gale.

The room beyond the entrance hall was furnished like that of a wealthy Kurdish chieftain of the past century: the floor not carpeted but overlaid by runners a meter wide and five meters long. Little but the edge of any single carpet showed beyond the edge of the next above; and so on, across the room, while stacked pillows turned the juncture of floor and walls into a continuous couch.

Ozel glanced toward the inner room, then took an elevator key from a pocket hidden in her housedress. Unexpectedly she gripped Kelly's free arm and, staring fiercely into his eyes, said, "This won't hurt Robert. Will it?"

She shouldn't know there was anything different about this one than there was about anything Bob did for his employer, NSA. *He* certainly hadn't told her. Kelly blinked, reassessing the mind behind those cowlike eyes. She would have gotten physical signals from Bob, but she had to be able to think to process the data.

"No," Kelly said in Kurdish. "Not if I'm alive to keep it from hurting him." He squeezed her hand in reassurance and led her by it to the elevator switch.

Bob had done a rather better job the second time around, Kelly thought as the cage descended. Or maybe he really needed both women, needed the balance.

And what did Tom Kelly need? Nothing he'd found in

forty years, that was sure. And not some of the things he'd never had; the love of a good woman, for a major instance.

Though the love of the right bad woman might be just the sort of stress a fellow like him needed to keep out of the really life-threatening forms of excitement.

Like the current one.

The ETAP Marmar was the tallest building in Istanbul, and from his sixteenth-floor room in that hotel, Kelly could easily look down on the room Elaine had booked for him in the Sheraton.

More to the point, his ETAP window looked down on Elaine's own room and permitted him to aim the microwave transmitter he had picked up from Ozel toward the cavity resonator he had earlier planted in the love seat. The fact that the woman's rubber-backed drapes were drawn did not affect the microwaves with which Kelly now painted 727.

The trunk acted as both carrying case for the transmitter and the camouflage necessary for an unattended installation like this one in a room that would be entered for daily cleaning. Five sides of the Turkish-made trunk were standard sheet metal over light wood, with corner reinforcements, but the metal sheathing had been removed from one end and replaced by dull black paint. The change was noticeable but unremarkable and it was through that end that the parabolic antenna spewed a tight beam of microwaves.

Kelly rested his elbows on the ledge of the window and scanned the south face of the Sheraton with binoculars, a tiny pair of Zeiss roof-prism 10×20's. He had left his own drapes open in the Sheraton, and the Sony radio on the ledge there provided the certainty of location which he could not have achieved simply by counting windows. The window to the left of his own was the target. . . .

This room in the ETAP Marmar had been booked for Kelly by a woman who had left Bianci's staff a year before to join an Atlanta travel agency. The only question she had asked about the false name and the cash payment was how it affected Carlo. Kelly's word, that it didn't, had been good enough for her. A north-facing room high on the ETAP was certain to overlook a room in the Sheraton with a view of Taksim Square. While there had been no certainty that Elaine would book her own room beside the one Kelly had demanded, there had been a high probability of it.

And after all, there was no certainty in life.

The veteran gave final touches to the antenna alignment, switched on the power, and closed and locked the case sitting on the coffee table beside the window. The unit ran on wall current, so it was possible that a maid would unplug it despite the note in Turkish: Air Freshener Within—Please Do Not Unplug—left with a thousand lire bill atop the trunk. Its weight, primarily that of the transformers, made it unlikely that anyone would move it. Short of hiring someone to watch the room, there was no better way to set things up.

Whistling, Tom Kelly locked the door and the purring transmitter behind him. He figured he'd walk back to the Sheraton, but by the long way around the park.

He felt pretty good. He had his ass covered from his own side, more or less, and he could now get on with the job they had asked him to do.

Kelly expected somebody to be waiting for him in the lobby, but George was instead at the further end of the first-floor coffee shop where he was less obtrusive and had a full, if narrow, view of the front door. The American nodded to him cheerfully. No problem. He needed to get some information through Elaine, and he'd just as soon that she was expecting him.

With his own key in his pocket, Kelly tapped on the door of 727—'shave' with his index finger, 'and a haircut' with the middle finger, he *was* feeling good—and the door opened before the veteran could rap 'two bits' with both fingers together. Elaine, alone in the room as she gestured him inside, was wearing a beige dress that could have been silk-look polyester but probably was not.

"Glad to have you back, Tom," the woman said without emphasis. "Learn anything useful?"

"Learned I could get my watch wound with no help from the USG," Kelly replied with a chuckle, flopping down on the love seat and spreading his arms as he had before when he set the cavity resonator. Somewhere up there beyond the curtains was a microwave transmitter aimed right at his breastbone, god willing.

Elaine grimaced involuntarily, but there was no sign that she wasn't taking the lie at face value. Not that it was a lie, exactly: Tom Kelly damned well *could* get laid without government assistance. The statement covered both the time he'd been gone and the new buoyancy with which he returned. The hair on his chest tickled, but that was psychosomatic rather than a real effect of the microwaves. If, worst come to worst, his visit to Miss Ozel was traced, it explained that too.

"Perhaps we can get to business some time soon," the woman said, with no more emotional loading than was necessary.

"Had dinner?" Kelly asked brightly.

"We can call room service." The grimace, a momentary tic, was back. Maybe she thought he was drunk too.

He hadn't drunk alcohol since that boilermaker in the Madison. . . .

"Get me full poop on a blond belly dancer named—and this is phonetic, through Kurdish—Gee-soo-lah," Kelly said. "Claimed to be a foreign national, claimed to be a top act. Probably in somebody's files even if the computer doesn't kick her up for some other reason."

Elaine raised an eyebrow. "Excellent," she said, "but it'll take some time."

"Right," agreed Kelly as he stood with the smooth caution of a powerful man with too many scars to move unrestrained except at need. "And I don't guess you'll be burning off copies of the file yourself, will you?"

"I don't suppose so, no," the woman said guardedly.

"So why don't I," Kelly said with a grin as he walked past her to the door, "go take a shower while you make the arrangements? And then we'll go to dinner."

He paused with his hand on the knob. "For which you're rather overdressed, m'lady, but that's your business."

"Oh-kay," Elaine was saying as the door closed behind Kelly, her voice as quizzical as the expression on her face.

Istanbul had the nighttime beauty of any large city, its dirt and dilapidation cloaked by darkness and only shapes and the jewels of its illumination to be seen. The view from Kelly's window had the additional exoticism of an eastern city in which street lighting was too sparse to overwhelm the varicolored richness of neon shop-signs. The minarets of a large mosque in the distance were illuminated from within their parapets, so the shafts stood out around the dome like rockets being prepared for night lift-off.

Kelly sighed and walked into the bathroom to shower as he had said. He undressed carefully and set his trousers on the seat of the toilet. He would wear the same outfit for the rest of the evening . . . and that arrangement put the snubbie near his hand in the shower without displaying it to the unlikely possibility of optical surveillance devices planted within the hotel room. It was as easy to be careful, that was all.

When Elaine tapped on the door of 725 a few minutes after he had gotten dressed, Kelly had a twinge of concern that his comment regarding clothing would cause her to change into slacks. Istanbul was as cosmopolitan as London, in one sense, but the underlying culture was Sunni Muslim. Smart visitors to London didn't slaughter sheep in the street there, and women didn't go around in pants here without insulting a proportion of the people who saw them. That would be true even if she were a foreigner wearing some $200 Paris equivalent of blue jeans with a couturier's tag on the fly.

He needn't have worried. Elaine wore a high-throated black dress with a long-sleeved cotton jacket over it. Hell, she was smarter than he was and at least as well-traveled. Kelly nodded approvingly and joined her in the hall instead of inviting her into the room.

"Want to tell me what comes next?" Elaine asked as they strode toward the elevators, "or is the surprise an important part?"

"Well, you know . . ." Kelly said, poking the call button. Damn! but she seemed tiny when she stood beside him; the full cheeks were so deceptive. . . . "You can get any kind of food in the world in Istanbul—though if you're big on pork, you're limited to places like this one."

He circled his hand in a gesture that indicated the Sheraton itself and its five-star equivalents on Taksim Square. "But I thought we'd be exotic and eat at a Turkish diner. You can find that too in the tourist hotels, with tables and the waitresses tricked out like they were on loan from the *Arabian Nights* . . . but I don't much feel like that."

The elevator arrived, empty. "Lead on, faithful guide," Elaine said as she stepped into the cage. When the door shut she added in a voice barely audible over the whine of the hydraulics, "The dancer is Gisela Romer, a Turkish citizen but part of an expatriate German community that settled here after World War II. There should be an extensive file in Ankara. I've put a first priority on it, so something ought to be delivered by courier as soon as it's printed out here."

"Nice work," said Kelly.

"I'm glad you're giving us a chance to help you, Tom," Elaine said seriously. "That's all that we're here for."

"I wonder if—" he started to say, timing the words carefully so that the elevator chugged to a stop at the lobby before he could complete the sentence. Elaine's face blanked, and she said nothing more until they had dropped off their keys and left the hotel.

Kelly did not see George or any other of her subordinates.

"I think we'll walk," he said, with a wave to the doorman and the leading cab of the rank beneath the hotel's bright facade. As they walked beyond the band of light, Kelly went on in a low voice, "You know, I wonder if you could find me a pistol if I needed one. I don't mean I do, I mean *if*."

"I'd have thought you had sources of your own, Tom," Elaine said. Her smile asked more than the words themselves did.

"Yeah, needs must," agreed the veteran with false frustration. "I mean, it wasn't a turndown. But things're tight now, *real* tight, with Ecevit trying to get a grip on things. Somebody could take a *real* hard fall if, you know, something went wrong and the piece got traced back."

"What do you want?"

"I don't *want* anything," Kelly insisted, "but you know—if I do, something standard, a forty-five auto, a nine millimeter. And it'll just be a security blanket, if I turn out not to have enough guts to stay on an even keel without something to wrap my hand around."

"Doesn't sound like a problem," the woman said, nonchalance adding weight to the words. "Doesn't seem to me either that you need to feel you're going off the deep end if you choose to carry a personal sidearm under the— present circumstances."

They were walking down Independence Boulevard, which was flooded with traffic noise and the sound of music, mostly Turkish, from the open doors of many of the shops. A triple-tier Philips sign over an electronics store threw golden highlights over Elaine's short hair. Kelly bent closer to her to say, "I used to carry a piece all the time I was in uniform, a snubbie that wasn't good for a damn thing but to blow my brains out if things got too tough. Just as soon not get into that headset again, you know?"

Elaine nodded; and Kelly, his task of misinforming his case officer complete, focused on finding a place to eat.

A few doors down a sidestreet shone the internal lighting of a red and blue Pepsi-Cola sign with, lettered below, the name Doner California. "*There* we go," Kelly said, pointing with his offside arm to direct Elaine.

"Authentic Turkish, right," the woman said in mock scorn as she obeyed. "Do they have a quartet lip-synching the Beach Boys?"

"I'll eat every surfboard on the walls," Kelly promised as he pushed open the glass-paneled door and handed her within. "Watch the little step."

The floor of the diner was of ceramic tiles with a coarse brown glaze. There were half a dozen white-enameled tables, several of them occupied by men or groups of men dressed much as Kelly was. The sides and top of the counter were covered with green tile, similar to that of the floor in everything but color; but there was a decorative band just below the countertop, tiles mixing the brown and green glazes in an eight-pointed rosette against a white background.

Elaine was the only woman in the restaurant.

Though the evening was beginning to chill fog from air saturated by the Bosphorus, warmth puffed aggressively from the diner, heated as it was by a vertical gas grill behind the counter. A large piece of meat rotated on a spit before the mesh-fronted grill that glowed orange and blue as it hissed.

All eyes turned to the newcomers—particularly to Elaine—as they entered. The owner, behind the counter in an apron, made a guess at what variety of Europeans they were, and called, "Wilkommen!"

"God be with you," Kelly responded, in Turkish rather than German.

Elaine slid onto a stool at the counter instead of a hoop-backed chair at one of the empty tables. "If we're going to do this," she replied to the veteran's quizzical glance, "we may as well do it right. And you were right about the surfboards."

A ten-year-old boy with the owner's features and the skull-cap haircut universal among prepubescent Turkish males set out two glasses of water with a big smile.

"You hungry?" Kelly asked.

Elaine set her palm across the top of Kelly's glass and held his eyes. "The water's almost certainly okay," she said. "Worst case is you'll do anything *we* need you for before you're disabled by amoebiasis. Your choice." She slid the glass toward him and removed her hand.

Kelly hesitated. "Look," he said, "I've drunk—"

"And if you were in the field," Elaine interrupted calmly, "you might have to now. Your choice."

"Two Pepsis," Kelly said, smiling back at the boy. "And two dinners with double helpings of doner kebab, please," he added to the father.

"Turkish for shish kebab?" Elaine asked as the boy opened small bottles with the familiar logo.

"Shish kebab *is* Turkish," said Kelly, "and you can get it anywhere in the world. Doner's pretty localized by contrast, so I'm making you a better person by offering you a new experience. Not necessarily better than the familiar, but different."

The woman's body tensed into her 'neutral' status while

she attempted to follow the ramifications of what Kelly had just said. Her legs crossed instinctively, then uncrossed and anchored themselves firmly to the footrail of the stool when she realized what she was doing.

Kelly, grinning broadly, turned to watch the owner slice doner while his son readied the plates with cooked carrots, cooked greens, and ladlesful of rice.

The meat rotating before the gas flame was not the roast or boned leg of mutton it at first appeared. It was in fact a large loaf of ground mutton, recompressed into a slab in the ovine equivalent of hamburger, homogenous and broiling evenly on the vertical spit.

As the Americans watched, the man behind the counter swung out the spit and the integral driptray onto which juices spluttered with a sound that would have started Kelly's saliva flowing even if he had not gone most of a day without food. With a knife the length of his forearm, the Turk sliced away a strip of mutton so thin that it was translucent as it fell onto his cooking fork. The man pretended that he was not aware of the foreigners watching him, but his boy chortled with glee at the excellence of the job.

Rotating the spit with his fork—the motor drive shut off when the spit was removed from the fire—the owner stripped another portion of the loaf's surface.

"Aren't many useful things you can do with a knife sharp enough to shave with," said Kelly approvingly, "but this is sure one of them."

"You don't believe in sharp knives?" Elaine asked in surprise.

"I don't believe in—work knives," Kelly replied with a grin, "so sharp that the edge turns when you hit, let's say, a bone."

The meal was everything Kelly had hoped, hot and good and profoundly real in an existence that was increasingly removed from what he had known and done in the past. If incongruity were the essence of humor, then what Tom Kelly was doing with and to Pierrard's little playmates ought to be the laugh of a lifetime.

He sipped his Pepsi, put on a serious expression, and said, "I can never remember: should I have ordered lemon sodas instead with mutton?"

Elaine laughed, relaxed again. "We could ask the maitre d', I suppose," she said with a nod toward the owner beaming beside his grill.

"Who would tell us," Kelly said, slumping a little, "Efes Pilsen—like everybody else." His eyes swept the tables of other customers, crowded with the fat brown bottles of Pilsener beer. "And he'd be right, it's great stuff, but I don't suppose . . ."

Elaine touched the back of his fingers. "Tom," she said, "you've got more balls than anybody I ever met in my life. And it isn't because you act like you could tell the world to take a flying leap."

"Which it damned well can," Kelly grumbled. He was pleased nonetheless at the flattery, even though he knew that the woman was a professional and would have said the equivalent no matter what she really thought.

"I'm so very glad you're using me the way I'm here to be used," Elaine continued without taking her hand away from Kelly's. "We both want the same thing."

Except that one of us would really like Tom Kelly to survive the next couple weeks, the veteran thought as he turned over his hand and briefly squeezed her fingers. And the other cares more about what the weather in Washington'll be like when she gets back. But nobody was holding a gun to his head just now.

"Let's go see," he said, rising with a broad smile for the owner and everyone else in the restaurant, "just how efficient a team we're all gonna be."

*   *   *

Elaine checked the clasp of her little purse as they approached the door of 727. Kelly caught the angry red wink of a light emitting diode and the woman stutter-stepped, not quite a stumble, before halting.

"Problems?" the veteran said, unaware of the growling catch in his voice as he stepped to the hinge side of the door.

"No, we were expecting a courier, weren't we?" Elaine mumbled back, but she tapped on the door panel instead of inserting her key.

Doug opened the door. The LED warning went off. "I've been *waiting* here with the file," the blond man said.

"Very tricky," said Kelly with an approving nod toward the intrusion indicator.

"Not in the goddam *hallway*," snapped Elaine, using the purse as a pointer to thrust her big subordinate back in the room.

Kelly closed the door behind them. "The light wouldn't come on if somebody hadn't opened the door?" he asked.

"Amber if the door hadn't been breached, no light at all if the transmitter had been tampered with," said Elaine absently. She kicked off her shoes. "Doug, thank you for bringing the file. You can leave us to it now."

She looked at Kelly. "Unless you want to be alone with this, Tom?" she asked, gesturing with the red-bordered folder Doug had just handed her from his Halliburton.

"We'll take a look together," the veteran said, seating himself at the desk. He felt momentarily dizzy and, squeezing his temples with both hands, brought the world he saw back into color and focus.

"Are you all right?" the woman asked. "Doug, wait a minute."

"No problem," said Kelly. "Haven't slept in, you know, the whole flight. And with food in my belly, the brain isn't getting all the blood supply it'd like to have.

But no sweat, we'll run through this and get a jump on what we need.''

"Blow?" Doug offered.

"You wouldn't like me on coke," Kelly said with a grin that widened like that of a wolf launching itself toward prey. "*I* wouldn't like me on coke."

He opened the folder and let his face smooth. "Quicker we get to work," he said, speaking into the frozen silence, "the quicker I get to sleep."

Elaine gestured Doug through the door, but he was already moving that way of his own accord.

"Well, what've we got here," Kelly murmured, not a question, as Elaine set a straight-backed chair against the doorknob to jam the panel if anyone tried to power through it from the hallway. She damned well *was* more paranoid than the agent she was running. . . .

What they had was a sheaf of gatefold paper, the sheets still articulated, printed on a teletype or something with an equally unattractive typeface. Each page was headed with an alphanumeric folio line, but beneath that the first page was headed: Romer, Gisela Marie Hroswith. Good enough.

Kelly began to read, tearing each sheet off when he finished with it and laying it facedown on the desk. The woman, sitting on the bed, leaned forward and took the pages as Kelly laid them down. Neither spoke.

Gisela Romer was thirty-one, an inch taller than Kelly, and weighed a hundred and forty pounds. At five-ten, that didn't make her willowy by Western standards, but it was as exotic a touch as her blond hair in a Turkish culture where a beautiful woman five feet tall would weigh as much. The telecopied newspaper photograph appended to the file was indistinct enough to have been Jackie Kennedy, but the high, prominent cheekbones came through.

As Elaine had said in the elevator, Gisela Romer was a Turkish citizen; but her father and mother were part of a sizable contingent of Germans who had surfaced in Turkey in the late forties, carrying South American and South African passports that might not have borne the most careful scrutiny. By that time, Berlin was under Soviet blockade and the Strategic Air Command was very interested in flight paths north from the Turkish bases they were constructing. Nobody was going to worry too much about, say, a Waffen-SS Oberfuehrer named Schneider who might now call himself Romer.

Information on Gisela was sparse through the mid sixties—no place of residence and no record of schooling, though her father was reaching a level of prominence as a power in what was variously called the Service League or simply the Service—der Dienst.

"Is there an annex on the Dienst?" Kelly muttered when he got to the reference in Gisela Romer's bio.

"You've got the file," Elaine noted simply. "I can give you a bare bones now if there isn't. An import-export cooperative for certain expatriate families. Almost certainly drug involvement, probably arms as well in the other direction."

"There's an annex," Kelly said as he thumbed forward from the back of the clumsy document.

The printout on the Dienst was obviously a synopsis. The organization had been penetrated decades before, possibly from the very date of its inception. The file was less circumspect than Elaine had been about drug and arms trafficking. CIA used the Dienst as one of the conduits by which it increased its unreported operating budget through worldwide drug dealing. Drugs were not, by the agency's charter, its problem; and morality became a CIA problem only when one of its officers became moral and went public with the details of what he had been doing while on the agency payroll.

Clients for the Dienst's gunrunning were a more catholic gathering, though various facets of the US government were prominent among them. A brief notation brought to

Kelly's mind the shipment of automatic rifles with Columbian proof markings which he had issued to his Kurds. It was useful—generally—to carry out policy through channels which permitted bureaucrats to deny government involvement. The Dienst was indeed a service organization, and not merely on behalf of the war criminals it had smuggled out of Germany.

"These guys are a bunch of Nazis," Kelly said wonderingly as he tossed the annex on the desk and returned to the main file.

"They appear to have no political ends, here or in Germany," his case officer replied. "There is—and it may not be here"—she tapped the paper with an index finger—"an involvement in espionage, with us and probably with the Russians. Perhaps just another way of buying safety by becoming useful to both sides."

'Which is where," Kelly said as he resumed reading, "Gisela Romer and her line of work come in, I presume."

Ahmed Ayyubi had called Romer "the blond whore," but there was nothing to suggest that the statement was literally true. The woman had been dancing professionally since she was fourteen. Her background and appearance would have gained her a following in any Moslem country, but her skill level was apparently equal to that of any competitor in Turkey. At over a hundred thousand lire per performance, her legitimate earnings approximated those of an international soccer star.

So the men she slept with were chosen for position rather than wealth: high police and military officials; bank presidents and airline officials, people who could facilitate movements of one sort or another; and members of the diplomatic community in both Istanbul and Ankara.

"Why the *hell* would she pick up Mohammed Ayyubi?" Kelly demanded as he flapped down the last page of the printout. "He's not in her *league*." He laughed. "Figuratively, I mean. Literally, hell, maybe he was."

"Does it say that there?" Elaine asked, picking up the sheet Kelly had just finished.

"Mohammed's brother says it," Kelly muttered, "more'r less. *God*, I'm tired. And what in *blazes* do either one of 'em have to do with that—thing in the freezer."

"Ayyubi isn't around to ask," the woman said dryly. "But if you want to meet Gisela Romer, that can be arranged."

Kelly stood up and stretched. Elaine waited tensely for her agent's face to take on an expression or for him to say something. The muscles of Kelly's shoulders bunched beneath his jacket and his eyes gave her the feeling that she was being watched over a gunsight.

"When. Where. How," the veteran said at last. The syllables were without tone, not even of interrogation.

"She'll be performing at a Turkish-American Friendship Society meeting tomorrow night. The file indicates her technique." Elaine fanned the sheaf of papers again. "If you attend with the US assistant military attaché here, she'll be interested."

The woman paused. Kelly gestured with one hand, palm upward. "Drop the other shoe."

"If we drop word of who you *really* are," Elaine continued calmly, "she'll hit on you for sure to learn what you're doing in Turkey again. And that could be the opening you need."

"Fucking *brilliant*," Kelly snorted. "And who else picks me up? I'm a bit of a target, don't you think, for what happened three years back?"

"That's not a problem with the Dienst," the woman said. "Quite the contrary. Nor with the Turkish government, which keeps the Israelis in line; you're not worth dynamiting the only diplomatic relations Israel has with an Islamic state. And we'll keep the USG off your back, now and from now on."

She bent forward, though that meant she had to look up

more steeply to meet the eyes of the standing man. "We're already doing that, Tom. That's the payment we're giving you that you couldn't buy with money."

"Convey my thanks to Pierrard and his budget officers," Kelly said with an ironic bow. They'd sell him to Shin Bet or for cats' meat—which might come to about the same thing—the moment it suited their purposes.

"All right," he continued, with a note of resignation, "she's the best handle I see just now." He held his fist out in front of him and stared at it as he raised his fingers one at a time. "I don't see very much, that's sure. What time's the party?"

"Seven-thirty," Elaine said, relaxing minusculely. "It's in the casino in the Hilton, five minutes walk, so that's not a problem. Probably better to have Commander Posner call for you here, though, so you arrive together."

"All right," said Kelly as he started for the door.

"What will you do till then?"

"Sleep," said the agent. "And probably nothin' else."

Which wasn't very much of a lie.

Kelly locked the door of 725 and turned on the shower.

He was taking a chance by deciding to review the tape as soon as he got back to his room, because the system could not record additional material while he was listening to what it had collected to date. A second tape recorder would have permitted both . . . but additional gear meant a greater chance of discovery, and anyway—he was Tom Kelly, no longer NSA, and there was only one of him.

So although there was a fair likelihood that Elaine was about to have a conversation Kelly would like to know about, he opened the false battery pack attached to the Sony and rewound the miniature metal tape. The shower was not to cover the sound of the tape—it played back through earphones attached to the radio—but rather as an explanation, if anyone were listening to the noises within his darkened room and wondering at the fact that he was not asleep.

The taping system worked. You never knew, when components had to be arranged separately and not tested until they were in place. And this installation had been trickier than most because the cavity resonator Kelly had planted in his case officer's room was nothing but a closed metal tube with a short antenna attached. One end of the tube was a thin diaphragm which vibrated with the speech of people in the room. There was no internal power source, no circuitry, nothing but the section of wave guide. The microwaves directed at it from the ETAP were modulated by the diaphragm, and the whole was rebroadcast on the FM band at a frequency determined by the resonance of the microwave signal, the wave guide, and the length of the antenna.

The recorder was voice-activated so the first syllable of any string was clipped, and there was the usual urban trash overlaying a weak signal. Kelly had been trained to gather content from as little as thirty percent of a vocal message, however, and he had no problem following the recording.

The first of it was the phone ringing followed by Elaine's voice, noncommittal but recognizable, saying, *"All right, good. Stay down there."* George reporting from the coffee shop that Kelly had returned to the Sheraton. That, and Kelly's own discussion with Elaine in her room, were of interest purely as a test of the system.

The next conversation was the case officer's side of an outbound telephone call which had to have been made while Kelly showered before they went out to dinner.

Click. *"All right, he's eye-deed Gisela Romer and wants her file. We're going out to dinner, so have it waiting. I don't think it'll surprise him. He expects us to be efficient, and there isn't much time to fuck around."*

Click. *"He says he was getting laid. . . . Maybe, maybe. I can't tell with him, he's spooky. . . . What—?"*

Click. "*No, for* god's *sake run off a fresh copy. How
are we going to explain photocopies of a dog-eared original? . . . I don't— . . . God* damn *it Doug, get somebody there who* can *run the printer, even if it means
dragging the* Consul *out of bed.*"

Click. "*All right. Oh—and tell Romer we'll try to have
Kelly at the dinner tomorrow night. She's to make contact
with him there.*"

Click. "*She's not* paid *to like it, she's paid to take
orders. We've* got *to have a check on what Kelly's doing,
and if it works out—he's perverse enough that he's just apt
to trust her. At any rate, they can talk politics without
getting into arguments. . . . Right.*"

The clunk of the handset returning to its cradle ended
the conversation. There were several identifiable sounds—
door opening and closing, someone muttering unintel-
ligibly—probably Doug entering with the requested files.
The discussion, the three of them and then the occasional
muttered comments of Kelly and the woman as he read
and she pretended to read the flimsies. Compression of the
silences made the tape jar against Kelly's memory, but
there was nothing really different about the conversation.

All but the auditory center of his brain was concerned
with what he had just heard, anyway.

It wasn't quite as bad as he'd feared; they weren't
setting him up for a long drop, not yet anyway. But they
wanted to make sure they had him on a leash, even if that
meant identifying him to a gang of Nazi criminals without
his say-so.

. . . *they can talk politics without getting into arguments. Christ!* didn't anybody realize that ideology, religious or political, didn't matter a damn to Tom Kelly? The
only things worth killing for—or dying for—were personal
. . . and if Kelly had personally kicked the whole state of
Israel in the balls, that didn't make him a Nazi. Given

cause and opportunity, he would have done the same to Britain or any political group in the US of A.

And the other thing they didn't seem to realize is that you don't own ideologues just because they take your money. Intelligence operatives, effective ones, cannot make decisions on political bases any more than they can for personal reasons. They tend, as a result, to devalue both. Perhaps Gisela Romer was simply venal, in which case she would take anyone else's money as quickly as she did Pierrard's. The personality Kelly had gleaned from the file, however, was that of a woman who would take US money for the same reason that she gave head to the KGB resident in Istanbul: the Dienst, the Service, required it.

In neither case was she going to jump through a hoop simply because Elaine Tuttle told her to.

Kelly sighed. The tape wound through several seconds of silence after recording the door closing as he left 727 for his own room. He reached for the Rewind switch, planning to reset the unit to record. A clear voice where there should have been only blank tape said, *"Mr. Kelly, we must speak with you. You need fear no harm. We need you to save yourselves."*

There was no click or other recording artifact before or after the voice. Its volume level was higher than that of the recording previously, and there was no background of white noise as had clung to the sounds broadcast by the cavity resonator.

Kelly backed the tape and listened again. The end of his conversation with Elaine, the door closing, and nothing. Nothing again.

The voice he had heard was gone, except for what now stuck in his mind like a drug-induced nightmare.

He rerigged the camouflaged recorder by rote. Kelly's hands could do that or strip a firearm with almost no support from his conscious mind; and just now, there was very little support available in that quarter. As he let himself down on the bed, he remembered the shower was running. It took an effort of will to get him to his feet again to turn off the tap, and that only because he had spent too long in arid landscapes to let water waste itself down the sewers now.

Short men in dark overcoats lurked at the corners of his eyes as he moved, but there was no one with him in the room and no light to have seen them by in any case.

Kelly dreamed while he slept, and his body flushed itself of the residues of tension and fatigue. There were no creatures with multijointed limbs, only men in tunics building and battling over a city on a river. Other rivers might have the sharp bank the swift-moving Tigris had cut through the soil of Mesopotamia, but there could be no doubt about the black basalt fortification: he was dreaming of Diyarbakir, or rather, of Amida—the city's name when it was part of the Roman and Byzantine Empires.

The walls rose and were ringed by Persian armies in glittering armor, a dream montage drawn from guidebook scraps Kelly had assimilated out of curiosity when he trained guerrillas nearby . . . but more than that as well, banners and equipment that he did not know, that very likely nobody knew at this distance from the event.

The besiegers raised a mound of earth and fascines, stripping the countryside of timber for miles. "No . . . ," Kelly muttered in his sleep, because he knew what came next, and he had himself soldiered through in the wreck of other people's disastrously bad ideas. The wall of Amida rose regardless, propped and piled and jury-rigged to over-match the encircling threat.

It was not a normal dream. It had the cohesiveness and inevitability not of nightmare, where fear makes its own reality for the duration of sleep, but rather of history. Kelly was an observer, and the frustration of watching rather than participating—even in a certain disaster—caused him to drench with sweat the bedspread on which he lay.

And the wall of Amida, thrown higher than reason to make the fortress impregnable, crashed of its own weight toward the Persian lines. The rubble of it lay in a broad entrance ramp, giving the besiegers a gentle slope up which they scrambled into the heart of the city, crying slaughter and the glory of their bloody monarch Shapur.

Kelly thought he would prefer anything to the rape and butchery his mind showed him in the same omniscient detail as it had the preliminaries. But what closed the dream at last was a nuclear fireball, expanding and devouring its way across not Amida but a thousand modern cities, each of them as clear in Kelly's brain as the screams of the first woman he had shot at close range.

He awoke standing, legs splayed and the snubbie in his right hand searching for a target in the dim light. He thought it must be dawn, but the digital clock in his little radio said that it was seven PM.

There was no one else in the room.

Kelly felt foolish as he put the revolver down, but coming alert with a gun ready had been a survival reflex for a lot of years. Hell, it probably was again. And if nothing was waiting for him in the room at the moment, then that certainly didn't mean that everything was normal.

He'd never had a dream like that in his life; and it seemed likely enough that whatever it was he'd just—imagined—it wasn't a dream.

The phone rang. Kelly jumped, cursed, and started to pick up the handset. His right palm and fingers tingled oddly, and not from his grip on the snubbie, that was too familiar a stress for him to notice its effect. Flexing his right hand, Kelly picked up the phone with his left and said, "Shoot."

"Thought I'd check in, Tom," Elaine said through a buzz of static more reasonable for a call from Lagos than from the next room over. "Commander Posner expects to meet you in the lobby in twenty minutes."

"No problem," said Kelly. "I was just getting dressed."

"Then I'll leave you to it. Good luck," the woman said and rang off.

She sounded cheerful enough, Kelly thought. Wonder if she'd be cheerful if she knew as much about the bug as the bug had told Kelly about her.

He should have been wrung out by the nightmare, but in fact he'd awakened feeling as good as he had in years. The length of time he'd slept didn't make sense, either. He'd *needed* eighteen hours of rest, but there was no way his mind should have let him get it. It didn't work that way when you were on edge. Catnaps maybe, but not uninterrupted sleep that genuinely refreshed you instead of just backing a notch or two off your tension.

The tingling in his right hand persisted for some minutes, finally wearing away at about the time he shrugged into the coat of his gray wool suit. It hadn't been anything serious, nothing that kept him from tying his shoes or would have kept him from putting all five rounds from the snubbie into a shirt pocket at fifteen yards.

But the feeling had been in the portions of his hand which had brushed the surface of the alien corpse in Maryland, and it could be that that meant something very serious indeed.

"I don't *like* this," said Commander Posner for the third time, lighting a fresh cigarette from the butt of the one he had just smoked through. "Associating me with you and whatever you're doing is a public provocation to the host country, and it'll do a great deal of harm in the long run."

Posner was in civilian clothes tonight, a fact that surprised Kelly as did nothing else about the assistant military attaché. Military attachés—of all nations—have an advantage over other intelligence officers in that there is no dichotomy in what they are doing. They are, openly and by reciprocal treaty, spies in foreign countries. Not spies thinly masquerading as newsmen, AID officers, or vice-consuls, just spies. Their status makes it difficult for them to achieve results more remarkable than photographs of military parades, but it also permits them to believe that the world is as ordered a place as the bridge of an aircraft carrier in peacetime.

Posner's wife, a slim woman whose smile seemed no more likely to slip than that of the Mona Lisa, bent close to her husband's ear and whispered. He swore under his breath, glared at the cigarette, and ground it out in the clean ashtray with which a waiter had just replaced the overflowing one.

Mrs. Posner smiled at Kelly.

"I know," said Kelly with a nod of false condolence to the naval officer. "It's terrible to work for people as ruthless and *clumsy* as high military officers, ready to force the most ridiculous orders down the chain of command."

Commander Posner sat up sharply, blinking as if he thought he had misheard the statement.

As perhaps he had, because the noise in the big room was even greater than was to be expected by Western standards. A significant sample of the American official community was at the party, and, Kelly noticed, a high proportion of the Turkish nationals was not in fact ethnic Turks. Men—almost all the women in the room were the wives of Americans—of the Levantine, Kurdish, East European, and even Jewish communities in Istanbul predominated here. They were the folk who, rightly or wrongly, felt they might need outside protection in or from what was basically an Osmanli—Ottoman Turkish—nation state.

The US was unlikely to supply that help, should it ever come down to cases; but when you're nervous, a bad chance is better than no chance at all. Tom Kelly knew the feeling right enough.

There was a rattle of cymbals from the far doorway. A man in evening dress on the low podium in the center of the hall cried, his voice echoing through the ill-balanced sound system, "I give you Gisela!" in both English and Turkish.

Turkish music began at the far end of the hall. A man as tall as Doug Blakeley came in, carrying a large, chrome-glittering ghetto blaster, and stood by the doorway.

With a clash of finger cymbals, Gisela Romer appeared there. She was of a height with her assistant, though part of that was the pumps she wore.

Nothing in the file, photograph included, had prepared Kelly for the fact that the woman came as close to his ideal of beauty as anyone he had ever met in his life. Her shoulder-length hair was not the ash blond he had expected, but rather a richer color like that of polished brass or amber that has paled during long exposure to sunlight. Her choker, bra, and briefs were of those materials, brass and amber, and the gauze 'skirt' depending from the briefs at her flanks and midline was silk dyed a yellow of low saturation.

The dancer moved down the hall toward the podium with a lithe grace and as much speed as comported with the need to make an entrance. Her arms reached above her head and twined at the wrists momentarily. Then, clashing the finger cymbals, she advanced, spinning with alternate hip jerks—each carrying her the length of a long leg closer to her goal. The man with the tape deck trailed her, accompanied by a shorter man playing what looked like a small acoustic guitar.

"I've never understood the attraction of Oriental dancing," said Mrs. Posner distantly, using the technical term not from concern for anyone's feelings but rather from a distaste for the word *belly*.

"Muscle control," Kelly said. He watched intently as the blond mounted the podium and went into a formal routine, rotating slowly around the semicircle of the audience. "I've never seen a dancer with muscle control that good. Well, once before."

Gisela's hips shimmied and threw the gauze draperies outward, drawing the eyes of most in the room. Kelly watched instead what the actual belly muscles were doing and was flabbergasted. The blond woman was taut-bodied and no more fleshy than the veteran himself was, so the horizontal folds which ascended one after another from briefs to rib cage were not accented into crevices by folds of subcutaneous fat. They were impressive nonetheless, and the precision with which they marched upward like the static arcs of a Jacob's ladder was nothing short of remarkable when combined with the flashier portions of the routine.

"Who was that?" someone asked.

Kelly glanced around him. Mrs. Posner waited, an eyebrow raised in interrogation, for the veteran's answer.

"Bev," said her husband with a grimace.

"A go-go dancer in Sydney," Kelly said, turning again toward Gisela as he spoke, "tucked six Ping-Pong balls up her snatch with the mouth of a beer bottle. While she danced"—from the corner of his eye he noted that Mrs. Posner's hand had lifted to cover her gaping mouth—"she spit 'em out into the audience again. I mean, she could really aim, and some of 'em landed in the third rank of tables."

The woman made a choking sound but did not say anything further. Kelly thought there was the least hint of a smile on Commander Posner's face.

The music thinned to a background of sharply-tapped drums, which Gisela counterpointed with her finger cymbals as she went into a long series of hip rolls, shifting position again with each thrust to make the whole audience part of the performance. Her face was not bored nor disfigured by slit-eyed, open-mouthed mimings of lust. Rather, she was alive and aware both of her audience and the fact that she was *very* damned good at what she was doing.

Gisela ran a full set on the podium before she began to work the room. Her stunning hair remained surprisingly still as her body, hidden from most angles in the narrow aisleways, shimmied and jerked.

Belly dancing was a form of gymnastics and, like other gymnastic routines, an acquired taste. The detailed muscle work, which distinguished this performance from that in a Sirkeci nightclub, was subtler than similar skill demonstrated on the parallel bars. As a result, the attention of most Westerners lapsed—even that of the men, who could see more flesh in cocktail bars in whatever city they called home.

But Christ! thought Tom Kelly, not flesh like that— unless they were dating gymnasts. And the Turkish citizens were noisily delighted, their enthusiasm making up for any lack of spirit among the foreigners present. Men at each table held up bills as the dancer swung close. In general Gisela smiled and shot a pelvis toward them, holding the pose long enough for them to tuck the money under the strap of her briefs.

The two music men accompanied her on her rounds, providing music—by Turkish definitions, rhythm by any— and a level not so much of protection as of presence, to keep matters from getting out of hand. Neither man was as young as Kelly, and the bigger one, for all that he looked fit, was closer to sixty than fifty. At intervals, as Gisela shifted her attention from table to table, the smaller fellow with the guitar plucked sweaty lire from the dancer's waistband and stuffed them into the side pockets of his jacket. Even granting that most of the bills would be hundreds—something over a US dollar—Gisela was making a respectable haul.

And there were exceptions. One table held a quartet of fat, balding men with features similar enough to make them brothers. They had been drinking raki, Turkey's water-clear national liquor that clouded over ice. Its licorice flavor disguised its ability to lift the scalp of an incautious drinker. Though these four were not inexperienced, the volume of their intake tonight had loosened them considerably.

"Ho!" cried the nearest one as Gisela did a shoulder shimmy before him. He raised a bill over his head and flapped it. Kelly could not see what it was, but somebody at a nearby table hooted and clapped.

The blond woman responded with a belly roll that progressed to an amazing shimmy, a rattle of finger cymbals that overrode the drum taps from the boom box, and finally a forward thrust of her chest that brought her breasts within an inch of the man's face. A bangle, either a large topaz or tawny paste, joined the two bra cups. It was beneath that that the man thrust his bill. There was a cheer and general applause from the surrounding tables.

The brother to whom Gisela now directed herself already had a bank note ready, but instead of waving it he shouted, "Wait!" in Kurdish to the hip-swaying woman and fumbled again in his wallet. The two others at the table who had not yet joined the performance were doing the same, bumping empty glasses in their haste to get out more money.

The second target—'victim' would be a misstatement; he was paying for the honor of momentarily starring before an audience of his peers and powerful foreigners—came out with a second bill, raised one in either hand, and was rewarded with a hip thrust, front and center, and a kiss on the forehead which, not coincidentally, shot Gisela's crotch away from him as soon as he had inserted the money between the briefs and her pubic hair. You could get a lot more sex for a couple hundred dollars, but it would be hard to beat what Gisela had just provided the man in the way of thrills and public recognition.

When the dancer swayed from that table, her bra cups, pubic wedge, and the crack of her buttocks had all spouted 10,000 lire bills. The engraved visage of Kemal Atatürk waved against the sweat-glistening flesh, and Kelly doubted that the hard-drinking old hero disapproved. Gisela left the crotch and tail pieces in place as encouragement for later tables as she continued her rounds.

The attendant with the recorder had swapped sides on his ninety-minute tape, and the blond dancer had been in motion from the time she entered the room. Kelly unconsciously caught a roll of flesh above his own beltline between thumb and forefinger. It wasn't flab, but it sure as hell wasn't muscle tone like that which Gisela was demonstrating. He hadn't been in shape like that when he was nineteen and humping nearly a hundred pounds of gear, rations, and ammo across a series of thirty-klick days. . . .

The woman swayed closer. The table Kelly shared with the Posners was, by chance or intent, almost the last on her circuit of the room. Commander Posner reached toward his breast pocket. His wife straightened with an expression of blank horror that would have suited her own impalement.

"Well, I don't know what the etiquette is," the naval officer muttered with a nervous smile. "This is the wrong sort of entertainment for a—for a diplomatic gathering, you see."

"Don't worry, sir," said Kelly dryly. "I'll sacrifice myself to uphold the honor of the flag."

He had two bank notes ready: thousands. The amount was a compromise between avoiding notoriety for a huge offering and the need to make reasonable the query on the scrap of paper between the two bills: *Later?* The three sheets were fanned slightly so that the note's white edge was visible between the engraved expanses of currency.

Gisela hip-jerked to the table, turning a full 360 degrees as she left the guests she had just milked and—by switching her pivot foot—striding six feet without appearing to have abandoned them. Those men would not feel plucked and foolish when they went home tonight. It was nice watching a pro work, thought Kelly; and it was not only the woman's dancing which was of professional quality.

She swung around, facing first toward Commander Posner, and did a slow belly roll with her arms twined above her. Posner clapped lightly in embarrassment but did not reach again for his wallet.

Close up, the two attendants looked as out of place as Kelly himself would have felt doing their jobs. There was quite a lot of similarity between what he saw behind their eyes and what he felt behind his own. . . . Both men could well be Germans, though the smaller one was as swarthy as Kelly and the taller one had certainly not been a 'Nordic blond' before his hair went gray. They were armed— there were flat bulges beneath either's left armpit.

Gisela blew a kiss at Posner, tinkled her finger cymbals toward Mrs. Posner (who winced) and switched to Kelly.

She was tired, the veteran could see, and her midriff glittered where sweat jeweled the tiny blond hairs which would otherwise have been invisible. She began a hip sway; and, as the taped music quickened to an accompaniment of chords clashed on the guitar, the sway sped into a shimmy.

"My wife could have done that," Kelly said in German, enunciating precisely so that he did not have to shout to be understood. "But belly muscles like yours I have never seen, fraulein."

The look on the woman's face had been one of wariness masked by fatigue. Gisela tossed her heavy hair in its blond net and, with a smile as real and wicked as Kelly's own as he watched her, went into a belly roll that speeded to the point that the movement but not the individual folds were visible.

"Ha!" she shouted after what seemed to have been a minute of frantic motion. She stamped her right foot and shifted back into a gentle hip sway as if a control had been thrown to a lower speed.

Gisela's pelvis was prominent above the line of her spangled briefs. Kelly reached toward the point of her left hip with the currency and question. Rather than thrusting her flank toward him, Gisela bent and jerked her shoulders back so that the tassles on her left bra-cup flicked out against the bills.

"There," she directed in a Platt-Deutsch accent, "for the thought. And I can do other things your wife never thought of, too."

Her breast was warm; but then, so were Kelly's fingers and everything else in the big room.

There was a louder cheer than expected from local tables, because very few of the Americans had gotten into the spirit of the affair as Kelly seemed to have done. Gisela strode and swayed liquidly to the podium to finish her act there. Kelly had fanned the note briefly to show the dancer it was there, but as she moved away from him he noticed that her fingers brushed the three pieces of paper into a thin sheaf so that the query was not visible amid the currency.

They were both actors, going through motions choreographed by others; neither able to admit to the other what their real purposes and intentions were, or what they knew of the other party's. It was human society in microcosm, Kelly supposed.

Within moments of the time Gisela sprang from the room with a series of leggy bounds and double-handed kisses toward the guests to either side of her path, chairs and a speaker's stand were set up on the podium by members of the hotel staff.

"We really ought to stay for the speeches," Posner said apologetically in response to a whisper from his wife.

"They'll be in *Turkish*," Mrs. Posner replied, and in a tone that suggested she had been asked to go mud-wrestling.

Kelly looked at her, amazed. She seemed to think that after-dinner speeches at an affair like this were likely to be more boring in a language you didn't understand than they would be in one that you did.

A waiter approached, so soon after the dancer had left that Kelly assumed he was changing the defense attaché's ashtray once again. Instead, the waiter offered a folded note to Kelly himself with a smirk. It was the paper he had slipped between the thousand lire bills, and beneath his own *Later?* was written in a loose, jerky hand, *Why don't we talk about it at the door to the parking lot?*

Well, that was fast. Kelly rose, setting his chair back with one hand while he balanced the weight of his torso over the table with the other. "Mrs. Posner," he said as he leaned toward the couple, "Commander, I appreciate your company, but I think I've found my own ride home." Or somewhere.

Mrs. Posner nodded distantly. Her husband, frowning, said, "Mr. Bradsheer—take care."

"Thank you, Commander." Kelly shook the naval officer's hand, then walked toward the exit.

The cooler, less smoky air of the hallway as he went to the elevators did not seem at first to clear Kelly's sinuses. Rather, motion and oxygen brought with them a pounding headache as smoke-constricted capillaries tried to adjust to the new demands.

The parking lot north of the big hotel was actually off the basement rather than on a level with the front entrance to the ground-floor lobby. A hotel here, where almost all the guests would arrive in and use taxis instead of their own cars, had less need for parking than a similar 450-room unit in Washington, but that meant there would probably be a great deal of congestion tonight. Kelly shrugged as he got off the elevator, loosening his coat and his muscles, trying to be prepared for anything at all.

Gisela Romer was, quite literally, waiting at the far end of the hall, beside the glazed outside door. The shorter of her two attendants was visible through the panel, glancing in through the door and out again toward the crowded parking lot with the wariness of a point man on patrol.

The woman wore a long cloth coat, belted and not buttoned. Kelly wondered momentarily whether she had simply thrown it on over her costume, but the beige frill of a blouse showed at the cuff when she waved at him. "Are you the sort of man a girl can trust in a wicked world, Mr. Monaghan?" she called. It was Kelly's war name from the time he trained Kurds rather than what was on his present ID as a Boeing Services employee.

"Well, you know," Kelly said as he strolled to her side. The man outside stared at him like a vicious dog which precisely knows the length of its chain. "If you drop a bowling ball, you can trust it to do certain things. You just have to know ahead of time if they're the things you want."

Gisela smiled, an expression that made the most of the width of her mouth. "I think I'll trust you to protect my life, Monaghan. As for my virtue, I'll decide later if that needs to be protected or not."

She made a quick, dismissing gesture toward the glass door without bothering to look around to see how it was received. Kelly saw the attendant's head go back in a nod of acceptance, but the motion might equally have followed a slap. The man strode away from the door, his back straight and his neck no longer swiveling. Christ, you'd think they'd be used to it, whatever the relationships were. . . .

"I'd like to talk, Mr. Monaghan," Gisela said as she

touched the sleeve of his suitcoat and rubbed the fabric approvingly between thumb and forefinger. "I have a comfortable place, if you're inclined. . . . and we can take your car or mine."

"Does yours come with a couple kibitzers?" the American asked, feeling his face smile as his mind correlated the two operations: meeting a valuable source who was not trustworthy, and meeting a woman whom he intended at an instinctive level to fuck. The second part of the equation should have been too trivial for present consideration; but, because Tom Kelly was as human as the next guy, it was going to get at least equal billing until he did something about it.

"They'll go in the van," said the woman. She had exchanged her pumps for flats, and still only the thick Vibram heels on Kelly's shoes put his eyes on a level with hers. "I have my own car—and it has only two seats." Definitely a nice smile.

"Let's go," said Kelly, thrusting the door open for his companion, after whom he stepped into the night.

Mercury vapor lights on tall aluminum poles illuminated the Hilton lot well enough for Turkey, but the effect was very sparse by American standards. The lot was overparked tonight, as Kelly had expected. Close to the sidewalk was a British-style delivery truck, with roughly the wheelbase of a full-sized American car but a taller roofline than an American van. The sides were not painted with *GISELA* or a similar legend, but the attendant who had been watching over the dancer was walking toward the passenger side.

The second through tenth floors of the hotel overhung the ground floor and basement so that the glow from lighted guest rooms curtained the wall near the doorway with shadows deeper than they would otherwise have been. Nonetheless, the eyes of Gisela's attendant had been dark-adapted, and it was inconceivable that someone had been standing close to the door without being seen.

"Thomas Kelly," said a voice as clear and recognizable as what the agent thought he had heard on the tape in his room. He spun around.

"Do not be afraid because we must speak."

There were three short men in overcoats and hats with brims, shadows amid shadows against the concrete wall. One of them carried a transistor radio, from whose speaker the voice issued. The figures would not have been there unnoticed earlier, they could not have stepped through the concrete, and Kelly would have caught motion from the corner of his eye had they come running toward him alongside the building. But they were there now, ten feet away, their radio speaking as the attendant just getting into the van shrieked a warning.

Gisela cried out also. A purse dangled from her left wrist, but it was toward the side pocket of her coat instead that her free hand dived.

First things first. The shorter attendant and his companion, who stood up on the driver's side-step and looked over the van's cab, were both reaching for hardware. Kelly threw himself sideways, toward the line of yews fringing the thirty-foot walkway to the parking lot. His hundred and eighty pounds meat-axed the dancer ahead of him, out of the line of fire.

It occurred to him as the first shot banged from the cab of the van that he might be getting a personal demonstration of how Mohammed Ayyubi had died: in the wrong place at the wrong time.

Ricochets have a soul-freezing sound that rightly suggests the flattened bullet may rip a hole through you from any direction. This round cracked twice from the concrete, wall and overhang, before thrumming viciously into the night. Ten yards is spitting distance on a lighted pistol range, but shock and darkness made the gunman at the van as great a threat to the world at large as he was to his target.

As they crashed through the prickly branches of the shrubs, Kelly expected to hit the ground on top of the woman he was trying to save. He had not considered the fact that she was his superior as an athlete. She twisted in the air, using Kelly's own weight as a fulcrum, and hit the hard ground beyond him on braced fingers and toes. The weight of the gun in her right side pocket twisted the tail of the coat around behind her.

"Kelly—" the radio voice in back of him called. There was a snap as the American scrambled to his feet. The sound was not a gunshot like the volley blasting from around the van; it could have been the release of a bowstring.

"Your *car!*" Kelly cried to the woman beside him. Glass shattered from the building, and the man shooting from in front of the van splayed like an electrocuted squirrel as he fell backward.

Crouching, Kelly aware that the woman's light-colored coat made as good an aiming point as his own dark suit was a bad one, the couple broke for the asphalt lot at an angle which thankfully spread them further from the second attendant, who continued to shoot over the cab of the van. The three figures stood like sandbagged dummies, unaffected by the bullets. One round vanished in a violet flash that lighted the wall of the hotel instead of ricocheting away.

"This one!" Gisela shouted, motioning with her right arm toward a car parked at the edge of the asphalt. It was a Mercedes coupe with the slight rounding of lines that marked it as ten or fifteen years old rather than brand new. The mercury-vapor lamp was reflected as a rich blue pool from the bodywork of metallic silver, a German hallmark which Japanese automakers attempted to match with less success than they showed in matters of pure mechanics.

There was a second *snap!* and the remaining attendant catapulted from the van. Gisela, instead of dodging around the front bumper of the coupe, vaulted the hood which her

dangling coattail struck with a clang. Kelly flattened himself on the ground, reaching up for the passenger-side door
as he twisted his head back to see what weapons were
being aimed. He had not attempted to clear the revolver
attached to his waistband. All it was going to do under
present circumstances was tie up his hand and make a
target of him.

A better target.

Two of the figures, the men if they were men, ran
toward him while the third's radio shouted, "Thomas
Kelly, for your planet's sake—"

The long burst of submachinegun fire from a parked
Audi sedan drowned the cough-*brap!* of the six-cylinder
Mercedes engine catching.

Kelly expected the coupe's door to be locked. It was
not. He threw it open and tossed himself into the passenger
seat of the low car, wishing he were half as agile as the
woman he was accompanying. The nearer of the two
figures running toward the car toppled limply. The second
froze and remained standing in a violet blaze as two or
three automatic weapons ripped at it.

The Mercedes was accelerating before Kelly got his
door closed. Gisela pulled a hard left turn, spinning the
little vehicle in about its own length. The 280 SL had not
been a dragster even when new, but its engine was in a
sharp state of tune and snarled happily as the driver revved
it through the powerband. Centrifugal force made the door
in Kelly's hand a weight worthy of his strength as he
drew it closed.

"Thomas Kelly!" the radio voice called over the roar of
gunfire and exhaust. Shots raked the building in a cloud of
pulverized concrete, lighted internally by spluttering arcs
from the figure who stood in the midst of the bullets until
he disappeared instead of falling.

As the coupe straightened in the aisle, heading in the
direction opposite to the way it had been parked, Gisela's

foot blipped the throttle so that the automatic clutch would let her upshift. There was a red and white glare from a second Audi, backing at speed across the head of the aisle to block them. The medley of tail and backup lights was as uncompromising as the muzzle flashes from the other German sedan.

The shriek of the Mercedes' brakes was louder than the angry whine of the Audi's gearbox being overrevved in reverse gear. The coupe's blunt nose slewed thirty degrees to the left as that front disk gripped minutely before its companion. Kelly's left hand was furiously searching the door panel for a way to roll down the window. Gisela had not switched on her lights, and the parking lot fixtures overhead did nothing to illuminate the car's interior to eyes dazzled by muzzle flashes and the electric coruscance which bullets had drawn from the three figures.

He poised the revolver in his hand, bumping the coupe's low roof with it as he readied to smash out the side window with the gun butt. Instead, Gisela flung his unbraced body against her as she downshifted again and cut the wheel right.

Inertia had carried the heavy sedan from its blocking position against the drag of its own brakes. As it lunged back against its springs when the tires got a firm grip, Gisela punched the coupe between the Audi and the rear bumper of the nearest parked car.

The sedan's bright headlights reflected explosively from the metallic side of the Mercedes squirming past it, accelerating. The Mercedes was too solidly built for competitive racing, but the little engine had enough torque to shoot them through a gap which neither Kelly nor the Audi's driver thought was present.

"Not yours?" Kelly shouted over the exhaust note reflected from the sides of parked cars. Lights scissored across the sky behind them as both sedans maneuvered in the parking lot.

"I don't know whose," Gisela shouted back, shifting into third up the short ramp to Mete Street. The headlights of a car parked illegally on the street flashed on. "What are you *doing?*" Her gearshift hand batted down at Kelly.

The car on Mete Street was a third Audi.

"You drive," said Kelly as he worked the gun from the woman's coat pocket. "I'll worry about the rest."

Gisela's hand touched the control standard on the left side of the steering column, throwing her headlights on and bright. That might have spooked the passenger in the third sedan into putting his burst of shots into the dirt and driveway curb instead of through the Mercedes' windshield. Alternatively, he might have been trying merely to disable the coupe by shooting out the left-side tires. Either way, the muzzle blasts and the ringing crash of a ricochet into one of the Mercedes' rocker panels confirmed a decision Kelly had more or less made already. The guy who shot at them had just clarified the rules.

Gisela had flinched as the bullet hit the car, but her hands were rock-steady now at the ten and two o'clock positions on the steering wheel. She crossed them right and straightened expertly to give the coupe room at the head of the drive if this Audi too attempted to drive across their path. The Mercedes lurched, brushing but not rebounding from the right-hand radius of the curb cut. Then they were in Mete Street, using the full considerable width of the pavement to hang a left turn while continuing to accelerate. There was more firing distantly behind them, but nothing passed close to the 280 SL.

The dancer's two attendants had carried pocket pistols, .32's by the sound of them: the highly-portable European answer to situations in which Americans tended to carry small revolvers. Both choices were guns you carried when you wanted to be armed but didn't expect to have to use your hardware.

The pistol Kelly hauled from Gisela's coat was something else again: a Walther P-38, old enough to have a steel frame and grooved wooden grips. It fired full-house 9mm Parabellum ammunition through a five-inch barrel, which, with the projecting hammer, safety, and front sight, made the weapon as bad a choice for pocket carry as could be imagined.

On the plus side, Kelly couldn't have asked for a better weapon to *use* if he had to be limited to pistols.

Behind them, the lights of a car bounced wildly as it plunged into Mete Street in pursuit. The Audi which had shot at them waited for its companion to clear the driveway before pulling a U-turn to follow. Kelly couldn't be sure through the rear window whether or not the third sedan was following also; but two, crewed by men with submachineguns, were certainly enough.

"God*dam*," he muttered, then raised his voice enough to add, "See if you can lose 'em. They may not want us dead."

Men with submachineguns, and possibly a woman.

The Taksim District with its broad streets and low-density development—public buildings and luxury hotels landscaped like no other area of the city—was as good a place to drive fast as anywhere in Istanbul. That made it the least suitable place for them to lose pursuers in cars which, for all the coupe's sporting appearance, had the legs of them. Metallurgy and the technology of internal combustion engines had not stood still during the past fifteen years.

Gisela sent the Mercedes snarling past the Sport Palace—the enclosed soccer stadium—without shifting up from third gear, and entered what was supposed to be a controlled intersection at speed. As it chanced, the light was in their favor—but a '56 Chevy, for *Chrissake,* being driven with almost as much abandon as the coupe, was running it from Kadergalar, the merging street.

Kelly's feet were planted against the firewall and his

shoulders compressed the springs of the seatback, anchoring him despite the violent accelerations of the car. Gisela yanked her wheel left, trusting the gap in oncoming traffic, as the driver of the Chevy slammed on brakes which grabbed on the right front and started his car spinning just before the moment of contact.

The result was something closer to elastic rebound than auto bodies collapsing within one another, though eight tires simultaneously losing their grip on the pavement sounded like a chorus of the damned.

The coupe's right headlight nacelle touched the left bumper of the taller American design, spraying glass and a cloud of tungsten which had sublimed in a green arc. The front ends counterrotated and the rear quarter-panel of the Chevy patted the Mercedes' back bumper with the control of a handball player's glove. Gisela, bracing herself on the wheel rim as her passenger did on the carpeted firewall, did not attempt input through the brakes or steering wheel until the tires regained enough traction to accept it.

The Chevy, its back end drifting to the right in response to the second impact, broadsided the end of the iron-tube barrier intended to separate cars and pedestrians at the intersection. The scattering of individuals waiting to cross the street at this hour leaped into recessed shop fronts or tried to climb the grated window of a branch bank as the car sawed itself in half with trunk and rear wheels on the sidewalk and the remainder sliding in the street.

Gisela's 280 SL swapped ends twice in a hundred yards of skidding while its tires shrieked without fatal overtones of metal dragging as well. The coupe's short wheelbase and tight suspension made the uncontrolled spin less physically punishing than it might have been in another vehicle, but the Chevy beside them separating in sparks both from friction and the sheared powerline feeding the traffic signal was a sight with heart-freezing elements of prophecy.

They missed an Anadol at the next intersection, marked

as a taxi by its band of black and yellow checkerboard, because its driver had braked hard to watch the Chevy disintegrate. The Mercedes' left front brushed the little Ford just hard enough to give Gisela control again. She could not have managed the obtuse angle required to turn left onto Bayildim Street, but there was a cobblestone alley directly across the intersection. The Mercedes dropped into it like a bullet through the muzzle of a smoothbore.

The alley ran between the dun-stuccoed courtyard walls of multistory apartment blocks. The coupe's single remaining headlight filled the passageway, save for the black fingers of shadow flung ahead of the car by projections from the walls. Gisela's eyes and mouth were both wide open in an expression more masklike than fearful. The engine stuttered and boomed as she downshifted, but she did not lose the car's minimal traction except for the instant a driving wheel slipped on garbage and the coupe's right side streaked the plaster silver.

Kelly's left hand massaged his thigh where the hammer of the P-38 had bitten him while the car spun. His thumb touched the safety lever. Christ, it was on safe! The woman knew a lot more about cars than she did double-action pistols. When he had clicked the safety up to fire position, he also checked the little pin which projected above the hammer to show that a round was chambered.

Kelly didn't expect to need the gun now, given the likelihood that the collision would have screened their escape and possibly even blocked pursuit. The Chevy had not exploded as it well might have done—and he was glad it had not. Kelly lacked the willingness to ignore side effects displayed by certain of his superiors who would cheerfully have incinerated scores of Turkish civilians in a gasoline fire if it suited their purposes. The victims would be nonwhites, after all, wogs; and *certainly* non-Christians.

Still, Kelly was not writing the Audis out; he unrolled his window as an unlighted lamp bracket beside a courtyard gate clacked against his door handle and Gisela braked hard. Only when she was sure of her clearance did she spin the wheel and the Mercedes hard right, up a slightly-wider alley leading back toward the Catholic church adjoining the grounds of the Technical School.

There was an echoing cry of metal behind them. The car plunging down the alley they were leaving had scraped twenty feet of stucco from the same wall the coupe had touched. The dazzle of headlights made the vehicle itself invisible, but the only reasonable question about its identity was *which* of the three Audis this one was.

"Pull right at the next street," Kelly ordered loudly in a voice as emotionless as the echoing exhaust of the twin pipes. "Drop me half a block down, and go like hell till I take care of the problem."

The woman glanced at her passenger. Kelly had reached across his body left-handed to unlatch his door and hold it ajar. He held the P-38 vertical beside his head, so that the muzzle was clear of his skull no matter what shocks the weapon received in the next moments.

"All right," she said, and the agent realized from her tone that she knew how sure she had better be that it *was* all right.

The Mercedes fishtailed onto Macka Street, losing just enough momentum in a downshift as it burst from the alley that it thrust a Fiat taxi out of the way, by presence rather than by collision, horns on both cars blaring. The taxi cut left, threatening oncoming traffic for a moment but giving the coupe what amounted to a third lane along the curb. Pedestrians and the shills in front of the few shops still open shouted more in enthusiasm than fear.

Gisela braked hard and the Mercedes slewed again, scraping the curb with the edge and sidewall of the front tire as the Fiat that had continued to race them for the slot in traffic shot ahead in a Dopplered howl of alarm. Three more subcompact sedans swerved outward from the coupe's blazing brake lights, honking and cursing but without real animus. Gisela's present maneuvering was not greatly out of the ordinary for the streets of the densely-built old city.

Kelly let the inertia of the door swing it open against the coupe's breaking effort, and stepped out onto the sidewalk. He immediately tumbled, balling his head and limbs against his torso to save himself serious injury from the unintended somersaults. Only to the agent's speeded-up senses had the car stopped. It and he were still moving at about ten miles an hour when his foot hit the concrete, and the small contact patch provided by his right heel could not possibly bring to a halt his hundred and eighty pound mass as he intended.

The 280 SL accelerated away, surely enough to save the door's hinges though not to latch it firmly again. Kelly skidded to a stop on his back, the suit coat bunched beneath his shoulders. He rolled to his feet and stood, looking back toward the alley they had left.

Men in sweaters or baggy suits who had run to help him up scattered when they saw the big pistol in Kelly's hand. There was holster wear at the muzzle and the squared-off edges of the slide, and the external bar that was part of the trigger mechanism had polished a patch of bluing from the frame. That only meant that the P-38 had been used, however, and guns were meant to be used.

Horns and tires competed in cacaphony behind Kelly, with the insistent note of rubber skidding on concrete probably the winner of the contest. He spun, bracing his left palm against the blistered paint of a light pole. He had expected the Audi which was their immediate pursuit to exit the alley momentarily; headlights already blazed from its mouth across the intersecting street.

But another of the German sedans had expertly circled the whole warren of alleys on Sport Street—named because of the stadium—and had been speeding north on

Macka Street past the Technical School when the driver caught sight of Gisela heading in the other direction.

The way the Audi changed front and scrubbed off velocity in an all-wheel drift was testimony both to the driver's skill and the fact that the sedan had four-wheel drive. Otherwise, the weight shift during braking would have unloaded the rear wheels and thrown the vehicle into an uncontrollable spin as the driver tried to change direction.

Gisela had made room for herself in the southbound lane by bluff and audacity. The Audi sedan was a 5000, heavy and as close to a full-sized car as anything made in Europe save for six-door limousines. It simply brushed aside a Skoda pickup which crashed to a halt against the barred front of an apothecary's shop twenty feet south of the agent.

A man Kelly did not recognize from behind was hanging out of the passenger-side window as the Audi regained forward momentum in its new direction. The P-38's thin front sightblade and its U-notch rear were almost useless in the bad lighting, but the Walther pointed like his own finger as Kelly squeezed the trigger through its first long double-action pull. The muzzle blast of the 9 mm, even from a relatively long barrel, was a deafening crash more painful than that of larger and more powerful cartridges operating at lower levels of pressure.

Handgun recoil was always more a matter of perception than physical punishment, and the P-38's was mild by reasonable standards in any case. The barrel had a right-hand twist, giving the gun a torque opposite to what a shooter expected as it recoiled and returned to battery, but neither that nor the lift of the light barrel kept Kelly from putting out a second aimed shot within a fraction of a second of the first. Ears ringing and his retinas flooded by purple afterimages of the huge flashes from the muzzle of his weapon, Kelly rotated back to the Audi which he had intended for his initial target when he jumped from the coupe.

Kelly had aimed not at the passenger, though the man presumably had a submachinegun, but rather at the side window behind him. Reflection from the smooth glass made the empty rectangle a good aiming point, and Kelly's quartering angle on the sedan meant that the bullets would snap across the tonneau and the space most likely to be occupied by the driver's head.

The Audi spun broadside as the driver's hands flung the wheel away and his foot came off the gas before he had quite compensated for the momentum of the vehicle's drift. An oncoming bus smashed into the right side of the Audi just as an Anadol hit the sedan from what would have been behind a fraction of a second earlier. The man leaning from the right-hand window rebounded twice between the door and window posts before sprawling, as limp as an official explanation, against the door.

It hadn't mattered to Kelly—and probably not to the driver bouncing inside the crumpling sedan—whether or not he actually hit the man at the wheel. The 9 mm bullets were supersonic. Their ballistic crack within inches at most of the driver's ears and the way the windshield exploded into webbed opacity as they exited were enough to throw the best wheelman in the world into a disastrous error in this traffic.

The people in the second Audi had seen enough of what happened to target Kelly even as he turned back to face them. The passenger opened up with an automatic weapon as the sedan, its side streaked surreally by the battering it had taken in the alley, pulled halfway up on the curb with a snarl of low-end power as it came toward Kelly.

God himself couldn't count on hitting anything from a moving car. That was why Kelly had jumped from the Mercedes when it became obvious that they were not going to shake the pursuit. The Audi gunner's long burst lifted the muzzle so that bullets spalled concrete from the sidewalk halfway between weapon and target, riddled the neon tobacconist's sign above Kelly's head, and sparked from a rooftop flagpole halfway down the block.

One ricochet gouged ten inches of fabric from the left tail of Kelly's coat unnoticed, and the spray of hot glass from above made him flinch and send an unintended third shot after the two he aimed at the Audi's windshield, at the place where the gunner's torso should be if his head was behind the blinding muzzle flashes of the submachinegun.

If the windshield was bulletproof, Kelly was shit outa luck—but surely no one could drive at night with the skill these men had shown if there was a thick plate of Lexan between their eyes and the road.

The submachinegun fell, banging off one more round as it hit the concrete and skittered. The gunner slumped back, his right forearm flopping against the outside of the door. The two bullets through the windshield had crazed most of it into a milky smear.

Kelly had stepped away from the light pole when he switched targets. The halogen headlights of the sedan bearing down on him flamed the plate glass of shop windows into dazzling facets and threw shadows like curtains over the door alcoves the lights did not penetrate.

The quartz-iodide lights did not blind Kelly as he shifted his left foot a half step to swing his gun and rigid arm. He fired pistols one-handed, not because he thought it was better than modern two-hand grips but because it was the way he had first learned—and thus was better for him. The car, twenty feet away and jouncing closer, was too near for the lights to interfere with his sight line toward the driver.

The Audi slammed to a stop so abrupt that the nose dipped and the undamaged portion of the windshield reflected flashes of advertising signs like a heliograph. The car lurched into reverse and, with its right front wheel still on the sidewalk, crunched again to a halt against some unfortunate econobox in the traffic lane.

Kelly held his fire, shielding his eyes now with his free left hand. The sedan was cocked upward, lights on and motor racing as the driver leaped out.

''No!'' he screamed to Kelly, throwing his own hands out before him in unintended mimickry. It was the first time Kelly had actually seen one of the men from the Audis.

It was George, the balding member of Elaine's team, who apparently handled driving chores as well as sweeping for bugs. Christ on a crutch.

Kelly fired, aiming between the Audi's headlights, the clanging of his high-velocity bullet against metal an instant counterpoint to the muzzle blast. George leaped as though he had been hit and ran across the street, regardless of the cars trying to extricate themselves from the chaos of multiple collisions.

Maybe the ricochet or flecks of metal ripped from the bullet and the car *had* hit him. More likely it had been pure terror, an emotion Kelly could well appreciate. His own thighs were wet with something, probably sweat or blood and lymph where the fall from the car had scraped him. But he could've shit himself; it happened more often'n anybody who hadn't been there'd believe.

And 'there' was a place Tom Kelly was back to this night for sure.

The right 9 mm loads had penetration up the ass, so it was possible that the bullet had holed the aluminum engine block. The steam that gushed from the sedan's grill proved that Kelly had taken out at least the radiator, which made the car undrivable even if somebody shut off the motor before it melted itself down. There was still one car not accounted for, but Kelly intended to limit further pursuit as completely as he could.

Without killing additional friendlies. More or less friendly.

Gunfire had cleared the sidewalks almost as thoroughly as if all the pedestrians had been shot. Cars still moved or tried to, and the windows of apartments on upper floors were thrown open by curious occupants.

Kelly was trying to look down the street, shielding his eyes from the Audi's halogen glare with his left forearm, when what had been the shadowed side of the pilastered wall before him brightened with light from a new direction. He spun.

The indicator pin told him there was still a cartridge in the chamber; but he couldn't remember how many shots he had fired, nor did he know whether the piece had originally been loaded to its full nine-round capacity. The snubbie was still where Kelly had dropped it on clearing the Walther, in the side pocket of his coat—and thank the dear Lord that he hadn't found time to refix it at the base of his spine before skidding down the sidewalk on his back. The short-barreled revolver was as bad a choice for shooting at vehicles as the P-38 was a good one.

A car was driving up the sidewalk toward him, opposite to the flow of traffic which the nearer lane would have had if George's Audi had not blocked it. A net bag full of soccer balls, dropped by some shopper or peddler to the sidewalk, burst and spewed its contents in all directions as the car neared at twenty miles an hour.

The car had only one headlight, the left one. Gisela had come back to fetch him, despite the tangle and the bloody violence that anybody with sense would've driven like hell to avoid. One thing about having the shit hit the fan: it taught you who you wanted to keep among the people you knew.

Kelly stepped off the curb to let the Mercedes by and flung open the door of the coupe that squealed to a halt beside him.

"There's another one out there," Kelly said, meaning the Audi and too wired to wonder whether or not he was understood. He flopped onto the low seat and pulled the door closed after him. "Hope to god it doesn't find us."

The dancer pulled around the tangled Audi and the car it had backed into, then cramped her wheel hard and bumped off the curb again with a clang from the low undercarriage. The vehicle immediately behind the cars paired by the collision had begun to back clear to skirt the obstacle. Gisela accelerated through the momentary gap, ignoring both the screamed curses and the clack as she smashed off her outside mirror against the fender of the higher car.

"I'm taking you to the pickup point," she said in German. They had spoken in English before, but stress had thrown the dancer back to her birth language. Kelly was fluent enough in German that the change didn't matter to him, but the fact of it was a datum to file. "We—we've needed somebody like you, for the people you know. This has proven how little time there is."

Kelly started to say, "Wait," although waiting was the last thing he really wanted to do in this confusion with its chance of fire and explosion and its certainty of heavily-armed patrols descending at any moment. Instead, as Gisela negotiated the acute turn onto Tesfikige Street, bumping over the curb again to clear the van stalled in the intersection, Kelly said, "Gisela, run me back to the Sheraton. There's something I need in my room there."

"Are you sick in the *head?*" she demanded, sparing him a glance.

"Didn't say it was a great idea," the American said as he met her eyes. "But I've never volunteered for a suicide mission, and that's what tonight'll have been if I don't have some way to cover my ass." He grimaced and looked away. "Yeah, and get a change of clothes, too. These"—he felt the back of his coat with his free left hand—"haven't come through the night much better than I have."

"But you'll come," the woman said. She was driving normally. The traffic now was Istanbul's normal dense matrix, and there was no reason to call attention to themselves by attempting to break out of it. There was no particularly good way to get from one place to another in the ancient streets laid out by donkey-drivers, so their present course was not a bad one from Kelly's standpoint.

"I'm with you as soon as we're outa my hotel," the agent agreed, sliding forward in his seat so that he could replace the little revolver at the back of his waistband. He didn't want it to clank against the Walther he intended to carry in his trouser pocket, screened by the coattail, when he got out of the car. "I go up to the room, grab my stuff like I'm just changing clothes to party some more, and I think anybody listening's going to leave me alone until they've got a better notion of what's going on tonight. Better'n *I* do, anyway."

Why in the *hell* had they shot at him, George and whoever had been with George or at least issuing his orders? Confusion rather than deliberate purpose, perhaps, but you don't issue somebody a gun in a civilized venue unless you trust him not to shoot first and ask questions later.

Except that to Doug and his ilk in their English suits and Italian shoes, Turkey *wasn't* civilized; it was part of the great brown mass of Wog-land, where a white man could do anything he pleased if he had money and the US government behind him.

So they might have thought there were—use the word—aliens in the Mercedes, and they might have thought it was Kelly about to pull something unstructured on his own. Either way, somebody had made the decision to stop the car at any cost.

They just hadn't realized who would be paying most of that cost.

"Got another magazine for this?" Kelly asked, tapping the slide of the P-38. His eyes searched traffic for anything his trigger reflexes needed to know.

"No," said Gisela. She had switched back to English, but the shake of her head was a bit too abrupt to have been without emotional undertones. "It was . . . it was my father's before they killed him. The *crabs*. They took even his body away.''

"It'll do," said Kelly, unwilling to remove the maga-zine and check the load on the off chance that he'd need the weapon fully functional during those few seconds. "Why did they murder your father?"

Nothing in the files Elaine had showed him said any-thing about direct contact between the aliens and the Dienst. More important, nothing in the conversation Kelly had bugged suggested that his case officer and her chief subor-dinate had any inkling of the connection. Maybe there was more in Kelly's meeting with Gisela Romer than a way of gaming his employers. . . .

"I don't know," she said miserably, reacting to the concern in her passenger's voice. It was genuine enough, concern that a human being had been killed by monsters; but Kelly displayed his feeling because it was politic to do so, the way it would have been politic to display affection if he were trying to get into the woman's pants . . . which might come yet, the aftermath of the adrenaline rush of the firefight accentuating his lust.

"We've known about them for three years," Gisela went on. She forced her way in a blare of horns onto Besiktas Street, through a light that had already changed. None of her memories were keeping her from being as aggressive a driver as Istanbul traffic required. "Ever since the—they made the Plan—my father and the other Old Fighters—the crabs, the aliens, have been attacking us one by one, all over Earth."

"Which plan was that?" asked Kelly mildly, to give the impression that he was just making conversation.

"You'll have to learn," said Gisela. A sudden distance in her tone implied the question had not been delicate enough. "But not from me, it is not my place."

Three truckloads of Paramilitary Police passed at speed with their two-note hooters blasting as Gisela turned past the open-air stadium on the Bosphorus side of the huge Taksim Park. Kelly kept his left hand over the pistol in his lap, knowing that the blue-bereted policemen hanging off the sides of their trucks might catch a glimpse into the interior of the low coupe. On a terrorist alert like this, a burst of automatic rifle fire through the Mercedes was a very possible response.

Perhaps because of a similar thought, the woman glanced at Kelly and said, "You saved my life, didn't you? Was it your job to do that?"

Wonder what Elaine's answer would be, Kelly thought, but he didn't wonder at all. Aloud he said, "Look, dammit, maybe I needed a driver."

It bothered him to be thanked for what he thought of as acts of simple humanity, getting somebody out of the line of fire, getting somebody to a dust-off bird. . . . It meant that either Kelly's vision of humanity was skewed, or that other people's perceptions of Kelly himself were very different from his own.

Two taxis and a BMW sedan were picking up passengers under the marquee of the Sheraton. Gisela pulled ahead of them and as far up onto the sidewalk as permitted by the posts set to prevent that behavior. "I'll be quick," Kelly said as he got out.

The driver's door thumped closed an instant before Kelly's own did. Gisela was already striding toward the hotel's uniformed attendant. The agent caught up with her just as she handed the Turk a bank note folded at a slant so that the numerical 1000 on two corners was clearly visible. "No trouble if we run in for a few minutes, is there?" she asked cheerfully in Turkish, smiling down at the attendant from her six-inch height advantage.

"Well . . . " the door man temporized, but his fingers had closed over the bill and were refolding it apparently of their own volition.

"Another one for you when we return," Gisela promised, taking Kelly's left arm with her own right hand and beginning to stride toward the entrance.

The doorman looked at the thousand-lire note, then toward the back of the leggy beauty who had given it to him. Kelly himself got only a bemused glance, though from the rear his coat and trousers were in worse shape than the coupe's battered right side.

"Listen, this may get hot," Kelly hissed in angry German as he pushed open a door for them. He had not spoken earlier because he did not know of any language he had in common with Gisela which the doorman did not share. "Having you along makes it worse." He was trying to read her expression at the same time that he searched the lobby and alcoves for an observer or even an ambush.

"It makes it *better*, darling," Gisela purred as her hand moved up to stroke his shoulder blades as they walked toward the elevator. "You want to convince them there's nothing wrong, it's all innocent—we'll convince them." She giggled—was the woman really *that* relaxed?—and added, "All *not* innocent, not so?"

Christ, thought Kelly as he stepped onto the elevator. She was probably right, but if the shit hit the fan again . . . The P-38 would be even harder to clear from his pants pocket than it had been from Gisela's coat, and the snubbie was positioned for concealment rather than instant use.

But maybe nothing like that would be necessary. Maybe he'd waltz into his room, change clothes—pick up the radio and tape recorder—and waltz out again. By now, Elaine or whoever had survived the mess in the parking lot and afterwards would know that something had blown wide open . . . but in the darkness, with at least four sets of participants involved, nobody might be absolutely sure of Kelly's own role in the business. Not even George, who, at best, saw not Kelly but a dark suit and a pistol aiming at him. They'd want to talk to him, but to brace Kelly now—with his target, if they recognized Gisela, or with an innocent bystander if they didn't—would be breaking too many rules.

Unless they knew already what their agent had done to the teams in the Audis.

There was no one in the seventh-floor hallway.

"Well, I tell you, honey," Kelly said as he slipped his left hand around Gisela's waist, "you give me a few minutes to change, and then you can show *me* how to show *you* the best time in Istanbul." He shifted Gisela to his other side and drew the Walther from his pocket, using the bulk of both their bodies to shield it from sight of anything but the door of 725.

Left-handed, he inserted the room key, which he had cut from its brass tag to make more portable. Kelly had not *expected* to reenter the Sheraton looking like something the cat dragged in, but he had considered the possibility that he would.

There was no sound from 727, the next door down, and there was no tense aura of someone waiting within Kelly's room. Electronics weren't the most trustworthy indicators available to a trained human.

He closed the door and bolted it before turning and taking a deep breath with his palms flat against the panel. That was as close to collapse as Kelly could permit himself to come for a good long time yet.

Moving again with deliberate speed, Kelly strode to the window and closed the mechanical slide-switch of the Sony 2002, shutting off the recorder hidden in the battery pack as well. He telescoped the antenna and locked it in place, then put the units, still linked so that no one would open the pack simply because of ignorance as to its outward purpose, in his limp attaché case.

"Say, honey," he called over his shoulder as he straightened, shrugging off his abraded jacket and turning instinctively so that the butt of the snubbie would remain concealed from his companion, "you wanna use the john, go ahead, it's——'' Kelly's tongue missed a syllable, two syllables, as he looked at the woman for the first time since they entered the room, ''just like America,'' he concluded.

The light between the twin beds had gone on when Kelly flicked the switch in the short hallway. Its shade was the color of old parchment and the wallpaper was cream. Between them they enriched the sheen of Gisela's hair, of her beige knit dress, and of the breast which she had lifted above the scooped-out neck of that dress.

''I want a good time right now,'' she said.

Kelly scowled angrily. He would ignore her, dammit! He started to bend to unlace his shoes since their thick soles would catch in his trouser legs if he tried to change pants without taking the shoes off first. The P-38 jabbed his thigh with its front sight and safety lever, it was a *terrible* gun to carry unholstered, and he drew it from his pocket to toss it on the bed next to the dancer's overcoat.

The Walther wasn't perfect but it did its job; so what was he bitching about?

''Come on, honey, that's right,'' the woman said, leaning her shoulders against the wall where the hallway broadened into the room proper and thrusting her hips out toward Kelly. There was a smile in her voice, but her face was as neutral as Kelly's own and the laugh with which she followed the words was brittle. She was tight, the American realized, tight as a cocked mainspring, but she was too accomplished a professional to let that show to the audience on the other end of the possible listening devices.

She seemed to know exactly how she wanted the show to proceed.

''Well, I don't know,'' said Kelly, fumbling at his shoe-laces so badly that he had to look down to see what he was doing. *Dammit!* ''I've got reservations. . . .''

The lie was an unintended pun, and in any case his *body* had no reservations at all. His erection was so obvious

when he stood again that it brought a really cheerful giggle
from the dancer's lips. "*That's* right," she said again.

Kelly stepped closer to Gisela as he tried to unbutton his
shirt. It, like the coat, was torn in back and probably
bloodied as well. Since his fingers didn't goddam work at
the moment, and he needed *some* sort of release under the
circumstances, Kelly gripped his shirttails and ripped it
open.

Buttons rather than fabric gave, popping and pattering
around the laughing dancer like the leading edge of a sleet
storm. The cuffs still held him, and he hooked his fingers
in the left one as he bent closer to Gisela. "How the *hell*
long do you think we've got?" he whispered. "Later!" He
jerked his hand downward and, after the sleeve button
popped off, the whole cuff tore away in his hand.

"How long did you think it was going to take?" Gisela
murmured back. There was nothing wrong with *her* fine
motor control as she unbuckled Kelly's belt. Kelly's trousers dropped around his ankles abruptly, pulled by the
hidden snubbie, leaving him bare though he scarcely noticed
it.

Gisela's whole body was taut as a guitar string, and like
a string it vibrated as he met her lips. He was thinking
with his dick, which was about as good a way to get killed
as he knew of; and right now, nothing he knew mattered
except the way that his left hand cupped her bare breast
and lightly pinched the already-erect nipple. She began to
lift her dress with one hand while the other gripped Kelly's
member firmly to the soft fabric still covering her groin.

"I was going to fuck you tonight, not so?" she whispered in German as she laid her cheek against Kelly's,
eyes closed. She tongued the lobe of his ear. "Why should
I not because you save my life and make me *want* you?"

Who the hell expects anything to make sense, thought
Kelly. His free hand fondled her buttock, bare now that
she had raised the hem of her dress high enough. There

could be somebody in the room after all, waiting for the right moment to deck him from behind, or a team in the hallway poised to smash through the door as soon as Gisela shouted the code word. She could have a dozen diseases, ranging from loathsome to incurable. God *knew* who'd dipped his wick in her over the years—

And none of it fucking mattered, because just now fucking was the *only* thing that mattered.

Gisela wore a slip, but no hose or underwear, which helped explain the speed with which she had changed from her costume to street dress in the Hilton. Her hip muscles were ripplingly powerful, but the layer of subcutaneous fat common to all women, whatever their level of exercise, was like plush beneath Kelly's palm.

Gisela's pubic hair was darker than that of her head or the fine down covering her body, but like the mane of a lion its bronze highlights made it more than simply brown. Kelly's shirt still dangled from the agent's right wrist; now he stepped on the tail and pulled off everything except the cuff itself.

The dancer rose onto her toes to increase her height advantage and, gripping Kelly's member firmly, rubbed the head of it against the lips of her sex. She was dry and tightly closed, her body in this event rebelling against her will. She was murmuring something, but Kelly could not tell whether actual words were intended.

He bent to the nipple of the breast he held awkwardly from the dress, aware that the pair of them must look ridiculous. He was more concerned at some level of his mind about that than he was over the fact that he had just killed a number of people and that he might die himself before the night was out. He chuckled mentally at himself and, though he did not lose his erection, fully regained intellectual control over what he was doing.

Kelly shifted his weight and cupped her groin from the front with his right hand. The knit dress spilled down and both of them made simultaneous left-handed clutches for the garment. "Good," Gisela muttered in German with her eyes still closed as Kelly inserted a finger. "Good. Good."

The one-syllable approval was delivered in a technical tone, but the dancer's muscles were in full operation, clamping with a rhythmic pulse which drew him more deeply within her.

Gisela's eyes opened and the corners of her mouth spread widely in a smile of beatific happiness. Like Kelly himself, she expected her equipment to work when and as required, and that included the hardware she had been issued at birth.

She turned away, still gripping the shaft of his member with her own right hand. "What . . . ?" Kelly said as her hips brushed his groin and he was nestled momentarily between her buttocks while she pulled the hem of the dress up to her waist.

"Now," Gisela said firmly as she planted her left palm and forearm on the wall and rested her forehead against them. She inserted the head of his member into her vulva where his thrust and her eagerness drew it home at once.

It also drew Kelly into a climax more sudden than anything he had experienced since being rotated to base after sixty-three days in an outpost with no female company save a ewe with a smile that had begun to look flirtatious.

Gisela's simultaneous gasp passed unnoticed, but her cry a moment later as her hips pumped was loud enough to be heard in the next room with no need for bugging devices.

No partner of Kelly's had ever come as quickly as that, and certainly the dancer was as well able to fake a climax as anyone he'd met. Still, the vaginal spasms as he continued to thrust *seemed* uncontrolled; and the Lord knew, they'd both been ready for this or it wouldn't have had even the chance to happen. The whole business had taken approximately a minute and a half; and hell, he'd needed to undress anyway.

"Oh," Gisela said in a fairly normal tone. She chuckled as she straightened up with a friendly twitch of her buttocks against the man. "Yes, a very good time. Very good."

Kelly leaned over and scooped the tatters of his shirt from the floor. He held it to their paired groins before he withdrew from her and began to wipe himself dry with the tail. "Wonder if you can buy terry cloth shirts," he murmured as Gisela mopped at herself with a sleeve. "Might lay in a stock before the next time you'n me get together."

Gisela turned, dropping the damp shirt sleeve and letting her dress fall normally. She kissed him lightly on the tip of the nose, knelt, and, brushing away Kelly's hand and the shirt, engulfed very nearly the full length of his still-erect member with a momentary pause for adjustment at the halfway mark.

She released Kelly, rising again and flashing him the smile which had already become his identification point for memories of Gisela Romer. "Another time, we will take *more* time, not so? When we come back tonight, I think. But now you must dress."

Perfectly, Teutonically, correct, Kelly thought as he shuffled to the closet and chose another pair of slacks. He palmed the snubbie as he stepped out of his ankle-lapping trousers, uncertain as to whether the woman had already caught sight of the gun or not. The point of a real hideout gun is the surprise it offers the user, not primarily its function as a weapon. If people already know you're armed, then you may as well go for something that'll really do the job—like an automatic rifle.

Not that the P-38 he also stuck into the side pocket of the clean pants would be a surprise to anybody likely to be interested in the fact. You did what you could. . . .

*   *   *

"If it's okay to ask where we're going," Kelly said as Gisela drove east on Ciragan Street, away from the hotel and beyond it the Old City, "then I'd kinda like to know."

He kept his eyes on the fender before him, bent up at a sharp angle like a foresight where it should have been curved smoothly over the headlight. If he looked at her while he spoke, it would imply that he was pressing for the information. He *did* want to know, but pushing her was a damned bad way to learn anything.

She looked at him, the planes of her face a pattern of reflections moving at the corner of his eye. When she did not speak for a moment further, he went on, "Look, this car's going to be pretty conspicuous. I've got an address'r two where we might find something a little less so." He turned squarely toward her and smiled. "Isn't going to be as nice, but maybe for a couple days . . . ?"

"First, we're going to Asia, Tommy," Gisela said, beginning to smile herself as her eyes returned to the traffic.

"For Chrissake, don't call me that," Kelly protested with a laugh. Fine, it was a friendly conversation and not an interrogation session. "Call me Tom—hell, call me muledick if you want . . . but not Tommy, huh?"

"Puh," the woman said, a plosive sound rather than an attempt at words. Her smile toward the bumper of the leading car, a late forties Mercury, of all things, broadened. "We go to Asia, Tom, where you will meet people with whom you will discuss, not so? And if we choose to proceed, as I think we will, then this car will remain at the place of meeting, yes."

Asia. Well, he'd known they were headed toward either the Bosphorus Bridge or the Black Sea, and the latter was a hell of a long way north. Kelly wasn't in control, hadn't *been* in control since the moment he agreed to meet Gisela Romer. His alternative had been to disappear, to hunt up acquaintances in Diyarbakir and hope that they'd lead him closer to the aliens.

Which might have worked. But gathering information was a lot like deer hunting: people who stomp around making noise are less likely to nail what they're after than are the folks who settle themselves in a suitable location and let targets step into range.

"It . . ." Gisela looked over at her passenger again before continuing. "The crabs may appear again and you will be ready." She was speaking in the didactic certainty of a teacher coaxing a student into proper behavior. "But usually they do not twice so soon between. And you *must* not threaten my colleagues. That would be worse for you and for your country than you imagine."

"No problem," said Kelly. "I don't generally threaten people anyhow."

He'd pulled the Walther from his pocket as they drove away from the Sheraton and lowered it between his seat and the door panel, where he held it now.

Pierrard's gang had given Kelly credentials with the Dienst so solid that, it crossed the agent's mind, perhaps it had all been part of the plan. That seemed unlikely, upon reflection. Even if they had been willing to write off six figures worth of cars and every operative within gunshot of Tom Kelly, both of those possible decisions by the Suits, there was simply no way to be sure that Kelly and the dancer wouldn't be added to the butcher's bill. That had been live ammo being fired from the Audis.

Perhaps they didn't know the extent to which these German exiles were involved with the aliens. But there was no reason to have Kelly penetrate the group. They already had adequate access to it through Gisela. Who seemed to have played her American 'employers' for right fools, feeding them information on illegal activities they would wink at—and hiding the very fact of the aliens, and of the Plan . . . which wasn't Kelly's job tonight either.

"We'll need the toll," Gisela said. "Do you—? My purse is in the back."

Kelly nodded and took a five hundred-lire bill from his breast pocket, left-handed. Gisela had tossed her purse behind the seat, into the coupe's luggage compartment, with a thump almost as solid as that which the Sony radio in Kelly's attaché case had made. He assumed she had another gun there, the standard place for a woman to carry her hardware, though it was a lousy choice unless she walked around with one hand under the flap the way Elaine Tuttle had done the night Kelly met her.

But why had Gisela tried to draw the awkward P-38 from her coat when the aliens appeared, rather than going for whatever she had in her purse? Well, people didn't always do what you expected them to in a crisis. Kelly would trade a bad decision on pistols for the way she brought the car back for him any day.

The Bosphorus Bridge was lighted into a display unique in Turkey as the Mercedes slowed and eased into one of the multiple approach lanes to the toll plaza. The bridge was a mile long; and while there might have been more impressive engineering feats elsewhere in the world, this one joined two continents. The nearer of the five-hundred-foot high suspension towers was in Europe, and the second was, as Gisela had said, in Asia. The span and its approaches curling uphill from either end were illuminated by closely-spaced light standards, and sidescatter from the floodlit towers picked out the higher portions of the suspension cables as well.

Gisela paid, then accelerated through the mass of other vehicles merging into the three eastbound lanes. There was no need for special haste, but the challenge had brought out the competitiveness never far beneath the surface of the dancer's mind. She flicked her passenger a glance, saw him facing forward, smiling and as relaxed as a sensible man ever is with his hand on a gun butt, and downshifted again to surge into a slot in the traffic.

"You don't like the way I drive," Gisela said flatly as they settled into a steady pace.

"I love it," said Kelly, patting her thigh with his left hand. "When I drive, I push when I don't need to and get all tied up in knots." He grinned.

"Yes, well," she said as her hand squeezed Kelly a little closer to her, "someone must lead and someone must follow, that is so. That it should be *we* who follow—the minutes do not matter, but *that* does matter, perhaps."

Kelly should have felt nakedly open on the bridge, with a two-hundred-foot drop to the water beneath them and a major sea to either side of the long channel over which they passed. There were people looking for him, and there were things that weren't people—he didn't need Gisela's warning to tell him that. They wanted something from him, but the Dienst might be able to tell him what that was. Maybe not the best way to learn, asking somebody's enemy what the first party intended, but it had the advantage of involving fewer unknowns than the direct approach.

There were some *real* unknowns in this one.

The lighting created a box around the huge bridge and the vehicles on it, separating them from sea, sky, and the feeling of openness. The illumination curtained even the city behind them, much less anyone searching the bridge with binoculars from the surrounding high ground. Someone could be following them, since there was no need of a close tail on a vehicle forced to a single direction and speed. Nonetheless, Kelly felt better for the blanket of light that hid his enemies from him. To the extent there was a justification for that emotional response, it was that when there was really nothing you could do, you might as well relax.

The contrast of the highway to Kisikli and Ankara beyond, lighted only by the heavy traffic, brought the American again to full wariness, though his left hand continued to rest on Gisela's thigh. Camlica and the heights which gave a panorama of the whole city, its blemishes cloaked by darkness, led off on a branching road.

Just beyond that, but before they reached the cloverleaf that merged the Istanbul Bypass with the major routes through Anatolia, Gisela turned off. After a hundred yards on a frontage road serving a number of repair shops, closed and grated, the Mercedes turned again past the side of the last cinder-block structure in the row.

The roar of traffic dissipated behind them as the coupe proceeded, fast for rutted gravel and a single headlight, down a road marked by Turkish No Trespassing signs. There was brush and scrub pine, but no hardwoods and very little grass along the route. The one-lane road itself seemed to have been bulldozed from the side of the hill to the right and the rushes to the other side suggested at least a temporary watercourse. The possibility that a car was following the Mercedes had disappeared at the moment they turned to the frontage road.

"How far—" Kelly started to say as the coupe twisted again with the road and a ten-foot chain link fence webbed the road in the beam of their headlight. The red-lettered sign on the vehicle gate was again in Turkish, stating that this was the Palace Gravel Quarry, with no admittance to unauthorized personnel. There was a gatehouse within, unlighted, and no response at all to Gisela's blip on the horn.

Kelly got out, closing the door quickly behind him to shut off the courtesy light. He walked a few steps sideways, knowing that the galvanized fencing still reflected well enough to make him a target in silhouette to a marksman behind him. Dust from the road drifted around him, swirling before the car as it settled, and the only sound in the night was a fast idle of the 280 SL's warm engine.

"It's chained," he said loudly enough to be heard within the car, through the window he had left open. He held the

P-38 muzzle-down along his pants leg, as inconspicuous and nonthreatening as it could be and still remain instantly available.

Gisela switched off the headlights and called, "There should be someone. Take this key and be very careful."

Her hand was white and warm when Kelly took the circular-warded key from her. A high overcast hid the stars and the lights of a jet making an internal hop to Ankara, but the sound of its turbines rumbled down regardless. If there was a gun in Gisela's purse, she had left it there.

At the loop-chained gate, Kelly loosed the heavy padlock and swung inward the well-balanced portal. There was still no sound but that of the car and of the plane diminishing with distance and altitude. He walked into a graveled courtyard, sidling to the right enough to take him out of the path of the coupe. He waved Gisela in with his free hand, the one which was not gripping the big Walther.

Subconsciously, Kelly had thought that the grunt of the Mercedes' engine and the crunch of stones beneath its tires would cause *something* to happen. Gisela circled the car in a broad sweep in front of the building which the fence enclosed, a metal prefab painted beige where it was not washed with rusty speckles from rivet heads and the eaves. The headlight and the willing little motor shut off when Gisela faced the car out the open gateway again, and the night returned to its own sounds.

Gisela's door closing and her footsteps were muted, not so much cautious as precise applications of muscular effort by a woman whose physical self-control was as nearly complete as was possible for a human being.

"Who are we looking for?" Kelly asked softly as the woman paused at arm's length.

"I'll try the building," she responded, with enough tremor in her voice to indicate that she was as taut and puzzled as the American—which, perversely, was a comfort to him.

They walked toward the warehouse door, Kelly a pace behind and to the side. The weight of the pistol aligned with his pants leg made him feel silly, but he was willing neither to point the weapon without a real target nor to pocket it when the next moment might bring instant need. It would have been nice if he had known what the hell was happening, but as usual he didn't—it wasn't a line of work in which you could expect to understand 'the big picture.'

Unless you wore a suit, in which case you probably didn't understand anything, whatever you might think.

The warehouse had a vehicular door, made to slide sideways on top and bottom rails, and next to it a door for people. There was also a four-panel window, covered on the outside by a steel grating and on the inside by something that blacked out the interior.

Kelly expected the warehouse to be pitch dark. He stepped close to the hinge side of the door as Gisela opened it, so that he would not be silhouetted against the sky glow to anyone waiting within.

The big square interior was as well-illuminated as the courtyard, and as open to sky; what appeared from the ground to be a flat-roofed warehouse was four walls with no roof, only bracing posts along the hundred-foot sides. It held a vehicle backed against one corner of the structure, a van like the one which Gisela's attendants had been entering when the shooting started. Apart from that, the interior seemed as empty as the courtyard.

"Come," snapped Gisela, motioning Kelly peremptorily within and closing the door behind him, a precaution the American could not understand until the woman switched on a flashlight she had taken from a hook on the wall.

"What—" began Kelly, unable to see anything worth the exercise in the flickering beam of the light.

"'Nothing, nothing, *nothing!*" the dancer said, her inflection rising into spluttering fury. She strode fiercely toward the van, the tight beam of the flashlight bobbing up and down on the windshield like the laser sighting dot of a moving tank. "They could've left a *note*, surely?"

The floor of the warehouse was gravel, marked in unexpected ways. There were the usual lines and blotches of motor oil and other vehicular fluids inevitable in any parking space. The drips, however, were absent from the center of the enclosed structure, so far as Kelly could tell. Why wall so large an area if only the edges were to be used?

Gisela jerked open the van's door. The courtesy light went on but had to compete with the beam of the flashlight which the dancer had angrily twisted to wide aperture. "Nothing," she repeated in a voice like Kelly's the day they told him what had happened to Pacheco and another hundred of the *White Plains'* complement.

"This is the one your—" the American began, touching the side panel of the van.

"Yes, Franz and Dietrich," Gisela snapped as she straightened to slam the door of the vehicle closed. "They must have come back from the hotel, told them I'd been"—her hands writhed in a gesture that aimed the light skyward until she thumbed it off, plunging them back into darkness—"whatever, killed, captured. And they went off and *left* me!"

"They could get a job with some of *my* former employers," the American said, briefly thinking of his own Kurdish guerrillas. "But look," he added with a frown, "I saw your people go down. There was a flash and they went over when the whatevers were trading shots with 'em."

"That doesn't mean they were dead," the dancer said bitterly as she walked back toward the door through which they had entered. She couldn't see any better than Kelly could, but she knew there was nothing in the way. "We've had it happen before, people they've shot but not taken away as they usually do, the crabs. They'll come around again, in half an hour or so, and have headaches for a week—but live."

"It doesn't sound like your crabs," Kelly said, frowning, as the woman opened the door and stepped out, "are quite as hard-nosed about what they're doing as maybe I'd—"

"*Tom*," the woman said.

It was too late to matter because Kelly was half through the doorway already and the hand-held spotlight that switched on was as blinding to him as it was suitable for sighting whatever guns were arrayed behind it. For a moment he thought of the P-38, but a voice from behind the screen of light said, "Try it, fucker."

It was Doug Blakeley's voice, and Kelly was in no doubt as to what would happen in a fraction of a second if his pistol didn't drop on the gravel.

As the Walther slipped from Kelly's fingers, an automobile engine spun to life with a whine and a rumble. There was nothing sinister in the noise—but every unexpected sound was a blast of gunshots to Kelly's imagination, and he almost dived after the pistol in an instinctive desire to die with his teeth in a throat.

"Assume the position, Tommy-boy," called Doug in a hectoring voice. Rectangular headlights replaced the spotlight even more dazzlingly. Doug and whoever he'd brought along had driven through the open gate and poised there, waiting for their quarry to exit. Now they were using the car's lights for illumination, the way somebody in Diyarbakir had lighted Mustapha and the alien the night they were gunned down.

Kelly turned to the 'warehouse' wall and gingerly permitted it to take some of his weight through his arms. The structure was less stable than it appeared—a roof contributed more to strength than any amount of bracing in the plane of the walls could do. To judge from the amount of weathering, however, this construct had survived at least a decade of wind and storms, and the wall only creaked when the veteran leaned against it.

Chances were that Doug Blakeley had gotten everything he knew about body searches from cop shows or watching other people do the work. Kelly took a minor chance, spreading his legs and angling his body—but not so much that he could not spin upright by thrusting himself off with his hands. The P-38 lay at his right foot, throwing its own flat shadow across the gravel to the base of the wall.

How many were there behind the lights? If Doug were alone, this was going to end *real* quick no matter where Gisela decided to stand in the business.

Which was an open question in Kelly's mind right now, because the woman had sidled a few steps from his and was shielding her eyes with an uplifted forearm. She looked disconcerted, but not nearly as shocked by this as she had been by the fact that her friends had gone off and left her.

The situation made reasonable sense to Kelly, waiting for a frisk or a gunshot, if Doug Blakeley was one of the dancer's friends.

The asthmatic wheeze of a turbocharged engine at low rpm's masked but did not hide the sound of footsteps. Kelly's eyes were adjusting to the glare. Without shifting the position of his limbs or body, he turned his head and squinted over his shoulder.

There were two of them approaching, one from either side, their shadows distorted by the corrugations of the metal wall. The man to Kelly's left said, ''Peter here told me I should shoot you right off, Tom-lad. Blink wrong and we do just that.'' It was Doug.

Kelly snapped his head around to center it between the lines of his shoulder blades. Peter has good sense, motherfucker, he thought, but not so good that he doesn't take orders from you.

Gisela moved unexpectedly closer to the American. ''I hadn't thought you would arrive like this,'' she said pleasantly, in English.

Peter, the bull-necked professional to the right, knelt

and picked up the Walther without removing his gaze or the muzzle of his weapon from Kelly's chest. He and Doug both carried compact submachineguns—Beretta Model 12's whose wire stocks were folded along the receivers. Beretta 12's were easily distinguished from similar weapons by the fact that they had handgrips both before and behind the magazine well. Given his choice of wraparound bolt submachineguns, Kelly would have picked an Uzi or an Ingram, where the magazine in the handgrip facilitated reloading in a tight spot.

But given his choice, Kelly would have held the gun instead of being at the muzzle-end of two goons who were at least *willing* to blow him away.

Peter handed the P-38 to Doug, the shadow of the transfer warping itself across the beige metal wall. Both men carried their submachineguns in what was to Kelly the outside hand: he could probably grab either of his captors, but not both, and he could not grab either of the guns.

The engine of the car suddenly speeded up. It was an automatic response triggered either by the headlights' load on the alternator or the block's need for greater cooling than the fan could provide at a low idle. Peter snarled something in Bulgarian toward the vehicle, however, indicating both that he was jumpy—as Kelly would have been, forced to hold a gun on Peter—and that there was at least a third member of Doug's present team.

Elaine might possibly speak Bulgarian, but it wouldn't be the gunman's choice of a language in which to address her, even at the present tense moment.

"He didn't have a gun," said Doug, "and then he's got this to use on us. How do you suppose that happened?"

Kelly was so focused on himself and his own problems that he did not realize he was the subject of the sentence, not the question, until Gisela said, "He took—" and Doug slapped her alongside the jaw with the butt of the pistol.

Had the weapon fired, it would have punched a nine-millimeter hole down through Doug's belly, pelvis, and buttocks, a good start on what the fellow needed. . . . But Walthers, save for those churned out with bad steel and no care in the last days of the Nazis, were about as safe as handguns could be. The wooden grips cracked loudly on Gisela's jawbone, and the wall rang as the blow threw her head against it.

The veteran turned a few degrees to the left, enough to give him a direct view of what was happening without providing an excuse for Peter who had backed a step away.

Doug flung the P-38 toward the darkness. The fencing, thirty yards away, rattled angrily when the pistol struck it. "Oh, 'I just made a mistake'?" shouted the blond American as he hit the woman again with his open hand. The blow had a solid, meaty sound to it, and this time Gisela collapsed as her legs splayed. The black gloves which Doug was wearing probably had pockets of lead shot sewn into the palm and knuckles, giving his hand the inertia of a blackjack.

"Did you expect to get *away* with that shit?" he screamed to the woman who toppled onto her face, away from the wall, when her hips struck the ground.

Facing the wall squarely so that nothing in his stance would spark anger, Kelly said, "Look, Mr. Blakeley, maybe we all oughta sit down with Elaine and see about—"

Doug hit him, and the question of whether the blow was backhand or with clenched fist was beyond the veteran's calculation. The blond American wasn't just big—he had real muscle under that fine tailoring, and he put plenty of it into the blow.

The roar to which Kelly awakened was real, not his blood; Peter was shouting something in anger to his employer. Kelly knelt on the gravel, his palms and forehead against the painted steel wall. All his senses were covered by a screen that trembled through white and red, attenuating the sights and sounds of the world. His skin was hot, sticky hot, with the exception of his left cheek and jaw where something cold had gnawed all the flesh away.

Kelly had blacked out for only a fraction of a second, but for moments longer he had no idea of where he was or what was happening. "Don't *point* that thing at me!" Doug shouted over Kelly's head. "You *hold* him like I tell you!"

"I—" Kelly found as he tried to look up at Doug that his neck hurt and his tongue was thick and fiery. A hand gripped his left shoulder from behind, grabbed a handful of fabric and lifted. Doug punched him in the ribs.

Kelly's breath sprayed out with blood from the tongue and cheek, cut against his teeth by the previous blow. The veteran sagged back, his knees brushing the ground, but Peter's strength was enough to hold him.

"Higher," ordered Doug, breathing heavily himself.

Kelly didn't think his ribs had cracked that time, but his whole chest felt as if it were swelling, bursting. He knew where he was now, being beaten by a hotshot American who had finally found a way to assert his authority—while a Third World thug waited to blow holes in him if he didn't sit and take it.

Stand and take it. Peter dragged Kelly fully upright and Doug punched him again.

He aimed at the veteran's face, but the lead-burdened fist moved slowly enough that Kelly was able to duck so that Doug hit the point of his forehead instead of the nose. Even though the blond man was wearing a sap glove, the result was more likely to break knuckles than to do Kelly serious injury.

The veteran blinked against the jumbled dazzle of light caused by his brain bouncing within the bone. He went limp again, at least partly by volition, and his weight forced Peter back a step.

The Beretta was short for an automatic weapon but still,

at seventeen inches, much longer than an ordinary hand-gun. In order to point the weapon at Kelly without letting the muzzle touch him, Peter had to hold the veteran out at arm's length with his left hand. The gunman was strong, but Kelly's solid weight was an impossible load under those conditions.

"Get Tomashek!" Peter growled in English.

"Big, bad man who thinks he can shoot my people," Doug said as he panted. He had been trying to keep his Beretta muzzle-up as he swung at Kelly with his right hand alone, but the eight-pound submachinegun pulled itself down toward the gravel as the blond man tried to catch his breath.

Peter swore bitterly.

The cold patch on Kelly's forehead was probably blood cooling, but it felt as if the blow had lifted off a patch of skin. Flashes of light moved across his vision like the rotary shutter of a movie camera, but through them he could see Gisela still slumped where she had fallen. Kelly couldn't be sure, but he thought one of the dancer's legs flexed minutely when the blond man's shoe brushed it.

"Straighten him up," Doug ordered, wiping his forehead with the back of his gloved hand.

"Look, I said get Tomashek," Peter said. "I'm not—"

"*Listen*, you bastard!" the blond American roared. "You want to spend the rest of your life in a cell in Buca, you just give me lip once more. *Lift him!*"

Peter grunted in a combination of anger and effort as he obeyed. He bent his left arm at the elbow and half knelt, then used his leg muscles to jerk the veteran into place for another punch.

Kelly hurt in more places than the glove had touched him directly, signals scrambled when his brain jounced, but the inexpert beating had not thus far made him non-functional. He'd been in worse shape after a night drop into steppe country once—and that hadn't kept him from blowing up hardware that somebody else shouldn't have left behind and trekking out again himself.

He wasn't a boxer, but neither was Doug, and the fist the blond man aimed at Kelly's face was slow and clumsy. The veteran jerked his head to the side instinctively, even though part of his mind knew that it might be better to accept the punch than to piss off Doug further by dodging it. The fist touched the lobe of Kelly's left ear before momentum carried it into Peter's shoulder.

Peter blurted a curse, again in Bulgarian. Doug screamed incoherently and swung the Beretta at Kelly's head.

The looping sideways blow was beyond Kelly's ability to dodge, but Peter's own flinching reaction gave the veteran enough slack to avoid the worst of it.

The submachinegun's stock glanced off Kelly's skull, just above his right temple, and the shock jarred the gun's heavy bolt off the sear. The bolt clanged forward and fired the top round in the magazine.

The muzzle blast of the nine-millimeter round was deafening to all three men; gas and unburned powder bloomed simultaneously from the muzzle in a yellow-orange flash, stinging Peter's cheek as the bullet itself gouged a long slot through the wall. Sparks flew, and the howl of the unstabilized bullet cut through the echoing crash of the sheet metal.

'You have pig shit for brains!'' Peter shouted as he grabbed Doug's weapon by the magazine and twisted until the muzzle was safely skyward. Kelly, sprawled on his back, tangled the feet of the two men who had been beating him a moment before. "Either you're going to get more help here or you're going to do it *alone,* I swear to you!''

Kelly reached under himself as his heels and shoulders lifted the small of his back from the ground.

The Beretta's wire stock had flexed enough on impact to keep the veteran's skull from cracking, but there was still

a four-inch pressure cut in his scalp, and blood had begun
to mat the black hair before his body hit the ground. It felt
as though he had been struck by an ax, laying his brain
open to the chill night air, and a part of him was quite sure
that he was dying.

"Watch—" one of the men above him shouted as Kelly
lifted the aluminum snubbie and shot twice, close enough
to Peter's belly that the shirt caught fire.

Kelly's vision was sharp, though he had no color sense
at the moment. Both submachineguns were still pointed
up, but Peter had started to lower his to cover the man on
the ground when the bullets hit him like punches in the
solar plexus. The gunman doubled up, clamping both elbows to his wounds. The muzzle blasts had jerked the
front of his shirt out of his pants, to smolder over the oval
entrance holes just beneath his rib cage.

The cup-pointed bullets had perforated the diaphragm
and meandered upward through the gunman's right kidney
and lung. Neither nicked his heart, but the blood vessels
they destroyed before they lodged under the skin of Peter's
upper chest were sufficient to pour his life into his body
cavity in a matter of seconds.

Hunched over and mincing because his knees were bent,
Peter tried to run along the front of the warehouse to
escape the glare of the car's headlights. Doug had stumbled back a pace when his employee released the Beretta.
The blond man's mouth was open in a snarl of disapproval. Kelly, still on his back, aimed for the center of
Doug's mass and fired twice more.

The muzzle flashes were red to the victim, bright gray
to the shooter, and black swirls on the wall where the
halogen beams were distorted into shadow by the balls of
powder gases.

Doug's wire-slim belt buckle pinged as a bullet scalloped a section through its upper rim, and there was a
black hole marring the mauve-gray-and-white striping of

his left shirt pocket. Minusculely later, blood spurted to distort the clean outline the wadcutter had punched in the shirt fabric.

The blond American started both to turn away and to lower the submachinegun. Gisela scissored her legs, catching Doug at the ankles, and sent the big man down in a sprawl.

The gasp of the car's intake manifold trying to increase flow coincided with a sideways shift of the headlights, throwing shadows along the wall in an exaggerated reciprocal of the car's motion. Doug scrabbled on all fours toward the vehicle, splashing dark blood on the gravel every time his damaged heart pulsed. When his arms failed him, his legs continued for several seconds to thrash and hump his buttocks.

As the car started to move, Kelly sat up and tried for the first time to aim his revolver. The short radius and tenth-inch blade sight would have made real accuracy impossible, even if the veteran himself had been up to it. He fired at the broadside of the vehicle as it turned. There was no clang or smack of glass to indicate that he had hit anything. About all Kelly gained by the shot, his last, was to learn from the flash that he was seeing in color again.

"Here," said the dancer. She handed Kelly the submachinegun she had wrestled from Doug during the moment that she and the wounded American had threshed together on the ground.

The car was turning so sharply that the power steering belts rubbed and screamed. It was by European standards a large sedan, very probably another Audi 5000 Quattro, now in silhouette against the chain link fencing which its own lights illuminated. Kelly aimed, wishing that he had enough leisure to unlatch the stock and butt the weapon firmly against his shoulder.

There were two push-through selectors at the top of the rear handgrip. One of them was presumably the safety, while the other selected single shots or automatic fire. Kelly had no idea what combination would permit him to fire the bursts he wanted; but the best way to tell was to align the rear notch with the hooded front blade and squeeze the trigger.

Which gave him a three-round burst and a new respect for the Beretta because the front grip and the comfortably slow rate of fire made the weapon perfectly controllable at its rock-and-roll setting.

There were no tracers in the magazine, but Kelly caught the spark of one bullet beyond the muzzle flashes, snapping through the air a foot above the sedan's roofline. He had been sighting instinctively on the fence, against which he could see the post and notch, for the car merged with the gunsights in a uniformly dark mass. As the Audi fishtailed to center itself with the gate opening, Kelly lowered the muzzle a fraction of an inch and squeezed off again. He was smiling.

Glass flew up like early snowflakes, winking in the powder flashes and reflected headlights. The car, which had begun to straighten, went into a four-wheel drift to the left instead. Kelly gave the broadside fifty feet away a long burst. At least half the bullets appeared as red flecks on the door panels as friction heated both lead and sheet metal when the nine-millimeter rounds punched their way through the car body.

These muzzle blasts were less shocking than the first had been. In part, that was a matter of psychology, but the earlier shots had been literally deafening, and Kelly's back was now to the warehouse wall that had acted as a sounding board initially.

The headlights swung across Kelly and the dancer once more; then the Audi came to a stop with the driver's door to them. The engine had died, but bits of metal cooling at differential rates hissed and pinged.

Kelly walked a final burst across both front and rear

doors, aiming six inches above the rocker panels to catch anyone cowering on the floor. Then for a moment, nothing moved at all.

Gisela dusted herself briskly with her palms, started for her Mercedes, and stumbled.

"Wait," said Kelly, and he began to walk toward the Audi, whose headlights seemed already to be yellowing as they drained the battery, though that might have been an illusion. He couldn't hear properly. There was a high-pitched ringing in his right ear, and cocoons of white noise blurred the edges of all the ordinary sounds, his voice or the scrunch of feet on the gravel.

Because of the pain, each step the veteran took threatened to topple him onto the ground. It wasn't the blow to his chest, though sharp prickles warned that at best the muscles there were cramping, while at worst they were being savaged by the edges of broken ribs. The battering his head had taken, from the leaded glove and the steel tube of the receiver, was a different order of problem. The brain has no pain receptors of its own, but it has ways of making its displeasure known. Kelly's stomach and throat contracted with transferred discomfort every time his heel touched the ground.

Holding the Beretta by the back grip as if it were a pistol, Kelly tried to open the driver's door. It resisted; though the door was unlocked, one of its edges had been riveted into the frame by a bullet. There was a sharp whiff of gasoline near the car which cut the sweetish, nauseating odor of nitro powders and the chemicals which coated them.

Nothing gurgled from a punctured tank, and the smell of gas was vagrant enough to result from the way the car had stalled rather even than a clipped fuel line. Whatever the cause, thank the *Lord* that the Audi hadn't ignited. They were too far from the highway for the shots to have been noticed, but twenty gallons of gasoline flaring up would arouse interest for sure.

The courtesy light shone directly on the face of a man Kelly had never seen before. His feet were tangled with the gas and brake pedals, but his upper body lay on the floor of the passenger side. The bullet hole above his left eye could have been either an entrance or an exit wound. Its greenish edges had puckered back over the puncture.

No one else was in the tonneau of the car.

Kelly turned and closed the door. Gisela stood ten feet away, rubbing her jaw and waiting.

The waiting was over for Doug Blakeley, who lay belly-down on the gravel with his limbs splayed into a broad X. The huddle beside the sheet-metal wall, twenty feet from the place shooting had started, was Peter. That one was too dangerous to have been safely forgotten, but there'd been no time to worry about him when the worries would have been justified.

And the poor anonymous bastard in the car, who might have reported to somebody if a jacketed bullet hadn't churned his brain to jelly . . . .

The veteran knelt down. Being hit on the head was making him feel nauseated.

Bits of safety glass which had shattered into irregular prisms now glittered at Kelly amid the crushed granite. Then his stomach heaved and splashed most of its contents onto the ground. A second spasm followed, with just enough of an interval for Kelly to move the submachinegun he still held a little farther away from his stomach's target area.

He couldn't say that he felt good as he panted on all fours, trying to catch his breath; but he felt a lot better.

Gisela Romer was standing beside the Mercedes. She had taken her purse from the coupe and was rummaging in it. Kelly heard sounds from her and thought for a moment that the woman might also be vomiting.

It sounded more like sobs, however.

Kelly rose, spat, and wiped his mouth with the back of

his left hand as he walked over to the dancer. He could feel his individual injuries separately now, even the dimples left on his knees by the rough stones while he lost his dinner. The long list of pains, however, was a lot better than the total malaise which had preceded it, and his skin was no longer swollen with what had seemed to be three degrees of fever.

Gisela lifted something from her purse and cracked it down on the fender of the Mercedes.

That was the side that had crumpled in the alley. The action shocked Kelly however, since the coupe was too well cared for not to be loved by its owner. "What . . . ?" the veteran said as his free hand closed over Gisela's when she lifted it for another blow.

The woman surrendered the object to Kelly's grip without struggling. He'd been right about the sobs.

"He told me it was to call for help," she said as Kelly examined the object. "He said I should be careful, that you were very dangerous. If I needed help, I should throw that switch."

The object was a prism, three inches by two and about half an inch deep. The casing was dark resin, featureless except for a thumb slide on one of the narrow faces.

Kelly reached into the car, twisting the ignition key to the auxiliary position and then walking the radio up and down the dial. There was a loud squeal at the bottom of the FM band, near 85 megahertz. Sliding the switch back and forth did not affect the signal.

"Just a beacon," the veteran said as he dropped the little signal generator on the ground. "The slide's a dummy. Doesn't look like they trusted you."

He brought his heel down on the center of the case. He couldn't feel anything give, but the squealing on the coupe's radio vanished in an angry crackle of static.

"Wouldn't help a lot in town," Kelly added in an emotionless voice, "but once we got out on the road where the signal doesn't get lost with all the buildings, it'd home 'em right in.'' He turned off the radio and the ignition.

Gisela still said nothing.

"Do you know where your friends've gone?" Kelly asked, pointing at the empty, roofless structure. "Unless Doug and his boys were who you were looking for?"

"No!" the woman snapped. She shook her hair out, her visage relaxing slightly now that she had been able to let some of her anger loose. She went on, "There should be someone in Diyarbakir. But it will take us days . . ."

Kelly shrugged. "Not if we fly," he said. "And I figure that's a lot better idea than sticking around here."

He closed his eyes and pressed the palm of his free hand against the bruise in the center of his forehead. "They deserved it, more'r less," he said very softly. His stomach threatened him briefly when a breeze brought him a reminder of Doug Blakeley, whose sphincter muscles had relaxed to empty his bladder and bowels as he died.

"Might not've made any difference," Kelly continued, speaking to something more shadowy than the blond woman beginning to frown at him. "Wasn't going to be a clean way out, maybe. But maybe if they hadn't knocked me half silly, I'd have tried harder. I can run on reflex, but it ain't real pretty."

He opened his eyes to meet Gisela's. "Is it?" he added, putting a period to words he already regretted saying.

Gisela looked around her, at the bodies and the silent sky, before she faced Kelly again. "All right," she said. "What do *I* need to do?"

"Drive us to Yeşilköy Airport," the American replied as he gathered his attaché case from the Mercedes, "and I learn whether my authorization codes are much use there at the military terminal. If you've got the keys to that van" —he waved toward the vehicular door in the wall—"then it might be politic to take it. Can't guarantee we've cleared up all the—road hazards—with these.''

"All right," the dancer repeated.

Gisela had a key to the sliding vehicular door. As she manipulated it, Kelly searched the shadows for his aluminum Smith and Wesson. It seemed none the worse for having been fired and dropped without ceremony, though it would get a proper cleaning if Kelly had the opportunity. He had no .38 Special ammunition, so the gun was useless for the moment, as well as a dangerous link to the killings here. Peter and the driver weren't going to be a problem: very likely they weren't Turkish citizens, and they *certainly* weren't Amcits. But Doug was another matter, one that could land Tom Kelly in shit to his hair line—on the slim chance that he survived long enough for that to matter.

He velcroed the snubbie back in place on his waistband anyway. It'd been a friend when he needed one; and people who ditched their friends at the conclusion of present need wound up real quick with no friends.

The door rolled back with the rumble of well-oiled trunnions.

"The only thing I can't figure," said the veteran easily as he followed Gisela to the van, "is you working so close with the Jews and not figuring what they'd do if they got ahold of me.''

The woman froze stock-still, then turned. "What?" she said sharply. "I do not understand."

Kelly blinked in false puzzlement. They were standing close; he could see her face was set like a death mask. "Well, you know about me, don't you?" he said. "About the *White Plains* and—an' all?''

"What do you mean about the *Jews*?" Gisela demanded. She had reverted to German, and her tongue flicked unintentional spittle when she said "die Juden.''

"Well, who the hell did you think Doug worked for?"

Kelly responded, adding an undertone of anger, equally false, at the woman's obtuseness. *"Surely* you knew."

Gisela was swaying. "The American Central Intelligence Agency," she said in a distant voice, a mother begging the surgeon for the answer his face had already told her was a vain hope.

"Christ, I thought you people were professionals," Kelly snapped. "He's Shin Bet, the section of Israeli intelligence that reports to their Ministry of Defense. They really *did* play you for suckers, didn't they."

And then he caught the blond woman as she stumbled forward into his arms.

"Easy," the veteran said as he patted her back, pretended concern in his voice and unholy joy in his heart for having won one, having manipulated a subject into total submission. In this case, on the spur of the moment and without any significant amount of preparation. . . . "Easy," he repeated gently. "Are you all right to drive? I just thought you knew."

Gisela straightened as if bracing herself to attention— shoulders back, chin out, arms stiff at her sides. "Yes," she said, and drew a shudderingly deep breath. "Yes, of course. I'll have to report this to the . . ."

She turned around abruptly, perhaps to hide her expression or a tear, but she reached back for Kelly to show that she was not trying to cut herself off from him. "Come," she said, "we must get first to the airport." She was speaking English again and her tone, if urgent, was not panicked.

"Right you are," murmured Kelly.

The doors of the van were not locked, nor did the vehicle have a lockable ignition. Gisela turned the switch on the steering column and stepped firmly on the clutch so that the back of the clutch pedal engaged the starter button beneath it on the firewall. The engine spun easily and caught at once. The woman turned on the headlights and cautiously engaged what turned out to be a sticky clutch.

"You must understand," she said, her face set, as she reversed to face the vehicle toward the door, "that I acted in accordance with my orders."

She braked, shifted gears, and went on, "We worked with the ones we thought were CIA, but it was always to further the Plan, to gain time until the day came. Not for—their purposes, though we did not know they were the Jews."

They drove out into the courtyard, past the parked coupe and the bullet-shattered Audi. "Soon it will not matter, but—whatever I can do to make it up to you, Thomas Monaghan, I will do."

"What you're doing already is all I could ask for," said Kelly, meeting the woman's eyes in the dash lights. "I need friends real bad. Take me to your top folks and, if they'll help me, I'll do everything I can about the crabs with them. With you all." He paused before adding, "And my real last name's Kelly, but Tom's just fine."

There was one thing more the veteran needed to do before he tried to talk his way—bluff his way, in a manner of speaking, but he was doing *precisely* the job he'd been tasked to do—onto a military flight at the airport. Kelly unzipped one pocket of his attaché case to remove his radio, the concealed tape deck, and the headphones. Working by the greenish light of the gas and temperature gauges, Kelly rewound the tape and set it to play back whatever it had heard in Elaine's hotel room.

The lengthy hash with which the tape began was, Kelly realized after a minute or two, neither jamming nor a malfunction: the maid had entered 727 and was vacuuming it. He advanced the tape and, as he was preparing to blip forward a third time, heard the wheezing vacuum replaced by a click of static and the recorded ring of a telephone.

Click. "*Go ahead*," said the voice of Elaine Tuttle,

who picked up the handset before the completion of the first ring.

Click. *"Having sex, he says. It's, I don't know. Could be true, certainly could be."*

Click. *"Doug, lis—"*

Click. *"No, just listen to me. He doesn't have a gun right now, but he could get one very easily. We don't want to push him, that's not what we're—"*

Click. *"Of course we don't trust him. I'm saying we've got to give him the room to do what he's tasked to do, or there was no point in—"*

Click. *"Except that wasn't your decision or even mine,"* Elaine's voice said, each word as distinct as a blade of obsidian set in a wooden warclub. *"If you want to take that up with those who made the assignment, then I'll give you liberty right now to get on the next plane."*

It was noticeable that though she had not raised her voice, this time she was able to finish her sentence without being cut off by the person on the other end of the line.

Click. *"All right, I'm not neglecting the long-term. Trace them, it'll be good to cross-check Kelly as well as adding to our database on those Nazis. But don't crowd him; he's still as good a chance as we've got of coming up with the link between the Dienst, the Kurds, and the aliens."*

Click. *"All right. But be careful, sweetheart, he's dangerous even if he doesn't have a gun."*

There was nothing more of interest on the tape, not even the slam of the door as Elaine went out. Twice, the toilet flushed loudly enough to trip the recorder, but there were no phone calls and no face-to-face conversations after Elaine had signed off with a warning that Doug Blakeley had chosen to ignore. She had waited in her room, ready to relay information or orders, and neither had come.

Doug should have reported on the shooting in the Hilton parking lot. Either he'd been afraid because he was sure that his career had ended in the melee; or, more likely, he was afraid that the orders he would get would clearly debar him from the revenge he intended to take on one Tom Kelly, the working-class slob who was the cause of all the trouble . . . because there *had* to be a single cause for Doug's mind to grip. Otherwise there was nothing at all to keep him from slipping into a universe with no certainties at all.

Kelly took off his headphones and touched the Rewind switch of the recorder. Wonder if there's anybody left to give'er a phone call, he thought, or if she's going to read about it all in the papers. Maybe George has the number to call.

"What?" asked Gisela Romer, over the rattle of the van's body panels in the wind of their passage.

If he was going to start thinking out loud, then he was an even bigger damned fool than he'd realized. "I was thinking," Kelly said truthfully, "that if people had been less interested in fucking with me, then I'm not the only one who'd have been better off."

The woman looked at her passenger's frowning profile. "You won't regret the help you have given me—given us," she said. "There has never been greater need for men like you, men willing to act resolutely."

Guess even Doug'd give me high marks for that, Kelly thought. Especially Doug.

"He's dead, so I guess he deserved to die," the veteran said aloud. "That's the only way there is to figure, just let hindsight do it."

"Pardon?" said the woman. "I don't understand."

"Me neither," said Tom Kelly. He squeezed her right thigh firmly to assure himself that it was real and the world was real. "But we'll do what we can anyway."

Kelly was almost glad for the way his head hurt because when everything started to slip away it slipped toward the crevasse that seemed to have been banged in his skull.

That focused him and brought him back to awareness of the heavily-guarded terminal building.

It still hurt like hell.

The airmen could be distinguished from the National Police because the former wore khaki and carried automatic rifles while the police were in green with submachine-guns. There were six in each party, pausing in their banter to track Kelly and the woman from the little-used portion of the parking lot to the military terminal.

Some airports pretended to be cities of the future, with ramps and glass and cantilevered buildings. Yeşilköy was by contrast an aging factory district, where the pavement was cracked and the structures had been built for function, defined by an earlier generation, rather than ambiance.

Tom Kelly wasn't feeling much like a man of the future himself.

Gisela Romer did not exactly stiffen, but her stride became minutely more controlled. The veteran could almost feel her determining which persona she would don for the guards—haughty or sexy or mysterious. Most of these Turks were moonfaced and nineteen—and the same stock as those who stormed through naval gunfire at Gallipoli to drive the Anzacs back into the sea at bayonet point.

"Keep a low profile, love," Kelly said, risking a friendly pat on the woman's shoulder. He winked at the troops, one GI approaching some others, and all of them on fuckin' government business. "This is exactly the sorta thing they expect if I'm doing my job, and I've got authorizations up the ass."

It just feels funny because the people I just blew away were supposed to be my support, he added silently. And of course, the general fucked-upness of trying to do anything through channels wasn't to be overlooked as a factor.

"No sweat," he said jauntily.

Kelly figured he could spot the head of the National Police contingent, but the Air Force section was under a

senior lieutenant with pips and a holstered pistol to make
identification certain.

"Sir," said Kelly in Turkish, taking out a billfold bulging
with the documentation his case officer had given him,
"we have urgent business with the flight controller's office."

The Turkish officer looked carefully at both sides of the
card he was proffered, feeling the points of the seal im-
pressed through the attached bunny-in-the-headlights photograph of Tom Kelly. The back was signed by a Turkish
brigadier general from the Adana District, in his NATO
capacity.

After a pause that wouldn't have been nerve-racking
except for the fact that Kelly had put so many bodies to
cool in the recent past, the Turk saluted and said, "An
honor to meet you, Colonel. Do you know where you're
going, or would you like a guide?"

Christ, he hadn't noticed the rank she'd given him for
this one. Tom Kelly couldn't remember ever meeting a
colonel with whom he'd have willingly shared a meal.

"Is there, ah," the veteran said aloud, "an American
duty section?"

"Of course," said the lieutenant; and, if his tone was a
trifle cooler, then Kelly was still speaking Turkish.

Too many of the Americans who entered the terminal
took the attitude that anybody understood English if you
raised your voice enough, and that Turks had about enough
brains to be busboys. There were no American bases in
Turkey; there were many Turkish installations dedicated to
NATO and manned by Americans . . . and if more Americans kept that distinction clear, a demagogue like Ecevit
would have found it harder to divert attention from the
corruptness of his government with anti-American rhetoric.

"Corporal," said the officer to one of the men with
worn-looking G-3 rifles, "take Colonel O'Neill to the
NATO office."

Kelly gestured the dancer ahead before he himself fol-

lowed the sturdy-looking noncom through the terminal
doors. Neither he nor the Turk had referred to Gisela, who
was not specifically covered by the authorization. On the
other hand, she was only a woman and as such under the
colonel's control. Much had changed since the Revolution
of 1919, but the Turks were still the people who had given
the word *seraglio* to the rest of the world.

What was now the military terminal had presumably
been built in past years for civilian uses, long outgrown. It
had the feel inside of a train station, with wainscots and
plaster moldings, now dingy but painted in complementary
pastels. The lobby, at present empty, was equipped with
backless wooden benches.

"Are you expecting a flight any time soon?" Kelly
asked, mostly to put their guide at ease.

The corporal turned and flashed a smile that was unwilling to become involved, the look of a well-dressed pedestrian faced with a man-in-the-street reporter.

Kelly shrugged.

As he and Gisela followed their guide down a side
hallway they saw a portly figure in khakis coming the
other way and calling over his shoulder, "Well for
Chrissake, Larry, get it off when you can, okay?" The
fellow spoke English with a Midwestern twang and wore
USAF sleeve insignia—master sergeant's, Kelly thought,
but it was always hard to tell with the multiplicity of
winged rockers the Air Force affected to be different.

The Turkish corporal gestured toward the sergeant, said
"Sir," to Kelly, and whisked himself back toward his unit
with a slight rattle of his weapon's internal parts.

"Yes, can I help you, sir?" asked the sergeant as he
paused in the doorway of an office which was lighted
much better than the hall which served it.

Kelly stepped close to the sergeant to use the light in
finding the right document this time. The blue nametape
over the man's breast pocket read Atwater. His moustache

was neat and pencil-slim, and despite carrying an extra forty pounds, he had the dignified presence called 'military bearing' when coupled with a uniform.

"Yes, sergeant," said Kelly, handing over a layered plastic card with an inset hologram of the Great Seal and another bad photo of Kelly. "My companion and I need to get to Diyarbakir soonest, and we don't have time to wait for the Turkey Trot."

"Ummm," said Atwater, frowning with concern at the card as he led the others into his office. "That could be a bit of a problem, sir. . . ."

The phone on his desk began to ring. He lifted the handset and poked the hold button without answering the call. The light began to pulse angrily. "You see," he continued, "there's some kinda flap on, and . . ." His voice trailed off again as he shifted the card between his thumbs and forefingers to move the seal in and out of focus.

Atwater was not giving them a runaround; he was genuinely concentrating as he stared at the card. Kelly, though his face did not change, was chilling down inside, and it was at the last moment before the veteran exploded that Atwater stood up.

"Look," he said, "I'll see what I can do. I don't have any equipment on hand and the Turkey Trot—there's not another for two days anyway." He raised his hand. "Besides you don't want to run that way, I know, sir."

Kelly nodded guardedly. Every week, a C-130 transport made a circuit of the major US-manned installations in Turkey like an aerial bus route. The delay would be a problem, but the questions and whispers of the military types and their dependents sharing the flight made that option even worse.

"I'm going to check with the indigs, see if I can pull a favor or two," the sergeant continued. "If it was just you, sir"—he spread his hands—"maybe we could stick you in the rear seat of something. Two of you, that's a bit of a problem—not anything to do with *you*, you understand, ma'am.''

Kelly had been sitting on the arm of one of the office chairs along the wall. Now he stood up but faced the plastic relief map of Anatolia instead of the sergeant to avoid making a threat by his posture. ''Ah, look, Sergeant Atwater,'' he said, getting his voice back under control after the first few syllables, ''that card really means what it says, *absolute* priority. If that means stranding the ambassador in Kars, that's what it means.''

He turned carefully, thrusting his hands in his hip pockets and looking at the desk before he added, ''And if there's a Logistics Support aircraft handy, it means that too.''

Gisela had judged the conversation perfectly. She sat as still as the chair beneath her, examining her nails. Because she so perfectly mimicked a piece of furniture, the two Americans were able to hold the necessary discussion for which she should not have been present.

''Yessir, I sorta figured that,'' said Sergeant Atwater with a grimace. He rubbed his forehead and thinning hair with his palm, then returned the card to Kelly. ''There's a bird here, you bet; only, you see, I don't dispatch 'em, exactly.''

The hefty noncom spread his hands again. ''It's not Logistics Support, it's Communications Service. For this week at least. But I won't BS you, it's just the situation that's the problem.''

''Well, you've got the codes, haven't you?'' the veteran asked in amazement. ''I know it's got to be authorized stateside, but it *has* been. Just punch it in and the confirmation'll be along soonest. This signature''—he raised the card so that the back was to Atwater—''ain't a facsimile, friend.''

''Right, Colonel, didn't think it was,'' the sergeant said.

He was sweating profusely, though his manner was one of angry frustration rather than fear. Atwater was within a year of retirement and he knew that if he did his job by the rules, his ass was covered no matter *how* hacked off anybody got about it. But that wasn't the way to do a job right; and, like most members of most bureaucracies, the sergeant really liked to do his job right.

"Look, the way it is, I can't *get* stateside on a protected line to check those codes," he said, gesturing with a crooked finger at the card Kelly held. "I can't even get Rome, which'd be good enough. All the secure lines're locked up with priority traffic. Somebody's really dumped manure in the blender"—he nodded to the silent Gisela and a drop of perspiration wobbled off his nose—"if you'll pardon me, ma'am. It don't seem to be Double-you Double-you Three from anything BBC or Armed Forces radio say, they're talking progress in Geneva . . . but it's a flap and no mistake."

"I think," said Tom Kelly, looking at the woman who was as still as a blond caryatid, "we'd better get to Diyarbakir."

Gisela raised her head and nodded.

"Right," said Atwater, sucking his lips inward so that his moustache twitched. "We'll go talk to the man, and if he'll fly you, I'll log it as authorized pending confirmation."

The sergeant led the way down the hall. The next room had a Dutch door, both halves closed, with the legend Messages on the top portion and a counter built out from the lower one. Kelly's face stiffened as he strode past and he felt the weight of the tape recorder in his attaché case. "Hang on," he said, though part of him knew he ought to wait until he was wheels-up from Istanbul. He rapped on the door.

The upper panel was opened at once by an American airman. Behind him a partition baffled the remainder of the room from the hallway. "Look, Don," he said, looking past Kelly to Sergeant Atwater, "it'll go when it goes. What can I say?" There was a muted clatter of static and machinery from behind him.

"I've got something to go out in clear," Kelly said, pulling the top sheet from the memo pad on the counter before he started to write on it with one of the stub pencils there for the purpose.

"Sir?" said the airman, raising an eyebrow.

"He's got authorization, Larry," said the sergeant, before Kelly, having finished with the cable address, could take out his card case again.

"I gather there's some problem with encrypted material," the veteran said, shuttling the code clerk's eyes back to him as he set the miniature tape deck on the counter. He opened the case to display the workings of the recorder within. "I don't want encryption anyway. For all I care, you can put this on the twenty-meter amateur band and beam it right off the tape."

He paused before locking his eyes with those of the young airman. "You *can* get it out in clear, can't you, despite the tie-up?"

"Yessir," said the airman. He blinked to break eye contact so that he could look at the camouflaged recorder.

"Output's through what would be the battery jack," Kelly said. "You people can handle that, I'm sure."

"Oh, yes sir," the airman agreed, turning the memo slip to face him. He blinked again and said, "Jesus."

The veteran smiled as their eyes met again over the counter. "No sweat, buddy," he said. "It'll give you something to play with while the priority channels're busy with other people's worries."

"Check, sir," agreed the airman. He managed a smile of his own. "It's just that—I thought NSA Headquarters got even requests for furniture polish encrypted."

"Not this time, my friend," said Kelly as he waved to chop the conversation, then turned away. "This time the idea's for a whole lotta people to know what went down. The medium damn well *is* the message.''

The door leaf swung closed behind him. ''That's that, sergeant,'' the veteran said to Atwater's expressionless face. ''Let's see about transportation.''

The hall ended in a metal door that gave out onto the airfield itself. They reached it just as a Turkish Airlines 727 was lunging skyward beyond the wire-reinforced window. As Atwater knocked on the unmarked door to the right of the metal one, the roar of the commercial jet's engines shook the building like a terrier on a rat.

''Shine!'' the sergeant called through the lessening rumble. ''I got a proposition for you.''

''Is she—'' said a voice as the door opened. The speaker was a black man, five-five or six, wearing a one-piece gray flight suit. His hair was cropped so close that he could have passed for a Marine in boot camp.

When his brown, opaque eyes flickered past Atwater's shoulder, the pilot paused with his mouth already shaped to speak the next word. ''Well, Jesus and his saints,'' he said instead, ''it's Monaghan, isn't it, or have I died and gone to hell?''

''We've been to hell, Shine,'' said Kelly with a sudden recollection of tracer bullets crisscrossing the makeshift flare path and the high-wing aircraft setting down. ''It didn't kill us, did it?''

He gave the pilot a lopsided smile. ''Ready for another little jaunt? A real piece a' cake, just a ferry run to Diyarbakir.''

Shine cocked his head and looked at the sergeant. ''He got his clearances?''

''We've got that problem with the message traffic, like you know,'' Atwater replied, looking at a corner of the Ready Room. A magazine lay open on the rumpled bunk from which the pilot had risen. ''We'll get through when we get through, but . . . Colonel here seems to think there's a bit of a crunch.''

"Colonel, are we?" said the pilot. "Hadn't heard you were on quite those terms, Tommy. Guess you figure I owe you one for not going in for the rest of your team when they pulled the plug on Birdlike?"

Kelly shrugged. "I'd walked away from that one before you did, Shine. We all do what we do."

The black grinned and traced a line across the side of his skull, miming the track of blood matting Kelly's hair. "So-o-o," Shine said, "a milk run, no flak a'tall. Till I come back and try to explain why I flew you, m'friend. There's gonna be a *lot* of flak then."

"Look, Shine—" began Sergeant Atwater with a puzzled frown.

Kelly touched the sergeant's arm to silence him and said with his eyes meeting the pilot's, "I'm not going to tell you you're wrong, man."

"Shit, let's fly," the pilot said, lifting a zip-lock folder and his flight helmet from the shelf beside the door. "*I* figure I owe you one. Or I owe somebody and you're closest."

The aircraft being rolled from a hangar to meet them, a Pilatus Turbo-Porter, was, like the pilot, on twenty-four hour standby with its preflight check already completed. Its straight wing, exceptionally long and broad for an aircraft of the size, was fitted with slotted flaps to lower the stall speed even further.

The Porter's undersurfaces were painted a dark blue-gray that better approximated the shade of the night sky than black would. The upper surfaces were whorls of black over brown and maroon almost as dark to keep the aircraft from having an identifiable outline from above.

Kelly knew where the Logistics Support unit in Istanbul had been flying three years before. Now that the political situation in Greece had stabilized—or reverted, depending on your bias—he was mildly surprised that an agent-transporting aircraft was still based here. Some things had their own inertia, especially when the secrecy of the operation kept it out of normal budgetary examinations. Score one for inefficiency.

Shine—his last name was Jacobs, Kelly thought, or at least it had been when he had been on the eastern border of Turkey supporting Kurdish operations—ducked through the port-side entry doors, springing off the step attached to the fuselage. The Porter was awkward to board because its fixed landing gear was mounted on long struts to take the impact of landings that closely approached vertical. Even the tail wheel was lifted by a shock absorber.

Kelly started to hand the woman up the high step, an action as reflexive for him as was her look of scorn as she entered the cabin unaided. Hell, the veteran thought, he was the one who needed help. Walking to the hangar had brought him double vision, and the two steps to enter the aircraft rang like hammers in his skull.

He'd been hurt worse before, plenty times; but he'd never been this *old* before, any more than he'd ever be this young again. If he didn't start using common sense about the things he let his body in for, the aging problem was going to take care of itself real quick.

A ground crewman closed the cabin door while the starter cart whirled the Porter's turbine engine into wailing life. Shine was forward in the cockpit, and Gisela eyed the sparse furnishings of the cabin. There was a fold-down bench of aluminum tubing and canvas on the starboard bulkhead across from the doors, and individual jumpseats of similar construction to port.

Kelly unlatched a seat, then the bench, as Shine ran the five-hundred-horse turbine up to speed. With his mouth close to Gisela's ears, the veteran said, ''You got any problem if I rack out on the bench?'' He pointed. ''I'm not

. . . I mean, I think I could use a couple hours, if that's okay.''

Gisela smiled grimly at what both of them recognized as an admission of weakness—and an apology for treating her like a girl moments earlier. ''Fine,'' she said, and nodded toward the cockpit. ''Do you think your friend will mind if I sit next to him?''

Kelly glanced forward toward the back of Shine's helmet, just visible over his seat back. The right-hand cockpit seat was empty. ''Not unless he's changed a hell of a lot since I last knew him,'' the veteran said with a chuckle. ''He'd screw a snake if somebody held it down. Of course, it'd have to be a *girl* snake.''

The woman laughed also and patted Kelly's shoulder as she slid her way into the empty forward seat. He could not hear the brief exchange between Gisela and the pilot a moment before the Porter began to taxi, but the dancer's laugh trilled again above the turbine whine.

Kelly seated himself and belted in as the aircraft waited for clearance. The belt wasn't going to do a hell of a lot of good with a side-facing seat bolted onto the frame of a light aircraft; but it was the way he'd been trained, and his brain was running on autopilot. Christ, it felt as if each revolution of the spinning prop was shaving a little deeper through his skull.

He'd be better for sleep. If he could sleep.

The runway could accommodate 747's, but Shine took off within the first hundred and twenty yards of the pavement. The Porter lifted at a one-to-one ratio, gaining a foot of altitude for every foot of forward flight. In a straight-sided gulley or a clearing literally blasted in triple-canopy jungle, such a takeoff might have been necessary. Here, it was necessary only because Shine needed to prove that he and the plane could do it every time—because next time it might not be a matter of choice.

They climbed at over a thousand feet per minute toward

whatever Shine chose to call cruising altitude for this flight. It had been possible that he'd fly the entire seven hundred miles on the deck to prove his capabilities in the most bruising way possible. Probably he wanted enough height to engage the autopilot safely—and leave his hands free, since Gisela had decided to sit forward.

Even before the Porter leveled off, Kelly had unbuckled his seat belt and stretched out on the narrow bench. A severe bank to port would fling him across the cabin lengthwise like a log to the flume, but Shine wouldn't do that except at need. The bench, trembling with the thrust of the prop and the shudder of air past the skin of the aircraft, made a poor bed . . . but better than some, and, in the event, good enough.

He dreamed again of ancient Amida, its black basalt walls shrugging off attack by the Romans who had raised them initially. And he dreamed of the Fortress; but in the way of dreams and nightmares, the two merged into a single, stark threat, in space and on the empty plains of Mesopotamia.

It was still dark when he awakened to the gentle pressure of Gisela's hands on his shoulder blades. Shine was making his final approach to the airbase at Diyarbakir, headquarters of the Turkish Third Tactical Air Force.

And perhaps the headquarters of the Dienst and its Plan, as well as whatever the aliens had been doing when one was shot with Mohammed. Rise and shine, Tom Kelly, there's no rest for the wicked in this life.

The airfield at Diyarbakir had been paved for fully-laden fighter bombers, but, as on takeoff, the pilot had his own notions of proper utilization. Kelly was scarcely buckled in across from the woman who had awakened him when the Turbo-Porter hit the ground at an angle nearly as steep as that at which they had lifted off.

The cabin bucked and hammered in sudden turbulence

as Shine reversed the blade pitch and brought the aircraft to a halt against the full snarling power of the Garrett turbine. The engine braked them to a stop within seventy feet of the point they first touched down.

Shine throttled back. Over the keening of the turbine as it settled to forty percent power through a medley of harmonics, he shouted, "You got ground transport laid on?"

"Ought to," Kelly answered, nodding and finding that the motion did not hurt him nearly as much as he had expected. The nightmares he had seen and joined had wrung him out mentally, but his physical state was surprisingly close to normal. He unbuckled himself and stood up, rocking as Shine changed blade pitch to taxi and tapped on the left brake to swing the nose.

Through the windscreen Kelly could see a control tower of dun-colored brick, with corrugated-metal additions turned a similar shade by the blowing dust. At the edge of the building was parked a Dodge pickup truck painted Air Force blue. While the pilot centered the Porter's prop spinner on the vehicle, its door opened and the driver got out.

Shine braked and feathered the prop again, only ten feet from the bumper of the pickup. "Door-to-door service a specialty," he shouted.

Kelly gestured Gisela toward the cabin door but stepped forward himself so that he could be heard, and heard privately. "Appreciate it, man," the veteran said, shaking the pilot's hand between the two seatbacks. "You done a good thing."

Shine laughed without much humor. "Yeah, well, Tommy," he said, "you meet up with any of the types who got back anyway, the ragheads—you tell 'em I'm sorry. There was orders, sure, but . . . you know, the longer I live, the less I regret the times I violated orders, and the less I like to remember some of the ones I obeyed. You know?''

''Don't feel like the Lone Ranger,'' Kelly said, squeezing the pilot's hand again before he turned to follow Gisela.

Moments after the two passengers had stepped onto the concrete and dogged the hatch closed, the Porter rotated and lifted again—a brief hop to the fueling point a quarter mile farther down the runway—instead of taxiing properly.

''Not exactly the least conspicuous vehicle,'' Kelly muttered as he and the dancer stepped toward the truck. ''But I didn't think we'd do better through Atwater, even if I kicked and screamed for something civilian. The folks who were supposed to arrange that sorta thing for me are either dead or wish I was.''

The man standing beside the truck was in his mid-twenties, wearing a moustache and sideburns which were within, though barely, the loose parameters of the US Air Force. ''Colonel Monaghan?'' he asked without saluting; neither he nor Kelly were in uniform, and there was a look in the man's eyes that suggested he didn't volunteer salutes anyway.

''Yessir,'' said Kelly, nodding courteously. The other man's eyes had drifted to the dancer. ''I much appreciate this. I know it's not the sort of thing you're here for.''

There were only a few US liaison officers at the airbase here in Diyarbakir. This man and the vehicle had to have been requisitioned from the NSA listening post at Pirinclik, fifteen miles west of the city, where the midflight telemetry of tests from the Russian missile proving ground at Tyuratam was monitored. Pirinclik was staffed by the US Air Force; but nonetheless, Sergeant Atwater must have called in personal chips to arrange for a vehicle over a general phone line.

''Here's the key, sir,'' the younger man said with a modicum of respect in his voice. ''There's a chain to run from the steering wheel to the foot-feed. No ignition lock, you know?''

Kelly nodded. ''Much appreciated,'' he repeated as he opened the driver's side door and handed Gisela behind the wheel. She knew where they were going, Lord willing. ''Hope you've got a way back?'' he added, suddenly struck by the fact that the airman looked very much alone against the empty background of runways on an alluvial plain. ''We're in more of a time crunch than . . .''

''So I hear,'' the younger man agreed with a tight smile. At a base like Pirinclik, there were more sources of information than the official channels. It struck Kelly that this fellow might know a lot more than he and Gisela themselves did, but there really *wasn't* time to explore that possibility. ''I'll call and they'll send a jeep. Just didn't want to tie up two vehicles on so loose an ETA.'' He nodded toward the Turbo-Porter, shrunken into a dark huddle at the distant service point.

Gisela cranked the engine, which caught on the second attempt, just before the airman called, ''Pump once and—''

''The gate's off to the left,'' Kelly said as he closed his own door, wondering how often he'd flown in or out of the Third TAF base. More times than he could remember, literally, because once he'd been delirious, controllable only because he was just as weak as he was crazy. . . .

They paused for the gate, chain link on a sturdy frame, to be swung open by Turks from the sandbagged bunkers to either side. There was no identification check for people leaving in an American vehicle, though the guards showed some surprise that the driver was a blond woman. Gisela turned left on the narrow blacktop highway and accelerated jerkily while she determined the throw and engagement of the pickup's clutch.

''You've been here before,'' Kelly said, noting that the woman turned without hesitation.

She glanced aside, then back to the road. ''Not here,''

she said in a cool voice, aware that the American was fishing for information—and willing to give it to him even though he had not, by habit, done her the courtesy of asking directly. "Not the airfield. But of course, I've spent a great deal of time at our base in the city."

The landscape through which they drove as fast as the truck's front-end shimmy permitted was as flat as any place Kelly had ever been. It appeared to be rolling countryside, but the scale of distance was so great that it gave shape to what would otherwise have been considered dead-level ground.

But the plains were neither smooth nor green—at least this early in the year; Kelly knew from experience that by early summer the oats and barley planted in some of the unfenced fields would have grown high enough to hide the rocks.

The soil of Mesopotamia had been cultivated for millennia, for virtually as long as any area of the Earth's surface. Every time a plow bit, it sent a puff of yellow-gray dust off on the constant wind and diminished the soil by that much. The rocks, from pebbles to blocks the size of a man's torso, remained . . . and from a slight distance, from a road, those rocks were *all* that remained of what had been the most fertile lands on Earth. One could still cultivate with care and hardship, however, and pasture sheep.

"We—concentrated here in Diyarbakir, when the Plan was developed," Gisela said deliberately, "in part for recruitment's sake—the Kurds." She looked over to make sure her student was following. Kelly nodded obediently.

"But more because it is, you see, not developed," the woman continued, "but still there are the airbase and the tracking station. Competing jurisdictions, do you see?" The tutor looked over again.

"So that if things should be seen that neither understands, your NSA or Turk Hava Kuvvertli"—Gisela used the indigenous words for Turkish Air Force within the English of her lecture—"both blame the other . . . but not *blame,* because of security."

She smiled toward the windshield as, downshifting the long-throw gearbox, she passed a horse-drawn wagon in a flapping roar. Communication among friendly forces was a more necessary ingredient of success than was intelligence of the enemy, but it was notable that whenever military bureaucracies set priorities, information flow came in a bad second to security. Perhaps that was a case of making a virtue of necessity, since it was almost impossible to pass data through a military bureaucracy anyway.

"So each thinks the other responsible and says nothing, so as not to embarrass an ally and to poke into what is not their own business," Gisela concluded. "Bad practice of security."

The road off to the right, past a small orchard of pistachio trees, could have been a goat track save that it meandered in double rather than single file. Gisela found the brakes were spongy and downshifted sharply to let the engine compression help slow the truck. They made the turn comfortably, though the pickup swayed on springs abused by too many rutted roads like this.

"Reach into my right coat pocket," the woman directed. She had crossed right arm over left to take the turnoff, and even in the moment it took her to reposition her hands afterwards, the steering wheel jibbed viciously.

Kelly obeyed, expecting to find sunglasses or something similar. Instead there was a round-nosed cylinder that could have been a lipstick, save that it was clicking against three others like it—and a fifth, buried deeply in a corner of the lining.

He drew out the handful of .38 Special cartridges, a full load for the cylinder of the snubbie now nestled empty against his spine. "Well, I'll be a sonofabitch," said the veteran softly as he drew the weapon to load it.

The rounds were US Government issue, bearing Lake City Arsenal headstamps and 130-grain bullets with full metal jackets. They were really intended for 9-mm autoloaders and would literally rattle down the bore of most .38 Special revolvers. When fired, however, they upset enough to take the rifling.

They weren't a perfect load for the aluminum snubbie, but they were a hell of an improvement over an empty cylinder . . . and the fact that Gisela had procured them for him, just before he was to be introduced to her associates, was a sign more valuable than any real protection that the weapon gave him.

"I got them from the pilot," Gisela said needlessly. "I thought you wouldn't ask, to call attention. So I asked, and it won't be reported."

Kelly hunched forward to replace the little revolver. He'd carried it a lot of years and never used it before the previous night, but that didn't mean he wouldn't need it again soon. Lightning was liable to keep striking the same place so long as the storm raged and the tree still stood in its path.

The ground became broken to either side of the road, lifting in outcrops of dense rock shaded by brush instead of sere grass. Gisela downshifted again into compound low. A moment later, the hood of the truck dipped as the ruts led into a gorge notched through the plain in two stages.

They drove down the upper, broader level; then Gisela cramped the wheels hard left to follow the track across a single-arched bridge of stone, vaulting the narrow center of the gully. There was enough water in the rivulet below to flash in the sun before the truck began climbing from the declivity with a shiver of wheelspin.

"How old was that bridge?" asked Kelly, craning his neck to look out the back window, an effort made vain by the coating of dust over the glass.

"Seljuk at least," answered the woman with a shrug

which merged into a shoulder thrust as the steering fought her when they rattled out of the gully. "Maybe Byzantine, maybe Roman, maybe—who knows? There's probably been a bridge there as long as men have lived here and farmed . . . and that is a very long time."

"And now you're here," Kelly said quietly. "The Service."

"Here." Gisela's smile was more arrogant than pleased. "And soon, everywhere. To the world's benefit."

The ground dropped a few feet on the left side of the road. Gisela swung to the right around a basalt rock face and then pulled left toward the recently refurbished gate of a han, a caravanserai, ruined by time.

The walls of basalt blocks weathered gray gleamed in the sunlight, but the shadowed gaps in the dome of the mosque which formed one corner of the enclosure were as black as a colonel's soul. The dome was crumbling; but, though the ages had scalloped the upper edge of the wall around the courtyard, it was still solid and at no point less than eight feet high.

The original gateway had been built between the mosque and a gatehouse, but part of the latter had been demolished when the new gate was constructed. This was steel, double-leafed and wide enough to pass a semi-trailer. The posts to which the leaves were hinged were themselves steel, eight inches in diameter and concrete-filled if they were not solid billets.

In the far corner of the facing wall there were arrow slits, in the walls and the blockhouse. It struck Kelly that the stone edifice was proof to any modern weapons up through tank cannon, and that the embrasures could shower machinegun fire on trespassers as effectively as the arrows for which they had been intended.

Gisela pulled up to the gate and honked imperiously. The dust cloud they had raised in their passage continued to drift forward, settling on Kelly's right sleeve and the ledge of his open window. The back of his neck began to tingle. He shifted in his seat, unwilling to draw his revolver but certain that a premonition of danger was causing his hair to bristle.

The woman honked again and said, "If somebody's asleep at *this* time, they'll—"

"Jesus *Christ!*" shouted Kelly. He unlatched his door so hastily that his feet tangled as he got out of the cab. He did not draw his gun, any more than he would have thought to do so if he found himself in the path of a diesel locomotive.

At first it was more like watching time-lapse photography of a building under construction, for the object was huge and silent and rising vertically in a nimbus of brilliant light. Hairs that had been prickling all over Kelly's body now stood straight out, and when he reached for the car door to steady himself a static spark snapped six inches from the metal to numb his hand.

It wasn't a cylinder rising on jacks from the han courtyard: it was a disk fifty feet in diameter with a bluntly-rounded circumference and a central depth of about twelve feet.

It was a fucking flying saucer.

Gisela was out of the truck also, shouting and waving her clenched fist in obvious fury. The underside of the saucer was clearly visible, so it could scarcely be called an unidentified flying object. The veil of light surrounding the vehicle as it rose was pastel and of uncertain color, shifting like the aurora but bright enough to be visible now in broad daylight.

The skin of the flying saucer was formed of riveted plates. The junctions of the plates and the individual rivet heads stood out despite the nimbus because the portion of the field emanating from those surface irregularities was of a shade which contrasted with that of the plates themselves.

The whole aura shifted across the spectrum and, as the

saucer continued to rise, faded. The craft climbed vertically. A bright line appeared from the rim to the central axis, as if the nimbus had been pleated there and trebled in thickness. The line rotated across the circular undersurface faster than the second hand on a watch dial, hissing and crackling with violent electrical discharges. The rate of the saucer's rise accelerated with the sweep of the line, so that there was only a speck of dazzling corona by the time the full surface area should have been swept. Then there was nothing at all.

"It was Dora," said Gisela brokenly. She touched the truck's fender with a hand for balance, looking as staggered as she had been the moment Doug had slapped her with a shot-loaded hand.

"Have the aliens come and taken your friend?" Kelly demanded harshly in order to be understood through the woman's dismay.

"No, not the crabs," Gisela said petulantly, turning so that both her palms were braced against the vehicle.

The breeze that was too constant to be noticed made enough noise in the background that she was hard to hear, since the truck separated her from Kelly. He stepped around the front of the vehicle to join her, though he was nervous that his appearance of haste would silence her. By focusing on the details of gathering information, Tom Kelly was able to avoid boggling inertly as a result of what he had just seen.

What*ever* he had just seen.

Gisela met his eyes and straightened. "That was Dora," she said in a firm, emotionless voice. "The first of the Special Applications craft, the prototype which escaped to the Antarctic base from the Bavarian Alps in 1945. She must have been sent to make the final pickup. And we have missed her."

The blond woman's face was as cool as that of a marble virgin, but tears had begun to well from the inner corners of her blue eyes. "We may as well go back into the city, Thomas Kelly. We'll be able to communicate from the office there, but I'm sure no one will have time for us until everything has been accomplished.

"They have begun to execute the Plan already, and I am not a part of it."

Tom Kelly took the woman's hands in support, but only a small portion of his mind was on Gisela anymore. He was far more concerned with the fact that not all of the UFOs being sighted were under the control of aliens whose motives were at least uncertain.

Some of the spacecraft were in the hands of Nazis whose motives were not doubtful in the slightest.

Kelly started back to Diyarbakir with Gisela slumped as his passenger against the other door. He drove with the caution demanded by the loose steering and his own unfamiliarity with the roads.

Besides, there was no longer any reason for haste.

"I didn't think they'd leave before dark," Gisela said.

A front wheel bucked in a rut, jolting her hard against the doorframe and recalling her to her dignity. She straightened in the seat and gave a body-length quiver like the motion of a snake casting its skin. "But of course, now it doesn't matter—secrecy. No need for it, no chance for it either. And they left me behind."

The sky had darkened abruptly, as if the flying saucer had punched a hole in the stratosphere and let the storm rush in. That was what had happened, near enough in the larger sense, Kelly supposed. Not asking the question wouldn't make the situation go away, though.

"Exactly what *is* the Plan?" the veteran asked, while his hands and eyes drove the truck and left his intellect free for things he would have preferred not to think about.

"To control the world by using your Fortress," the

dancer said, destroying with her flat voice any possibility that Kelly's imagination might have run away with him.

"At first we had the base in Antarctica," Gisela continued. "My father was commander of the detachment guarding the salt mines at Kertl, in Bavaria. When British troops were within five kilometers and they could hear Russian guns in the east, so near were they, a motorcycle arrived with orders that they should leave at once for Thule Base in the Antarctic, taking all flyable Special Applications craft."

The woman was speaking in German, and her voice had the sing-song texture of a tale which had been repeated so many times.

"Only Dora, the fourth prototype, could be flown," said Gisela. "Some of those at Kertl wished to wait still further for the aircraft from Berlin Tempelhof they had been hoping would arrive. Others would have fled to the British in order to escape the Bolsheviks, but they feared to entrust themselves to a journey of twenty thousand kilometers in a craft which had thus far been the subject only of static testing.

"But my father understood that orders must be obeyed, not questioned; and he understood that there was sometimes no path but that of ruthlessness to the accomplishment of a soldier's duty."

Kelly's hands gripped the steering wheel more fiercely than the road itself—the highway to Diyarbakir, now—demanded. The American agent had seen enough things in his own lifetime to be able to imagine that scene in the foothills of the Alps close to the time he was being born. Electrostatic charges from Dora, the prototype built so solidly that she still flew like nothing else on Earth, must have lighted up the salt mine in which the laboratory hid from Allied bombers. It would have been like living in the heart of a neon lamp while the powerplant was run up to takeoff level.

But the machinery was only part of the drama. The rest was that of the men and women wearing laboratory smocks or laborers' coveralls, the personnel who had decided to ignore the order from Berlin and stay behind. As Dora readied to attempt her final mission, those who were not aboard her would have begun to understand exactly what decision they had *really* made.

The guard detachment of Waffen SS would have been in spatter-camouflage uniforms and carrying the revolutionary MP-44 assault rifles which could not win the war for Germany but which armed a generation of liberation movements after the Russians lightly modified the design into the AK-47. Even the pick of Germany's fighting strength there at the end would have been a far cry from the triumphant legions of the Blitzkrieg: boys, taller and blonder, perhaps, than their classmates, but still fifteen years old; and a leavening of veterans whose eyes were too empty now to show weariness, much less mercy.

Tom Kelly had been a man like that for too many years not to know what it would have been to have stood with those guardsmen; and how little he would have felt when Colonel Schneider gave the order to fire and the bellow of a score of automatic rifles echoed itself into thunder in the walls of the tunnel.

"Thule Base was safe, unapproachable," said Gisela. In her voice was a memory of ice and snow and a constant wind, with even bare rock so deep ice had to be excavated to reach it. "But it was useless save as a place to hide while we reorganized and gathered the wealth required for the task. Three U-boats of the Type XXI rendezvoused with the refugees from Dora, and there was the original complement of Thule Base . . . but still very few, you must understand?"

A few oversized drops of rain splattered down, followed by a downpour snaking across the highway in a distinct line. The dust on the hood and windshield turned immediately to mud which the desiccated wiper blades pushed across the glass in streaks when Kelly found their switch.

"Others provided aid, supplied us with connections and part of the money required," the woman said, raising her voice over the drumbeat of raindrops as though addressing a hall of awestruck, upturned faces which hung on her words. "But there were two secrets which the Service kept: those original stragglers at Thule Base and their descendants like myself. We kept the secret of Dora. And we kept the secret of the last flight from Tempelhof, a special Arado Blitzbomber as planned—but north, to one of the Swedish islands, where those who flew in it transferred to a U-boat which would proceed to Antarctica to meet us."

They were getting close to the incorporated area of the city. Diyarbakir had spread to the north and west of ancient Amida. The city walls to the south loomed on an escarpment, free of modern buildings, and the eastern boundary was the steep gorge of the Tigris—now and as it had been for millennia.

In the heavy traffic they were entering, bad brakes and the universal-tread pattern of the pickup's tires made Kelly concentrate more on his driving than he wanted to. The rhythm of outside sounds and the greasy divorcement of the rain-slick highway were releasing Gisela's tongue, however. They were in a microcosm of their own, she and Kelly; not the universe that others inhabited and one which had secrets that one must never tell.

"We could buy equipment easily," the woman said. "Through sympathizers, sometimes, but easily also through those who wanted drugs or wanted arms that we could supply. However, there was no place on Earth where we could safely produce what we needed for the day we knew would come, when the Service would provide thousands of craft like Dora for the legions of New Germany to sweep away Bolshevism and materialism together."

Brake lights turned the road ahead of them into a strand of rubies, twinkling on their windshield and on the rain spattering toward the street. A major factory, one of the few in a city almost wholly dependent on agriculture, was letting the workers out to choke the road with motorcycles, private cars, and dolmuses—minivans that followed fixed routes like buses, but on no particular schedule and with an even higher degree of overloading than was the norm for Turkish buses.

"Turn here," Gisela said with a note of disapproval. "You should have turned at the last cross street. We enter the Old City best by the Urfa Gate."

Kelly nodded obsequiously. Colonel Schneider's—Romer's—daughter was telling him things now, in a state divorced from reason, which she had not told even when she was convinced that he had saved her and her Plan from Israeli secret agents. Then she had been willing to take him to those whose business the explanations were—but not to overstep her own duties. Irrational snappishness when he missed the turn to a location unknown to him was a small price for the background he was hearing.

Gisela cleared her throat with a touch of embarrassment as she ran her comment back. "I apologize," she said in English. "Our office is to the right on the inner circumferential, facing the walls."

"No problem," the veteran answered in German. He inched forward, thankful for the rain-swept traffic that kept them from what might be the terminus of their conversation. "How did you get over the problem with fabrication, then?"

"By putting the assembly plant on the Moon," said Gisela calmly.

Kelly, shifting from first into neutral, lost the selector in the sloppy linkages of third and fourth when his arm twitched forward. "Okay," he said when he thought his voice would be calm. "I guess I thought maybe you had a satellite of your own. Like Fortress."

"It was easier to armor against vacuum than it was the winds and convection cooling at Thule Base," said the woman. "And the Moon had what neither Antarctica nor an orbiting platform could provide: ores. Raw material to be formed into aluminum for the skin and girders of the fleet. Dora had been built of impervium, chromium-vanadium alloy; but that was not necessary, the scientists who escaped with my father decided.

"The instruments and the drive units, the great electromagnetic engines that draw their power from the auras surrounding the Earth and Sun, had to be constructed here; but that was easy to arrange, since the pieces divulged little of their purpose. They are shipped as freight to our warehouse at Iskenderun and there loaded on a motorship which the Service owns through a Greek holding company. It sails with only our own personnel in the crew and, hundreds of miles from the coast, the cargo is transferred to Dora or one of her newer sisters."

Traffic surged forward like a clot releasing in a blood vessel. The wall above the Urfa Gate was whole and fifty feet high, with semicircular towers flanking the treble entrances and rising even higher. Only the arched central gateway, tall enough and wide enough to pass the heaviest military equipment of Byzantine times, was used for vehicular traffic. It constricted the modern two-lane road; Kelly swore under his breath as he watched the cars ahead of them slither on the pavement, threatening traffic in the other lane and stone walls that had survived at least fifteen centuries of collisions.

"And then you Americans started to build your nuclear Fortress, and we knew that fate was on our side, despite the disasters of the war and the hardships that we underwent while the Service huddled in Antarctica and—and after."

There was a tendency, in Kelly as surely as in other people, to assume that what somebody did in the course of his job—or her job—was what he liked to do. It made him mad every time somebody read his file and looked at him with face muscles stiffening as if that would armor the person against the monster calling itself Tom Kelly.

But he did the same thing, even knowing better; even knowing that there were worse things in the life of Gisela Romer than years spent on the Antarctic ice, but you did what had to be done. . . .

There had been a pitiable attempt to landscape the approach to the Urfa Gate with trees. Those which still survived at twenty-meter intervals along the boulevard were trees like those found throughout the inhabited Middle East: stunted, the major branches a yard or so long from the point they forked, and a burst of first-year twigs splaying from the cut ends like the hair of a drowned woman. Firewood was at a premium, and each year these trees would be pruned back secretly by those whose only choice was to freeze.

And sometimes the long-term choices people made for themselves and for mankind weren't a whole lot prettier; that was all.

Pedestrians hurried along the sidewalk within the circumferential, bent and squinting as though they could shut themselves off from the battering rain. The hooped iron barrier which separated them from the vehicular way gleamed silver in the lights of cars turning into the Old City, providing a touch of fairyland for a scene otherwise harsh and squalid. The girdered tower holding a transformer substation just within the walls could as well have been the guard post of a concentration camp. Life is not exotic while it is being lived. The walls which made Diyarbakir an archeological treasure were proof of a past reality as cruel as anything that put Fortress in orbit above the Earth today.

Kelly knew now why he had been dreaming about ancient Amida and her walls, past which he now drove a pickup truck, turned against their builders. He had a pretty good idea of who—of what—had caused him to have those dreams.

But he was damned if he knew what he'd been supposed to do about the situation.

"What was the message you sent out from Istanbul?" Gisela asked unexpectedly. She had talked her way through her shock at being left behind at the crucial juncture. She had reason to ask the question, and Kelly had no reason at all to lie in his answer.

"I was set up last night," he said, leaning forward for a better angle through the windshield. At least it had been raining hard enough to wash the dust from the glass. Presumably he would get further directions when it was time for them.

"*We* were set up," Kelly went on, amending his initial words. "I got a tape of it, back at my room. What we picked up before heading for the airport, too late for it to do *us* any good right then."

The woman grinned as the same memory struck both of them simultaneously. She ran her fingertips up Kelly's right thigh, then cupped his groin firmly. "There will be more of that, you and I," she promised with a wink.

Kelly laughed. "There isn't a bad time to think about sex," he said. But there were more important things to think about which were very bad indeed.

"Set up by my own people," the American continued because Gisela expected him to. "I—" He paused, then went on, "Assuming I get through this in one piece, I'm going to be deep in shit for blowing away the people I did."

The woman nodded. "Yes," she said seriously, "we know how closely your country works with the Jews. That is why it was so, of so much importance to us to find someone like you who had access to your intelligence community but who could be trusted not to be a puppet of the Jews.''

Yep, thought Kelly, that's exactly why they handed me to you, Elaine and her bosses. Tom Kelly's a fuckin' Nazi, he'll get along just fine with these other Nazis, and maybe we'll learn what kinda games the Service's been playin' with the funny-looking gray guys in the flying saucers.

The hell of it was, things had worked out just about the way Pierrard would've wanted them to—except maybe in detail, though Suits didn't like being bothered with details about who'd been killed and where and how many. The thing Pierrard really wouldn't like was the fact that he'd been so slow off the mark that the information was probably getting to him through the evening news.

Knowing the type, the delay was going to turn out to be the fault of some subordinate—very possibly the fault of Tom Kelly. Officers called that ''delegation of responsibility.''

''So,'' the veteran continued, ''I figured that the tape of that conversation sent clear text so there's no way in *hell* they could be sure who'd heard it, all over the world— that'd give 'em another bone to gnaw instead of me.''

His tongue touched his lips again. ''Besides,'' he added so softly that his passenger could not have been sure of the words, ''they gotta learn: If they stick it to me, I stick it right back. Whoever they are.''

''We can either park here,'' Gisela said, ''or you can go left at Gazi Boulevard and left again at once in the alley, unless somebody's blocking it.''

She had the same trick he did, Kelly noticed, of giving directions without raising her voice unless they were very goddam important. Him driving around in the rain because he was too dumb to listen to a normal voice wouldn't have been that important; and he *wasn't* too dumb to listen.

''Here'' was an area within an angle of the walls, set off

from the occupied portion of the city by law and the circumferential road. The big circular tower at the apex of the angle was a famous one, the Married Tower, though Kelly couldn't remember the reason for that name if he ever had known. The clear area would have been a park if it were landscaped. At the moment, it was a wasteland whose dust had been wetted to mud by the rain—too unusual a circumstance for grass to have secured a foothold.

There were bushes planted at the edge of the circumferential, but the hard conditions had opened several gaps in the attempted hedge through which the truck could drive without doing further damage. The truck with US Air Force plates could sit undisturbed there, and, in this downpour, more or less unnoticed. The buildings across the circumferential were raised on common walls, and the alley behind them would have been laid out when donkeys were the sole form of transportation.

Kelly shifted down into the granny gear, standing on the brake pedal as he did so to warn the driver behind him. He pulled hard right, and the truck bumped over the curb with less commotion than it had negotiated the road to the han where Dora hid.

The shock of recognition which Kelly felt was real enough to send a tingle up his arm from the finger which was switching off the headlights. He swore softly as the rain-streaked glow faded in his memory.

Not that it should have been a surprise.

"This is where Mohammed Ayyubi bought it," Kelly said, gesturing with his chin toward the walls thirty feet away. The rain paused, then sent a fierce lash of droplets across the hood and windshield. The stark battlements were hidden beyond the rain and glass, but Kelly's mind superimposed the videotaped scene in Congressman Bianci's office on the image his headlights had just shown: the same wall, the same dripping illumination. . . . Bodies only in what the camera had recorded; at least so far.

"Yes, Mohammed made the initial approach and screening for the Kurds we recruited for the Field Force," Gisela agreed. "We couldn't recruit in Europe, not safely. And besides, Europeans—even the Aryans—have grown soft."

The woman shrugged; the act gave her the look of a person rising from catastrophe. "He was coming to meet me at the office here. There were the shots and many vehicles. We scattered, of course, though there was no attempt to make arrests . . . and afterwards, who can say? The crabs, we thought once, but they do not use guns—though one was killed there. A colonel of police was full of tales of the *thing* that the Americans had bundled away from the site."

Her eyes had been on the inner curve of the windshield, on her reflection or her memory. Now she turned to the American agent and said, "He spoke of you often, you know, Tom Kelly. I think now perhaps it was the Jews who killed him."

"Something like that," said Kelly as he opened his door and felt water drip on the bare skin of his wrist. "Could well be."

There was no street lighting, and the lights of the traffic hid rather than illuminated Kelly's surroundings by levering shadows through the sparse hedge in a counterfeit of nearby motion. The courtesy light in the cab winked as Gisela got out on her side. The vehicle neatly plugged the gap through which Kelly had driven. He stepped around the front of the pickup, toward the woman and another opening in the hedge.

"Thomas Kelly," said a voice that he recognized, "we must speak with you. It may be that there still is time to save your world."

There were three of them again, one on either side of the pickup and the third facing the vehicle's hood and the two humans. The pair on the flanks were utterly motionless, but white noise surrounded them in a palpable cloak. The words were coming from the little radio in Kelly's attaché case, though its power was turned off. The rain that fell with fitful intensity was disintegrating away from the standing figures, without the fiery enthusiasm of bullets the night before but with an accompaniment of sound.

Gisela, arm's length from the American, made a grab for the gun beneath his waistband.

She was lithe and very strong; but not so strong as Kelly, nor as quick. He caught her right wrist in his right hand and, with the other, tried to grip her about the waist. "Wait!" he cried.

One of the frozen-seeming pair of strangers changed appearance. He—it—remained motionless, but the frosting and sizzle of rain that did not quite touch the form now wetted it normally. *"Wait!"* Kelly screamed again, this time to the figures who stood like wooden carvings of humanity.

Kelly was not willing to hurt the dancer, and she was willing to do whatever was necessary to escape. During the preceding day he had twice saved her life—so *she* thought at any rate—and gained such intellectual trust as a person like Gisela Romer had to offer. But her fear and hatred of the aliens were matters ingrained for years and redoubled by the fate of her father.

Her muscles flexed against Kelly's grip by habit, sure from experience that she could tear herself free from any man before he realized her strength. Kelly held her like a band of iron. The point of her shoulder jarred his forehead hard enough for pain to explode in sheets of light across his optic nerves. Even then the veteran's grip did not loosen, but his eyes missed the motion of her free hand.

He knew what she'd done surely enough when her knuckles slammed him in the groin.

On a conscious level Kelly thought he was still winning, still in control. He could block the pain while he reached for Gisela's left hand also and his lips ordered her to—

His lips passed only a rattle like that of a strangled

rabbit. His belly muscles had drawn up so tightly that he could not breathe, much less speak. And the will was there, but the strength had poured from his muscles like blood from the throat of a stuck pig. Gisela lunged back and away from him. Kelly still did not feel the pain he knew must be wracking him, but he could not feel anything at all between his knees and his shoulders.

Christ, that woman could break rocks with her bare hands.

He toppled as she twisted aside and froze, a splendid Valkyrie, in a dazzle of light as sharp and sudden as a static spark. Neither of the man-looking figures Kelly could see as his shoulder hit the ground had moved, though the one to the truck's side began to hiss and shimmer again at the touch of raindrops. One or both must have shot the woman, but Kelly could only deduce that from the result. He reached back toward the Smith and Wesson he had refused to draw a moment before.

"*Please,* Mr. Kelly," begged the radio voice. "She is not harmed. Please, we *must* speak with you while there may be time."

"Christ," muttered Tom Kelly as mottlings of shadow and light from the roadway quivered across the fully-human face of one of the strangers. The rain on his own face and forehead felt good because it both cooled and dampened skin which felt as though it had been parching in an oven. He had feeling throughout his body again, an ache radiating from his groin in steady pulses with random flashes of pain to add piquancy.

Gisela'd done her usual professional job. If this trio didn't want to shoot him the way they had her, they'd have plenty of time to stomp Kelly down into the muddy gravel before he, in his present state, could clear the snubbie.

Hell, he'd needed to talk with 'em anyway. And if Gisela was as dead as her boneless sprawl implied—there'd be a time to fix that, the only way a man like Tom Kelly knew to fix things. . . .

"The neuroreceptors of her brain are blocked," said the voice of the stranger, who/which might either be reading Kelly's mind in good truth or making a shrewd estimate on the basis of file data. They must have files, or they wouldn't have found reason to track him across Anatolia; though the Lord knew what those reasons might be.

"She will be well in half an hour," the central stranger continued as Kelly rose carefully to his feet. The other two figures in dark overcoats, darkening further as the rain wet them, minced in slowly from either side. "You must believe me, Thomas Kelly, that we will not kill even to save a world. Even to save your world from itself."

"Keep away from her," Kelly grunted to the silent figures as they began to kneel beside Gisela. He stepped to her, steady enough, though the muscles in his thighs trembled as if with extreme fatigue.

The stranger across from him paused, looking up at the veteran with a bland face that almost certainly emanated from the medallion on the figure's chest. Kelly shouldered the other one aside. He could feel the give of bones and joints that were as inhuman as the corpse in the freezer back on Fort Meade.

"Alive, is she?" Kelly said as he, himself, knelt, and touched the woman's throat. The carotid pulse was as strong and steady as Kelly's own.

"Oh, boy," the veteran said. He rocked back on his haunches and exhaled the breath which he had not realized he was holding. Gisela's throat felt warm, not hot, and that reminded him that his own bare skin was chilled by the rain. The woman needed to be under shelter, or her final state would be the same as if the—hell, the aliens— had used .45's.

"Look—" Kelly began.

The two silent aliens knelt again, reaching for the woman,

and the radio's speaker said, "We will carry her within the office of her organization." The central alien pointed with his whole arm past the hedge and road to the two- and three-story building facing the walls.

"There is no one there now," the alien voice continued as the figure refolded his arm against his chest with a motion which was grossly wrong for what he appeared to be. "But she will be warm and dry and recover quickly."

Kelly frowned, but he stepped back to allow the other pair to lift Gisela. They were lighter than men and Kelly had assumed they were frail, but they handled the dancer's solid form as easily as two humans of the veteran's own build could have done.

"Another time," the alien voice said as his companions walked the woman through a gap in the hedge like men with a friend who had drunk herself insensible, "we would have held her as we hold others of her organization, so that they could not execute their Plan. But we did not hold enough of them. Now it is too late for prevention, Thomas Kelly, and the cure is something that we cannot do for you.

"We cannot kill, even to save a world."

Tom Kelly stretched his arms out stiffly behind him and bent forward, then back, from the waist. His head spun in slow circles when he lowered it, and the throb radiating from his groin picked up its tempo when the motion of his torso thrust his hips out. For all that, he felt better for the exercise; felt human at any rate, and that was an improvement over the way he'd felt since Gisela punched him in the balls.

Since he thought he saw her killed. No point in kidding himself about what the worst part of the shock had been.

Kelly stepped to the open door of the truck and picked up the radio, shielding it from the continuing drizzle with the flap of his coat.

"Somebody told you I was the right guy to contract out

killing to, did they?'' said Kelly. He was relieved enough
that she was alive and he was alive—and for Chrissake,
that somebody saw a way clear of a world disaster that was
real clear even without the details—that the implications
that he had just made overt didn't bother him the way they
usually did.

Not that it wasn't true. The Lord knew he'd painted his
reputation in the blood of more men than Doug and his
buddies . . . and women too, bombs weren't real fussy,
and he'd used bombs when they seemed the choice.

The two of them were alone now, Kelly and the alien
who talked. The other pair were jaywalking Gisela across
the boulevard; safer, perhaps, than it looked because the
traffic was crawling despite being bumper to bumper—but
he'd let 'em go ahead for lack of a better idea, and he
wasn't going to second-guess matters now. ''Do you have
a name?'' he demanded, wishing that it wasn't raining,
wishing a lot of things.

''Call me Wun, Mr. Kelly,'' said the alien through the
speaker beneath Kelly's coat, and the face smiled as a
fragment of headlight beam trolled across it. The 'skin'
surface reflected normally, even showing streaks of rain,
but Kelly knew from the corpse and the videotape that the
perceived features were wholly immaterial.

''One as in bir, digit?'' Kelly asked, translating the
word he understood into Turkish and raising a single index
finger.

''No, Mr. Kelly, more like the Spanish Juan,'' said the
other. ''But just Wun. Are you not comfortable here?'' He
raised his arm toward the sky. ''Should we go inside your
vehicle?''

Kelly chopped his hand like a blade in the direction of
the ancient walls. He didn't feel like putting himself in a
metal box, no, but the basalt ramparts were shelter of a
sort against both rain and the breeze. He wondered if

Mohammed Ayyubi had thought the same thing the night those stones had backstopped the bullets which killed him.

"Come on," he said aloud. "Dunno that I'm ever going to be comfortable, but we can get outa some of the rain."

"The Dienst has taken over your Fortress," Wun said as they walked together, man and not-man, toward walls that were a stone patchwork of more than a thousand years. "They think to rule the Earth, at least to their satisfaction, because they are invulnerable and have the power to destroy whatever targets they may choose."

No sign of bullet pocks on the hard stone, no certain sign in this light at any rate. The rubble and concrete foundations were Roman; the sections of large ashlars which sprawled across the fabric like birthmarks were probably Byzantine repairs; and the Turks, both Seljuk and Osmanli, had rebuilt the upper levels, perhaps many times, with squared stones of smaller and less regular size. The presence of the massive edifice gave Kelly a feeling of protection which he knew was specious, but anything to calm his subconscious was worthwhile so long as it let his intellect get on with what it needed to do.

"All right, then," the veteran said, focusing his mind by planting his right palm against the wet stone, "it's government level now and I'm tactical. So hell, it's in somebody else's court, and I don't know that Gisela and *her* buddies are much crazier than some of the folk who've had their fingers on the button officially."

"It *is* your business, Mr. Kelly," said Wun. His dark-coated body was almost invisible, close to the basalt and farther from the light flickering from the circumferential. Kelly thought the alien was shivering, however.

"Don't *tell* me my business," the American snapped. "Look, I walked into this, and if I'd been in time I'd've done something about it, sure. I don't need to be tasked before I'll blow my nose. But it's *gone*, fucked—and that's *not* my problem."

"The Soviets will not believe the space station has changed hands, Mr. Kelly," Wun said with inhumanly-precise enunciation. "They are convinced that the events of the past hours, including the nuclear destruction of the shuttle launching facilities at Luke and Kennedy Space Command bases, are all part of American policy. When the Dienst presses its demands on Russia by attacking major cities in addition to the space launching facilities which have already been destroyed, the Soviets will react against those they believe to be the true aggressors. Your world will survive the result, Mr. Kelly; but your civilization will not, and your race may not."

Kelly's mouth opened to repeat that there was nothing he could do about it. Before he spoke the words, he heard them in his mind, being spoken by everyone he'd heard say them in the past, every cowardly shit who wouldn't act and wouldn't let Tom Kelly act when something really had to be done.

"Christ," said the veteran, and he took a deep breath. "All right, what is it that I can do?"

"You must enter Fortress and destroy it," replied Wun as calmly as if he had not considered that Kelly might make any other answer. "We can bring you from orbit to the structure, but we cannot enter a solid object, and we will not help you further in a work of death."

"*Christ,* you're sweethearts!" Kelly said. "You oughta run for Congress, you'd fit right fuckin' in with the clean-hands crowd."

"We do not have to ask you to understand principles, Mr. Kelly," the alien said. "You have principles yourself. They differ from ours; and yours will permit you to save your world from consequences which could never occur to our race. We *will* not kill."

"Yeah, sorry," the American said, turning his eyes toward the stone, tracing the irregular courses upward till they blended with the sky and the rain washed the embarrassment from his face. They might be crazy, Wun and his buddies, but they were crazy in a better way than most anybody else Kelly knew. You had to draw lines, and no damn body else in the world had a right to complain about lines *you* drew and chose to live by.

" 'Fortress' isn't a public relations gag," he said aloud. "If those Nazis've really taken it over, then its going to be a bitch to get close without getting blown into dust clouds."

"We can get you to the satellite unnoticed, Thomas Kelly," said Wun. "We can do no more."

"Guess that oughta be enough," said Kelly, stretching his arms overhead and pulling the wet fingers of one hand against those of the other. He *had* to think that way; he'd have gone off in a shivering funk *years* ago if he hadn't believed at bottom that he could do any job he was willing to undertake.

The movement of Kelly's body worked the slick metal of the revolver against the base of his spine. "Why me?" he demanded flatly, fixing the alien with his eyes as firmly as he could in the half-light. Now that he'd made his decision, he had to have the background information that anyone with good sense would've demanded earlier.

"Because of the physical contact," the alien said. His hand mimed a face-rubbing gesture, and Kelly recalled the way he had touched the corpse of the alien that night on Fort Meade. He'd done that to prove to the Suits that he wasn't afraid—and to himself, that he could do whatever he had to do, even if he *was* scared shitless. . . .

"We could find you then, Mr. Kelly," Wun was saying, "and even before we found you, we could begin to speak to you, through your mind. You felt us, surely? We are not expert on your race's psychology. Though we have observed you for a century, it is only in the past three years, since you achieved stardrive, that we have been permitted to interact with you. We still have much to learn."

"Stardrive," the American repeated, filing the remainder of the statement to be considered at some other time.

Wun, space travel's something I'm paid to know about. We're still talking chemical rockets here, unless you mean the monocle ferry—and that's a low-orbit system, pure and simple."

"The researchers at Cambridge University who are responsible for the discovery," Wun replied, "still think they are working with time travel. We know better, however, and that is sufficient for those to whom we must report on the progress of our oversight. Without that, Mr. Kelly, we could not have attempted to immobilize the members of the Service; and I could not now be talking to you."

"Okay," said Kelly, pressing his hands firmly against his face, fingertips to forehead. The tight skin over his nose and cheekbones crinkled and lost some of the numbness that the tension and cool rain had brought. His coat was soaked across the back. "Okay. But you'll have to get me there, all the way. I doubt I can get outa Diyarbakir the way things are. There'd be too many people to convince. Christ, there's like as not a scratch order out on me right now. And my chances of even getting a message out, much less listened to, when I'm in West Bumfuck and there's been nukes going off in ConUS—zip, zed, zero."

He pointed toward the dark sky. "If you need me, Wun, you carry me all the way in your ship."

"Our ships are not on Earth. We cannot carry you to them as we are carried, because you—were not there already, Thomas Kelly," the alien said.

Wun *was* shivering, though his seeming face and bare hands were motionless. Wun's arms and torso quaked beneath the dark overcoat, however. "Whatever message you need to pass, we can pass for you—to anyone, anywhere. For now, you must move yourself on your own world and from it."

"You *did* leave a message on my tape," Kelly said "Told me you had to see me or like that. It wasn't in my head; I was really hearing it through the earphones?"

Wun nodded. "Yes," he said, "of course. We dared not leave a longer message for you then until you had seen us in person."

Kelly laughed. "You know," he said, "I was thinking there was no way you'd be able to get into the Tank . . . and maybe there isn't. But if you can punch my message through to the heart of the Pentagon, then it's going to save a whole lot of time. Because even if they don't believe me—which they won't, not after some of what's gone down lately—they'll damn well hop to meet whoever can play games that way with their codes.

"Come on," he added, striding back toward the truck. "You may not need this written out, but I need paper to compose it. There'll be a destination sheet and a clipboard in the pickup, and we'll just use the back of that."

The funny thing was, Kelly thought, that he felt pretty good. Oh, he'd been in better physical shape than he was now—but hell, he was functional, and that was a long sight better than he'd felt in the recent past. Hurt didn't matter; he'd been hurt before.

And he was in the middle of something that was either going to work or it wasn't—but it wouldn't fry its circuits just because the folks he depended on for support made a policy decision to do something else. He trusted Wun in a way that he had never trusted a human in a suit or an officer's uniform. Partly, that was crazy; and a gut reaction was, by definition, irrational.

But he *could* find reason to justify the way he felt. They'd come a very long way to lie to Tom Kelly, if they were lying, and what Wun had just told him about Fortress was exactly what the veteran had extrapolated from Gisela's words.

The aliens didn't have to be altruists—they could want

Earth for themselves, for any damn reason you cared to name. If they managed to save the place from a bunch of Nazis with H-bombs, then what else they wanted could be dealt with in its own good time.

And if Tom Kelly could do something to help with the problem, then it was about the first time in twenty years he'd been tasked to do something he really believed in.

It occurred to Kelly that he might simply get lost in the sprawling airbase.

Third TAF was one of the two combat divisions of the Turkish Air Force, and the bureaucracy at its Diyarbakir headquarters was both extensive and unfamiliar to the American. If all went well, someone in Washington would shortly be sending a message about Tom Kelly to someone in Diyarbakir Air Division. Whom the recipient was going to be, and through what combination of Turkish, NATO, and American channels the message would be delivered, were both questions at whose answer Kelly could not even guess; and that meant that he hadn't the faintest notion as to where on the base he ought to be waiting to be noticed when the time came.

The veteran smiled as he approached the main gate of the airbase again, visualizing the end of the world in nuclear cataclysm while Turks sped through the halls and grounds of the great airbase, too intent on what they understood were their own duties to pay any attention to the American screaming himself hoarse.

Like a lot of things, it didn't cost any more to laugh.

In the hours since Kelly had driven the borrowed pickup out the main gate, there had been some subtle changes. Instead of a squad on duty to check IDs, there was a platoon—and the earlier relaxed atmosphere was gone. A barrier of concertina wire on a tube-steel frame had been swung across the road, and behind it waited an open-topped Cadillac-Gage armored car with an airman ready at the pair of pintle-mounted machineguns.

The guards must have recognized the truck's markings, and a few of them probably recalled Kelly himself driving away in the vehicle. Whatever word was out regarding the world situation—nothing on local civilian radio, Kelly knew from sweeping the shortwave and AM band with his portable—it had sure convinced Third TAF to raise its state of readiness.

Three airmen and a lieutenant with automatic rifles were waiting outside the barrier. They ran to the truck from both sides as soon as Kelly stopped, and the way their guns pointed caused him to get out and remove his card case with slow, nonthreatening motions.

It made his decision as to where to wait relatively easy, however.

While two airmen peered at the—empty—bed of the pickup to make sure that it was not packed with explosives and acetylene tanks, Kelly handed his Turkish ID to the lieutenant.

"Sir," the American said in the officer's own language, "sometime in the next—I don't know, it might be a day"—it might be never, but there was no point in thinking that—"there are going to be orders sent regarding me. Then things will have to move very fast. For now, I think it's best that I remain here at the gate, outside if you prefer. But it is absolutely critical that the Officer of the Day and the head of base security both be informed immediately that I *am* here, and that I'll stay right here until sent for."

He paused, but before the Turk could frame a reply, Kelly added, "In addition to the name on this card, they may come looking for Thomas Kelly."

Elaine would very likely have been furious had she known Kelly was carrying his own North Carolina driver's license with him, but there were times you simply had to have real ID. The Lord only knew which of Kelly's various cover names the Pentagon would reference him under—assuming the message had gotten through—but at bottom, they would probably include the real name.

Kelly gave the driver's license to the officer; if it saved only five minutes in the course of the next twenty-four hours, then five minutes could be real important.

"One moment, please," the lieutenant said. His lips pursed and he frowned as he looked at the cards, practicing the unfamiliar names under his breath. Then he walked back to the regular guard post, stepping through the narrow gap left between the gate post and the barbed wire barricade.

"Any notion of what's going on?" Kelly said to the airmen, primarily to make conversation; people don't let their guns point at folks with whom they're holding a friendly conversation.

"It's a full alert, sir," one of the Turks responded. "They're fueling and arming everything that'll fly."

The lieutenant, watching Kelly through the glass of the guardpost, hung up the phone and barked an unheard order. Six airmen trotted past the officer as he strode toward Kelly. They grabbed crossbars extending from the concertina wire and began to drag the barricade to one side.

"You may come in, sir," the lieutenant said, a little less dourly hostile than he had seemed before. Perhaps he had just been afraid of being chewed out by his superiors for reporting something nonstandard. Now he handed back the two identification cards. "Your pass permits that, and for the rest—it will be as God wills. The Officer of the Day says he will report your presence to General Tergut, as you requested."

"Thank you, Lieutenant," the American said as he got back into the truck. The rain had stopped by the time he made it out of the walled city, but the vehicle's heater had not even begun to dry his soaked clothing. He sneezed as he put the pickup in gear, wondering whether after everything he had gone through he wasn't going to wind up a casualty from pneumonia. Inshallah—as God wills it.

That was about as good a philosophy for a soldier as any Kelly had heard. And right now, it might be as much as you could say for the world itself.

Kelly saw the lights at the same time the phone rang in the guard post beside which he was parked. There were two vehicles speeding toward the gate from the heart of the installation, both of them flashing blue lights and crying out the hearts of their European-style warning hooters. The road was asphalt-surfaced, but the vehicles raised plumes of surface dust to reflect the headlights of the follow-car and the rotating blue party hats of both.

It hadn't been a long wait, but Kelly found as he stepped out of the truck that his muscles had stiffened. The Turkish lieutenant ran to him, leaving his rifle behind this time. "Sir!" he shouted to Kelly, "they're sending a car for you!"

"Thank you, Lieutenant," the veteran said as he twisted some of the rigidity out of his torso. "I thought that"—he nodded toward the oncoming flashers—"might be me being paged."

Wun was on top of things for sure, Kelly thought as the vehicles—a van followed by a gun jeep, both of them blue and marked HP for Air Police—skidded to a halt with their hooters still blaring.

Of course, it was just conceivable that this was a result of the shootings in Istanbul and hadn't a damn thing to do with Fortress.

Kelly jogged to the passenger side of the van even before the doors unlatched. There was an empty seat in the jeep, but he had no intention of being carried any distance in it if there were an alternative. A short wheelbase and four-wheel independent suspension made jeeps marvelously handy; but that also made them flip and kill hell outa everybody on board when the driver turned sharply at speed. There was nothing about the way the Hava Polis driver had approached the guard post to make Kelly trust his judgment.

The man who jumped from the van was heavyset and wore a US Air Force uniform with rosettes on the epaulets. In the colored light of the flashers, Kelly could not be certain whether the rank insignia were the gold of a major or a lieutenant-colonel's silver.

"Thomas Kelly?" the Air Force Officer shouted through the chest-cramping racket of the hooters. He thumbed toward the doors at the back of the van being opened by a Turkish airman. "Hop in, we've got a flight for you to Incirlik."

"*Colonel* Kelly," said the veteran. "And *you* can ride in back if you need to come along, Major Snipes." The name tag over the officer's pocket was clearly visible, and he obeyed Kelly without objection.

"Yes?" said the Turkish driver when Kelly slid in beside him. The back door banged and latched.

"Take me where we're going," Kelly replied in Turkish, giving the airman a lopsided smile.

Grinning back, the Turk hauled the van around in a tight, accelerating turn that must have spilled the occupants of the side benches in the back onto the floor and into one another's arms. Kelly, bracing his right palm against the dashboard, smiled broadly.

To the veteran's surprise, the two-vehicle entourage did not halt at one of the administration buildings. Instead they sped along access roads to the flight line, passing fuel tankers and firefighting vehicles. Men bustled over each of the aircraft in open-topped revetments which would be of limited protection against parafrags or cluster bombs sown by low-flying attackers.

Or, of course, the nukes that Nazis in orbit could unload here in the event they decided it was a good idea.

But that made him think about Gisela, and the blond dancer was one of the last things Tom Kelly wanted on his mind right now.

The van's right brakes grabbed as the driver stepped on them hard, making the vehicle shimmy against the simultaneous twist on the steering wheel to swing them into a revetment. There was already a car there, a Plymouth, and the men waiting included some in Turkish and American dress uniforms besides those in coveralls servicing a razor-winged TF-104G.

"This one's Kelly!" called Major Snipes, throwing open the back of the van before Kelly himself was sure that they had come to a final stop.

He opened his own door and got out. Two Turkish airmen, followed by a captain, ran up to him with a helmet and a pressure suit, the latter looking too large by half. "Who gave us the size?" the captain demanded. "Come on, we'll take him back and outfit him properly."

"Wait a minute," an American bird colonel said as he grabbed Major Snipes by the coat sleeve, "how do we *know* this is the right guy?"

"Look I'll pull it on over my clothes," said Kelly, taking the suit from the now-hesitant airman. "So long as the helmet's not too small, we're golden."

"Well, he had ID—"

"No, the suit's no good if it doesn't fit," insisted the Turkish captain.

"*Any* body could have ID—"

"What the *fuck* do you expect me to do, Colonel?" Kelly roared as he thrust his right leg into the pressure suit, rotating a half step on the other foot to forestall the captain, who seemed willing to snatch the garment away from him. "Sit around for a fingerprint check? How the hell would I know to pretend to be me if I wasn't?"

"He is not the man you wish?" asked a Turk with a huge moustache and what Kelly thought were general's insignia. His English was labored rather than hesitant, suggestive of bricklaying with words.

"Robbie," said Snipes to the colonel, "it's all copacetic. The fat's in the fire now, and the last thing we need is for a review board to decide it was all the fault of US liaison at Diyarbakir."

"Colonel," Kelly put in more calmly as he checked for torso fasteners, "I'm the man they're looking for. It's not the usual sort of deal"—he tried on the helmet which, for a wonder, fitted perfectly—"but it's the deal we've been handed this time."

He started walking toward the plane that had obviously been readied for him, hopeful that the colonel wouldn't decide to shoot him in the back. Sometimes Kelly found it useful to remember that during the disasters of Ishandhlwana and of Pearl Harbor, armorers had refused to issue ammunition to the troops because the proper chits had not been signed. The military collected a lot of people to whom order was more important than anything else on Earth. Trouble was, the times you really *needed* the military, the only thing you could bank on was disorder.

No bullets. No shouts, in fact, though squabbling in Turkish and English continued behind him as he strode away.

The TF-104G was a thing of beauty, the two-seat conversion trainer modification of the aircraft which had seduced the top fighter jocks of the fifties and sixties and had killed literally hundreds of their less-skilled brethren. The F-104 was fast, quick, and maneuverable. It also had the glide angle of a brick and offered its crew no desirable options when the single J-79 turbojet failed on takeoff.

But this was also a situation in which a fast ride was preferable to a safe one. For that matter, the Turks—one of the last major users of the F-104 in several variants—

hadn't had nearly the problem with crashes that others, particularly the Luftwaffe, had experienced. West German maintenance was notoriously slipshod, and the F-104 simply didn't tolerate mistakes.

That wasn't an attitude Kelly could object to, even in a piece of hardware; and anyway, like he'd told the colonel behind him, it was the deal he'd been handed this time.

Turkish ground crewmen helped Kelly up the narrow steps to the rear seat in the cockpit. They grinned and gestured to point out the warning arrows setting off the jet intake. The rushing whine of air to the turbine would have overwhelmed human speech.

Kelly dumped himself into the seat behind the pilot. He flew enough that he sometimes thought he'd spent five years of his life in airplanes; but he was strictly a passenger, with neither knowledge nor interest in the sort of thing that happened in the cockpit. That included, he began to realize, matters like where to put his feet, and how to buckle himself into the ejection seat, which he supposed included a parachute.

The pilot—Turkish or American?—didn't care any more about Kelly's problems than Kelly would have had their positions been reversed. As soon as the passenger dropped into the cockpit, the TF-104G's brakes released with a jerk and the aircraft slid out of its revetment on the narrow undercarriage splaying from its fuselage. The wings were too thin to conceal a tire.

The cockpit canopy closed smoothly, bringing blessed relief from the howl of the jet being reflected from the berm. Kelly found the oxygen mask and fitted it while the right brake and the delicate, steerable nosewheel aligned the aircraft with the runway. There had been a minimum of rollout; this was a combat installation, not a commercial operation handcuffed by the need to serve thousands of passengers.

There was probably a connection for the radio leads

dangling from his helmet, the veteran thought while the turbojet shrieked and shuddered as the pilot wound it out. Then acceleration punched him back into a seat which seemed remarkably uncomfortable.

The hell with the radio, Kelly thought as the needle nose lifted and the Earth fell away so sharply that he had nothing with which to compare the sight.

It occurred to him, however, that this was only a foretaste of what awaited him in El Paso if things worked out the way he had planned.

He also found himself thinking that the F-104, even at its worst, had never approached the hundred-percent failure rate that the monocle ferry held to date.

Knowing that he was still in Turkey, Kelly could have told from the air that they were over Incirlik Airbase by the planes deployed on the ground: C-141 Starlifters and a flight of F-15's. Incirlik had no home squadron of its own, but it was American-staffed and trained, in rotation, all the US tactical wings based in Europe. Turkey herself could afford neither the big cargo aircraft nor state-of-the-art fighters like the F-15. Despite that, the performance of Kelly's pilot and his aging F-104, without notice and on a nontasked mission, suggested that the Turkish Air Force would hold up its end just fine if it came to a crunch.

They touched down firmly, jarring off knots, and the thump and shock that lifted their nose again startled Kelly until he realized that a drag chute was deploying behind them. The F-104 slowed abruptly. Presumably in response to instructions from the tower, the pilot braked to a near stop and turned onto a taxiway.

As the cockpit canopies began to rise again, the veteran looked to the side and saw that a car was driving parallel with them, a midsize American station wagon. Well, he couldn't complain that he wasn't getting the full treatment. Not red carpet, of course, but he didn't *want* red carpet, he wanted functional. If they decided to parachute him out over Fort Bliss instead of landing, he couldn't rightly complain.

Though as long as it'd been since he last jumped, he'd probably wind up cratering the mesquite.

The TF-104 halted in the middle of the taxiway. An American, carefully donning his saucer hat as he stepped out of the back door of the car, waved to Kelly and shouted something not quite audible. The man's upturned face looked anxious in the aircraft's clearance lights.

Kelly started to get out and was pulled up short by the feed of his oxygen mask. He unhooked it and swung himself out of the cockpit. He felt as if someone had conducted a search and destroy mission in his sinuses. He could not find the last of the miniature toeholds in the aircraft's polished skin. Grimacing, the veteran let himself drop. The officer who had just gotten out of the car gave a squawk when Kelly sprawled at his feet, but there was no harm done.

"Mr. Kelly," said the officer, gripping the veteran by both forearms and lifting, "we have a flight waiting for you. They've just been cleared."

Kelly wasn't in any shape to object to the manhandling. He ended it the quickest, simplest way by entering the car as if it were a burrow and he a fox going to ground. The greeting officer, another captain, hesitated a moment before he ran around to the far door. The driver, watching them in the mirror, had the car rolling even before the door closed.

"Where am I cleared to this time?" Kelly asked, enunciating carefully. He straightened himself in the seat as precisely as if he were a diplomat arriving at a major conference. He wasn't so wrecked that he couldn't act for a few minutes like the VIP these people had been led to expect. He didn't know of any reason why he *had* to put

on a front, but it was cheaper to do so than to learn later
that he should have.

"Sir, I really don't have that information," the captain
replied. "From, ah—from rumor, I'm not sure that the
flight crew does. This flight was originally headed for
Rome, but that's maybe been changed along with the—the
cargo."

They were speeding toward one of the C-141's, whose
white-painted upper surfaces drew a palette of colors from
the rising sun and made the gray lower curves almost
disappear. The wings, mounted high so that the main spar
did not cut the cabin in half, now drooped under the
weight of four big turbofans, but in flight they would flex
upward as they lifted the huge mass of the aircraft and
cargo.

Kelly was thoroughly familiar with C-141's, the logistics
workhorse of the Lebanon Involvement. They were aluminum cylinders which hauled cargo very well and very
efficiently, so this one was of particular interest to him
only because he was apparently making the next stage of
his journey on it.

The scene on the pad was a great deal more unusual.

Separated from the aircraft by thirty yards and what
looked like a platoon of Air Police was a huge clot of
civilians, women and children. The driver had to swing
wide around them in order to approach the plane's lowered
tail ramp. As he did so, a number of civilians darted from
the larger group and blocked the vehicle's path.

The driver swore softly and slammed the transmission
into reverse.

A woman struggled up to Kelly's window. Her rage-
distorted face might have been cute under other circumstances, and the amazing puffiness of her torso was surely
because she was wearing at least six outfits on top of one
another. A child of perhaps three, similarly overdressed,
tugged at the tail of the long cloth coat on top; and because

she held an infant in her left arm, she had to drop her
suitcase in order to hammer on the window while she
screamed, "You bastard! You've got to let Dawn and
Jeffie aboard! What kind of—"

An airman wearing a helmet instead of a cap caught the
woman from behind by wrist and shoulder, dragging her
back as the car reversed in a quick arc. More grim-faced
police spread themselves in a loose barricade against the
would-be refugees while the driver accelerated toward the
ramp.

"My god," said the captain, "I've never seen anything
like that."

"Goddam," said Kelly, trying to mop his forehead and
finding that he still wore the flight helmet.

There were no additional officers waiting for Kelly at
the ramp of the C-141. The captain who had greeted him
at the TF-104 now shepherded him onto the ramp alone.
"Good luck, sir," he said, and offered his hand.

Offhand, Kelly couldn't remember anybody saying that—
and sounding like he meant it—since this business began.

"I appreciate that," the veteran said as they shook
hands. "And—folks pretty high up"—which described
the aliens as well as anything could—"tell me it'll all be
fine if I do my job. Which I do."

"Door's lifting," said the loadmaster at the cargo bay's
rear control panel, but his hand did not actually hit the
lifter switch until the captain had sprung back down the
ramp. As the ramp started to rise, the loadmaster called a
terse report on his commo helmet, glanced at Kelly, and
then looked down the nearly empty cargo bay.

The benches were folded down and locked in place
along both windowless sides of the fuselage. During the
Starlifter's usual 'passenger' operation as a troop transport,
the broad central aisleway would have been loaded with
munitions and heavy equipment. It was empty now. Be-

neath one of the benches, however, was a child's suitcase of pink vinyl.

The loadmaster strode over to the piece of miniature luggage, jerked it from its partial concealment, and hurled it underhand toward the tail. The suitcase bounced from the ramp and out the narrowing gap to the concrete.

The C-141 was already moving, rotating outward in a manner disconcerting because nothing outside the cargo bay was visible. Kelly took off the helmet; he would not need it on this flight. The curving sides and roofline gave him the feeling of being trapped in a subway tunnel which echoed to the roar of an oncoming train.

"Well, that kid'll need it more'n we will, won't she?" the loadmaster demanded loudly as he walked over to the veteran. He was a burly man, unaffected by the motion of the aircraft through long familiarity.

"Got a problem, friend?" asked Kelly as he sat down on the bench. If anything *did* start, the bulkhead anchoring him would be better than a fair trade-off for the height advantage that he surrendered.

"You really rate, doncha?" the crewman continued. "Had 'em all aboard, over two hundred dependents. Another three minutes and we'd have been wheels-up for Rome. Then, bingo! Off-load everybody and prepare to take on a special passenger. Not, 'a special passenger *and* the dependents.' Oh, no. And the ones who don't *move* quick enough, there's nightsticks to move 'em along. So my wife and kids are out there on the fuckin' *pad*, and you've got the plane to yourself, buddy."

"Think Rome's going to be a great place if they nuke it?" Kelly asked in a tone of cool curiosity. His right hand gripped the strap of the helmet, ready to use it as a club if things worked out that way.

"I'd be with them, at least," the loadmaster said harshly.

"There's people who think if I get back to the World quick enough, there won't be any more nukes," Kelly snapped in a voice that could have been heard over gun-fire. He stood, dropping the helmet because it wasn't going to be needed. "Who the *fuck* do you think I am, Sergeant? Some politician running home from a junket? Don't you *want* this shit to stop?"

The loadmaster blinked and backed a step. "Oh," he said. "Ah . . ."

"Christ, I'm sorry, buddy," Kelly said, looking down as if he were embarrassed. "Look, I'm really tight. I left some people behind too, and—" He raised his eyes and met the crewman's in false candor. "—Wasn't a great place, you know? Even if this other crap quiets down."

"Ah. . . ." said the crewman. "Aw, hell, we're all jumpy. You know how it is." He tried out a rather careful smile. "Want to go forward before we lift?"

"Lemme strip this suit off," the veteran answered with an equally abashed smile, textured for the use. "After we get the wheels up, I'll go say 'hi' . . . but this is the part of the plane I'm used to."

He grinned, this time genuinely—not that the difference was noticeable. "Only thing is, it's a *lot* bigger'n the ones I've had to jump out."

"You bet your ass," the crewman agreed proudly, then reported on his commo helmet as he settled himself in a seat by the tail ramp.

The flight was uneventful. It would have seemed un-eventful even if Kelly had not spent much of the air time asleep. The crew had a job to do, and they were cruising at twenty knots above normal speed; even with the agreed need for haste, there was no reasonable way to wring more out of a big bird optimized to move cargo.

The cockpit windows showed the clouds below or, through the clouds, the Mediterranean. The wall of gauges and displays in front of each flight engineer had more potential interest, at least—the possibility that boards would suddenly glow red and the sea would take on a reality beyond that of a backdrop for the hole the C-141 was punching through the sky.

But sleep was useful, once the demands of socializing had been met. The new routing was to Torrejeon, just outside Madrid. That could change at any moment; since this Starlifter was a B model with air refueling capability in addition to a lengthened fuselage, their final touchdown could be El Paso—if the Powers That Be decided.

Kelly dreamed of Fortress, but not as he had seen it in photographs and artists' renderings. Now there was a trio of saucers tethered near the docking area. Their design prevented them from using the airlocks in normal fashion, but a saucer was still connected to Fortress by a thick umbilicus configured at its nether end to mate with the station in the same manner as the nose of a Space Command transporter.

Fortress showed no sign of the struggle in which it had been captured. The outer doughnut of raw bauxite and ilmenite from the Moon, the same material that was refined and extruded in the solar furnaces with which Fortress built itself, was beginning to weather into greater uniformity under the impact of micrometeorites and hard radiation. It was not scarred by anything more major, the high-explosive or even nuclear warheads against which it gave reasonable protection.

The close-in defense arrays visible from the north pole of the space station were empty, the spidery launching frames catching sunlight and shadowing one another at unexpected angles. Two of the launchers were missing, sheared down to their bases when their rockets gang-fired.

The space station itself was a dumbbell rotating within the hoop of shielding material. Each lobe of the station was a short length of cylinder connected by a spoke to the spherical hub. Now the dream-viewpoint shifted, angling across the center of the doughnut toward the windows, through which mirrors deflected sunlight into the living quarters of Fortress. Polished slats repeatedly re-reflected light while filtering the radiation which would otherwise have entered through the windows as well.

As Kelly's mind watched, the trailing end of one of the lobes flew outward in slow motion. The aluminum panels twisted under stress but kept their general shape and even clung in part to the girders on which they had been hung. Glass-honeycomb insulation disintegrated, providing a spinning cloud which mimicked the bloom of white-hot gases to be expected from a normal explosion.

The real blast had been only a small one—strip charges laid along the inner frame of the panel. The difference in pressure between hard vacuum and the part of the space station which had just been opened to that vacuum was sufficient to void most of the chamber's contents, however. Flimsy furniture, sheets of paper, and over a hundred living men spewed into space along with the metal and shredded glass.

Some of the men flapped their arms vigorously, as if they were trying to swim to the hub or the brightly-sunlit saucers docked there. In the event, when a few of them did collide with bracing wires, they spun slowly away; they had lost the ability to comprehend what might seem a hope of safety, though they still were not legally dead.

The viewpoint narrowed on the opened chamber itself, though with none of the mechanical feeling of a camera being dollied. When a gun fires, some residues of the reaction remain aswirl in the breech. Similarly, there was a single human figure still drifting in the chamber from which his fellows had been voided. At one point he had been trying to grasp the screw latch of the airlock to one of the adjoining compartments. His grip had lost definition, though it had not wholly relaxed, and now he floated with his fingers hooked into vain claws.

The victim had been a stocky man of medium height.

His beard, moustache, and white tunic had been sprayed a brilliant red with blood when air within his body cavity expanded to ram his empty lungs out his mouth and nostrils. Kelly did not recognize the rank insignia on the tunic sleeves, but the SS runes on the collar were unmistakable.

Kelly knew the victim, and that knowledge was not the false assurance of a dream. He could not recall the fellow's full name, but he was known as ben Majlis, and he had been leader of a squad of Kurds while Operation Birdlike was up and running.

The body twitched harshly, mindlessly, not quite close enough to a bulkhead or the floor for the movement to thrust against something solid. The corneas of ben Majlis's eyes were red with ruptured capillaries, and ice crystals were already beginning to glitter on them.

One of the hands flopped toward Kelly's point of view, driven by the Kurd's dying convulsions. As it did so, something touched the veteran's shoulder in good truth. He leaped up with a cry and a look of horror that drove back the loadmaster who had just awakened Kelly to tell him that the C-141 was making its final approach to Torrejeon.

The Starlifter's crew greased her in, the instant of touchdown unnoticed until the thrust reversers on the big turbofans grabbed hold of the air and tried to pull the aircraft backwards. Skill in a fighter meant quickness; skill in a transport was a matter of being smooth, and sliding a hundred and some tons onto a concrete slab without evident shock was skill indeed.

"What's the drill from here?" Kelly asked the loadmaster, who now had his helmet's long cord plugged into a console near one of the forward doors. Neither of the men in the echoing cargo bay could see anything save the aluminum walls around them, but the crewman was in touch with the flight deck through his intercom.

The loadmaster spoke an acknowledgment into the straw-slim microphone wand and stepped closer to Kelly in order to explain without shouting, "We're going to taxi to N-2. There's a bird waiting there for you already."

He paused, then touched the intercom key of his helmet to say, "Gotcha." To Kelly he then went on, smiling, "Seems like you're stepping up in the world, Colonel Kelly."

"It used to be 'sergent,' and right now it's 'civilian'— whatever I tell people that have more use'n I do for brass," the veteran said with a smile of his own. "I gonna need the flight suit?" He had surprisingly little stiffness or specific pain from the battering he'd taken in the past few days, but he found when he shrugged that his whole body felt as if there were an inch of fuzz growing on it.

"On an Airborne Command Post?" the loadmaster said. "Nossir, I don't guess you will."

The big crewman paused again, this time in response to memory rather than a voice in his earphones. "Look sir, you were serious about putting a lid on this? Word is . . . word is, they've already pooped a nuke. If they did . . ."

"Thing is"—Kelly frowned as he chose words that could explain things simply—and hopefully—" 'they' aren't the Reds, not yet. They're a bunch of terrorists. And I can't do a damn thing for what's gone down already; but yeah, I can put a lid on it."

He grinned a shark's grin. The loadmaster remembered the fight he had tried to pick when his passenger came aboard. "I can put some people," Kelly said, "where they won't be a problem till Judgment Day."

One of the three men waiting in civilian clothes atop the truck-mounted boarding steps was General Redstone. That was good because the other two had the look and the size of folks who'd be sent to take Kelly out of play.

If they'd wanted to do that, of course—especially after

what had happened at the landing site near Istanbul—there were going to be more than two guys sent.

"Christ, that's *beautiful*," Kelly blurted as he stepped from the Starlifter onto the landing of the boarding stairs.

"Hang on," directed Redstone, and the two—call them attendants—each grabbed Kelly firmly with one hand while anchoring themselves to the railing with the other. "Somebody thought this'd—"

The truck backed away from the C-141 in an arc, then braked sharply enough that Kelly gripped one of the attendants and the closest portion of the railing himself. The big men's touch had shocked him, but they had not tried to immobilize his hands. The truck accelerated forward, toward the open hatch of the plane that had drawn Kelly's exclamation.

The aircraft was a Boeing 747 which had few external modifications beyond the slight excrescence on the nose for accepting a refueling drogue, and the radome which recapitulated in miniature the bulge of the flight deck on which it rested.

Kelly's vision of the Strategic Air Command had been molded by the tired B-52D's which had flown to Lebanon out of Akrotiri, painted in camouflage colors and carrying tens of tons of high-explosive bombs under the wings. But an Airborne Command Post was as close to being a showpiece as SAC had available; and in these days, when budget cutters reasonably suggested the nuclear strike mission be left wholly to Space Command and Fortress, the manned-bomber boys weren't going to miss any opportunity for show.

The big aircraft was painted dazzling white, with a blue accent stripe down the line of windows from nose to tail. Above the stripe, in Times Roman letters that must have been five feet high, were the words *United States of America*. The forward entrance hatch was swung inward, awaiting the motorized boarding stairs.

"Geez," Kelly muttered, "do they paint 'em like that to make 'em easier to target on?"

"Maybe somebody told 'em white'd make the damn thing more survivable in a near nuke," responded Redstone with a grimace of his own. Red hadn't been the smartest fellow Kelly had met in the service, but his instincts were good and he'd been willing to go to the wall for his men. How he'd made general was a wonder and a half. "Of course," Redstone continued, "that flag on the tail's going to burn seven red stripes right through the control surfaces."

"Purty, though," Kelly observed. He was squinting. Twenty miles an hour seemed plenty fast enough when you hung onto a railing fifteen feet in the air.

Grit was blowing across the field, along with fumes from the big turbofans of the aircraft they approached. The odor left no question but that the bird was burning JP-4 rather than kerosene-based JP-1. The gasoline propellant could be expected both to significantly increase speed and range, and to turn the aircraft into a huge bomb if it had to make a belly landing.

Well, Kelly's taste had always been for performance over survivability. His plans for Fortress didn't strike him as particularly survivable, even if everything worked up to specs.

The truck slowed. An attendant in the doorway of the 747 was talking the driver in. A flat-topped yellow fuel tanker pulled away from the other side of the aircraft which it had been topping off. Kelly wondered how long the Airborne Command Post had been idling here, ready to take off as soon as the Starlifter from Incirlik landed its cargo.

"Something you might keep in mind, Kelly," said General Redstone as the truck began to nestle the stairs' padded bumpers against the 747, "is that a lot of 'em don't like you, and I don't guess anybody believes *everything* you put in that cable—me included. But nobody knows what the fuck's going on, either. If you keep your temper—that's *always* been the problem, Kelly—and you keep saying what you say you know . . . then I guess you might get what you say you want.''

The boarding stairs butted gently against the aircraft. Kelly rocked slightly and the two attendants released him. '' 'I say,' '' he quoted with a grin. '' 'I *say*.' You know me, Red. I say what I mean.'' He took the precedence the general offered with a hand and strode aboard the Airborne Command Post.

"This way, please," said a female attendant whose dark skirt and blazer looked like a uniform, though they had no insignia—military or civilian. Kelly followed her, keeping the figure centered in a hallway which seemed extremely dim after the sunblasted concrete of the Spanish airport outside. The corridor was enclosed by bulkheads to either side, so that none of the light from the extensive windows reached it.

There was a muted sound from the outer hatch as it closed and sealed behind them, and all the noises external to the aircraft disappeared.

Offhand, Kelly couldn't think of any group of people with whom he less cared to share a miniature universe than the ones he expected to see in a moment.

"They're here," said the female attendant to the pair of men outside the first open door to the right. The guards could have passed for brothers to those who had received Kelly on the boarding stairs and who now tramped down the hall behind him. The aircraft was already beginning to trundle forward.

One of the guards turned his head into the room and murmured something. The other shifted his body slightly to block the doorway, but he focused his eyes well above Kelly's head so that the action did not become an overt challenge.

"Yes, of course!" snapped a male voice from within,

and the guards sprang aside with the suddenness of the
Symplegades parting to trap another ship. Kelly gave the
one who had blocked him a wry smile as he passed.
Working for folks who got off by jumping on the hired
help wasn't his idea of a real good time. By now, at least,
they must realize that Tom Kelly wasn't part of the hired
help.

The plaque of layered plastic on the door said Briefing
Room, and within were thirty upholstered seats facing aft
in an arc toward an offset lectern. "*Good* morning,
Pierrard," the veteran said to the miasma of pipe smoke
which was identifiable before the man himself was, one of
a score of faces turned to watch over their shoulders and
seatbacks as the newcomers arrived.

"Sit down and strap in, Kelly," directed the white-
haired man in the second of the five rows of seats. "We're
about to take off." He pointed to the trio of jump seats
now folded against the bulkhead behind the lectern.

Kelly slid into the empty seat nearest the door instead.
The upholstery and carpet were royal blue, a shade that
reminded the veteran of Congressman Bianci's office. For
a moment he felt—not homesick, but nonetheless nostal-
gic; he didn't really belong in that world, but it had been a
good place to be.

Redstone, whose seat the agent had probably taken,
grimaced and found another one by stepping over a naval
officer with enough stripes on his sleeves to be at least a
captain. "It's no sweat, Red," Kelly called over the rumble of the four turbofans booting the 747 down the runway
on full enriched thrust. "I'm cool, I just like these chairs
better."

Everyone waited until the pilot had lifted them without
wasting time, though with nothing like the abrupt intent of
the Starfighter at Diyarbakir some hours before. It was still
a big enough world that traveling across it took finite
blocks of time. Within the atmosphere, at any rate; the

orbital period of Fortress was ninety-five minutes, plus or
minus a few depending on how recently the engines had
been fired to correct for atmospheric friction.

That was the maximum amount of time before any
particular point on Earth became a potential target for a
thermonuclear warhead on an unstoppable trajectory.

After less than two minutes, despite what it felt like to
all those in the briefing room, the big aircraft's upward
lunge reached the point at which cabin attendants on commercial flights would have begun their spiel about compli-
mentary beverages. Kelly turned his eyes from the windows,
past which rags of low cloud were tearing, and took a deep
breath. He might or might not switch planes again. Either
way, this room and these men—they were all men—were
the last stage of the preliminaries.

"Will somebody tell him to get up there where he
belongs?" demanded someone in a peevish voice.

"Bates," said Pierrard in a voice whose volume and
clarity suggested the anger behind it, "we'll proceed more
smoothly if only those with business choose to speak."

The room paused. Kelly nodded approvingly to the
white-haired man, who then continued into the silence he
had wrought. "How *did* you manage to insert your report
that way, Mr. Kelly?"

The veteran laughed. Everyone else in the room was
twisted in the bolted-down chairs to see him, save for
those in the last row—behind him—who had a direct view
of the back of his head. He would've gone to the lectern as
directed except that he *had* been directed; and besides, it
would feel a little too much like being a duck in a shooting
gallery.

"Oh, that wasn't me," Kelly said, looking down. "NSA's
good, but we're not *that* good. That was the aliens you
sent me to find." It had been disconcertingly natural for
him to verbally put on a uniform again the way he just
had.

There was a ripple of talk, more of it directed at neighbors than at the veteran. Pierrard was giving himself time by lifting his pipe to his lips, though smoke continued to trickle from the bowl in indication that he was not drawing on it.

Kelly rose, resting his buttocks on the seat back and curling his right foot directly beneath his hip to lock him there. "Look," he repeated, "I *couldn't* have gotten through any way I know about, not from Diyarbakir, not if I were the *President*."

The veteran's eyes were adjusting to the light and his mind was locking down into the gears suitable for the present situation. He nodded to a man he recognized from the office of the National Security Advisor—not the Advisor himself, a political opportunist whose pronouncements always sounded as though he were still a Marine battalion commander.

"Anyway," Kelly continued, finding that his new perch was less stable than he had thought—the 747 was still climbing—"the important thing is dealing with the situation. I can do that with a little cooperation. A lot less cooperation than it took to put all you people together in one room, believe me."

Kelly's mind was cataloguing the faces turned awkwardly over their seats toward him, and he found that he recognized a surprising number of them from his years on Capitol Hill. They were not the men who discussed crises on-camera. They—like Kelly—were the ones who did the groundwork, or the dirty work, required to solve the real problems.

"What *is* the situation, in your view, Mr. Kelly?" asked a Space Command colonel named Stoddard. Kelly had been on a 'Tom and Jim' basis with him for over a year, ever since Stoddard became the Command's liaison—lobbyist—with Congress. Kelly couldn't blame him for not making a big thing about their association just now, when the veteran's status was at best in doubt.

"A small group of Nazis," Kelly said, projecting his voice and his gaze at the men around him with consciousness of the power which knowledge gave him, "and I don't mean Neo-Nazis; these're the real thing, holdouts and their kids. Anyway, they've taken over Fortress, using trained Kurds as shock troops. I assume all the station personnel are dead. I *know* the Kurds have been eliminated now that their job's done, so there's no possibility of outsiders within Fortress being turned, even if you had a way to contact them."

He paused, but added through the first syllables of response, "*I'm* your way to contact Fortress, and I've told you how."

"We don't know they're actually Germans because they say they are," said the shorthaired, red-faced man, whom Kelly now recognized as Bates. "Maybe they're Russkies, maybe they're these aliens you claim you're right about."

"Maybe if you had a brain in your *head*, Bates," Kelly snapped, "you'd have some business here." Almost in the same breath, he said, bending toward General Redstone, "I'm sorry, Red, I didn't mean to do that. S'okay now."

"Bates, for *god's* sake, keep your mouth shut," Pierrard said angrily. He followed it with a spasm of coughing from which spurted pipe smoke that he had not exhaled properly before speaking.

"Yeah, they're for real, the Nazis," Kelly said quietly, making amends for his outburst. "They call 'emselves the Service, the Dienst, and I guess everybody here's data bank's got a megabyte of background on 'em."

He smiled and shook his head ruefully. "You know, they'd be just as harmless as they look, except they got outa Germany in '45 with a flying saucer"—he spread his hands toward his audience, recognizing the incredulity they must be feeling—''and engineers to build more of the damn things.''

''I suggest,'' said Pierrard, touching the wave of his white hair with the fingers of his left hand, ''that for the present we ignore the question of responsibility and move on to a discussion of Mr. Kelly's proposal for action.''

One of the men Kelly remembered from the orderly room at Fort Meade slipped out of the Briefing Room in response to a signal the veteran had not seen Pierrard give. Checking on the Dienst, no doubt, through the Airborne Command Post's shielded data links with every computer bank in the federal government. The question the old man said he would ignore was obviously one that had already been answered to his satisfaction.

Pierrard was a bastard, but Kelly had never assumed he was a stupid bastard. The fact that the veteran had been met by this particular aircraft and the men aboard it suggested more clearly than Redstone had that a sufficient 'they' were willing to go along with, if not trust, Tom Kelly.

''I was told,'' Kelly said carefully, ''that the ferry pads on both coasts, and the Russian equivalent at Tyuratam, have all been nuked.''

''*Who* told you?'' demanded a man who'd been a GS-16 in Defense when Kelly last talked with him. ''*No* information on that subject has been released.''

''They'd know at Pirinclik!'' someone else suggested excitedly. ''Has he been allowed into the compound at Pirinclik?''

''*Look,*'' Kelly shouted, exasperated by men who were stuck with their own functional areas instead of focusing their minds on the real problem. ''It was the fucking aliens, I *told* you, the little guys like the one in the freezer at Meade—and it doesn't *matter*. All it means is, unless you've got another way to lift me to orbit, I go up on the monocle ferry at Bliss. You got a better way, let's hear it, because I'm just counting on enough of the bugs to be worked out that it does like it's supposed to one time.''

"Yes, well," said Pierrard, meeting the veteran's eyes while his right hand played with his meerschaum pipe, "there's also the question of who goes up in the ferry if we do choose that option. There are—''

"That's not a question," said Kelly. "I go."

"There are younger men with better training both in—'' Pierrard began.

"God *damn* it," said the veteran, stepping forward from his perch and leaning toward Pierrard across the intervening seats and startled men. "Just one time in my life there's going to be something I did that I point to and say *I* did it; good, bad or indifferent. You *chose* me. I'm *going!*''

"We didn't choose you for this, Kelly," said General Redstone, the only man in the room willing to argue calmly in the face of the veteran's obvious fury.

Kelly took a deep breath. "Sure you did, Red," he replied in a husky, low-pitched voice as he rubbed his eyes and forehead with both hands. "Sure you did, even if you didn't know it just then."

"I—'' Pierrard said as the stocky agent paused.

"Look," Kelly continued, loudly enough to interrupt but without the anger of a moment before. "Used to be something'd come up and I'd be told, 'Right, but that's not in your area any more. It's in the hands of the people who take care of that.' This is what you made my area, folks.'' He looked grimly around the room. "This is what I've done for you for twenty years. Killing people.''

"Not for *me*, buddy," someone unseen rumbled.

Kelly turned in that direction and smiled. No one else spoke for several seconds.

"The aliens won't take orders from you, Mr. Kelly," said Pierrard, using the word *aliens* with none of the incredulous hesitancy that had plagued others when they found they had no alternative.

"Won't they, Pierrard?" replied Kelly, continuing to smile as he reached overhead and stretched his legs up on tiptoes besides. His fingers couldn't touch the ceiling. This was a hell of a big plane, and as steady as a train through the skies besides. "How do you know? You can't even speak with them."

"Do you—" someone began.

"One moment," snapped Pierrard, his eyes meeting Kelly's as the veteran lowered his hands and stood arms akimbo, relaxed in the way a poker player relaxes when he has laid down a straight flush to the king.

Pierrard got his moment, got several, while smoke from his pipe wreathed him and the hand with which he stroked his hair seemed as rigid as a claw. "Mr. Kelly," he said at last, "there are quarters provided for you, and there's a lounge. If you'd care to—"

"My room have a shower?" the veteran interrupted.

"Yes." The syllable Pierrard spoke held no emotion, but there was rage in his eyes to equal that of Kelly a few minutes before.

"You've got my address," Kelly said with a brittle smile.

When Kelly opened the hall door, the two guards snapped to alertness. "Take this gentleman to room sixteen," called Pierrard from behind Kelly, just before the veteran closed the door again.

One of the guards touched the key of his throat mike. "Bev, report to the Briefing Room," came from his lips and was syncopated by the same order whispering down the corridor from a speaker forward.

"Christ, people, I can find a room number myself," the agent said with a grimace. He had done so and was opening the door when the earnest-looking female attendant scurried past. High levels of government were the wrong places to look for women's liberation. Generals and their civilian equivalents liked perks to remind them of their power, and chirpy girls in menial positions were high on their list of requirements.

The room wasn't huge, though it had two windows with a nice view of clouds a hell of a long way down. The fittings were more than comfortable—chair, writing desk, and a bed which seemed a trifle longer than standard. VIPs tended to be men of above-average height, and the Strategic Air Command certainly had its share of officers who could not be comfortably fitted into fighter cockpits.

There was the promised shower, not an enormous luxury so far as space went . . . but the weight of the water to feed it and the other similar facilities was something else again. No wonder the bird in this configuration had an all-up weight of four hundred tons.

The water felt good, as it always did. Soap, dust, body oils, and dried blood curled down the drain as a gray slurry. By adjusting the taps as hot as he could stand it, Kelly was able to knead with his fingertips the injury that seemed most bothersome: the welt across his right temple where Doug had slapped him with the submachinegun. The general pain of the hot water provided cover for him to work loose the scabs and get normal circulation flowing.

The pain had another benefit. It made Kelly think of Doug as a figure beating him . . . displacing, for the moment, at least, memory of Doug as something recently human, huddled now and forever in a pool of blood and feces because Tom Kelly had made him that way.

Kelly hadn't locked the door, hadn't even looked to see if there *was* a lock.

It was no surprise to hear the door open, and a relief but no surprise that the intruder—water sprayed toward the bed when Kelly swung open the stall's frosted glass door without first closing the faucets—was General Redstone, rather than six or eight of the husky attendants.

"Hey, Red," said the veteran, shutting off the water, "good to see you." Which was true on a number of levels.

"I thought you'd, you know, hold it against me I didn't come with you when you left," Redstone said, settling himself in the swivel chair bolted down in front of the desk. Light gleamed from his bald scalp, and the older man had gained at least twenty pounds since he had last toured the training camp outside Diyarbakir in a set of khaki desert fatigues.

"Hell, I'd rather have a friend in court than somebody to hold my hand," said the agent.

He hadn't left Redstone behind as a friend, exactly. Red was the sort of guy who would sacrifice his firstborn if God in the guise of the US government demanded it. Not that he wouldn't argue about the decision.

But Kelly also knew that Redstone wasn't going to let one of his boys be fucked over just because that seemed like a good policy to somebody in a suit. He would spend Kelly or spend himself; but, like Kelly, only if that were required to accomplish the task.

"Well, what they going to go with, Red?" the agent asked as he spilled the cartridges onto the bunk and began to clean the revolver. "Me or nothing?"

"We've got a preliminary report from Istanbul," Redstone said, looking toward the windows instead of the nude, scarred body of the man who had once served under him. "About Blakeley."

"That mean I'm out, then?" Kelly asked in a bantering tone. His hands concentrated on feeding a corner of the towel into each of the chambers. He hadn't had a chance to clean the weapon properly since he'd used it on Doug. . . .

"Funny world," said Redstone idly. He looked at Kelly. "Convinced some folks you meant what you said. God knows *I'd* tried. Means you're on, on your terms. Nobody had a better plan that didn't include you, and nobody seemed to think you were going to mellow out any time soon."

"Jesus," said Kelly. He sat down on the bed, still holding the towel-wrapped gun but without pretending any longer that it had his attention. The cartridges rolled down the bedspread and against his right thigh. "Well, at least they got that'n right."

"Now," said the older man, leaning forward with his hands clasped above his knees, "are you going off and do it your way, or are you willing to listen to reason on the hardware?"

Kelly pursed his lips. "I'm willing," he said slowly, "to talk things over with somebody who knows which end of a gun the bang comes out of . . . which"—he grinned—"is you and nobody else within about seven vertical miles."

"Then take an Ultimax 100 instead," the general said earnestly. "Twelve and a half pounds with the hundred-round drum, rate of fire low enough to be controllable even in light gravity, and absolutely reliable in or out of an atmosphere."

"Sure, nice gun, Red," said Kelly, the individual words agreeable but the implication a refusal. He resumed the task of cleaning the Smith and Wesson while the air and bedspread got on with the business of drying his body. "But all thumbs'd be mild for the way I'll be, rigged out in a space suit. A machinegun won't cut it."

"Well, there's been some talk about that . . ." said Redstone. Both men were relaxing now that the conversation had lapsed into routine and minutiae. The general locked his fingers behind his neck and stretched out his legs, demonstrating in the process that the chair back reclined. "If you blow each segment as you go through, then everybody's on the same footing. You say they terminated the Kurds, right?"

"Sure." Kelly held the revolver with the cylinder open so that light was reflected from the recoil plate through the barrel to his eye. "I'm probably on better'n even terms with each one of the maybe twenty Germans. Not great odds, buddy, and I can't watch both directions at once. I need something that'll take 'em out section by section—fast, because it's *me* that's gotta move to get to the control room. If I wait to blow doors instead of just opening them, they'll sure as shit get around behind and scrag me.''

"You'll be awkward as a hog on ice, lugging all that gear, baby.'' Redstone grimaced, though his relaxed posture did not change.

"I'll be awkward as hell in a space suit anyway,'' Kelly agreed with a shrug. "Red, you got anything thin enough to feed through this bore or do I tear off a bit of the sheet?''

Redstone fished in his top pocket for a handkerchief. "We can probably hunt you up a proper cleaning kit,'' he grumbled. "Carry a backup, hey? Those things fuck up more ways than a seventeen-year-old kid.''

"Thought maybe a shotgun,'' the veteran agreed, keeping his eyes on the gun. "Look, Red. You find a way to put a platoon in orbit *fast,* then we'll do it that way. Otherwise, this is the choice, and I don't need any shit about it. I'm *right.''* He glared fiercely at the older man.

"Never said you weren't,'' Redstone agreed with a shrug. Businesslike again, he went on, "I'll call in, have 'em cut down a Model 1100 and put a pistol grip on it.''

Kelly cocked his head. "Figured a pump gun from stores,'' he said. "Why an autoloader?''

"You figure to have both hands free, Kelly?'' the general replied with a grin. "Besides, it'll function better, especially with you in a suit and likely to shortstroke the slide.'' He raised his hand. *"Don't* tell me it wouldn't happen to you. It *won't* happen if you let a gas valve do all the thinking the times that you've got other things on your plate.''

"Yeah, okay,'' Kelly said. He began reloading the cylinder of his snubbie. "Suppose anybody thought to bring me a change of clothes? *I* didn't think of it.''

"We'll rustle something up," the general said, evaluating the veteran's body with a practiced eye. "You're in pretty good shape, Kelly. Be nice if you were nineteen and still had your experience, but I guess the experience's the choice." He nodded toward the door, then started to get up. "There's people waiting to brief you on layout and the control sequence as soon as you're ready to hear about that."

"Right," said Kelly. "Find me a pair of slacks at least and send 'em with the briefing team."

"Right," Redstone agreed, but big hands stayed on the back of the chair, which he swiveled in a pair of short, nervous arcs.

"Spit it *out*, Red," the veteran said sharply, his eyes narrowing. "Hard to tell when you'll get a better chance."

"Why'd you blow her that way, Kelly?" Redstone said, each word chipped from stone. "Elaine, I mean. Why'd you fuck her over?"

"Goddam," Kelly said in surprise. "Red, I didn't know you knew the lady."

"Answer the goddam question," the general whispered.

"Roger," said Kelly coolly. "Because she lied to me, and because she set me up. Any more questions?"

"Goddammit, she *didn't* set you up!" Redstone burst out. "I heard the fucking tape! You were supposed to get the kid gloves treatment, and except for that shithead Blakeley you'd have gotten it!"

He turned toward the wall, and for a moment Kelly thought the older man was going to break a hand trying to punch a hole in the bulkhead. He sagged instead, bracing himself with his hands flattened on either side of the doorframe.

"I'm sorry, Red," Kelly said as calmly as he could. "If I'd known a little more, maybe some things I'd have done another way. But I'm not psychic, man."

"Shit, Kelly, shit," General Redstone muttered to the

door. He faced the agent again. Moments before he had been flushed, but now he looked sallow and very old. "We all lie," he said. "Sometimes it's hard to draw the line, I guess." Redstone shook his head violently from side to side, as if to clear it of something clinging. "Sorry," he muttered. "Sorry."

"Red." Kelly waited until the other man met his eyes. "Somebody greased Mohammed Ayyubi in order to get me into this whole thing. I told his brother I'd even the score." He took a deep breath. "I'm going to, Red. Someday I'll learn who gave the scratch order, and then I'll handle it. If that's something you need to pass on, then that's how it is."

"Oh, Christ, Kelly," the general said with an operational smile that relaxed the veteran as no words could have done, "you already took care of that one. It was Blakeley, and—and it got cleared afterwards because of the other, the funny gray guy. But that was when they decided that somebody ought to be brought in over Blakeley to ride herd."

Redstone nodded a period to his thought. Then, in a voice that could have been Tom Kelly's in a similar case, he added, "And if you hadn't nailed him, soldier, I would've done it myself after the bucket he put—a whole lotta people in."

He turned quickly, mumbling as he opened the door, "I'll see to your pants."

"*Damn*, it's bright out there," said Tom Kelly as Redstone slid closed the door of the van. The latch stuck and the panting general had to bang the door again to jar loose metal covered with El Paso's omnipresent yellow-gray grit. "I ought to eat more carrots."

"It's an old wives' tale that carrots improve vision," said the passenger who had arrived with the van. They were idling beside the low terminal building until the rest of the entourage had mounted up. The cavalcade of locally available transportation included a pair of canvas-topped Army three-quarter-tons. At least they'd put Kelly in something air-conditioned, though that was probably because he was riding with Pierrard. "Are you having trouble with your eyes?"

"You're a doctor?" Kelly asked, squinting. The thirtyish man had short hair and a short-sleeved shirt with a tie.

The car radio sputtered. The driver with a plug earphone turned and said "Sir?" to Pierrard.

"Drive on," ordered the white-haired man, scowling.

"I'm an MD, if that's what you mean," the passenger said. "Also a PhD. Name's Suggs." He offered Kelly his hand.

The veteran shook it, saying, "Then you ought to know that carotene helps the eye adapt to rapid changes in light level—which is the only eye problem I've got."

Dr. Suggs jumped as though Kelly had hit him with a joy buzzer.

"Kelly, calm down," said General Redstone. "Doctor, you're here to do a quick physical, not to talk. Why don't you get on with it?"

The landscape beginning to slide past the van's windows was not dissimilar to that in the vicinity of Diyarbakir, though the mountains in the distance here seemed neither as extensive nor as high.

"Will you roll up your sleeve, please?" said the doctor distantly as he took a sphygmomanometer from his case.

"How tight's the timing?" Kelly asked Redstone. The van rocked more violently than the condition of the road seemed to require. The vehicle was loaded well below its normal capacity of nine persons and luggage, so the springing seemed unduly harsh.

"This isn't the time to discuss the situation," Pierrard said in a flat voice.

"It's the goddam time we got," Kelly snapped back as

Suggs started to fit the rubber cuff on him. "Look"—Kelly waved and the doctor sucked in his lips with a hiss of anger, poising as if to capture the arm when next it came to rest—"you've got a lieutenant colonel *driving,* for Chrissake. If you'll go that far for a secure environment, then *use* it. Even if you don't like me, okay?"

The uniformed driver's eyes flickered back in the rearview mirror, though he neither spoke nor turned his head.

Pierrard had taken his unlighted pipe from a side pocket of his suit. Unexpectedly, he dropped it back and said, "I don't like very many people, Mr. Kelly, and that has not in general affected my performance."

He smiled, and though the expression itself was forced, the attempt was significant. "I think it may be that you don't cringe enough."

"Naw," said the veteran. "When I'm scared, I fly hot. And you scare the crap outa me, buddy, that I'll tell you."

Redstone, seated behind Pierrard and kitty-corner across the van's narrow aisle from Kelly, looked from man to man and squeezed unconsciously against his own seatback.

"The gun in your pocket," said Pierrard, nodding toward the borrowed trousers over which Kelly let the tail of the borrowed shirt hang. "That's the one that killed Blakeley?"

"That's the one," Kelly agreed. He kept his hands plainly in sight on the back of his seat and the one in front of him. Suggs, on the other half of the double seat, tried again to fit the cuff.

"I assumed so," Pierrard said. "I think I can say that at least we share common emotions, Mr. Kelly, when we're forced to deal with one another."

The old man paused, then went on. "We—the proper parties—are in negotiation with the parties who claim to have captured Fortress."

"Claim?" repeated Kelly, glancing over at Redstone.

"I misspoke, Mr. Kelly," Pierrard said. "Litotes when bluntness would have been appropriate. They have accurately targeted and released a number of the nuclear weapons from Fortress, so common sense indicates that they are fully in control as they claim.''

Pierrard's hand began to play with the hidden meerschaum. ''They did not,'' he continued, ''expect that news of a nuclear attack could be obfuscated; I cannot claim that it was totally concealed for over a day in both the countries which were victimized. There has been a considerable outcry at 'launching disasters' with attendant loss of life . . . but the, the 'Aryan Legion,' as they choose to style themselves now, has received no publicity. As you can imagine, the capabilities designed into Fortress do not include general broadcast equipment.'' He permitted himself a tight smile.

''So you figure they're going to up the stakes with something you can't cover up,'' Kelly suggested.

''Moscow and Washington, we feared,'' agreed Pierrard. ''Perhaps only Moscow, if they are what you tell us, Nazi holdouts . . . but the result will be the same, since the Soviets can be expected to respond against the presumed perpetrators, the West.''

''Yeah, I've heard that estimate already,'' the veteran agreed, remembering the rain-swept walls of Diyarbakir and the thing, Wun, that spoke to him there. ''Shit.'' He made sure he held the older man's eyes as he added, ''How did the X-ray lasers work?''

Something else he hadn't any business knowing, Kelly thought and Pierrard knew quite well. *That* one wasn't going to be decoyed into answering a question whose premises went beyond anything Kelly was cleared for.

''Perfectly,'' Pierrard said coolly. ''The Soviets attacked with three flights of twenty missiles apiece. Each salvo was destroyed by a single unit of the defensive constellation, operating presumably in an automatic mode. We do not know that the''—he coughed—''Aryan Legion can launch additional defensive satellites as the normal com-

plement would have done . . . but since on the next pass
both the silo farms from which the Soviets launched received multiple bombs from Fortress, neither superpower
is likely to proceed further in that direction.''

''Yeah, well,'' Kelly said. He turned to look out the
window, although without seeing much of the scenery—
one-story buildings, mesquite bushes, and dust. ''Yeah.
Well, I'll be glad to get it over with myself.''

''You can't see out the cockpit windows,'' said Tom
Kelly cautiously. ''*I* can't see through the windows.''

''Ummm,'' agreed Desmond, the project scientist who
had been the bright spot in Kelly's previous visit to the
Biggs Field installation. ''You're going to have enough
problems, Mr. Kelly, without being cooked by the beams
that raise the ferry. They're very precisely directed, but
both the distances and velocities involved are considerable
and will magnify slight misalignments.''

''Check,'' said Kelly, nodding ruefully. ''And we're
talking the same wavelengths as the warming racks at the
local hamburger joint. Sorry, should've thought.''

The suit—the space suit, though it shocked Kelly to
think of it that way—was bulky and constricting because
of its weight and stiffness, though it did not feel tight. His
mind was treating the garment as protective armor rather
than a burden. That was good in a way, but the suit really
was both—and the fact that his subconscious was more
concerned about the threat to him than the object he had to
achieve was more than a little bothersome.

''You won't be able to do anything with the controls
anyway.'' The scientist seemed to think he was offering
reassurance. ''So it doesn't matter whether or not you can
see.''

''Great.''

The makeshift crew vehicle pulled up at the ferry pad.
Well, it wasn't really any different from a night inser-

tion by helicopter; you couldn't see a damned thing, you couldn't change a thing either, and you had to trust not only the hardware but the skills of the man in control of it. On the plus side, nobody'd be shooting at him on this leg of the operation; lift-off would occur while Earth eclipsed Fortress from El Paso. The battle station was not a reconnaissance satellite, but there was no point in risking disclosure because some Nazi glanced at southwest Texas and wondered what the bright flash was.

Desmond opened the door of the van. This one had been modified by the removal of the three seats across the middle to provide more room for a man wrapped in the bulk of a space suit with breathing apparatus in place. "I'm sorry," said the physicist, "you'll have to walk the remainder of the way. We don't have proper equipment for this."

Kelly ducked to look out the door at the monocle ferry, over which waited a castered framework meant for the maintenance crews. There *were* no crew accommodations here; all the testing was ground controlled, as this flight would be as well. "Guess I can make twenty yards," he said, and, when Desmond did not precede him, he stepped past the physicist onto the ground.

The pad was hexagonal, for no particular reason, and four feet above the surrounding soil, in higher than most of the dust stinging along on the constant wind. A tank truck preceded by dust and steaming with the blow-off of its remaining load of liquid hydrogen drove away, downwind.

Kelly led the scientist to the pad's steps, realizing as he walked that his center of balance was farther back than he was used to. Desmond, who carried the helmet, was simply making sure that he was in position to support the veteran if he stumbled backward. The ferry looked larger at each of the six upward steps. That was reassuring. Though Kelly had been close to the Frisbee-shaped vehicle before, his mental image throughout the planning was of a tiny disk beneath his seat in the helicopter, preparing to disintegrate as an even tinier speck above him.

"How will you arrange for transfer?" Desmond asked as Kelly reached the top of the pad. Several men in coveralls stood beside the ferry, but they were service crew rather than a send-off committee. The brass was all in the control bunker; there were no choppers orbiting today.

Kelly tried to glance over his shoulder, but the suit got in the way and his balance wasn't that good anyway. "Honest to god, I don't know," he called against the force of the breeze. He had no idea of how much the physicist had been told. From the fact that Desmond had scrupulously avoided comment on the attempt, whose risks he knew and for whose failure he would feel responsible, Kelly assumed that the man must know a great deal.

"Right up here, sir," said a technician, steadying the tube and steel mesh service bridge with one hand and gesturing toward the nearer flight of steps with the other. "Please don't touch the mirrored surfaces when you step into the cockpit."

The bridge was two flights of metal steps supporting an angle-iron walkway that skimmed the upper surface of the cockpit, either closed or clam-shelled open as now. The railing appeared to be one-inch ID waterpipe, and the whole ensemble had clearly been built in a base workshop. It was sturdy, functional, and almost certainly superior to anything General Dynamics would have achieved with a $350,000 sole-source Space Command contract to the same end. There were advantages to being the poor relation.

The upper surfaces of the ferry were dazzling, the structural members even more so than the sapphire hexagons that accepted the laser beams. Kelly had expected the windows to be bluish, but the segments had only the color of what they chanced to be reflecting—the bridge, the pale sky, or the sun like the point of a blazing dagger.

"We'd better lock this down," Desmond said, offering the helmet to Kelly.

The agent bowed slightly so that Desmond could fit the helmet instead of just handing it over. "There's a certain amount of dust on the surface anyway," he said without inflection.

"Yes, the raised platform was only to lessen the accumulation," the physicist agreed as he lowered the helmet, "not to eliminate it." His voice becoming muffled as the padded thermoplastic slid down over Kelly's ears, he continued, "It burns off cleanly in the laser flux. We've retrieved enough of the earlier test units to be sure that wasn't the cause of failure."

The locking cogs began to snap into place around the base of the helmet. Very softly, the veteran heard Desmond conclude, "Enough pieces."

There was a crackle in Kelly's ears as the project scientist connected the earphones to the power pack. "Do we have a link?" demanded a compressed voice. "*Dancer One*, do you read me? Over."

"Yes," Kelly said as he mounted the steps, bending forward at the waist because the base of the helmet cut off his normal downward peripheral vision. The pure oxygen he was now breathing flooded his sinuses like a seepage of ice water. "Now get off the air. Please."

"*Dancer One*, are you having difficulties with the boarding bridge? Should we get you some personnel to help? Over."

Kelly paused, found the power connection with his gloved hand, and unplugged the radio. Then he resumed trudging to the middle of the walkway where the railing had been cut away. He lowered himself carefully, one leg at a time, into the cramped cockpit. Where they thought there'd be room for anybody to lend a hand with the process was beyond him. Maybe a gantry, but there weren't any available on-site.

His position in the saucer was roughly that of an F-16 pilot or a Russian tank driver: flat on his back with his head raised less than would've been comfortable for reading in bed. In the contemplated operational use, there would have been a condenser screen in front of the pilot and a projector between his knees to throw instrument data onto that screen.

For this run, the heads-up display had been removed so that the fuel and pressure tanks of Kelly's additional gear could fill the space. More than fill it, as a matter of fact; what would have been a tight fit now nearly required a shoehorn. The boarding bridge clattered as a technician and Dr. Desmond climbed on from opposite ends.

"I'm all right, dammit!" Kelly snapped, his scowl evident through the face shield, though his words must have been unintelligible.

The physicist nodded approvingly, reached down for the throat of the fuel tank, and lifted it the fraction of an inch that permitted Kelly's legs to clear to either side. The veteran sank back thankfully onto the seat, aware of his previous tension once he had released it.

The technician began to close half the cockpit cover. His hands were gloved; a handprint in body oils on the reflective surface would dangerously concentrate the initial laser pulse. Desmond stopped the man, pointed at Kelly's helmet, and then mimed on his own neck the process of reconnecting the veteran's radio. It would be next to impossible for Kelly to mate the plugs himself in the strait cockpit.

Kelly smiled but shook his head, and the doors above shut him into blackness.

Then there was nothing to do save wait; but Tom Kelly, like a leopard, was very good at waiting for a kill.

Kelly's mind had drifted so that when the monocle ferry took off, its passenger flashed that he was again riding an armored personnel carrier which had just rolled over a mine.

That—the feeling at least—was an apt analogy for the event. The ferry lifted off without the buildup of power inevitable in any fuel-burning system. The laser flux converted the air trapped between the pad and the mirrored concavity of the ferry's underside into plasma expanding with a suddenness greater than the propagation rate of high explosive. Kelly left the ground as if shot from a gun.

The roaring acceleration was so fierce that it trapped the hand which reflex tried to thrust down to the shotgun holstered alongside Kelly's right calf. The ferry shifted to pulsejet mode as soon as the initial blast lifted it from the pad. The low-frequency hammering of the chambers firing in quick succession, blasting out as plasma air that they had earlier sucked in, so nearly resembled the vibration of a piston engine about to drop a valve that anticipation kept the veteran rigid for long seconds after g-forces had decreased to a level against which he could have moved had he continued to try.

The rim of the ferry with the firing chambers spun at high speed around the cockpit at the hub. Kelly had expected to be aware of that gyroscopic motion, to feel or hear the contact of the bearing surfaces surrounding him. There was no such vibration, and it was only as he found himself straining to hear the nonexistent that the veteran realized he had not been blown to fragments above the Texas desert the way the test units had gone.

Worrying about minutiae was probably the best way available to avoid funking in the face of real danger.

There was a pause. Thrust was replaced by real gravity: lower than surface-normal, but genuine enough that Kelly felt himself and the couch on which he lay begin to fall backward.

Instinct then told him falsely that there had been a total propulsion failure. His mind flashed him images of air crashes he had seen, craters rimmed with flesh and metal shredded together like colored tinsel, all lighted by the flare of burning fuel—

Fuel. And the slamming acceleration resumed. The chambers began valving the internal hydrogen as reaction mass in place of the atmosphere which had become too thin to sustain the laser-powered ferry's upward momentum.

This was *worse* than insertion by parachute—at least Kelly'd done that before. If the Nazis didn't scare him any worse than the manner of the reaching them was doing, he was still going to wind up the mission with white hair.

Though that, unlike carrots for the eyes, *was* wholly myth.

Because operation of the monocle ferry was new to Kelly, the occurrence of something that would have amazed Dr. Desmond did not cause the veteran to wonder what was happening. The reaction chambers continued to blast in rapid succession, but the feeling of acceleration faded into apparent weightlessness. Only then did the vibration stop, leaving Kelly to think about when and how Wun and his fellows would reach the ferry.

Whether they would reach the ferry.

And then the cockpit opened, the two halves moving apart as smoothly as if they were driven by hydraulic jacks instead of the arms of gray, naked monsters like the creature dead at Fort Meade.

Kelly's first thought was that the pair of aliens stood in hard vacuum, having somehow walked to the rising ferry without a ship of their own. He began to lift himself against the cockpit coaming, gripping the metal firmly with his thick gloves for fear of drifting away. There was, to the veteran's surprise—weren't they in orbit?—gravity after all; a slight fraction of what he was used to, perhaps a tenth, but enough to orient and anchor Kelly while he untangled his suited legs.

The monocle ferry floated against light-absorbent blackness that held it as solidly as had Earth gravity and the concrete pad. The aliens who had undogged the cockpit had firm footing also, on something invisible a hand's breadth above the mirrored surface.

Kelly could see the monocle ferry, his own suited limbs, and the aliens clearly, though without the depth that shadows would have given. There was, however, no apparent source of light nor any sign of stars, of the Sun, or of the Earth, whose sunlit surface should have filled much of the spherical horizon at this low altitude.

The veteran was still supporting himself on the lip of the cockpit. Grimacing, he took his hand away and found that he did not fall back onto the seat. He reached down into the cockpit for the equipment he had brought with him, noticing that he moved without resistance but that, apart from volitional actions, his body stayed exactly where he had last put it.

"Very well done, Mr. Kelly," said Wun's voice through the helmet earphones that Kelly had not reconnected. "How much time do you need before we place you at your Fortress?"

"Wun, can you hear me?" Kelly asked, turning and wondering whether he should open his face shield. The two visible aliens, stepping back on nothing now, wore no clothing, protective or otherwise.

Wun stood a few yards behind the veteran. Unlike his fellows, he wore a business suit and a human face which was at the moment smiling. "Yes," he said, his lips in synch with the voice in Kelly's earphones, "very well. And please do not open your helmet. It will not be necessary."

"Yeah, right," said Kelly. He pursed his lips. "Wun, where the *hell* are we?"

"It does what a ship does," said the alien. "Therefore I described it as a ship. We will be able to return you to Earth whenever you please now that you have reached here."

"Yeah, that's great," said Kelly, checking his equipment. Looked okay; and if it wasn't, he'd use the shotgun that weighted his right leg. Hell, he'd tear throats out with his teeth if that was what it took to get the job done.

Or he'd die trying . . . but that would mean he failed, and failure wasn't acceptable.

"How quick can you get me to Fortress?" the veteran asked, returning to Wun's initial question but not answering it until he had further data.

"Momentarily, Thomas Kelly," said the alien, bobbing his head in what was either an Oriental gesture or something indigenous to his own inhuman species.

"Okay," Kelly said, a place holder while he thought. He met the alien's eyes, or what passed for eyes in the human simulacrum. "You showed me—the dream, I mean—the balance half of the dumbbell was blown open. If that's still the case, can you land me at that opening instead of the docking hub?"

"Yes," Wun said simply, bobbing again.

"You know—" Kelly began and caught himself. Of *course* the aliens knew that the lobes were spinning around their common center. If Wun said they could land him there, that meant they would match velocities and land him there.

Now that he was within the alien 'ship,' he could understand Wun's confidence at being able to avoid the radars and X-ray lasers guarding the space station. Previously, he had taken the alien's word for that simply because there wasn't a damn thing to be done if Wun was talking through his hat.

The Nazis had probably achieved surprise by approaching in a wholly-unexpected trajectory, claiming to be from the American lunar base when they were finally challenged—and having only a minimal German crew with the Kurdish shock troops aboard the leading saucers, the ones that would take the salvos of Fortress's close-in defenses. Even so, the highest leaders of the Dienst would have waited well apart from the attack, in Antarctica or on the Moon, until the issue was decided.

"Okay," said Kelly again, hefting his gear. "Gimme a hand with this. It's been modified to strap on me, but the suit doesn't bend so well I can even get the straps over my shoulders myself."

He was starting to breathe fast. Hell, he'd hyperventilate on oxygen if he didn't watch out. "And then," the veteran concluded, "you set me aboard Fortress. And keep your fingers crossed."

Between the air supply on his back and the weapons pack slung across his chest, Tom Kelly looked like a truckload of bottles mounted on legs. The bulk felt friendly, though, even without the weight that should have accompanied it.

The thing that nobody who directed war movies understood—and why should they? It would have come as news to rear echelons in all the various armies as well—was that the guys at the sharp end carried it all on their backs.

The irreducible minimum for life in a combat zone was water, arms and munitions, and food. In most environments, heavy clothing or shelter had to be factored in as well; exposure in a hilltop trench would kill you just as dead as a bullet.

Helicopters were fine, but they weren't going to land while you lay baking on a bare hillside traversed by enemy guns; so you carried water in gallons, not quarts, and it was life itself. If you ran out of ammo, they'd cut you apart with split bamboo if that was what they had . . . so you carried extra bandoliers and extra grenades, and a pistol of your own because the rifle you were issued was going to jam at the worst possible time, no matter who designed it or how hard you tried to keep it clean.

Besides that, you carried a belt of ammo for one of the

overburdened machinegunners or a trio of shells for the
poor bastard with the mortar tube on his back. You were
all in it together; and besides, when the shit hit the fan
you were going to need heavy-weapons support.

And the chances were that, if you were really trying to
get the jump on the elusive other side, you had a case of
rations to hump with you as well. Every time a resupply
bird whop-whopped to you across hostile terrain, it fin-
gered you for the enemy and guaranteed that engagement
would be on the enemy's terms.

So you didn't move very fast, but you moved, and you
did your job of kicking butt while folks in strack uniforms
crayoned little boxes and arrows on acetate-covered maps,
learnedly discussing your location. That was the way the
world worked; and that was why Tom Kelly felt subconsciously better for the equipment slung on his body as he
shuffled into combat.

"All right," Kelly said with his shotgun drawn in his
right hand and his left extended to grasp the first hold
chance offered. Recoil from the charge of buckshot would
accelerate the veteran right out of business if he hadn't
anchored himself before he fired. Not that there was supposed to be anybody in this half of Fortress.

"Just walk forward, Mr. Kelly," said Wun's voice, "as
if it were a beaded curtain."

There wasn't supposed to be a gang of Nazis in control
of Fortress, period—if you were going to get hung up on
supposed-to-bes.

"Right," said Tom Kelly, shifting his weight and stepping through a wall that was nothing, not even color, into
Fortress.

The alien ship—the *place*, if even that did not imply too
much—from which Kelly stepped could be seen only as an
absence of the things which should have been visible
behind it, and even that only in a seven-foot disk without

discernible thickness. The disk, which could only be the point of impingement between the universe which Kelly knew and wherever the hell the aliens were, rotated at the same speed as the space station, so that the veteran had not expected to notice motion as he stepped aboard Fortress.

He had forgotten the shielding doughnut of lunar slag within which the two lobes of the dumbbell spun at a relative velocity of almost two hundred miles an hour. The gap between the portal and the space station was only a few inches wide, but that was enough to give Kelly the impression that he was watching a gravel road through the rusted-out floorboards of a speeding car. This job was assuredly finding unique ways to give him the willies.

The first thing he noticed when his feet hit the bare aluminum planking of the dumbbell's floor was that he had weight again, real weight, although not quite the load that he would have been carrying in full Earth gravity. Fortress spun at a rate which gave it approximately .8 g's at the floor level of either dumbbell. The arms revolved at nearly two revolutions per minute, fast enough to displace a dropping object several inches from where it would have fallen under the pull of gravity instead of centrifugal force. It would play hell with marksmanship also, but Kelly with his gloves and helmet hadn't the least chance of target accuracy anyway.

The corpse in the SS uniform lay exactly where it had in Kelly's dream.

The chamber was brightly illuminated by sunlight reflected through the solar panels above. Where it fell on the dead Kurd, his skin appeared shrunken and darker than it had been during life—a shade close to that of waxed mahogany. One outflung hand was shaded by a structural member, however, and it gleamed with a tracery of hoarfrost. Ice was crystallizing from the corpse's body fluids and from there subliming into vacuum, leaving behind the rind of a man that would not age or spoil if it lay here until the heat death of the universe.

Perhaps houris were ministering to ben Majlis's soul in Paradise. Ben Majlis deserved that as much as any soldier did; and as little.

The next part was tricky. Kelly stepped past ben Majlis's body to reach the door the Kurd had tried to open. The doors of Fortress did not lock, but it was possible that the Nazis had welded this one shut before blowing their Kurd-ish cannon fodder into the void at the end of their per-ceived usefulness. If the door *was* welded, Kelly would have to punch his entrance with explosives, and that was almost certain to warn those who had taken over the station.

Awkward because of his glove and the fact he was using only his left hand on a mechanism meant for two, Kelly rotated the large aluminum wheel that latched the door between this compartment and the remainder of Fortress. The dogs freed with no more than the hesitation to be expected when plates of aluminum are left in contact long enough for their oxide coatings to creep together.

The agent pulled. Nothing gave. His lips curled to rip out a curse; and as he reached back for the self-adhesive strip charge hanging in a roll from his left hip, he noticed that the panel was beveled to open away from him instead of toward him as the plans and instructor on the Airborne Command Post had assured him. Somebody had misread the specs, or else the construction crew had reasonably decided that it didn't matter a hoot in hell which way they hung the doors so long as the seal was good.

Kelly hit the panel with a shoulder backed with all his mass and that of the equipment he carried. The seal popped enough to spray air from around half the circumference. Then the door opened fully, and the veteran lurched inside behind his shotgun.

The air that escaped around Kelly scattered and softened

the light which until then had lain flat on the panel of aluminum/ceramic fiber sandwich. It ruffled the sleeve of ben Majlis's uniform as it surged past, but it lacked the force and volume that would have been required to eject the corpse from the open chamber.

As soon as he was inside the undamaged compartment, Kelly thrust the door shut and fell to his knees with the ill-controlled effort. Despite the air that had puffed into the void, the residual pressure within the compartment slammed the door firmly against the seals.

This compartment was about as empty as the one whose wall had been blown away. It had attachment points up and down both long walls, but nothing was slung from them and there were no bodies on the floor. The vertical lighting did display a line of oval punctures stitched at chest height across one wall: bullet holes punched at an angle through the metal facing but swallowed harmlessly by the glass core—all save one which was covered by a piece of Speedtape. Somebody from the original complement of Fortress had made it this far; and then, no doubt, made it into vacuum as just another body, shortly to be followed by the Kurds who had gunned him down.

And now it was the turn of the Nazis.

The atmosphere-exchange vents which had swung closed when air surged through the open door had reopened when the pressure drop ceased, bringing the chamber back in balance with the remainder of the space station. Kelly turned the inner door wheel to lock the dogs home, keeping his eyes and gun on the door at the far end of the chamber.

The quantity of air lost when Kelly entered the space station had probably registered somewhere; but since the 'leak' had shut off immediately, the new owners of Fortress would probably not notice anything amiss. The pointed shotgun was cheap insurance, however . . . and by the time Kelly had finished latching the door, he was sure that

the chamber's oxygen level had returned what was normal
for Fortress, a partial pressure equal to that of Earth at sea
level, although the quantity of nitrogen in the atmosphere
was only half that of Earth by unit volume.

With the atmosphere back to normal, Kelly could unlim-
ber the flamethrower he had brought as his primary weapon.

The two cross-connected napalm tanks and the smaller
air bottle which pressurized them weighed almost fifty
pounds here, even though all were constructed of aluminum. The flame gun itself had a pistolgrip with a bar
trigger for the fuel valve, easily grasped and used despite
Kelly's protective clothing. The ignition lever just behind
the nozzle was of similar handy size.

The veteran went to the far end of the compartment and
twisted the latch wheel of the door which would be,
according to the plans, the central one of the five in this
lobe of the dumbbell. Then, with his hands on both controls of the flame gun, he kicked the panel open.

The third compartment was stacked with crated supplies, primarily foodstuffs, and one cage of the dual elevators waited beside the helical staircase which also led
toward the hub. There was nothing alive to see Kelly burst
through the doorway.

Each of the elevator shafts was fifteen feet in diameter,
large enough to handle any cargo which could be ferried to
orbit on existing hardware. The elevators' size had determined the thickness of the spokes connecting the lobes of
the dumbbell to the hub, since strength requirements could
have been met by spokes thinner than the thirty-five feet or
so of the present structure.

The elevators were intended to move simultaneously and
in opposite directions, one cage rising as the other fell,
though in an emergency the pair could be decoupled. As a
further preparation for emergency, stairs were built into
part of the spoke diameter left over when the elevator

shafts were laid out, and it was this staircase by which Kelly had intended to cross to the hub.

Using the elevator that gaped like a holding cell would be crazy, Kelly thought as he shuffled to the stairs. With one hand on the railing to keep from overbalancing, he bent backwards to look up the helical staircase. Dabs of light blurred like beads on a string on the steps and the closed elevator shafts beside which the steps proceeded upward. From the bottom they seemed an interminable escalade.

Hell, he'd take the elevator. If he weren't crazy, he'd have stayed home.

Kelly hadn't been briefed on the elevators, but the controls could scarcely have been simpler. The door was a section of the cage's cylindrical wall. It slid around on rollered tracks at top and bottom when Kelly pulled at its staple-shaped handle. The door did not latch, nor did there appear to be any interlock between it and the elevator control.

After considering the situation for a moment, Kelly slid the door open again, faced it, and prodded the single palm-sized button on the cage wall with the muzzle of the flame gun. Nothing happened for long enough that the veteran reached for the door handle again, convinced that he must have been wrong about the interlock. The cage staggered into upward motion before his arm completed its motion. There was simply a delay built into its operation, probably tied to a warning signal in the other elevator, which would start at the same time.

That might or might not be important. Holding the flame gun in a two-handed grip, Kelly grinned toward the elevator shaft that slid past his open door.

He did not see the metal sheathing, however. His mind was trying to imagine the face of the next person it would direct the veteran's hands to kill. Over the years, he had come surprisingly close a number of times. . . .

* * *

The elevator shaft was almost nine hundred feet high—or long, in a manner of speaking, because the cage ceased to go 'up' as it neared the hub and the effect of centrifugal force lessened. The drive was hydraulic and very smooth after the initial jerk as the pumps cut in. As the impellers pressurized the column to raise the cage in which Kelly rode, they drew a partial vacuum in the other column to drag the cage down from hub level. Ordinary cable operation would not work in the absence of true gravity, and a cogged-rail system like that of some mountain railways would have put unbalanced stresses on the spokes, whose thickness and mass would have had to be greatly increased to avoid warping.

The portion of the design that was critical at the moment was the fact that the pumps were in the lobe, not at the hub, and that the elevator's operation was therefore effectively silent at the inner end. It didn't mean that the approaching cage would not be noticed; but at least there would be no squalling take-up spool to rivet the attention of all those in the hub on the elevator shaft.

Kelly's hands were clammy, though his gloves would keep them from slipping on the triggers of the flame gun. This wasn't like Istanbul, where he was in too deep too quickly to think. Three hundred yards, three football fields end to end, with the cage moving at the speed of a man walking fast. Plenty of time to review the faces of the men you'd already killed—only the ones you'd really *seen*, not the lumps sprawled like piles of laundry on the ground you'd raked. . . .

Some people had nightmares about the times they'd almost bought the farm themselves. Kelly saw instead faces distorted by pain or rage or the shock waves of the bullet already splashing flesh to the side. He was as likely to awaken screaming as those who feared their own death;

and he was surely as likely to slug his brain with alcohol to blur the memories he knew it could not erase.

But it was the only thing Tom Kelly did that his gut knew he could win at, and he was only really alive during those rare moments that he was winning.

The edge of the spherical hub began to rotate past the open door of the cage. A gray-haired woman in a skirt and bemedaled jacket glanced over her shoulder toward the cage. Kelly squeezed the valve lever in the pistol grip and, as the nozzle began to buck, fired an ignition cartridge with the lever under his left hand.

Recoil from Kelly's shot, a five-pound stream of napalm, thrust him back against the wall of the elevator cage, but that was of no significance to the effect of the short burst. The veteran had only a momentary glimpse past the uniformed woman before his flame obliterated the scene, but there were at least two dozen figures in the center of the hub. They all wore formal uniforms and were attempting to stand braced in formation, despite the tendency to float in the absence of gravity.

Kelly's flame devoured them. The effect of his weapon under these conditions was beyond anything he had seen or dreamed of on Earth.

The compressed air tank could send the jet of fuel fifty yards, even with gravity to pull it down. Here it easily splashed the thickened gasoline off the far side of the hub, barely a hundred feet from the weapon. The lowered air pressure, half that of Earth, combined with the high relative oxygen level to turn what would have been a narrow jet of flame into a fireball which exploded across the open area like the flame-front filling the cylinder of a gasoline engine on the power stroke.

The gush of orange blinded Kelly and kicked him back against the wall from which he had begun to recoil from the thrust of the napalm itself. The suit he wore was designed to protect its wearer against the unshielded power

of the Sun and insulate him against the cold of objects
which had radiated all their heat into the insatiable black
maw of vacuum. Its design parameters were sufficient to
shield him here against the second of ravenous flame he
had released. Blinking and wishing he had flipped down
the sunshield over his faceplate before he fired, Kelly
thrust himself off the wall of the stationary elevator and
into the hub proper.

The great domed room was filled with violent motion.
Smoke and occasional beads of napalm still afire swirled
in the shock waves rebounding from the curved walls.

The men and women who had shared the room with the
fireball cavorted now like gobbets spewed from a Roman
candle. Their hair and uniforms blazed, fanned by the
screaming, frantic efforts of the victims to extinguish them.
Nazis, blinded as their eyeballs bubbled, collided with one
another and sailed off across the dome on random courses,
pinwheeling slowly.

Slender poles were set every twenty feet or so in the
floor and walls of the room to give purchase to those who,
like Kelly at present, were drifting without adequate control. The veteran snagged one of the wands in the crook of
his left arm. He locked his body against it to kill the spin
he had been given by the elevator cage which rotated with
the spoke. When he had anchored himself, he was able to
survey the room and the possible threats it held.

The bodies, some corpses and some still in the process
of dying, which drifted like lazy blowflies over carrion, were
no danger to anyone. A touch on the back of Kelly's leg
caused him to twist in panic, cursing the way the helmet
limited his peripheral vision. Something smoldering had
brushed him, surrounded by a mist of blood from lungs
which had hemorrhaged when they sucked in flame.

Here in the hub there was a walkway seven feet wide at
the point the spokes mated with it and the elevators
debouched.

The plane of the walkway was continued by solid flooring across the hub, so that the sphere was separated into slightly unequal volumes. The larger one was the open, northern portion which served for zero-gravity transport between the lobes and from them through the docking module to the rest of the universe. Beneath the flooring, the other moiety of the hub was given over to the controls which ruled both the defensive array and the three thousand fusion warheads waiting for the command that would trip their retro rockets to set them on the path to reentry.

The elevators to the other lobe of the dumbbell were not moving, and the circular doorway to the control section was closed and flush with the floor across which Kelly's boots floated. The portal to the docking module above him, however, at the north pole, was sphinctering open. Keeping the pole within the circle of his arms, Kelly leaned backward and aimed the flame gun toward the opening portal.

The recoil of two gallons of thickened gasoline shoved him down against the floor this time, but the pole anchored him well enough to send most of the three-second burst into the docking module. Ammunition carried by some of the men inside blew up with a violence that sprayed bits of metal, plastic, and bodies down into the dome.

Only after the explosion did it occur to Kelly to wonder whose arrival had caused the personnel who had conquered Fortress to draw themselves up for inspection. Well, it didn't matter now.

The second jet of flame, though of longer duration than the first, had a more limited effect because the chamber's oxygen had been depleted faster than the ventilation system could replenish it. Napalm spluttered, each drop wrapped in a cloud of black smoke as it drifted lazily back toward Kelly.

It was time to move anyway. He dropped the flame gun

and let it trail behind him from its hose as he thrust himself toward the control room door.

The doorway was surrounded by a waist-high trio of inverted U's made of aluminum girder. There was room for a man, even suited and laden as Tom Kelly was, to walk between each adjacent pair, but the U's provided not only handholds the way the wands did but also protection for the doorway in the event that any high-inertia object sailed down from the docking module.

Kelly braked himself left-handed, tensing his muscles fiercely to halt his considerable mass without using his gun hand as well. The trigger guard of his shotgun had been cut away so that he could use the weapon with gloves. He was by no means certain that his motor control in his present garb was fine enough that he could count on not putting a charge of shot god knew where.

He might well need all five of the rounds in the gun.

The door handle was a flat semicircle that the veteran had to flip up before he could turn it. The men who briefed him on the Airborne Command Post assured him there was no locking mechanism, but that didn't mean the Nazis hadn't welded a bolt in place after they took over. There was the explosive tape if they had, but—

The handle turned. Kelly swung the door up, gripping a stanchion between his booted feet so that he could point the shotgun muzzle down the opening with his right hand.

If the job Kelly set himself had been to clear Fortress of the Nazis who had captured it, he would have squirted his remaining gallon of napalm into the control room before he went in himself with the shotgun. Some of the men arguing on the Airborne Command Post had considered that at least the most desirable option.

The trouble was that the Soviets, driven to the wall by the fact of Fortress, had almost certainly been pushed beyond that point when the weapon was actually used against them. If something very final did not convince Moscow of America's good faith, the Soviets would themselves precipitate the holocaust they assumed was certain in any event.

And a final, unequivocal act of good faith meant that the controls had to be intact.

Kelly went through the doorway, swinging the panel closed behind him against the rain of napalm—though most of the droplets had sputtered to expanding globes of soot by now. He expected someone to meet him in the enclosed hallway—a squad of aroused gunmen at worst, at best a trembling technician left on watch while the ceremony went on above. But there was no one in the hall, and no one in the computer rooms past which the veteran drifted, their cryonic circuitry made practicable by radiation through heat exchangers on the shaded surface of the station.

Even the control room itself, at Fortress's south pole, was empty, though the defensive array was live and programmed, according to its warning lights, for automatic engagement.

He couldn't possibly have been the one who had been arriving? Christ, he'd have been almost a century old. Though in a low-gravity environment like the Moon . . .

It didn't matter. There was a job to do.

The control room of Fortress was designed to have three officers on duty at all times. Under full War Emergency Orders any two of the consoles could be slaved to the third—with an appropriate accompaniment of lights and sirens. The arrangement was a concession to the paired facts that nobody in his right mind wanted a single individual to have the end of the world under his fingertip—and that if Fortress really had to be *used,* there wasn't going to be time to screw around with authorization and confirmation codes.

The Nazis had, as expected, linked the consoles already.

Kelly unstrapped the flamethrower and settled himself into the seat at the master unit, drawing himself down by chair arms deliberately set wide enough to fit a man in a space suit. There was a palm latch that would have permitted Kelly to move the back cushion to clear his life-support package. Rather than fool with nonessentials, he scrunched forward, aimed the waiting light pen at the screen, and began to press the large buttons.

Kelly was not trained to operate the console, to understand the steps of what he was doing. There had been neither time nor need for that aboard the Airborne Command Post. This was rote memory, the same sort of learning that permitted his fingers to strip and reassemble a fifty-caliber machinegun in the dark.

There were twelve weapons in the first rota which the Nazis had punched up on the screen. Their targets were given as twelve-digit numbers, not names—zip codes to hell. Warhead data appeared on the line beneath each target designator. The first target was selected for a 1.1 megaton warhead. Rather than change those parameters, Kelly flashed his light pen to target two, already set for a 5 megaton weapon, and engaged the launch sequence with the button whose cage was already unlocked.

When the launch button was pressed the first time, the printing on the screen switched from green-on-white to black-on-yellow. All data for the other weapons in the rota shrank down into a sidebar in the left corner, while ten additional data lines for the selected target appeared in large print. A black-on-red engagement clock began to run down from 432 in the upper left corner.

Kelly drew the light pen down the screen to the seventh data line, time delay, and pressed the cancel button. The number 971 blinked to yellow-on-black. Kelly keyed in the digit one, bending awkwardly to see the alphanumeric pad through the curve of his faceplate. He palmed the Execute key.

A gong went off loudly enough that Kelly heard and felt it through his suit. The top two inches of the screen pulsed Invalid Command in blue and yellow. The engagement clock continued to run down, but the top half of its digits changed from red to blue. Kelly hit the Execute button again. The data line changed from 791 to 1, and the visual and aural alarms ceased.

The veteran's hand reached for the Launch button to confirm. He was warned that something was happening behind him, not by the sound but rather because when the door to the north section of the hub opened it reflected a shimmer of light across the console at which Kelly was working.

Reflex sent his hand to his gun instead of completing the motion it had started; instinct wrapped his gloved fingers around the butt of the weapon he had laid across his lap, though he could neither see nor feel it, garbed as he was. He twisted in the seat.

Three men, all of them wearing what looked more like aircraft pressure suits than anything intended for hard vacuum, were groping hand over hand down the passageway, past the computer rooms. Kelly fired before he could see whether or not the newcomers were armed. He had to aim overhead, and, even though gravity was not a factor, the awkwardness of the position made the fact that his buckshot missed almost inevitable.

The newcomers were in straggling echelon across the width of the passage, so one pellet glancing from the wall paneling gouged its way across the flank of the rearmost man—without drawing blood. The cut-down shotgun recoiled viciously from the heavy charge, making the veteran's right palm tingle through the glove. Kelly clamped his left hand on the fore-end before triggering a second round.

If the trio of newcomers had startled Kelly, then the clumsiness with which they started to unsling the submachineguns they did in fact carry suggested that they had not recognized him as an enemy until that moment. The veteran could not tell whether they came from the other lobe of the dumbbell, from the docking module and the vessels positioned there, or even from some other location. All that mattered was that the chest of the nearest surrounded the front sight of the shotgun as Kelly squeezed off.

Recoil thrust the veteran against the seat cushion as he swung the muzzle toward the next man; the buckshot punched a dozen ragged holes through the first target's chest in a pattern the size of a dinner plate. Kinetic energy chopped the victim backward, into his fellows, with his limbs windmilling and a spray of blood swirling from the pellet holes.

The third of the newcomers fired wildly as the dead man tangled with him, the muzzle blasts cracking sharply despite Kelly's muffling helmet. The veteran switched his aim to the man who had his gun clear. He fired, shattering the face shield and hitting the target's own weapon with several pellets which drove it off on a course separate from that of the man who had used it.

The German in the middle of the group still had not managed to unsling his gun when Kelly's buckshot slammed his lower abdomen and spun him back up the aisle. The center of the passageway was now a fog of blood.

Kelly paused a fraction of a second to be sure that the trio's movements were the disconnected thrashing of dying men. Then he turned his head down to the console and the screen on which the engagement clock had run down to 221 seconds. Enough time. He thumped the Launch button again, setting the new parameters which would detonate the 5 megaton warhead one second after Fortress released the reentry vehicle.

There wasn't a prayer of getting out the way he had entered the space station, but the docking module was a relatively short path to vacuum. There was at least a chance that Wun would be waiting wherever Kelly exited Fortress. Might as well hope that, because otherwise Kelly didn't have a snowball's chance in hell of surviving.

He launched himself up the passageway, suddenly terrified by knowledge that in a little over three minutes, Fortress was going to reach the orbital position from which it would automatically release the weapon he had cued.

Thrust in weightlessness had its own rules. The veteran moved in a surprisingly straight line, but his body tumbled slowly end over end, so that he had to catch himself with his free hand on the jamb of a computer-room doorway at the midpoint of the aisle. One of the men Kelly had just killed floated in the same doorway. The German looked to have been about Kelly's age when he died . . . and there was a radio with a loaded whip antenna set into the right side of his helmet.

The veteran, poised to jump the rest of the way to the door, had an instant to wonder what his victims might have reported. The burst of fire from the doorway answered the question even as it was being formed.

Lighting in the passageway was dimmer than that in the domed room above, and the gunman was sighting past the bodies of his fellows besides; his target was not Kelly, lost among the corpses, but rather the motion down by the control console. The burst of submachinegun fire rang on the flamethrower twisting gently in the air currents, rupturing the pressure tank with a bang louder than that of Kelly returning the shots from his doorway.

The last charge of buckshot lifted the German, now faceless, up in a slow arc toward the top of the dome.

The flamethrower air bottle was still pressurized to several hundred atmospheres when it burst, so bits of it gouged deep holes in the aluminum panels nearby. The control consoles had been protected from the blast by the napalm tanks, so the engagement clock continued to count down, unimpaired.

Kelly snatched the submachinegun, a Walther, from the unresisting fingers of the body beside him. The three-shot burst he fired emptied the doorway of the figures already poking guns over the circular lintel . . . but there was no way the veteran was going to escape in that direction.

He pushed himself fiercely back toward the control consoles. No one had briefed him on the way to abort a launch sequence, and the clock was down to 97 seconds. A shot through the console or bursts into each of the incredibly complex computers up the hall would probably shut down the operation—but that would not save Kelly, only delay his end until hostile manpower overwhelmed him, and it would pretty well guarantee the failure of his mission. Fortress contained too many warheads for their release onto Earth, even unguided, to be an empty threat.

Tom Kelly was a fox with hounds waiting to rend him at the mouth of his burrow. Well then, he'd dig out the back—and if it didn't work, it was still a long step up from resigning himself to his fate.

The south pole of the hub, like the north with its docking module, was clear of the doughnut of shielding which surrounded the lobes of the dumbbell. Kelly flattened himself against the curve of the control-room floor which corresponded to the roof of the dome at the other axis. Locking his boots around the chair bolted in front of a console, the veteran reeled off a strip of his blasting tape. He was duck soup for any gunman who came through the door just now—but if the survivors weren't more cautious than their fellows had been, they were bloody suicidal.

The adhesive was only on one side of the thick tape, so when Kelly folded the strip at an angle to make a corner, the second length did not stick to the bulkhead against which it lay. Fucking bad design, but he should have checked it on the ground himself, and anyway it'd have to do. . . .

Kelly stuck down the third side of the square he was

taping as a long burst of automatic fire squirted from the north side of the sphere. The muzzle blasts were blurred by the helmet and the shots' confusion, with their own multiple echoes, but the ringing of bullets which hit the bulkhead near Kelly was clear enough. Dust puffed, and the tip of his left little finger, extending the final length of tape, flicked away from a hole in the aluminum.

The veteran had been wounded in worse ways, but nothing had *hurt* him like this since an ant buried its mandibles in the joint of his big toe. Kelly screamed and crimped the igniter lever in the end of the roll an instant sooner than he had intended. Five seconds—and at least the pain of his missing fingertip as he lunged away gave him something to think about besides the blast radius and the question of whether the gunman was aiming shots or just spraying them down the passageway.

There was movement in the direction of the door, the floating bodies twisting under the impact of bullets and fresh men plunging down the passage to finish the job. The submachinegun Kelly had appropriated had vanished, drifted off unnoticed while the veteran worked with the blasting tape. He looked desperately for the gun, wondering if the Nazi bullets had already shattered the launch control mechanism. The attackers were acting with a furious disregard for the equipment on whose capture they had invested so much effort. Maybe they—

The outline of PETN explosive blew a square out of the bulkhead so sharply that a green haze quivered along Kelly's optic nerves. He dived forward blindly, over the console that had shielded him from his own blast and into the stream of air rushing out the open. Vacuum would not affect the suited Germans, but neither should it harm the control-room hardware. The shock of the blast might or might not cause an abort. It'd be okay if the designers had done a proper job of isolating the computer banks from the structure of Fortress, and it was too late to worry about that anyway.

Kelly's head and the hands he had thrown up to protect his faceshield were sucked neatly through the opening, but his thighs slammed the edge. He hadn't realized just how fierce was the outrush until that blow; it felt as though a horse had kicked him with both hind legs. Kelly spun head over heels from the space station, like a diver in an event which would continue throughout eternity for anything he could do to change it.

The tip of his left little finger stung. The veteran reached for it instinctively with the other hand and squeezed the glove instead against the portion of finger above the second joint—the part that remained. The tears that burned worse than the blood freezing on the stump were not shed for pain but rather for loss. A part of Tom Kelly's body was gone as surely as his youth and his innocence.

The plume of air from the hub was dazzling where the reflection of the north polar mirror caught it. Closer to the hull from which it spewed, the venting atmosphere was a gray translucence lighted only by rays scattered higher in the plume.

The array of nuclear weapons through which Kelly tumbled was as black and brutal as a railroad marshaling yard at midnight.

The weapons that were Fortress's reason for being were anchored to the south hub by a tracery of girders, balancing the docking module and lighting mirror at the other pole of the axis. In schematic, the framework suggested precise randomness like that of a black widow spider's web, each crossing of strands supporting a nodule of thermonuclear warheads. The blunt curves of individual reentry vehicles were encased in aluminum pallets which supported clusters of small solid-fuel rockets.

The rocket motors simply counteracted the orbital momentum which each bomb shared as part of the space station. The pallet dropped away from the reentry vehicle after no more than thirty seconds of burn. For the remainder of its course, the warhead followed a ballistic trajectory governed by the same principles which had controlled the projectile fired by a fourteenth century bombard.

It was only after the reentry vehicle reached its target that advanced technology took over again, and the warhead detonated with more force than all of the explosives used in all the wars until that time.

There was no sign of the aliens who Kelly had prayed would meet him.

He had come out of the hub at an angle, but the nest of warheads was spread widely. Kelly saw that at each of his own slow rotations, an outlying node of bombs—six of them attached like petals to a common center—was growing in silhouette against the blue-white splendor of Earth. Distance was hard to judge in the absence of scale and atmosphere, but it looked as if the array were going to be close enough to touch.

The bomb should have gone off by now; he had drifted for what seemed at least five minutes. His strip charge or the flying bullets must have aborted the sequence. Kelly twisted, trying to follow the framework as it floated behind his head. He could not move even his body for lack of a fulcrum, but if he could catch hold of some solid object he could halt himself. Then he could wait for the aliens. Or for the Germans to locate and riddle him. Or for the moment he emptied the air pack from which he had been breathing since the monocle ferry was sealed.

The bombs were coming into sight again, past Kelly's toes. He *was* going to collide with them; the retro rockets of the nearest were within two yards and growing as the—

The rockets fired.

There was a puff of exhaust that clouded the metal from the ablative coating of the reentry vehicle itself. Then the cold vapors became three glowing blossoms while the bomb broke away from the cluster, the equivalent of five million tons of TNT fused to detonate one second after release.

With a horrified scream in his throat, Tom Kelly drifted through an invisible portal that left him collapsed at the feet of Wun, who still looked like a swarthy businessman in his human suit and face.

When Kelly wanted to watch the destruction of Fortress a third time, the aliens looped the final twenty seconds of the event and played it over and over while they worked on the human's finger.

"Does that hurt, Mr. Kelly?" Wun asked through the speakers of the helmet now resting beside Kelly.

"Just a little," said the veteran, though his wince a moment before had been diagnostic. "Look, it's okay."

Three aliens with no concession to human design or accoutrement bent over Kelly's outstretched left hand. Beyond them and seemingly as much a part of present reality as the five figures—theirs and Kelly's and Wun's—hung a vision of Fortress from about a kilometer away. The doughnut was viewed at a flat angle from the south pole, so that the four saucers at the docking module were partly visible over the curve of shielding material. Dora had joined her three dull-finished aluminum sisters and was linked to Fortress by an umbilicus.

The webbing holding the nuclear weapons was illuminated by a flash so intense that aluminum became translucent and only the warheads themselves remained momentarily black.

Most or all of the weapons which absorbed the sleet of radiation from the first 5 megaton warhead also detonated a microsecond later. Fortress—the space station, the saucers which had brought the Nazis to it, and the kilotons of shielding material—became vapor and a retinal memory in a blast that devoured the entire field of view . . . and faded back to the start of the explosion.

"Mr. Kelly," said Wun peevishly, "the question is not whether you can *stand* the pain but rather if we can eliminate it. Which we can do unless you pretend stoical indifference."

Another of the aliens poked toward (though not *to*) the stump of Kelly's finger with an instrument that looked like a miniature orange flyswatter. "Does *that* hurt?"

"There's a dull ache on the—the lower side," said the veteran, pointing with his right index finger. He hated to look at the amputation, though the aliens had closed the wound neatly with something pink the texture of fresh skin. He'd get used to the loss, as he'd gotten used to other things.

The orange instrument twisted. The ache disappeared. Fortress vaporized again in the ambiance beyond.

"Where will you have us place you when your injury is repaired, Mr. Kelly?" asked Wun, his eyes on Kelly while his voice came disconcertingly from the helmet at an angle to the figure.

"You're going to get in touch with governments now?" Kelly said. Lord knew what that blast would do to communications on the planet below, but there'd be auroras to tell the grandkids about. There'd *be* grandkids for those who wanted them, and that made it worthwhile. "Formal contact, I mean?"

Hell, it'd have been worthwhile if Tom Kelly had become part of the ball of glowing plasma he'd created with the help of Wun and a lot of luck.

And whatever.

"We can return you to the base from which you were launched into orbit, for instance," said Wun. The other three aliens stepped back as if to admire the repair work they had completed on the human's finger. It was as perfect as it could be without the portion the bullet had excised.

The loop of destruction flared again. Cheap at the price.

"I've been told in worse ways I oughta mind my own business," said Kelly, grinning at Wun. "And no, I don't want to go back to El Paso any time soon."

The stocky human stood up and stretched. It felt good to move without the bulk of the suit, good to breathe air that smelled like Earth's on a spring day. It felt very good to win one unequivocally.

It would have felt even better to have forgotten the scene in the dome as he left it, the drifting, smoking bodies. At the time, that part had seemed like a win also. . . .

"No," he said, "there's a couple people I owe . . . I dunno, maybe an explanation. Maybe just a chance to take a shot at me."

Kelly's face softened as he thought about his past, recent and farther back, as far as he could remember. "If I had good sense, I'd just walk away from that," he said. "But I never did have much use for people who walked away from things."

The three evident nonhumans had vanished. "You wish to be returned to the neighborhood of the woman Tuttle or the woman Romer?" said Wun, who either was psychic or understood how Kelly's mind worked better than anybody born on Earth seemed to have done.

"You can do that?" the veteran demanded.

"Either one," responded the alien. "Which would you prefer?"

"I—" began Tom Kelly. He laughed without humor, a sound as sharp as the warheads outlined against the first microsecond of the destruction of Fortress.

Then he reached into his trousers pocket to see if there were a coin he could flip.